Ale

SCOFFING THE PRIMROSES

Earl's Eye Publishing

By the same author:

Who Does Your Garden Grow? ISBN 0 9518 1330 7
- the stories and characters behind many favourite garden plants

SCOFFING THE PRIMROSES
First published in the UK in 2003
by Earl's Eye Publishing
Lamb Corner, Dedham, Colchester CO7 6EE
earlseyepublishing.com

Alex Pankhurst is hereby identified as author of the work in accordance
with section 77 of the Copyright, Designs and Patents Act 1988

ISBN 0-95181-331-5

Printed and bound in Great Britain by
St Edmundsbury Press Ltd, Bury St Edmunds, Suffolk

To everyone, both friends and strangers,
who helped with this book,
my warmest thanks.

Chapter One

'Roger, if you do that one more time there will be big trouble.' Zinnia Peasemore's tone carried unmistakable menace, and Roger's black tail twitched as he decided against further claw-sharpening on the young quince tree, and suddenly remembered a nearby mouse hole that needed inspecting.

'The thing is,' Zinnia continued without missing a beat, 'whatever am I going to do with this girl?'

'What do you mean, "do"?' asked Julia Trugglestone. 'I thought you said she was nearly thirty. Surely she'll be able to entertain herself – go up to London, hire a car and do touristy things? Americans are usually well able to look after themselves.'

'Hm. Perhaps you're right. But she's not really coming as a tourist.' Having billed the situation as a problem, Zinnia wasn't prepared to have it soothed away like a child's tummy ache. 'Her mother died last year, although that was probably a blessing as you know, and now my brother's gone, I'm her nearest relative. Mind the step. The moss is slippery.'

The early March sunshine felt warm on their backs, as the two women walked slowly along the brick path from the back door, through the formal part of Zinnia's garden towards the old chalk pit. They made an incongruous duo, like a gnu and a gazelle. Tall, with a large nose and deep-set eyes, Zinnia Peasemore had the leathery look of an outdoor person who abhors sun hats. Of late she had taken to cutting her straggly grey hair herself, a saving that the unkind might have considered an economy too far. There was a small rip in the knee of her brown corduroy trousers, and her navy anorak was sun-faded on the shoulders. Its sleeve ends were shiny with use, and the pockets bulged with plant labels and trailing bits of string.

By contrast Lady Julia Trugglestone was petite, with soft, hazel eyes, and that innate, feminine elegance which women trying hard, and failing, to achieve, find so irritating. Her almost white hair was neatly drawn back into a loose knot, which emphasised the fine bones of her face, and she wore a calf-length skirt, tailored jacket and knotted scarf, in blending colours. Walking with a stick, her slightly stiff gait suggested a spinal problem, which somehow managed to add to her delicate appeal.

Zinnia watched her friend manage the step safely, before adding, 'I do hope the girl's not coming to "find her family". Don't think I could cope with a surrogate daughter at my age.'

'Really, Zinnia, there are times when I wonder whether family means anything to you at all,' Julia reproached her. 'You dislike your daughter-in-law, and criticise your son - when actually Derek's very good to you. And if we hadn't virtually bundled you on to that plane, you'd have ducked out of your only brother's funeral, on the grounds that you hate travelling, and hadn't seen him for years.' She paused, but perceived no sign of repentance. 'The way you're going, they'll be dancing on your grave.'

It had crossed both women's minds that if they'd met later in life, mutual incomprehension and dislike would probably have kept them apart. But as it was, more than five decades of intertwined lives had made each so comfortable with the other's idiosyncrasies, it had long since been accepted that their differences simply didn't matter.

'I wanted you to see the Anemone blanda,' Zinnia changed the subject, as Julia negotiated the sloping track that led down to the Pit Garden. 'They're simply wonderful this year, after I had a blitz on the ivy.'

It never ceased to amaze visitors that the old chalk pit was so big, and yet standing by the house, you could be completely unaware of its existence. In the ninety odd years since commercial working had ceased, hawthorn, ash and sycamore seedlings had established themselves on the steep sides, and grown tall, while roses and other shrubs disguised the edge so that, from the house, the area could easily be mistaken for a patch of woodland. It was only as they descended the ramp up which horses had once hauled laden carts, that the scale of the huge hole in the ground made people gasp. Digging for chalk had resulted in two linked pits, a small one, now completely smothered in undergrowth, and the main site. Over the centuries this had been gouged further and further into the hillside, so that although the edge nearest the house was about fifty foot in height, the far side towered far above, the layer of topsoil clearly delineated against the grey of the chalk, even tenacious plants unable to get a hold.

Trees had grown on the floor of the pit, but had been severely thinned, letting in warming sunlight, like approval in a strict household. On one side they had been completely cleared to make space for a tennis court, green with disuse, and an ornamental pond. At the far end was an octagonal wooden summer house, its felted roof now steaming gently in the warm sun. Paths led off enticingly, and even in early spring, it was clear that this was a sheltered paradise for flowers. Big clumps of snowdrops were giving way to the uplifting simplicity of primroses, and patches of purple and white violets were fighting for territory with periwinkles and the intriguingly patterned leaves of hundreds of cyclamen. Drifts of acid green euphorbias gleamed among the trees, and in a huge carpet of vivid blue, dotted here and there with pink and white, Anemone blanda turned up their daisy faces to the sun.

'Such a wonderful blue,' Zinnia said, as they stood in admiration. 'I like things that get on with life and don't fuss. No attention, and they've gone from ten corms to this in... it must be forty-four years.'

'Heavens, is it really?'

'Well, I planted the first ones just before Derek was born – do you remember, you said I shouldn't bend so much, or I'd fall over and lie there helplessly like a beetle.'

'I thought you were crazy even to venture down here,' Julia responded, 'let alone try and make it into a garden. You could hardly see the summer house for brambles and ivy. Just clearing all that undergrowth would have daunted most people.'

'Oh I couldn't have left it like that,' declared Zinnia unequivocally. 'It was a challenge.'

'None of us ever imagined what you would make it into. It's been a great achievement, something to be really proud of. But don't you think...' Julia hesitated, and Zinnia interrupted.

'Did I tell you that a horticultural photographer rang, wanting to come and photograph the garden last week?' She added dismissively, 'Sent him away with a flea in his ear, of course.'

'Why "of course"?'

'You can't trust any of them.' The tone indicated photographers and hyenas had much in common. 'Once someone's got transparencies of the garden, you never know where they'll be used – plant catalogues, birthday cards, chocolate boxes. For which they pay me precisely nothing.'

'Surely you can expect some payment?' Julia was shocked.

'I wouldn't put it past an unscrupulous journalist even to take chunks out of my columns and cobble together an article to go with the photographs,' retorted Zinnia, who considered scepticism an essential raincoat in a showery world. ' "Garden Writer's Hideaway", or some such sick-making title. No thanks.'

'But wouldn't you like a set of photographs?'

She shook her head. 'I've got a reasonable record in slides already, and Basil Berriman will always come and take more. He may only be an amateur, but he knows his plants, and I can trust him.'

Julia didn't seem convinced. 'Well, I think it would be a good idea to have a professional photographer record all this while it's still...' She stopped, and brushed back a stray hair uneasily.

'Still what?'

'Er, while it's still... at its best. Look Zinnia, I could do with a rest, can we sit down a moment. I want to talk to you.'

The bench seat that almost encircled the summer house was green with algae, a fact which gave Zinnia no pause at all, as she plumped herself down, while Julia fastidiously tried to find the driest spot. A nearby Daphne odora was casting its sweetness on the air, and perched in the Witch Hazel, with its fading yellow blooms resembling the woollen hair of a rag doll dragged across mud, the Pit Garden's robin twittered at them sociably.

'You know how I always pictured myself back in the Dower House, when Clive and Susan took over Trugglestone Hall,' Julia began, in carefully conversational tones. 'Well, both of us actually. I just assumed that Richard and I would have years of pleasant retirement, doing the things we enjoyed but never had time for.' She paused, twisting her wedding ring. 'That's partly why it was such a shock,' she said in a low voice. 'Do you know, I just can't get used to describing myself as a "widow" on forms.'

'Horrible word,' agreed Zinnia, who had secretly thought of herself more as a liberated prisoner than a widow, for the past five years.

'I had such fond memories of the Dower House,' Julia continued wistfully. 'I suppose you do of your first married home. And I don't agree at all with Clive selling it. Or any of the other things he's doing. But he won't listen. You do know that don't you?' She looked at Zinnia anxiously.

'Anyway,' her voice became brisker, 'what I wanted to say was that now I've come to terms with it, and bought Riverside Cottage, I'm beginning to feel that a whole new chapter of life is opening up.'

'Going to run a betting shop, or start up as a clairvoyant, are you?' Zinnia teased. '"Lady of the Manor Kicks Over the Traces". The local paper will love it.'

'No, silly,' Julia smiled faintly. 'What I mean is, it's small, and all mine. I can live in it exactly how I like. The central heating really works. You've no idea how wonderful it is to be warm enough! And when Berrimans have finished building the raised beds, I shall be able to do the garden if I feel like it, or go away and leave the place for weeks at a time. No ties, just do what I want, when I want. Wonderful.'

'Hm.' Zinnia thought this rosy outlook sounded more like 'happy ever after' than real life, but no sense in pricking an illusion. 'Is that what you wanted to tell me?'

'Yes. No. That is...' Julia struggled for words. 'The point is, having to start afresh, on a small scale, has made me realise that it's no bad thing. And... and, I think you should too.'

The robin flew off and a thrush shrilled a cry of warning. A sinuous dark shape was catching up with them, like something shameful done in youth.

'Are you seriously suggesting,' asked Zinnia incredulously, 'that I should sell my house, give up the garden, and move into some "cosy cottage" in the village just because I'm eligible for the old age pension?' She shook her head, nonplussed. 'Julia, it's very nice of you to be concerned, but I assure you I anticipate living in my cold and inconvenient house for a good many years to come.'

Julia was fidgeting with her stick uncomfortably. 'But you surely don't expect to be able to do this for much longer,' she tried again, waving her hand at their surroundings. 'Let's face it, you're not getting any younger, Zinnia. A pity for it to deteriorate, and have to tell people it was a wonderful garden once.'

She saw the expression on her friend's face, and hurried on. 'Better to quit while it's really something to be proud of, and start again on a more manageable scale. After all, an old chalk pit with steep sides, and sycamore seedlings and ivy forever having to be kept at bay is hardly an ideal garden for one's old age.'

'You may consider yourself old at sixty-five,' retorted Zinnia, who was blessed with a spotty mirror in a dark bathroom, 'but I certainly don't. And I know you like gardening, Julia, but you would be the first to say it's not exactly a consuming passion. Whereas plants and gardening are my life.' She gestured expressively. 'It's what I do. I've spent over forty years making this garden – just walking away from it is unthinkable. I'm surprised at you even suggesting it.'

As they made their way back to the house a few minutes later, the sun disappeared behind dark clouds, and a cold breeze brought a hint of rain. Roger darted in front of them, ostentatiously dashing up trees in an effort to gain attention. 'Damn cat,' remarked Zinnia without rancour.

She still couldn't get over her companion's strange suggestion. Walking back up the ramp, she indicated the smaller, precipitous quarry on the left, and admitted, a trifle huffily, 'If it's any comfort to you, I've decided not to try and tackle the Little Pit after all.'

'I didn't know you were still planning to.'

'Well, the ivy's a nuisance invading from there, and I thought people might stop tipping rubbish from the road, if they could see it was cultivated,' said Zinnia, 'but just clearing the undergrowth would be an enormous task. Can't do it myself. That I will admit.' She shrugged. 'Derek isn't interested in helping, and it's no good trying to bribe Matthew. He says "Yes, Gran", but he never will.'

Julia smiled at the tone, knowing it belied Zinnia's soft spot for her grandson.

'So it'll have to be left. It does infuriate me though that people just come and tip stuff. If I ever catch anyone chucking rubbish down there, they'll find themselves shoved over with it,' she added with the robustness of a market trader defending his pitch.

'Was that what those boys were doing last week?' enquired Julia, pausing to rest as they reached the top.

'The one who fell in? No, they were cycling along the footpath above the main Pit. And playing silly dare games, apparently. The path is several feet from the edge up there, but the fence is a bit dodgy, and they got under it.'

Zinnia didn't sound unduly sympathetic. It was a quality that over the years had withered with disuse, like a biped's tail.

'I'm going to have a word with your son about getting that fencing renewed,' she warned, as they went on again. 'It's his land, and his responsibility. He's lucky the boy managed to cling on to the ledge, and only ended up with a broken leg. I wouldn't have thought the family are planning to sue, but they might have a case.' She paused. 'When would be the best time to go and see Clive?'

'Er, he's impossible to pin down, just now. Terribly busy,' Julia said hurriedly, as if Zinnia had just suggested dunning the family for thousands. 'Don't bother trying. I'll tell him what you said about the fencing. Must go – I've got someone coming to see about a bit of damp on the kitchen wall.'

'Not entirely Paradise then, your cosy cottage,' Zinnia commented drily, escorting her to the car.

'It will be, when I'm settled.' Julia got in and started the engine, then wound down the window. 'Tell your American girl she's welcome to call in. They always like Elizabethan beams and inglenook fireplaces. She'll probably tell her friends that Haydon Settleworth is just the cutest village, and they can't imagine how quaint we all are.'

'Hm.' Zinnia seemed unconvinced.

'Don't worry,' Julia assured her, 'I'm sure you'll get along just fine.'

****

A week later the subject of Zinnia's forebodings found herself battling similar feelings, along with sudden queasiness, as the Boeing 747 headed out of Boston.

Just my luck, Rosemary thought with resignation, to be sandwiched between a mother with a baby and small child, and some olfactorily challenged, middle-aged woman. That perfume of hers – phew, she must have ladled it on. She caught the immaculately made-up dragon's eye, and smiled insincerely.

The expectation of conversation with stimulating travelling companions succumbed to the weight of reality, and her spirits sank like a miners' cage. Think positive girl, she instructed herself. Think brief flight, and then broad horizons, people to meet, whole new world.

The trouble was, she wasn't convincing herself. You don't when you're miserable. The doctor had given her anti-depressants, declaring in a breezy manner that grieving was only natural, and she would get over it. How many times a day does he say that? she'd wondered, dismissing the verbal Prozac along with the pills. But then, doctors have to remain aloof, Bill said, they had it drummed into them in training. Otherwise they would never be able to get out on the golf course with a light heart and unbowed shoulders. Huh.

'My name's Jason,' the small child on the other side of her announced, with a five year old's certainty of audience interest. Blond, curly haired and with big blue eyes, he reminded Rosemary of the cherubs that infested Renaissance paintings. Except that they were usually plumper, and – inevitably, given the states of undress all around – inclined to knowing expressions. Jason was looking up at her with open friendliness.

'We're going to see my Daddy,' he confided. 'Do you have a Daddy?'

The child ceased to appear quite so favoured in Rosemary's eyes.

'No,' she said woodenly, and opened her bag looking for the newly-bought paperback.

If he'd asked about her Mummy, there'd have been no trouble, she reflected guiltily. 'She'd been badly injured in a car accident, you see,' she was used to explaining lightly, 'and was paralysed and brain damaged for nearly ten years. Dad and I did most of the nursing between us, but she had no life really.'

People said it was a release, and Rosemary agreed. Only she'd been thinking of herself and Dad. What kind of a daughter did that make her? she thought reproachfully. Not wonderful.

She located the book, and with a meaning glance at Jason, opened it, but her mind had gone into the familiar loop.

Not going away to college, and taking an unloved job at the university library hadn't been out of pure, selfless love for the dependent lump that her mother had become, as friends and neighbours assumed. It was because she couldn't let it all fall on Dad. And the pity of it was, she thought sadly, he hadn't needed to devote himself to looking after her. The huge compensation the judge had awarded would have allowed them to put her in a really good nursing home, and get on with life, while other people did all the caring. But Dad wouldn't hear of it, on principle. Damn all principles.

'This is Skiffy,' Jason pushed a strange hybrid creature, like a bear with rabbit ears, in Rosemary's direction. 'He wants you to say hello to him.'

'Hi Skiffy.'

Some stimulating travelling companion! she thought, searching now for her sense of humour. A blue, stuffed animal with an identity crisis.

'He likes aeroplanes,' the child went on chattily. 'Do you like aeroplanes?'

'Well, I haven't been on many.'

He stared at her as if she'd just confessed to having a nose that unscrewed at night.

'We fly all the time.'

The Wright brothers could hardly have imagined that in 1997 some precocious tot would consider it natural to flit across the globe in an aeroplane, Rosemary reflected, failing to warm to the diminutive traveller. There was no mistaking the dismissive tone.

She felt like telling him that she would have had a great time flying the world. That had been the plan, after Mum died. Money no problem, there were so many things they were going to do. A trip to Africa had been imminent. Dad wanted to go to various mines, and visit old contacts. And she was looking forward to seeing for herself the things he'd mentioned in his letters home. Mining engineers and their daughters don't necessarily find the same things of interest, but she very much wanted to drive through the beautiful Drakensberg Mountains, and spend a few days in the Kruger National Park, to balance against his work-related plans.

And Europe. Why not go on a modern Grand Tour, absorbing the flavour of Italy, Spain, Austria and France in a leisurely meander, they'd thought? Bill had been all in favour, even if it meant missing her for a few months. That was nice of him.

Rosemary noticed the blue bearbbit was now being put through his life-saving routine.

How comforting was it knowing that you had a life jacket in the event of the plane going down? she wondered. It was rather like being handed an aspirin to take after the cyanide pill.

Bill had helped to keep her afloat though, when she'd felt as if she was drowning. Of course he was almost one of the family already. It was pleasing that he and her father had got on okay, even though they didn't have much in common. Dad was interested in so many things – history, anthropology, climate, engineering, geology, Rosemary thought with pride. Just about any subject that came up, you found he had a view, based on a store of knowledge gleaned from somewhere. Bill and he eventually agreed to disagree about psychology and human behaviour, because her beloved would spout his medical school notes, while her father had, as usual, linked together factors from many different fields, and mulled over them to form an unorthodox conclusion. Eclectic – was that the word for it?

Bill just didn't work that way. 'If we spent all our time questioning established knowledge, we'd be forever reinventing the wheel, and make no progress at all,' he maintained, and she had to admit there was something in that.

'Why don't you have a Daddy?'

Give me strength! Rosemary experienced rising dislike.

'I just don't, okay,' she informed her small neighbour shortly.

'But why?'

She glanced across for help, but his mother was cooing softly to the baby, and had the absorbed air of a parent determinedly off answering duty.

'Well he...he fell downstairs,' she responded unwillingly.

'Why?'

'I don't know why. I wasn't there. He probably walked in his sleep.' It was like tearing a plaster off a fresh wound. 'Why don't you go to sleep,' she suggested fiercely, suppressing the urge to stuff sleeping pills down her tormentor's throat.

If only she hadn't agreed to go away that weekend with Bill, she reproached herself, yet again. It was to be a fun time, a day's walking in Boxford State Forest (she'd made him promise to leave his bird book and binoculars at home), meals out, a concert in Boston. He wanted her to admire his new apartment too, which she did, but with a certain misgiving. It was so *tidy*, and spotlessly clean. She couldn't picture her own belongings homing in on the place, collecting informally in corners, like leaves in the Fall. No doubt about it, she would have to become more disciplined.

Oh God, that awful weekend. The telephone call on Sunday morning, the frantic journey home, interviews with the police. Had her father been depressed? Were there money worries? Did he sleep walk? She'd been lost in a blur of distress.

Now stop it, *stop it,* Rosemary told herself fiercely. This is not 'getting over it' behaviour.

With a determined effort she managed to smile and shake her head as the flight attendant came down the aisle offering drinks. She looked again at her book, but gave up. There was no hope of the words meaning anything.

Bill had steadied and helped all he could, Rosemary thought, with gratitude, and she had managed to get through those weeks, clenched, but not mad, and not ill. She would now be able to put down on her meagre list of skills, 'Knows how to organise a funeral, and sell a house. Dealing with lawyers a speciality.' She'd sold all the furniture too, and kept only a few possessions and mementos she couldn't bear to part with. They'd been sent down to Bill's. He wouldn't mind just a few things cluttering up his apartment, surely.

Including her. That was the idea anyhow. She could slowly unwind, decide what she wanted to do, look around for another job. Adjust. Get over it.

And then he'd casually trodden on her fingers, clinging to the ledge. 'Eight months in Antarctica!,' she'd protested, aghast. 'You can't mean it.'

But he did.

'A colleague's dropped out, and they want me to take his place studying Seasonal Affective Disorder at the US National Science Foundation . It's a wonderful opportunity,' he enthused to Rosemary, and indeed she'd never seen him so animated.

Antarctic winter conditions will soon put paid to that, she'd thought sourly. And what am I supposed to do for the next eight months, alone in a strange city?

'The timing isn't good, I know,' Bill tried to be consoling. 'But it really is a once-in-a-lifetime opportunity. And you wouldn't want me to miss out, would you?'

That was four-star blackmail.

'It'll look great on job applications. Besides, you won't be lonely,' he'd assured her, with the glib certainty of a salesman selling a racy Cadillac to an octogenarian. 'I've got a contact at Harvard who reckons there's a vacancy coming up in the library, and I'm sure they'd be interested in your previous experience. And my sister says she'll teach you to play bridge, and then you can hop on the train to Beverly and join in her Bridge Evenings. You'll soon make friends.'

Jeez, what a prospect. How to leap from twenty-eight to middle-age in a few short weeks. Well no thanks. Rosemary's chin lifted in remembered defiance. If Bill could swan off (or more aptly in the circumstances, penguin off), for months, so could she. What are distant relatives for, if not to visit?

So here she was, a poor little orphan girl, sitting on a plane to England. She pulled herself up sternly. You're not a girl. Lots of people my age are knee-deep in small children. God help them. She glanced at Jason, who had now found a fascinating, loose thread in Skiffy's black nose, and was pulling it to see what happened. She thought of alerting his mother, but ungallantly decided against it.

Several contemporaries were climbing career ladders, gazing calculatingly at the feet above. No, she might be an orphan, but she wasn't a girl. And you're not poor, for heavens sake, she told herself. What was it the financial advisor had said? 'You are very comfortably off, Miss Keel. Always supposing you don't succumb to drugs, alcohol, gambling, saving the world, or a wastrel husband, you should be well provided for.'

The bulk of it was her mother's compensation, of course. Then her father had turned out to have a hefty life insurance policy, and the proceeds of the house sale and contents were added to that. But she hadn't earned a cent of it, and it just didn't feel like her money.

The meals were being brought round, and she opened her bag to replace the unread book. It had an improbably beautiful girl on the cover, hair flying in a wind which somehow didn't make it too cold for a revealingly low-necked blouse. Wryly, Rosemary compared herself with this fictional apparition. Financially well-endowed, instead of physically. And plain. What was the point of pretending otherwise? She had years ago come to terms with muddy-coloured eyes and hair, and an untidy face, as if put together by someone in need of more practice. Nice wide mouth, but a nose too large and long. Not the kind of looks that prompt men to glance lustfully across a crowded room and demand of their hostess, 'Who is that girl over there? You *must* introduce me.'

In any case, Rosemary reflected with realism, she would have been incapable of making the playful small talk that seemed to come easily to attractive girls. The whole ritual of flirtation, and falling in love simply made her impatient. She and Bill were great friends, that was the important thing.

Jason was now eagerly consuming some kind of brown stew, and Rosemary envied him his appetite. She gazed at her own food without enthusiasm. You have to manage half, she thought with discipline, and found herself idly wondering what happened to the leftovers. After all, it's not as if they could chuck them out of the window, like a discarded apple core. An airlocked disposal chute would be handy though, and conjured up a diverting picture of hungry hordes eagerly tracking airliners in the hope of manna from heaven. Or Duck a l'Orange.

She smiled, and felt better. Her world had suddenly collapsed, but it hadn't ended. The best thing would be to regard the next few months as a breathing space in which to sort herself out, get used to the new horizons, shake down.

Maybe Bill ratting on her could turn out for the good, although it would never do to say so. A remorseful partner is a wonderful thing. As long as he felt guilty of course. She wasn't entirely sure that he did.

Also she owed it to Dad to stop feeling sorry for herself, and try and take an interest in the world as it was now. Her disintegration would only have made him impatient.

So, Rosemary my girl, she ordered herself, you can start by talking to the harridan in the next seat. Even if she does ladle on a perfume that smells like cheap soap and wet dogs, she has to be an improvement on Skiffy. Boy, what a pong! Stuff probably costs the earth.

****

The gaggle of passengers, who last night had thronged, chatting brightly, onto the plane, looked weary and crumpled as used tissues, while they waited silently for their luggage off the carousel at Heathrow. Rosemary was not only tired, but apprehensive. She felt like the control in an experiment in which all the others had had prior training.

'Do you know what your uncle looks like?' her odorous seat companion enquired, as they wheeled their luggage trolleys towards a small crowd of expectant-looking people.

'No, but apparently he's got a photograph of me.'

She scanned the faces, expecting someone to brighten with recognition and greeting, but their eyes slid over her like car lights on an empty building. Shamingly, rivulets of fear solidified in her stomach, and she was trying to think what to do if she found herself stranded alone in a strange country, when her flight acquaintance nudged her, and pointed.

Near the end of the the line of people stood a tall youth, untidy, dark curls emerging from beneath a chauffeur's cap. He was holding up a placard with the printed heading, 'Explicit Films Inc' above a logo of a pair of voluptuous breasts, and on the sign was scrawled, 'Rosemary Keel.'

'Is that for you?' Her companion's voice was brittle.

The young chauffeur had spotted them. 'Miss Keel?' he enquired with a bright smile.

'Yes. Er, no. I mean, that is my name, but maybe there's someone else with the same…'

'Miss Rosemary Keel, from Ann Arbor, Michigan?'

'Well, yes, but there must be some mistake…'

'I'll take your luggage,' said the chauffeur cheerfully, commandeering her trolley. 'My, you have brought a lot of clothes! Won't be needing *those*,' and he winked lasciviously at her companion, who turned on Rosemary with ice in her eyes.

'Librarian indeed!' she snapped. 'Fetching books from top shelves in fishnet tights and mini skirts, I suppose. Huh!' And giving her trolley an angry shove, she pushed off into the crowd, glowering like an ousted politician.

This can't be happening, thought Rosemary, helplessly following the young man through the throng, as if she was a stray dog on a string. I'm not rich enough to be kidnapped – am I? The words 'white slave trade' passed ridiculously through her bemused brain. Oh come *on*, she scolded herself. Authors don't even have the nerve to put that in fiction. And you haven't the face for it either, for heavens sake. It was far more likely her luggage was being hijacked. She had just decided to insist on reclaiming it while there were still plenty of people around, when they came to a waiting area. Her chauffeur stopped, removed his cap and handed it to a uniformed man who was leaning against a coffee bar.

'Thanks, mate,' he said cheerily. 'Do the same for you some day.' And turning to the uncomprehending Rosemary, he gave a delighted grin and held out his hand.

'Hi, I'm your cousin Matthew.'

****

'I can't believe what you did to me,' Rosemary, still shaken by the experience, admonished her capless chauffeur, when he had extricated them from the airport, and was heading north.

'Good, wasn't it.' Matthew was clearly impervious to reproach, like a foreign exchange student smiling uncomprehendingly whatever is said. 'I did the placard on the computer last night. Great logo, don't you think? I got it off the internet. And your face was priceless.' He chuckled at the thought. 'That woman's too.'

'If I ever met her again, I wouldn't know where to put myself',' Rosemary protested.

'Well, you're not likely to, are you. Who was she anyway?'

'I didn't ask her name. Some bore who'd been on a lecture tour of the States to promote her latest book. Apparently she's famous on both sides of the Atlan...' Rosemary stopped, and leant towards her companion, examining his curls intently. 'What's that on your hair? It's not...' Her voice registered reproach and disgust. 'Surely you haven't got head lice, Matthew?'

'*What*!'

'Your hair's crawling with them.'

Matthew clutched at his head, attempting to look in the mirror at the same time, causing the car to swerve, and the driver behind gave a blast on his horn.

'Watch it!'

There was a pause while he sorted out his driving.

'You probably got them off that chauffeur's cap.' She struggled in vain to keep the amusement off her face at his horrified reaction.

'You're having me on.'

'Might be,' she said with satisfaction. 'But you can't be sure he didn't have head lice, can you? It would serve you right if he did.'

The score a bit more even now, Rosemary felt better. 'Why was it you at the airport?' she asked. 'I was expecting to be met by Uncle Derek.'

'Dad realised yesterday that he couldn't come. Trouble at t'mill,' Matthew answered enigmatically.

'Trouble at what?'

'You'll have to get used to us native English speakers, m'lady,' he said, in an exaggerated country accent. 'He's General Manager for a company called Thornways, owned by Gerry Thornway, who's a total prat, and hasn't a clue how to run the place. Sends Dad up the wall. They were having some kind of crisis meeting today, and that's why he couldn't come.'

'And he sent you instead? I thought you were still a little boy, at school.'

'I growed,' Matthew informed her, somewhat unnecessarily, 'I'm nineteen now.'

'Are you at university or something?'

'Er, no,' was all he said, and changed the subject. 'Dad's not your uncle, you know. I was working it out last night. He's your cousin, and that makes me your cousin once removed. Or was it second cousin?' He gave up. 'Anyway, he won't like being called uncle. He and Mum are going through middle-age denial at the moment.'

The earliest trees were showing a hint of green, giving the drab countryside a promise of hayfield days to come, although some were white with blossom, as if they'd experienced their own private snowstorm. But the warm car and lack of sleep caused Rosemary to close her eyes wearily. She awoke just as they passed a roadside sign announcing the county of Suffolk

'Are we nearly there?' she asked, immediately regretting the child-like question, which Matthew seized on with delight.

'Well, now,' he said, like a determinedly kind uncle taking a small child out for the day, 'if you can hold on just a bit longer, it won't be much further.'

She made a face at him, and looked out of the window. They were crossing a river, whose wide, grassy valley, was bounded by low wooded hills, a distant village marked by a tall church tower.

'This is pretty,' she said.

'Constable Country,' announced Matthew. 'You know – the valley that John Constable made famous with his paintings. That's Dedham over there.' He indicated off to their right. 'In the summer we must hire a boat and take you rowing up the river, and have a cream tea afterwards. When I was small it was one of my favourite treats. How long are you staying, by the way?'

'Well, maybe...' she began uncertainly, and shrugged. 'See I don't know really. It depends. On how I get on with Zinnia, for a start. I hardly had time to talk to her when she came over for the funeral.'

'Oh, Gran's not a bad old stick,' her cousin informed her, as if explaining his unfriendly mongrel was really only fierce for show.

'I'm kind of apprehensive about the whole thing,' she confessed. 'I only know what happens in English country houses from books and things. Is she very grand?'

'Kiln House isn't large, you know. It probably belonged to the Tudor farmer who originally started the chalk pit. I don't think you would use the word 'grand' either.' He gave a sideways glance at his passenger. 'But she is a stickler about using the silver every day, of course,' he told her seriously, 'and changing into evening dress for dinner, that sort of thing.'

'Oh dear,' she said, feeling inadequate already. This was going to be an ordeal.

****

How will I know when hypothermia sets in? Rosemary asked herself at four o'clock the next morning, when gnawing cold had made sleep impossible. And how crazy would that be? Bill goes off to Antarctica, coldest place on earth, only to hear that his fiancée has frozen to death in England. She couldn't ever remember being so chilled, it was like trying to doze off in a snowdrift.

'I hope you'll be all right in here,' Zinnia had said. 'There's no central heating, but the Rayburn in the kitchen keeps the house quite warm.'

Warm! Maybe she really thinks that, Rosemary reflected, in an effort to be charitable. Her aunt's bedroom was above the kitchen, after all, while she had been given a large room at the far end of the landing.

'Extra blankets in the wardrobe, if you need them,' she suddenly remembered Zinnia had added. Need? Jeez, they could save her life. Turning on the bedside light, she shivered her way across the room in search of warm clothing in her suitcase, the wooden floor unkindly stealing the last vestiges of blood heat from her bare feet. A large and ugly closet stood against the far wall, a door at each side, full-length mirror in the middle. Rosemary caught a glimpse of herself, hair dishevelled, cotton nightdress now unglamorously gathered beneath a polo-necked sweater. What a way to be found as a stiff, she thought wryly, turning the rusty key of the right hand door.

A fusty smell escaped, reminding her of old bookstores at the library. There was a small amount of hanging space, occupied by suits and large tweed jackets, but the majority of the inside was taken up by drawers and shelves. Binoculars in a leather case, together with a silver whisky flask, and what looked like a bowler hat in a dusty plastic bag, confirmed that this was, or had been, a man's closet.

Guiltily, feeling as if she was prying, she scanned the shelves in vain for the promised blankets. Standing on tiptoe, she reached up to the top shelf, and felt something rough and woollen, just as a shower of mothballs rolled over the edge, bounced on her head, and dropped noisily to the ground.

Rosemary braced herself for Zinnia to come and investigate the evident sound of her guest playing pin-ball in the small hours, but nothing happened. She had hold of the blanket now, and pulled it forward, only to be struck in the face by a little cardboard box, which flew open as it hit the ground, followed by the sound of small objects rolling across the floor, like beads from an unstrung necklace. Sheesh!

Unnerved, she closed the door and retreated back to bed, clutching what seemed to be a tartan travelling rug. It wasn't much, but maybe, with the thick sweater, it would be enough to prevent frostbite. She added the rug to her bedclothes, wriggled down till they came up to her ears, and waited, shivering, for some warmth to return.

Sleep hardly seemed likely. She was too cold, and her mind seethed like a witch's caldron, as it struggled to come to terms with the last thirty-six hours.

She had often wondered how astronauts coped with the mental shock of being on earth one moment, bracing themselves for blast-off, and then, just a few minutes later, there they were all alone above the atmosphere, the strangest environment possible. It might be unfair comparing her aunt's house to outer space, but the gap between her own, vague, expectations and the reality had proved intergalactic.

Her own fault, of course. She'd pictured an elegant, Jane Austen-type house, set in beautiful grounds, probably complete with a wizened and faithful cook/housekeeper. She had been taken in by Matthew's tease about changing for dinner precisely because it was half what she was expecting. The thought now of putting on an elegant evening dress and eating with polished silver caused a disillusioned smile. Zinnia undoubtedly had silver cutlery, but it was probably black with decades of neglect, and stashed away under the stairs.

And the house. Oh boy, the house. Dad had told her about it once. His family had moved to Haydon Settleworth towards the end of the war, when he was ten, and only stayed three years, but he remembered tagging along with his older sister when she was invited to tennis parties at Kiln House. He had a great time, exploring the huge, overgrown chalk pit, occasionally retrieving balls that had been lobbed too enthusiastically, and he was included in teas afterwards up at Kiln House.

It had been owned by a Mr and Mrs Peasemore, who relished their pivotal role, as they saw it, in the village's society. The teas were delicious, he recalled, laid out in the dining room, or in the garden if the weather was fine. There were staff on hand to make sure everyone had enough, and the family always had the latest gadgets before anyone else. Everything was impressively stylish. Years later, his sister had inexplicably married Howard, the Peasemore's son, but Dad had never been back to the village. He remembered the extraordinary chalk pit though, those wonderful teas, and Mrs Peasemore being very particular that her house was clean and smart.

Not now, it wasn't. The place was giving a good impression of dereliction, or the beginnings of it, anyhow. At first sight it had looked attractive, with old Tudor beams and a big tiled roof. But although the front of the house faced south, a small wood over the road shaded out all but the highest sun, so that the roof tiles were mottled with moss, like a Martian's acne. A large, studded front door peered out from a brick porch, which had garnered a crunchy harvest of dead leaves, in no apparent danger of eviction. The back door into the kitchen, round the side of the building, was evidently the only one ever used. Two bay windows, at odds with the sixteenth century style, flanked the front door, but like most of the other window frames in the house, they were afflicted with rot, and evidently hadn't seen paint for years. Inside the house, buckets were suspiciously located under brown ceiling stains in various rooms, and there were long cracks in the plaster here and there. Ancient linoleum on the kitchen and passage floor was worn through to the canvas backing in hard-worked places, and the whole feeling of the house was dark and dingy.

Zinnia evidently lived in the kitchen, which was the heart of the house. A solid pine dresser, displaying blue and white plates, dominated one side of the room, and on the wall beside it, as unexpected as a tiara on a tea lady, was an arrestingly beautiful oil painting of primroses arranged in a vase. By the window, the sink unit and surrounding fitted cupboards had an unlovely, fifties style about them.

But although the room would have given an interior designer the screaming habdabs, it nevertheless managed a shabbily comfortable air. The four chairs round the central oak table had cane seats that sagged just the right amount, and a worn armchair invited ease, snuggled up to the cream-coloured Rayburn cooking range which gave out blessed warmth day and night. Mind you, the thing exacted a price. Rosemary had been shocked to discover her aunt lugging a great hod of anthracite in from an outhouse, and pouring it into the beast's mouth. The whole set up was like something out of a post-war film, and it felt as if she had travelled back in time, not just across the Atlantic.

So it had been frustrating, but not altogether surprising, to discover in the afternoon, that her laptop computer refused to work properly. She'd promised to e-mail Bill on arrival, and to find that it wasn't possible made her feel even more cast adrift.

'Matthew will be able to sort it out for you,' Zinnia had said with certainty. 'He's a real expert. Earns quite a bit of money by sorting out people's computer problems locally, although goodness knows how he picked it all up.'

So that would be the first problem to be tackled, Rosemary decided, huddled under the bedclothes, her legs slowly beginning to feel less like cheese rolls in the chilled food cabinet.

And the second, no kidding, would be how to make herself comfortable in this strange household.

There was, admittedly, a strong temptation to jump on a plane and speed back to the comfort of the States, but that would be just cowardly. This may be one big mistake, she told herself firmly, but, Rosemary Keel, you are not going to run away. Plain, undistinguished and directionless she might admit to being. But a quitter? No way.

Chapter Two

'Down the lane, keep going for nearly a mile, and you come to the village. Theirs is one of the last houses on the far side,' were Zinnia's directions for finding Matthew's house next morning, adding, 'I'm sure you'll enjoy the walk.'

And Rosemary was finding it invigorating.. Clouds tumbled across the sky, fleeing a chill breeze, which was largely defeating the spring sunshine, but she was soon glowing with exercise-induced warmth. Maybe, she thought, that's what I should have done last night – indulged in a strenuous workout to bring back the circulation. Except that all her bedroom floorboards creaked, and she could imagine Zinnia's pained comments to friends. 'She's an odd sort, that one. Takes violent exercise in the middle of the night, and I found mothballs in the strangest places. Goodness knows what she'd been up to.'

Actually Rosemary had collected up all she could find, and put them back in the wardrobe, to continue their malodorous guard duties. Likewise the contents of the small box – odd-shaped, shrivelled little brown things. The lid rather doubtfully claimed that they were Denis's Lincolnshire Pig Powders, and Rosemary formed a pleasing picture of sows fussily powdering their snouts, as she put the small box with its replaced contents back on the shelf. She felt rather foolish about the whole episode, especially after discovering in the morning that the other side of the closet had been cleared for her use, and contained a whole stack of blankets.

She'd hardly noticed the village when driving through with Matthew yesterday, but now, at walking pace, was able to take it in properly. The main street of Haydon Settleworth was most attractive, its assortment of ancient-looking buildings on both sides of the road leaning together companionably, the colours of the plastered cottages mingling in harmonies of cream, deep ochre, pink and even a raspberry red. Halfway up the street they drew back, as if in respect, for a flint-built church with a square tower, surrounded by a well-kept churchyard.

The village, although not large, still managed to support a food store, post office come newsagents, and a pub, The Oak. There was also a rather forlorn looking junk shop with 'Antiques' ambitiously emblazoned over the window, but a dusty 'Closed' sign on the door, like a woman flaunting a teasing bit of ankle, then donning heavy boots. There was a timeless, aged quality about the place that pleased in the same way as a centuries-old oak tree. According to Zinnia, the village had largely been built in Tudor times, trading with travellers using the ford on the road to Bury St Edmunds.

Rosemary made a detour, taking the road that joined the main street, and walked down to a low bridge to gaze into the reed-fringed water. The little river glittered in the clear air, as if sunlight were woven into the water, and a cluster of ducks rushed to congregate beneath her, quacking competitively but, finding she was foodless, they soon drifted away in disappointment. Leaning on the brick parapet, she looked back at the village. From here the church tower seemed to gather the houses to itself protectively, and in the foreground a row of cottages along the river, with not a straight roof between them, made a picture that should have graced a calendar, or birthday card. Probably did. Although today a photographer would have had to asked for the removal of some newly-washed jeans doing an energetic salsa on a washing line, and a row of trash cans. It was too bad that people led untidy, twentieth century lives in picture postcard properties. Mind you, Zinnia's living conditions appeared to be several decades in the past, but whether this was from choice or financial circumstances, Rosemary wasn't sure.

She retraced her footsteps, and continued up the main street. Some way beyond the church the twentieth century had asserted itself, in the form of a side road with identical, houses on either side, some of them rather scruffy, and further on, next to a gracious old house, a whole new estate was under construction. A sign directed potential buyers to the 'Sleepy Hollow Development Show House'. It was difficult to imagine how people would view them in a few centuries' time, but she couldn't help feeling that, even when aged, these rather bland buildings with their own little squares of land would still lack the character and visual beauty she'd been admiring from the bridge.

The houses had petered out on the opposite side now, to be replaced by a meadow dotted with mature trees, and crossed by a drive ending in a pair of large, wooden gates.   A modest plaque on one of the gateposts announced 'Trugglestone Hall', and a high brick wall continued on the far side.   This must mean she was getting near to Matthew's house, and indeed, across the road there were now a series of redbrick houses, variously with 1895 or 1896 incorporated into the brickwork above the front doors, the last one, Warren Lodge, being her destination.

Matthew effervesced like a shaken beer can, and Rosemary was curious to meet his mother, confidently anticipating a warm and bubbly personality. She knocked on the front door, and it was opened by a dumpy little woman, smartly dressed in a green pleated skirt, and blue mohair sweater.

Veronica Peasemore had the same dark, curly hair, greying now, and worn shoulder length, but it took only a few moments in her company to conclude that the son's charm owed nothing to his maternal inheritance. She had probably been quite pretty once, but now at forty, her face had settled into a discontented expression with deeply incised frown mark. Double chins were gathering, and she had not yet twigged that an essentially young hairstyle round an older face merely emphasises age.

Matthew was out, she told Rosemary, inviting her in for coffee. The idea lacked appeal but, in the circumstances, saying, 'I'd sure like that, too bad there isn't time,' hardly seemed a plausible option. Besides, she was interested to find out more about this side of the family. There seemed to be an undercurrent of animosity between Zinnia and her daughter-in-law, which needed to be understood.

The kitchen she was shown into was bright and spotlessly clean, worktops gleaming emptily, like a fish shop on Sunday, and the floor tiles were polished to danger point. Cookery books occupied two long shelves on one wall, beneath a vase of flamboyant paper poppies, their scarlet picked up by the flowery curtains, in turn carefully matching the cushions on four chairs. These were set neatly round a table in the middle of the room, which sported only a bowl of ceramic fruit and a glossy magazine. A huge spice rack, stocking more intimidating ingredients than Rosemary knew existed, was situated conveniently by the ceramic hob, and above the worktop glowered a graduated row of steel knives. There were no signs of family living at all.

It was as if Veronica was expecting a photographer from some flick-through magazine any moment. When such kitchens were featured,

Rosemary always assumed someone had rushed round, loading the everyday clutter into trash cans, and hiding them in the next room, until the photo-shoot was over. Clearly not. Wondering whether she'd wiped her feet sufficiently, Rosemary sat at the table while Veronica made coffee.

'What a lovely kitchen,' she remarked, feeling like a chat show host with a difficult guest.

This elicited a small smile of satisfaction. 'Well, you might as well have it nice,' Veronica said, pouring boiling water into the cafetière, 'it's the room you spend most time in, after all. I was just thinking about doing that recipe,' she added, indicating the open magazine on the table. 'That's Country Harvest, by the way, the magazine Zinnia writes for. She does their gardening column.'

Rosemary looked through it with interest, and surprise. She had already heard her aunt pass disparaging remarks about people who just dabbled in gardening. 'Not proper gardeners,' was her term, and yet, even to Rosemary's untutored eye, this was a magazine for exactly the kind of people who went for image and not substance. It seemed to purvey a romantic idea of idyllic rural life, taking care to promote as many of its advertisers' wares as possible. She searched the contents page for Zinnia's name.

'You'll find her column near the back,' Veronica told her, reaching into a cupboard for cups and saucers.

Turning to the page, Rosemary glanced through the article.

'A new Features Editor's just been appointed, I think.' Veronica put the pot of coffee on a tray. 'And they're not seeing eye to eye about things. Zinnia says the man knows absolutely nothing, and she's invited him down to see the garden, but I don't suppose he'll come. Bring the magazine through with you, if you like.'

Rosemary failed to see why they couldn't stay at the kitchen table, but obediently followed her through to a small lounge, equally unwelcoming in its unreal tidiness.

'Do sit down,' suggested Veronica formally, putting a plate of tempting, home-made cakes on a low table in front of her guest. She refrained from eating herself, but enquired, with self-conscious politeness, 'And how are you settling in? Staying with Zinnia must be quite a contrast from what you're used to, I imagine.'

Rosemary began a light-hearted account of her need for arctic training, before her listener's expression indicated that this was a mistake.

'I've tried and tried to get her to see sense about that place,' Veronica interrupted. 'It would be so much better for her to sell Kiln House and move to something modern and convenient. One of the new Sleepy Hollow houses would be perfect. But she won't listen.'

She had a rather nasal voice, which tailed off at the end of sentences, like a harmonica with narcolepsy, and Rosemary didn't imagine Zinnia being overwhelmed by the force of her daughter-in-law's argument.

'Well, wouldn't just a bit of modernising do the trick?' Rosemary countered, failing to visualise her aunt in one of the neat little boxes she'd passed.

'No, the place needs too much doing to it. Derek says it really should be re-roofed, and the cost of putting in central heating, new windows, and all the other things... She just hasn't got the money. She only has a small pension to live on, you know, plus what she earns from her gardening column.'

Rosemary had been wondering about Zinnia's financial circumstances, so this was useful information, but it didn't feel right to be discussing her behind her back, especially with Veronica.

'I love what I've seen of Haydon Settleworth,' she said, diplomatically, trying not to drop cake crumbs on the carpet. Have you lived here long?'

'About fifteen years – yes, Matthew was four when we bought this house. It's a bit small though. I've always wanted to have a conservatory on the back, and put in an Aga, and extend the kitchen, but...' Veronica didn't finish the sentence. It was obviously all right to state that her mother-in-law had money constraints, but shameful to acknowledge the same problem herself.

'It was kind of Matthew to come and collect me yesterday,' Rosemary said quickly. 'I was hoping he could sort out why I can't get my computer working properly. One of his many talents, according to his grandmother. Will he be back soon?'

But Veronica didn't know. 'I'm always the last to be told what he's doing,' she complained. He's supposed to be studying for his A-levels, and I keep telling him that he'll fail again if he doesn't put his mind to it, and really do some work.' She brushed hair out of her eyes with irritation. 'Not that he listens to a word I say. He's helping to set up The Walled Garden at Trugglestone Hall at the moment. The best thing would be for you to call in, on your way back, and tell him what the problem is.'

The telephone rang in the hall at that moment, so Rosemary had to restrain her eagerness to depart, while Veronica went to answer it. She wasn't at all comfortable in this forbiddingly tidy house. The contrast with shabby Kiln House was almost comical. She didn't feel at home there either, but at least it had a warm, welcoming kitchen. Nor did she much take to the disapproving Veronica, a feeling that she sensed was reciprocated.

The phone call was short. 'That was Zinnia,' Veronica reported coming in from the hall, 'sounding agitated. She wants us all to come over this evening for a meal and a Family Council of War, as she put it. She wouldn't say what it was about. Any idea?'

'I only know she was going out to see someone this morning, but I don't know who,' was all Rosemary could contribute, as she rose to go.

'I've told her I'll make a large casserole and a trifle, and bring them over,' Veronica said, seeing her to the door, 'so she won't have to worry about food. And could you make sure Matthew knows about this evening, when you find him?'

That was nice of her, Rosemary reflected, as she walked towards the gate, past a row of daffodils, fidgeting in the wind. She's let herself in for a whole afternoon's cooking, just to be helpful to her mother-in-law. The trouble with you, my girl, is that you come to conclusions about people far too quickly.

The peeling gates of Trugglestone Hall sagged like a glutton's stomach, and gave the impression of having retired from active service some years ago, as Rosemary walked uncertainly through them in search of Matthew. A pot-holed drive stretched away towards the house, but to the left was a large, cobbled stable yard, where a cement mixer was toiling noisily, beside a heap of sand. A builder's lorry loaded with rubble was just emerging, and the driver stopped and leaned out obligingly.

'The Walled Garden? See those arched doors, it's through there.'

The high brick wall that flanked the road had turned a right angle, and now formed a side of the stable yard but, pushing open one of the large, wooden doors, she found that on the other side it was the boundary for an extensive garden.

Venerable old fruit trees were trained against three of the walls, with the fourth largely taken up by a long greenhouse, in need of some refurbishment. Together, they seemed to represent an old regime, pushed defensively to the edge by the upheaval going on in the rest of the garden. A large circle, intersected by paths, had been laid out in the middle, creating orange-segment beds, and in the four corners, separate little areas had been formed, all of them newly-planted, or still bare earth . Most of the paths too, were just ribbons of muddy soil, ridged with tyre marks and footprints. In the far corner Matthew was loading bricks into a wheelbarrow.

He hadn't seen her, and Rosemary was just wondering whether to shout across to him, or brave the mud in loafers she cared about, when a slight woman in her mid thirties, with a freckled, snub nose and bob of sun-bleached hair, came through the arched door behind her.

'I was hoping to speak to Matthew Peasmore,' she explained, guiltily, and the young woman gave her a warm smile.

'Hi, I'm Susie,' she said. 'You must be Rosemary – I've heard all about you from Matthew.' She put out her hand, then withdrew it and wiped it on her faded jeans. 'No, sorry,' she said laughing, 'I'm still too filthy.'

At the sound of their voices Matthew looked up, and Susie called across. 'It's your glamorous American cousin to see you. Look lively.'

'Glamorous, are you kidding?' Rosemary protested.

'Well, look at us Country Bumpkins,' Susie said, with smiling disparagement. 'Toiling away in scruffy clothes, mud up to our elbows, and everywhere else. Come and have some coffee, it's about time we had a break.'

They were soon sitting on upturned beer crates in one end of the old greenhouse, drinking instant coffee from assorted mugs, and Rosemary again found herself recounting her nocturnal experience, this time to a sympathetic audience.

'Bed socks,' Susie pronounced firmly. 'That's what you need. I found out they were one of life's essentials when we moved into the house a few months ago. We haven't any central heating either, and I used to wake up in the morning and find ice on the *inside* of the windows. The trick is to dress up to go to bed. Thick tights, pullover – and bed socks.' She laughed. 'Next winter, when the central heating's been installed, I shall buy myself a really glamorous nightdress in celebration. That's if we can afford the oil to run it, of course.'

Rosemary was torn between amusement at the picture painted, and dismay at the thought of not being able to banish the numbing cold of her bedroom.

'Well, I had thought, perhaps, an electric heater...,' she began.

'Good idea,' Susie agreed. 'And I don't suppose there's any warmth left in those old blankets either, what you need is a really efficient duvet.'

She took in the girl's strained face. 'Tell you what,' she said kindly, 'I'm going into Ipswich tomorrow. Would you like to come with me, and we'll buy all the things you've discovered you need.' Susie smiled at the answering look of relief , and glanced down at the loafers. 'A pair of wellington boots, for a start,' she suggested cheerfully.

Walking back, Rosemary felt like a struggling swimmer who'd suddenly touched bottom. It was immensely cheering to have found in Susie a potential friend and ally, to whom she could turn for help. Also Matthew seemed to think the problem with her computer would be easy to fix. It was probably just an unsuitable modem, he reckoned, and promised to look at it this evening, when they were all coming over.

She'd been surprised by the enthusiasm with which he was working. It was good to see he wasn't lazy, despite his laid back attitude, and her liking increased. Having now encountered Veronica, she was increasingly intrigued to meet his father, and found herself rather looking forward to the evening.

****

Matthew had promised to come well before the meal, in order to act as Information Technology consultant, and duly burst through the back door as Rosemary was clearing the last pile of stuff from the kitchen table, before laying it.

'Hi Gran,' he greeted Zinnia, 'They're here again, scoffing the primroses you've grown for them. Shall I chase them off? Mind you, that's your job, old Roger the Lodger.' He gave the cat's tail a friendly tweak, and pointed to the door. 'Out boy. Kill!'

'Oh not my primroses *again,,*' Zinnia lamented exasperatedly. 'The double ones are their favourites. And that's the third time this week. Yes, get rid of them please, give them a good fright if possible. Rosemary can come and help.'

'Well now, I wouldn't have called our Rosemary a fright, myself,' protested Matthew, giving her a mock appraisal 'But now that you come to mention it...'

'Hit him,' his grandmother suggested, aware that her guest was probably unused to family banter. 'He needs to be taught some manners. And so do those wretched things. Sort them out for me will you, or I won't have any garden left.'

Rosemary found herself outside, without any idea what manner of beast or human was supposed to be given a hard time.

'There they are,' Matthew indicated a flowerbed by the greenhouse, where two peacocks were happily pecking at the plants.

'Peacocks!'

'Yeah. Old Fart Features next door has started keeping them, and Gran's really getting her knickers in a twist about them. You go that side, and we'll try and drive them back through the hedge.' He spread his arms wide and emitted an aeroplane engine noise, followed by the ack-ack of a firing machine gun, as they closed in on the birds, who were affecting nonchalance, like shoplifters deciding to brazen it out. 'How good's your stone-throwing?' he asked over his shoulder. 'A few near misses might give them something to think about, as well.'

The peacocks were disinclined to cut short their epicurean outing, but eventually the male's resistance crumbled, and he retreated towards the hedge, found a hole, and disappeared. His mate ran up and down in growing alarm until she found another gap to scuttle through.

'I thought they were heading for the Pit, at one point,' Rosemary remarked, when they were walking back. 'We'd have had some job getting them out of there. I was exploring it this afternoon. What an amazing place.' She stopped. 'That reminds me, we can't find the summer house key, and I probably left it in the door. Better go and look.'

'When I was little, my friends all wanted to come and play down here,' Matthew told her, as they made their way down the ramp. 'We used to make great dens. They still come sometimes, at least the ones in the Group do.'

'Group? What's that, a secret society or something?'

'Yeah. Satanic rituals, naked dancing at full moon, and...' he eyed her speculatively, 'sacrificial virgins.'

Rosemary had a fleeting vision of an attractive, blue-eyed Devil, horns emerging from dark, curls.

'Give me a break,' she said good humouredly. 'Tell me about your Group.'

'Didn't Gran say. I play guitar in a band called The Heebie Jeebies.'

'The what?'

'Great name, isn't it. One of Gran's expressions.'

'Sure, but what does it mean?'

'Search me.' He shrugged. 'She always says something "gives her the heebie jeebies", and I thought it was a funky name. You must come to one of our gigs some time. We're really cool. But none of our families will let us practice at home now.'

'Amazing.'

Matthew flashed her an appreciative grin. 'Yeah, you'd think they'd jump at the chance of jazzing up their sad lives, wouldn't you. Anyway, Gran lets us jam down here, because the Pit muffles it a bit.'

Rosemary could believe that. The sound of birdsong seemed magnified by the steep sides, but all other background noise was suddenly absent, as if the surrounding world had taken a rest break.

'What a great place,' she said. 'It's like a private little kingdom, isn't it.'

They had made their way to the summer house, and sure enough, there was the key.

'Oh tut,' Matthew teased her. 'Gran'll have your guts for garters.'

'I think she's making allowances for my uncouth, colonial background,' Rosemary responded, unperturbed. She pocketed the key, and they stood looking at the garden, across a carpet of scented, white narcissus glimmering in the soft light, like motifs embroidered on a dusky veil.

'Those flowers – aren't they just something. Did Zinnia make all this?'

'There was just the tennis court and the summer house here originally,' Matthew told her, as they turned to go back. 'But as long as I can remember there's been a garden. And if ever you wanted Gran, she'd be working here, making it bigger and better every year.'

'I used to help sometimes,' he remarked as they started up the ramp. 'She wants me to start clearing down there,' he indicated the precipitous sides of the Little Pit to their left. 'And I might have a go... But, sorting out people's computer problems makes more dosh.'

'Oh, you charge do you. Am I going to be able to afford the highly talented Matthew Peasmore's services to sort out my humble machine?'

'Not a hope,' he assured her happily. 'I'll put it on the family slate.'

****

Matthew's IT skills were the subject of his parents' discussion, as Derek wearily changed out of his working suit.

'Having a way with computers is all very well,' Veronica was complaining, 'but he can't just mess around doing bits and bobs like this.'

'It does seem to earn him quite a bit, though.' Derek had been through this conversation before, and was still inclined to stick up for his son.

'Yes, but he'll need university qualifications, won't he, to go into it as a career. That computer course he applied for last year would have been perfect. Why did he have to go and mess up his A-level exams?'

'Mm.' Agreeing sounds were really the best policy.

'It's just that I can't see him passing them this summer either, because he isn't doing a stroke of work, Derek.' Veronica stood at their bedroom window looking out towards the trees that screened Trugglestone Hall. 'He's spending most of his time as unskilled labour at The Walled Garden, and then there's that band of his, and a few computer jobs squeezed in between,' she continued disparagingly. 'Not to mention the hordes of girls who flock round here, asking where he is.'

Trust a woman to see that as a fault, thought Derek, knowing better than to say so.

'You'll have to speak to him, and have a serious father and son talk. He doesn't listen to a word I say,' she added resentfully.

'Mm.' Derek had let the words flow over him, but suddenly realised this might not be the appropriate response. 'Oh I'm sure he does...er... know what you think.'

'Yes, but he doesn't take any notice. I *keep* telling him.'

This wasn't getting them anywhere. 'I'll try and have a word with him sometime,' Derek assured her, with all the enthusiasm of a man in a cosy armchair instructed to unblock the sink. 'To be honest, I hardly see him these days. By the time I get back from Thornways he's already gone out with the band or something. He went on ahead to Mum's did he?'

It seemed a chance to change the subject.

'What's this Family Council of War for? Let's see, who can we have declared against now? Oh no,' he groaned, 'don't tell me, it'll be Gerry Thornway. That's all I need. I spend the entire day fighting him at work, as it is. What have we done to deserve him as Mum's next door neighbour as well?'

'Your mother didn't say what it was about. But I thought things were okay with Elaine and Gerry now.' Veronica drew the curtains. 'Their cat has decided it wants to live at Kiln House, and they've finally accepted that. I don't think there are any other problems.'

She sounded rather defensive, and he suddenly remembered her weekly Health Club mornings with his boss's mousey little wife.

'I know you're friendly with Elaine,' he said, 'and she's nice enough, but that husband of hers is totally useless.' Sitting on the bed to put on his socks, he looked up at her, a worried frown on his normally good-humoured face. 'If he carries on the way he's going, Thornways will go to the wall, and I'll be out of a job.'

Veronica was alarmed. All complaints about their wayward son were suddenly banished as the consequences of what Derek had said sank in.

'Things can't be as bad as that, surely? I know you haven't been very happy there since Old Man Thornway died, but it was always a good business. What's Gerry been doing?'

'Taking large amounts out of the company and putting nothing back, that's what.' Derek was contemptuous. 'Old Thornway put him through accountancy training, but he was wasting his money.'

'Well, he doesn't know the ropes as well as you do,' she pointed out. 'Surely if you gave him lots of support and guidance...'

'Support and guidance – that pompous git! He doesn't have the first idea how to run a company, Veronica, and isn't interested in it anyway, except as a source of money for a flashy lifestyle.'

'Oh dear.' This was unsettling. It wasn't at all like Derek to get upset, and out of character for him to be pessimistic. Normally she had to drag him to uncomfortable facts, and make him face them. And clearly he had been bottling all this up for ages.

Tying his shoes, he said in a flat voice. 'There was a rumour going round today that he's looking for a buyer for the company.'

'Oh that's all right then,' Veronica was relieved. 'The new owners would keep you on, and probably expand it, wouldn't they.'

'Hm.'

She'd said that as a statement. No point in including her in his fears that they would be unlikely to do any such thing. He was trying not to admit it to himself.

'I don't want to talk about it,' Derek told her, reaching for his car keys. 'I've had work up to here,' he drew a line under his chin. 'When I get home, the last thing I want to bother about is that posturing twit, Gerry Thornway. And I'm ravenous as well. Let's get that wonderful-smelling casserole over to Mum's and demolish it, before I faint with hunger.'

Her husband's thickening figure was hardly giving a good impression of a starving man, but Veronica looked pleased. His obvious appreciation of her cooking was one of the cords that held them together.

A few minutes later, backing the car down the drive, he remarked, more cheerfully, 'On second thoughts, if Mum has declared war against Gerry Thornway, she's just acquired an enthusiastic general.'

****

Derek greeted Rosemary warmly. 'Ah, the long-lost American cousin, come to observe your quaint English relations, eh?'

'I'm deeply disappointed,' she responded, sounding pained. 'Where's the grand house, and the servants? There wasn't even a lady's maid to unpack my case.'

'And no-one to light a cosy fire in your bedroom, I hear,' he laughed, with a naughty glance at Zinnia's back.

She had expected an older version of Matthew, and instead he was shorter, and rather thickset, a paunch settling comfortably round his middle, but they clearly shared the same relaxed amusement at life. Throughout the meal she couldn't help sneaking glances at him, intrigued to find that, both physically and in his mannerisms, there were unmistakable shades of her father. Derek was his nephew of course, and perhaps it wasn't surprising that there should be shared family traits, but, raw with grief, she found it both fascinating and disturbing, like glimpsing your reflection in a distorting mirror.

'Come on Mum,' Derek urged, when they had made short work of Veronica's delicious beef casserole, and had started on the trifle. 'You'd better tell us who you've declared war on, so the Peasemore army can be mobilised to pulverise them forthwith.'

'It's the other way round,' Zinnia's tone was serious. 'We, or at least I, have been declared war upon. I haven't said anything before, because it wasn't certain. And I couldn't believe it anyway.' She paused, and announced dramatically, 'Clive Trugglestone is selling the Pit.'

There was an astonished silence.

'I've known Clive all his life, I just don't know what's got into him,' she continued angrily. 'Julia's very unhappy about the things he's doing too – she was telling me.' A thought struck her. 'She must have known about this when she was here, and never said anything! No wonder she's been avoiding me the last week or so.' The sense of betrayal stung like an unseen jellyfish. 'My oldest friend!'

'Well, maybe no-one will buy it,' put in Veronica soothingly.

'No. I found out this morning that a sale has already gone through.'

'Will you have to pay garden rent now, or something, Gran?' asked Matthew. 'How about turning the tables, and charging the new owner, whoever it is, for upkeep?'

'Who's bought it?' Derek wanted to know, more sensibly.

'That's the trouble. It's Mike Swathe.'

'Any connection with Swathes at Stockleigh? They're on the same trading estate as Thornways, right behind us in fact.'

She nodded. 'He runs it,' adding, with emphasis, for the others' benefit. 'It's a waste disposal business.'

'Well, what would he want with an old chalk pit?' Veronica was puzzled, but Derek had made the connection.

'You mean he's going to use it for tipping?'

'What else would he want it for?'

This wasn't making any sense to Rosemary. 'I'm sorry, but I don't understand. The Pit is part of your garden isn't it?'

'No, it belongs to the Trugglestone estate,' Derek explained. 'You don't even pay rent, do you Mum?'

She shook her head. 'There was just an informal arrangement. But it's unthinkable that he should use it for tipping. I'm not having it. Just not!' She looked round the table her face flushed, like a sitting hen defying a fox. 'I didn't spent years of effort making a garden down there, just to see it disappear under tons of rubbish. We've got to find a way of stopping them.'

'Now hold on a minute,' Derek tried to calm things down. 'You may not own the Pit, but you do own the access. They'd have to come through your entrance and across the garden to get to it. They could tip from the road into the Little Pit, I suppose, but they wouldn't be allowed to – it'd block the road. So unless you sell that land to Swathe, or agree to let lorries through, he can't do anything.'

'That's what I thought,' his mother said bleakly. 'But Clive has sold him the field above too. There's a farm track across that, which he could use to reach the side of the pit, where it's not so high, and tip from there.'

'I'll make some coffee.' Like a child with a comfort blanket, at times of stress Veronica always took refuge in preparing sustenance.

'What about squatter's rights?' suggested Matthew. 'You've had the use of the place for over forty years. Doesn't that give you some rights?'

'Apparently not. I've been taking advice on that this morning. Although no money was involved, father-in-law did draw up an agreement with the Trugglestone Estate. It says that he can have the use of the Pit "without prejudice", or something. Anyway, my solicitor says their ownership is clear. We've just got to find some other reason to stop Mike Swathe.'

Rosemary paused in the middle of clearing the plates. 'Are you sure he's going to fill it with garbage? Why on earth would he want to do that?'

'We've got a real problem in this country,' Derek told her, 'Too much rubbish, and we're running out of places to put it. If councils try to incinerate the stuff, there's an outcry about poisonous gases. And dumping at sea isn't allowed any more. So a hole in the ground that would take thousands of tons of rubbish would be worth a lot of money.' He paused. 'If Swathe just charged, say, twenty-five pounds per lorry load...' the arithmetic stretched away impossibly, 'he'd be making a fortune.'

'He's got one already. Odious little man.' Clearly Mike Swathe had failed to engage Zinnia's affections.

'How about getting a Preservation Order put on it,' was Veronica's unexpectedly sensible suggestion, as she put out five cups on a tray. 'After all, it has been quarried for centuries, and lime making was an important industry once. Wouldn't it qualify as Industrial Heritage or something?'

'Hm,' Zinnia nodded approvingly. 'We could look into that. But I think my esteemed father-in-law might have messed up the industrial archaeology scene, by demolishing the old lime kiln.'

'Why?' Rosemary was finding a lot of things puzzling, but decided now was not the moment to ask what a lime kiln was anyway.

'It was just after the war, when there was a shortage of bricks, and he wanted to build the garage. The Trugglestones said he could. Nobody cared about such things then.'

'Okay, why don't we do that in reverse?' suggested Matthew flippantly. 'We'll knock the garage down, and secretly rebuild the kiln. At night. There's an old photograph of it, isn't there Gran. It was sort of bottle-shaped.'

A rather absent smile was his response. 'I did wonder,' she said carefully, 'whether we couldn't suddenly discover an ancient skeleton down there.'

'A sort of Piltdown Man, you mean, Gran?'

Derek could see Rosemary was lost. 'Piltdown Man was a skeleton found in a quarry before the First World War,' he told her. 'He was supposed to be an ape-like form of early man, and the discovery had the scientists jumping up and down.'

'It was only found to be a hoax forty years later,' Zinnia added, with satisfaction.

'Ace idea!' Matthew could picture himself appearing on television to tell the world how he'd seen this bone sticking out of the cliff, when he and the band were jamming. It'd be great publicity for the HJ's.'

'Do you have a convincing skeleton lying around?' Rosemary enquired. 'I'd hate to spoil a good scam, but it does seem a slight problem.'

'There's an even bigger one,' cut in Derek amiably. 'This is a chalk pit we're talking about, and chalk was formed from the remains of tiny marine creatures, under the sea. You don't find the remains of Homo anything in the stuff. How about a mermaid?'

'Coffee,' announced Veronica, laying the tray on the table, and passing round the cups. 'You know, when I was down at the school this week, they'd put a big poster of a stag beetle up in one of the classrooms. Horrible thing, with great black pincers,' she shuddered. 'But apparently it's very scarce now, and the kids have been asked to look out for them. I'm sure there must be some down in the Pit. Wouldn't that help?'

'A rare species.' Zinnia considered. 'Yes, that is an idea. Can't say I've seen any lately, but we could always scour the countryside, and transport them back to form a nice little colony.'

Rosemary was already mentally composing a missive to her beloved. *'Today I crawled across the fields and captured thirty-one stag beetles, at no small hazard to myself. They have been taken to Oflag Pit One, and given quarters that are adequate, if not comfortable. The prisoners are subject to inspection at any time, and will remain under guard for the duration. Having a lovely time.'*

'Why stop at one rare species?' Matthew was suggesting, as she regretfully came back to reality 'What about the Horseshoe Bat? And Natterjack toads. Oh yeah, and every time some pond is threatened with development, they find Greater Crested Newts living in it, don't they. That stops the builders because they're rare.'

'Actually, Mum, haven't you got the answer, in the Pit Garden itself?' Derek had been thinking along simpler lines. 'Surely you've got a number of rather special plants down there?'

'Yes, I have.' She stirred her coffee thoughtfully. 'Not only rare things, but a few unique ones – crosses between plants that are totally original. There's a little hebe, a wonderful dianthus, and a peachy-coloured crocus, for starters. I had thought of possibly cashing in on them one day.'

'Well, wouldn't that do the trick then?'

'I don't think so. Well, probably not. They're easily transplanted, for one thing. And they're garden plants as well. The powers that be don't care about those. Now if they were wild flowers...'

'Or if they were endangered, *and* had exciting medicinal properties,' put in Rosemary. 'There was a travel article in the flight magazine, coming over, which mentioned some mint plant that Cornell University just discovered produces a really effective insect-repellent. They reckon it's very exciting. And the plant had almost died out in the wild.'

'It'd see off the stag beetles then,' commented Matthew irrepressibly.

She made a face at him. 'I didn't mean bring it over here. I meant find something like it. Isn't there some British wild flower that's not only rare, but would have the drug companies interested, so they wouldn't allow its habitat to be damaged?'

'Not that I can suggest,' Zinnia answered regretfully. 'And don't forget that we'd have to go and dig it up from somewhere, and replant it in the quarry. Even I draw the line at that.'

She shook her head, thinking about it. 'The tantalising thing is that there used to be a medicinal plant called Settlewort, which modern scientists would sell their mothers for. *And* it grew here, in the village. In fact that's why the place is called Haydon Settleworth. But the damn thing's extinct.'

'Why, what happened to it?' Rosemary wanted to know.

'Apparently it was difficult to grow. The Romans brought it over, and demand always outstripped supply. It got scarcer and scarcer, and just died out in the end.'

'Well, how about smuggling this plant back from the Mediterranean, or wherever, and pretending it was growing here naturally?' she suggested.

'Unfortunately, it was driven to extinction there too.' Zinnia noted her niece's unorthodox attitude, with approval. 'It no longer exists anywhere.'

'Couldn't we grow something else, Gran, and say it was Settlewort? Does anyone know how it should look?' Matthew was beginning to envisage television cameras again.

'I know what it looks like,' Zinnia told them unexpectedly, 'at least I think so. I was a little girl when the last known plant was found, growing. People suspected that's what it was, anyway. It was in an old bomb crater, where Gerry Thornway's house is built now, in fact. They reckoned the seed must have been in the soil for years, and suddenly germinated.'

'But did experts come and look at it?' Matthew remained hopeful. 'I mean couldn't we still fool people by growing something else in the Pit, and calling it Settlewort?'

'Surely it would have produced more seeds, and they could have been planted,' observed Derek, who hadn't heard this story before.

'In answer to your question, Matthew, no, the thing wasn't officially identified. It was just after the war, and people had more important things to occupy them than a possibly rare plant.' Zinnia shrugged. 'But old

Peasmore – my future father-in-law, Rosemary – took a great interest in it. He collected the seeds, and attempted to grow them on.' She paused, remembering. 'I know that for a fact, because we weren't allowed to come and play tennis here for several weeks, while he was trying to get them to germinate.'

'Sorry?' The logic of this statement was entirely escaping her family.

'Well, he tried planting them in several places. He put some seed into pots, and some in flowerbeds, and in the greenhouse,' she explained. 'They kept a few hens then, because of food rationing, and normally the things had the run of the garden. But he was afraid they would scratch up his precious seeds, so he caged them in the tennis court.'

'And he didn't get any plants out of the seeds?'

She shook her head. 'Unfortunately not. He gave some to his old gardener to try, and he had no joy either. After a while they lost interest, and we reclaimed the tennis court. I've always looked out for any possible seedlings though, even just a seed, in case it was biding its time in the soil. They were particularly distinctive too. I remember we sniggered because they looked like little brown buttocks.'

Rosemary appeared suddenly thoughtful, and Derek caught her eye.

'What you'd call your butt,' he told her helpfully, and Veronica sent him a restraining look.

Zinnia sighed. 'Thanks for your suggestion, Matthew. Something to try as a last resort maybe. But I suppose before anything else, the sensible thing is to find out if Swathe's applied for planning...'

Rosemary had got up, and was quietly leaving the room. Her aunt paused, while the others looked at her enquiringly.

Leaning back through the doorway, she gave them an enigmatic smile.

'Buttocks,' she said pleasantly, and closed the door.

There was a silence.

'Now look what you've done to our Rose,' Matthew chided his father delightedly. 'A nicely brought up girl, comes over here expecting relations who know the proper way to behave, and you shock her to the core with your coarse language, and bottom fetish.' He wagged his finger at Derek. 'It's not good enough, is it. Poor girl's probably had to go and lie down now.'

Zinnia regarded him indulgently. 'I think the washing up beckons, my lad.'

Footsteps could be heard coming downstairs.

'Talk amongst yourselves,' he hissed theatrically, 'pretend we haven't noticed,' adding loudly, 'No the thing about little green men, Gran, since you ask, is that they're never around when you want them. But if you're certain, we could try signalling at the next full moon that they'd be welcome to set up home...'

Rosemary came through the door holding a small cardboard box, which proclaimed the efficacy of Denis's Lincolnshire Pig Powders. Removing the lid, she put it down in front of Zinnia, who could see that it contained a number of brown seeds. Even though shrivelled with age, they had a distinctly cleavaged look.

'Don't suppose these'd be any use to you,' her niece enquired, with the elaborate casualness of a schoolchild announcing a coveted scholarship. 'Would they?'

Chapter Three

There had been rain overnight, and Rosemary walked through the village after breakfast the following morning in her inadequate shoes, avoiding the puddles. Dampness darkened the mossy roof tiles of the cottages, in places leaky gutters were still dripping, and the sharp air smelt tangy.

At this earlier hour of the morning there was more bustle in the village than she had noticed yesterday. Cars were speeding through, as people departed for work, some stopping to buy newspapers and suddenly remembered necessities from the two stores. The road with the unprepossessing houses was busy with mums and children, evidently school-bound, and she was surprised and pleased when several smiled and said good-morning to her.

Susie Trugglestone had suggested collecting her from Kiln House, after dropping the children at school, but her kind offer had been refused, as being an added inconvenience. Now Rosemary was glad of the chance to stretch her legs, also relieved that any possible confrontation between Zinnia and Susie had been avoided. It had in fact taken her some time to work out that yesterday's cheerfully muddy young woman in jeans and scruffy anorak, the saviour who was going to help her buy survival gear, was Lady Susan Trugglestone.

She didn't have long to wait by the peeling gates, before an unwashed Volvo, evidently treated as a pack animal, drew up beside her, Susie at the wheel.

'I didn't know you were a Lady,' Rosemary remarked ingenuously, buckling on her seat belt, and realising too late that that didn't sound quite right.

Susie laughed. 'Still can't get used to it myself, and it's been nearly a year now.'

'But I thought the English aristocracy were very grand.' This wasn't earning prizes for tact either. 'Heck, I'm sorry...'

'Not any more,' her ladyship was amused. 'Especially when they haven't got money. Titles are a load of hokum anyway.' She paused, concentrating on passing a rider with a frisky horse. As the car gathered speed again, she went on, 'All it means is that I married a man whose ancestor was a successful merchant in the eighteenth century. Probably did some small service to the Crown. No big deal, is it? Poor, but genteel, that's us. And,' she added matter-of-factly, 'my esteemed mother-in-law might even disagree with the genteel bit, where I'm concerned.'

Having finally kicked her sense of diplomacy into life, Rosemary decided this was a track it might be best not to explore. She would ask Zinnia for elucidation. But there was one thing she had to get straight, however tempting it was to avoid.

'I hardly dared tell my aunt that I was going into town with you,' she confessed hesitantly. 'It's consorting with the enemy in her eyes.'

'Enemy!' exclaimed Susie in genuine surprise. 'What do you mean?'

'No-one with the name Trugglestone is on her list of favourite people at the moment. She's just found out that her beloved Pit Garden has been sold, and she's spitting mad.'

'Ah, the chalk pit. Clive hadn't planned on selling, but a silly offer was made for it, and the field above,' said Susie, 'and the estate trustees agreed it would have been daft to refuse, in the circumstances. I don't think your aunt has any need to worry, though. The change of ownership isn't going to affect her, is it.'

'Well, she's afraid the man who's bought it wants to tip garbage there.'

'Oh surely not.' Susie sounded reassuringly certain.

'Why else would he want it?'

'Mike Swathe was brought up in Haydon Settleworth apparently. Julia, my mum-in-law, knows him. In fact she's gone to live next door to his mother's old cottage. Julia thinks he's intending to move back here, and maybe wants to build a house on the hill above your aunt.'

This certainly did put a new complexion on things.

'Besides, he'd never be given planning permission for tipping. You wouldn't believe the trouble we're having with the Council Planning Office over the changes we want to make at the Hall and the Walled Garden.'

Rosemary was soon hearing about her plans to open up a Herb Display Garden within the walls, with shop attached, selling refreshments, plants and herb products.

'I'm going flat out to get it ready for opening in the summer,' Susie told her eagerly, 'but it'll be touch and go. The planning people have been quite reasonable about Clive's plans for running the Hall as a conference centre, but for some reason my modest little venture is seen as a blot on the village. Commercialism – shock, horror!'

'You're interested in herbs then?'

'Oh they're fascinating.' Her face lit up. 'I first got interested at Kew – The Royal Botanic Garden – when I was training there. The place was originally important for medicinal plants, you know, and how to use them.'

'And they taught you all about that?'

''Well, not specifically. But when you start looking into herbs, they link so many things – cookery, medicine, gardening, folklore, history...' Susie's animation indicated this was her great enthusiasm.

Rosemary was on the verge of asking about Settlewort. Susie would surely know all about it. But her awakened sense of diplomacy growled warningly.

'Did you have a job with herbs then, after you trained?' This seemed a safer question.

'Would have liked to. But for the past few years I've been working at a big general nursery called Berrimans, over towards Cambridge.'

They were joining a busy dual carriageway, and Susie checked over her shoulder before moving out. 'Herbs are what I really want to specialise in though,' she continued. 'And we've simply got to make Trugglestone Hall earn its keep. It's been coasting downhill for years, and so much needs doing to the house, it's daunting.'

Reproach and resentment were detectable, as if she'd been handed a wonderful book, only to discover several years of library fines owing on it.

'We can't make it into the kind of conference centre Clive wants without spending vast sums,' she added, then her tone lightened. 'But if I can turn The Walled Garden into a tourist attraction, it'll really help pay the bills.'

She smiled at Rosemary. 'Planning officers, obstructive old gardeners, complaining mothers-in-law - nuts to the lot of them! Now, let's think about the things we need to buy for you today. Have you made a list?'

****

Back at Kiln House, Zinnia was pleased at the prospect of being able to concentrate on seed sowing, with Rosemary gone all morning.

Life was full of unexpected twists, she reflected, lacing up the comfortable old boots seized on with triumph in a charity shop sale. The prospect of losing the Pit Garden filled her with anger and despair. It was like losing her identity. That place was her great achievement, the one thing she could be really proud of.

She stood up and reached for the little brown box, fingering it reverently. This was not just a box of old seeds, she thought to herself with a thrill, it was an opportunity to save the garden, and have her name in lights in the horticultural world as well. Not that fame and fortune were things she hankered after, (although a very small fortune would be nice), but she was contemptuous of the glibness that seemed to have overtaken the gardening world.

People just seem to want bigger this, and brighter the other, she grumbled to herself in the outhouse, like a bad-tempered badger, while counting handfuls of compost into a large enamel bowl. They put in fully-grown shrubs and trees, for instant effect; plant unsuitable things in full flower; pretend that all you do is just lay out a garden and forget it. It's not proper gardening.

Zinnia would have had some difficulty defining this term herself, but extended horticultural friendships only to those she considered 'proper gardeners', of which there were none in Haydon Settleworth.

But both serious gardeners, and the horticultural establishment would sit up and take notice if she could successfully resurrect Settlewort, she thought, adding sand to the compost. Clearly that wasn't going to be easy, but there was no doubt in her mind that it could be achieved.

Until late last night, she'd been up, searching for books that would give some clue as to how to proceed. But she couldn't find the old herbal that might have helped, and the rest were a waste of time. Settlewort was absent from most indexes, and Solanum regale, its botanical name, didn't yield much more than a mention that the plant had been known for medicinal properties, but was now extinct. No guidance as to how to grow the thing. Not surprising really. How would anyone know?

Lying in bed that morning, she'd decided on a plan of campaign for sowing the thirty-two seeds the box contained. Most important was not to sow them all at once. It would have been ideal to try sowing them sparingly, every few weeks, over a whole year. But if the Pit was going to be saved by having Settlewort growing there, time was not on her side. So she decided to try with half the seeds straight away, all under different conditions.

Germination might require quite a high temperature, she reasoned, if Settlewort had originally been a Mediterranean plant. She would put some in a propagator on high heat, and some under cooler conditions. Alternatively, it might require a bit of frost to start the germination process, so a couple were going to be planted in a pot outside, in the hope of a really cold night. She had already put one seed in an envelope, labelled, 'Whoever you are, your life will not be worth living, if this is opened', and placed it in the fridge. Another would join it, after being soaked in water for a day or so, in case that was also a necessary part of the process.

In fact, there were almost more permutations to try than seeds available, for the first sowing. One method was bound to work, she told herself confidently, sliding open the greenhouse door and savouring the warm, damp atmosphere. Then it would be simple to treat the remaining seeds exactly the same, and achieve maximum germination.

After that, there would be the little matter of quietly transplanting the seedlings to realistic looking positions in the Pit. Shouldn't be difficult. A plausible explanation as to why a plant believed to be extinct had suddenly sprung to life in a cultivated chalk pit, was a problem that could be addressed later. Zinnia didn't believe in anxiously peering into the mist of times to come. Better to stride through it confidently, and if you fell off a cliff, too bad.

She was concentrating on the delicate task of making a little nick on one of the seeds with a sharp knife, when she heard a voice, and looked up to find approaching a chubby man of about forty, with light brown hair, a fringe and glasses. Oh dear. Basil Berriman.

'Knew I'd find you here, Zinnia,' he called cheerfully. 'Happiness is a warm greenhouse, and sowing seeds in the sunshine.'

A gardening friend like Basil would normally have been a welcome visitor, but Zinnia was wary of someone expert enough to ask awkward questions, and quickly put a trowel over the seed, before turning to greet him.

'Thought I'd call in to see you,' he slid the door shut to retain the warmth. 'Maurice sends his love.' He kissed Zinnia on both cheeks. 'He's hoping you'll come and see his potager garden this summer. He's desperate for an expert's view. I don't count, of course. And he makes such a fuss if I pick anything for cooking!'

In anyone else, Zinnia might have considered the manner off-putting, but she respected Basil as a fellow enthusiast, and a visit from him was always pleasurable, a chance to talk about plants with someone as knowledgeable as herself.

'I wondered whether your wonderful, dark blue pulmonaria might be out,' he went on, 'so I can take another shot of it. Didn't have the right film in last year, and the wretched thing came out mauve.'

'Of course you can, it's looking very good at the moment. Photograph anything you want,' Zinnia told him, glad of an excuse to leave the greenhouse.

'I've been going through my slides, for a talk I'm putting together that complements the Nursery's stand at Chelsea this year,' he explained, as they walked together along the path, pausing to admire the double primroses. 'It's our Centenary Year. Did I tell you our theme is Conservation. Fashionable, and commendably worthy, don't you think?'

'Conservation? What sort – wildflowers, rainforests…gardens?' Zinnia enquired, with the cynicism of one accustomed to watching bandwagons come to grief in potholes.

'Cultivated and wild plants. We're steering clear of vegetables, because there are specialist organisations busy saving those.'

'You don't sell them, either,' she commented, and Basil chuckled. One of the things he liked about Zinnia was that she saw through hype and flannel, and hadn't time for anyone who tried it on.

'Of course, it has to have a commercial base,' he agreed, removing some dead leaves from the pulmonaria he was about to photograph. 'The Micropropagation Unit has been working hard to produce batches of Franklinias, a small tree which may well be extinct in America now, plus Mazzard trees from Devon, and you wouldn't believe how many Hot Chocolate Plants it's been churning out.'

Zinnia raised her eyebrows at him.

'Well okay,' he countered her unspoken objection, 'we're not necessarily featuring plants that are rare in cultivation, as long as they're scarce in the wild. The idea is that the gardening public should see itself as keeping the plants safe for posterity, in their gardens. Have to buy them from Berrimans first, of course,' he added with a twinkle.

'You're not usually involved with Chelsea, are you?' Zinnia regarded him with tolerant affection. In the past Basil had been less than fulsome about Berrimans' choice of plants for their stand, and the two of them were agreed on the artificiality of the whole garden exhibition scene.

Crouching down for a close-up, he concentrated while pressing the camera shutter. 'No, I'm kept well out of the way, as a rule, being only a Lesser Being from the Design Department.' He straightened up. 'But all the usual bods found themselves a bit at sea with this one. So the call came, and suddenly glory is mine.' He smiled at her, as he wound on the camera.

'And are you pleased with how it's shaping up?'

'Reasonably. My brief was to find as many garden-worthy things as possible from the Red List of rare plants, which we could produce in bulk. But I wish I could have found something really arresting, a horticultural coup that would get us lots of publicity.'

'Mm.' Zinnia's brain was whirring, wondering if there was any way in which she could turn all this to advantage. If Settlewort plants were growing in the Pit Garden by the end of May, then maybe the Chelsea Flower Show would be the ideal place to announce the fact. She could ask Berrimans Nursery to do it, in conjunction with their stand.

Now that *would* get the press buzzing, she thought with satisfaction. The resulting publicity would mean an outcry if its habitat was in danger after that. Mike Swathe and his rubbish could go to hell. But as they moved off along the path a thought struck her. If Berriman's helped to publicise Settlewort, their considerable reputation would be on the line. It would be vital they had no doubts about the plant appearing spontaneously. So probably best not to mention the threat hanging over the Pit for the moment.

'Maybe something will turn up,' she told him blandly, 'you never know. Now, I want your opinion on a hybrid hellebore that's appeared in the Pit Garden. Come and have a look at it.'

A walk through the garden with someone knowledgeable always ended up being a slow affair, with many pauses to discuss various plants on the way. And when they reached the Pit, Basil gazed round in admiration.

'This place is amazing, Zinnia. I don't know how you do it.'

'It's a constant battle with sycamore seedlings, and the blasted ivy from the Little Pit,' she admitted with a sigh, although pleased at the praise. 'And the dispiriting thing is that I'll never win. Just the slightest let up, and between them they'll smother everything. But I had a real blitz this winter.'

'Well, it's looking just wonderful.' His eye rested on a drift of mauve and white. 'I took shots of that Corydalis solida two years ago, but they're even better now.'

'I don't suppose,' Zinnia asked hesitatingly, 'that is, would you consider taking a whole lot of photographs of the garden through the year, for me? I'd pay your costs, of course. I'd just like a ... record as it were. Of how it is now.'

'Of course, it'll be a pleasure. And I'll have an excuse to come and talk plants with you more often.' He beamed at her. 'You really have achieved something special here, you know. You'll have to fight off hordes of eager gardeners on the Gardens Festival day.'

'What Gardens Festival?'

'Oh I thought you'd be bound to know. I've just been to check how we're progressing with Lady Julia's garden, and she was saying that's going to be the village's big fund-raising effort this summer.'

'First I've heard of anything.' She made it sound as if he'd brought news of religious fervour sweeping the village.

'The plan is to have a Flower Arranging Competition as well,' he continued, 'and she wants my *dreadful* sister to come down for it!'

'Oh dear.' It was difficult to keep the smile out of her voice. Zinnia had been shaking her head over Loretta Moss's pretentious column in Country Harvest only yesterday. Author, exhibitionist, and doyenne of the flower arranging world, Basil's stories of his half-sister's extended ego, and abrasive manner were always entertaining.

'She's the blight of my life,' he wailed plaintively. 'We'll have to ask her to stay. And she always manages to upset Maurice dreadfully. Takes him weeks to recover.'

'Well, it's quite simple. Don't ask her to come. Tell Julia to get lost.'

Even as she said it, Zinnia knew this was impractical advice. Dear Basil telling anyone to get lost was as likely as a teddy bear stamping on a scorpion.

'Oh I couldn't,' he sounded appalled. 'Berrimans was originally started on Trugglestone estate land, so the family links go back a long way, as you know. And my uncle wants to use the garden we've designed for Lady Julia as part of our promotional brochure, next year. She's an important client.'

'She wouldn't stop you doing that though.'

'We've just been taken on to do the upkeep of Trugglestone Hall grounds, as well. Plus of course, my uncle is one of the estate trustees now.'

Zinnia's face darkened, and she was about to give Basil a piece of her mind about trustees who couldn't be trusted not to sell off other people's precious gardens, but stopped herself in time.

'A Gardens Festival?' she queried, instead. 'When? And what gardens was Julia thinking of?'

'I didn't ask, but she wanted to know if I thought hers would be presentable by July. Such a difficult month. I told her we'd have to plant it up with that in mind. Many more annuals, and half-hardy things.' Basil sounded aggrieved. 'Not at all the subtle planting that I'd planned for her. Really, clients can be so *difficult*.'

He suddenly remembered that Zinnia was a friend of Lady Julia's, and apologised, in embarrassment.

'Feel free,' she told him flatly.

'I'm sure the organisers are going to include your wonderful garden,' he went on hurriedly, assuming she was hurt not to have been approached already. 'It would be unthinkable not to. Such a lot of people would be thrilled to see it.'

They were making their way back towards the ramp. 'Oh, isn't that just a poppet! Clever you! They're so difficult to grow,' Basil exclaimed in delight as they passed a double, pink hepatica, and Zinnia's response failed to penetrate his consciousness.

'Let 'em ask, that's all,' she muttered grimly. 'Just let 'em ask.'

****

Next morning, Lady Julia Trugglestone's flapjacks emerged from the oven smoking and inedible, which made her feel even more fussed than she was already. It was perhaps not her fault that they'd turned mole-coloured brown – her new oven was still revealing its eccentricities – but the disaster seemed to duplicate her own hardening resentment.

Struggling to open a packet of digestive biscuits instead, she thought crossly that she simply hadn't pictured herself hosting meetings in her retirement cottage. At Trugglestone Hall it had been easy. People sat at the big dining room table, tempted by Mrs Chitting's delicious cakes and biscuits, and Julia was used to managing the discussions through to a conclusion with the minimum of wasted time. People liked their historic surroundings, and the authority of her position was an added help.

Even when she and Richard were young, and living at The Dower House, she'd helped her mother-in-law with these things, as a sort of apprenticeship. She might not have come from such a background herself, but fully realised that duties came with the family she'd married into. Julia paused unseeingly, thinking back. As a surgeon's daughter, she could have been said to have made a good match. She smiled faintly. Her parents were certainly not displeased. But, she told herself, she'd married Richard simply because he was a thoroughly nice man. The locked cupboard in her mind containing doubts about that was, as always, not even acknowledged.

She laid the biscuits out on two plates, and took them through to the dining room, which she'd decided was the best place for the meeting.

Being 'lady of the manor' had not come easily at first to someone who was reserved and instinctively private, but the number of charities and county committees she was expected to sit on soon grew. Inevitably, in the village she was a school governor, helped to run and allocate the almshouses, sat on the Parish Council, and generally did her bit. People joked about 'noblesse oblige and all that', but to Julia it meant something. The recognition and respect that people gave to a position such as hers had to be balanced by involvement with the community. You gave something back. It was your duty.

But she'd done more than her duty all these years, she thought, returning to the kitchen, and hunting for the ground coffee. And what's more she was no longer living at the Hall. She gave up the search impatiently, and decided that this morning's meeting could jolly well have instant, it was much less trouble. Then she got cups and saucers out of the cupboard, taking some small pleasure from the china she'd chosen for her new home. Good thing she'd bought eight of everything. And she could just about fit eight at her dining room table, although it would be a squeeze.

She opened the door into the garden, and breathed in the fresh spring air. A pity there was no time to make a tour of the garden before people arrived, but the birds were twittering at her reproachfully, so she unhooked the nut dispenser, her granddaughters' house-warming present, and brought it in for refilling.

How different things were from last spring, it suddenly came home to her. There'd been no clue then that Richard wasn't well. Indeed the shock of his heart attack and death had left her an automaton for months. It was a blessing that Clive and Susan were only a short distance away, and Clive had been wonderful, sorting out legal and financial matters manfully.

Bringing out a large bag of peanuts, she began spooning them into the narrow mouth of the dispenser. Clive and Susan had sold their Cambridge house as soon as they could, joining her at the Hall. That had been a very fraught period, she reflected, wondering impatiently if there was a quicker way to transfer the nuts. She'd had lots to think about of course, buying and refurbishing her cottage, but as the months went by family relations steadily deteriorated, and it wasn't just the two-women-in-the-kitchen problem.

Julia was not a weak woman, but she'd always felt estate affairs were not her province. She left that side of things to Richard, and of course the other trustees, who strictly speaking owned both Trugglestone Hall and its land. But she'd been shocked at the very different ideas Clive and Susan had about running the place. In particular the sale of the Dower House, and part of its garden for that horrible new estate, had been strenuously resisted. 'Sleepy Hollow' – the very name made her cringe.

She gave up on the spoon, made a lip in the bag of peanuts, and tipped it carefully towards the opening in the dispenser.

Perhaps because he'd feared his mother's reaction, she thought angrily, Clive had now sold Zinnia's precious Pit Garden without saying a word, until the deed was done. It put her in a hugely embarrassing position. A deep frost had descended on the friendship, and Julia hadn't dared make contact with Zinnia these past two weeks. Really it was too bad of Clive.

The ruining of the stables and the kitchen garden, though, that was all down to Susan.

Julia lost concentration, and the nuts cascaded out of the bag too fast, over the worktop, and on to the floor with a steady putter, like a pacifist's machine gun.

'Oh damn, *damn*!' she said out loud, and the white and tan head of a Springer spaniel appeared round the kitchen door enquiringly.

'I'm just being clumsy, Bracken,' she told the dog. 'No, you won't like them – leave them alone. I'll clear up the mess.'

She fetched a dustpan and brush, and began sweeping up the peanuts, telling herself she must try and think of her daughter-in-law with more charity.

Julia completely accepted the system whereby estates were passed down the generations. She had been at Trugglestone Hall for forty-four years, and regarded it as her home, yet had lived with the knowledge that she and Richard were really just its guardians. In due course it would be handed over to Clive, and the older generation would move without fuss to the Dower House, and enjoy a tranquil retirement. She paused in mid-sweep, and sighed. That was what should have happened anyway. And the system worked because the unwritten rule was that you didn't do things to the house and estate that were irrevocable. You could tinker, and improve as necessary, but your responsibility was to keep it for future generations.

Susan patently didn't understand this. Julia felt sure she was a bad influence on her son. Clive surely wouldn't have sold off parts of the estate otherwise. He certainly didn't listen to his mother, these days, she thought crossly. And now Susan was busy turning the kitchen garden into a Herb Garden, and knocking the stables about to make some horrible tea shop, of all things. It simply wasn't right.

She stood up, and used the corner of the dustpan to tip the nuts into the bird feeder. Then she clipped it shut, trapping her finger painfully. Nothing was going right this morning.

Carrying the replenished feeder through the sitting room to the garden door, she brooded on a further irritation.

The creation of this ridiculous Herb Garden was being used by her daughter-in-law as an excuse not to take on any of Julia's responsibilities. Susan declared that she couldn't possibly join anything, her hands were full. Julia had tried broaching the subject with Clive, but he brushed off her concerns, and sided with his wife. Susan was working flat out. The idea of sitting on 'worthy committees', as he put it, was out of the question.

She hung the feeder on its bracket, and stood for a moment watching to see which bird would venture down first.

That was all very well. What Susan didn't seem to realise (or maybe she did), was that this just wasn't fair. Julia needed to shed her workload of committees, and pass them on to the present Lady Trugglestone of Trugglestone Hall. They went with the role.

Susan had two girls to look after of course, and the house to run, but she could employ help with both, as Julia had. Dear Mrs Chitting, Julia's help in all things, had offered to stay on, but Susan had made it clear that she'd rather cope herself. It even looked as if she would push out old Harry Trench. A nice thank you for a gardening life devoted to the Hall.

If only Susan had come from a similar background to Clive, then she would have understood her obligations, personal and public, Julia reflected unworthily. It was a pity you couldn't choose your son's wife, as they did in other cultures. Not that she had had anyone in mind, but she would have known what to look for. And it wouldn't have been a solicitor's daughter from Cheshire, she thought sourly, making sure there was a clean towel for visitors. Her choice would have been someone who knew what was expected of her, even to producing an heir for the title. You just went on trying until you produced a boy. It went without saying.

That she herself had been lucky to produce a boy before her back problems made a second pregnancy inadvisable was conveniently brushed away, like fluff under the bed.

She checked the thermostat, turning up the central heating on her way into the kitchen. A few seconds later she walked back and turned it down again. If everyone was cold, perhaps they would want to go home sooner.

Why am I hosting yet another wretched village meeting? she asked herself resentfully, getting milk out of the fridge and pouring it into a jug.

'You're a fool, Julia,' Zinnia had told her bluntly, several weeks ago, 'a real sucker for punishment. These committees are just talking shops for the local bores anyway, who've got nothing much else in their lives. Makes them feel important. I've never sat on a committee in my life, and don't intend to.'

Clive's response was, 'If you don't want to do these things any longer, Mother, just resign from everything.'

But it wasn't as simple as that. Mostly because Susan wouldn't take her place. But also after Richard's death people had been very kind, and so many had told her the thing to do was keep busy. Throw herself into local affairs, make sure she didn't have time to think too much.

The sharpness of grief for Richard was certainly beginning to dull, as she came to terms with what had happened. But in its place was a mourning for the relaxing years she had pictured for them both. This was to have been their sunlit uplands, after finally shedding their respective responsibilities. What was her retirement going to be now – a barren waste of dutiful meetings? But if not that, then what?

That jibe of Zinnia's about people sitting on committees because they had empty lives she found uncomfortable to think about. Because, a small voice whispered, if she resigned from everything, as Clive suggested, what would she have left?

These thoughts bore little relation to the rosy retirement picture she had painted to Zinnia recently, it suddenly occurred to her. I do love living in my own little place, she reassured herself, looking about. It's just that...

She went upstairs to tidy her hair. 'You're just being negative,' she reprimanded her mirrored reflection. 'Yes this morning's meeting will be tedious, but organising a Gardens Festival might be fun. And it's in a good cause.' The face still looked downcast. Have a bet over how many times that dreary Daphne Stalker will mention her equally humourless husband, she told herself. If it's more than ten times, you can open some smoked salmon for lunch.

****

'So, we'll really have to get out skates on,' Daphne Stalker said, in a summing up voice, two and a half hours later. 'But we've got the bones of it sorted out this morning, which is a useful start. My husband Prentice to be Treasurer. I'll talk him into it, and he's always excellent at that sort of thing. And he'll contact the Millennium Commission to find out exactly how much the village needs to raise itself before they'll release the promised grant for the village hall.'

Julia added a further mark to a row of them on her note pad.

'Publicity, car parking, hire of marquee for the Flower Arranging Competition, we've covered. Stockleigh and District Flower Arranging Club to run the Competition itself. Teas – the Women's Institute are going to organise, in the village hall if wet, outside if fine.'

The vicar cleared his throat uneasily. 'We, er, we didn't really come to a conclusion about activities for the children,' he said tentatively. 'If we are going to have this Flower and Gardens Festival instead of the usual fete, I do think it's important to keep the youngsters involved.'

Daphne looked at him over her glasses impatiently. Sometimes she felt that chairing meetings and herding sheep had much in common. And it never did to let one break away. 'Oh I think we'll have enough to deal with, without that sort of...' she was going to say 'nonsense' – traditional frivolities were not favoured – but he interrupted bravely.

'This is all for outsiders, which is fine, if we're trying to raise money. But there needs to be something just for the village children. How about a Fancy Dress competition. They always love that.'

There were nodding heads and murmurs of approval, and Daphne sensed a mass escape from her control.

'And a dancing display,' Nigella Picket added eagerly. Her daughter Angelica's current ambition was to dance in front of the Queen at some Millennium celebration.

Julia watched the gathering slipping from its chairman's grasp with mixed feelings. Although her sympathies were with the rebels, she could see this meeting never ending, if they got the upper hand, and she was looking forward to her smoked salmon. Thoughtfully, she regarded Haydon's organising choir mistress.

'I have a suggestion,' she said quietly. 'Some of the children will be involved with helping to run the stalls that the Cubs and Brownies are organising, but a Fancy Dress Parade wouldn't take much arranging, and the vicar's right, they love it.' She saw Daphne's frown of displeasure, and gave her a little smile. 'And we're lucky to have such a good choir in the village,' she continued evenly, 'that I think we should have a recital, and a dancing display. That should involve just about everyone, and give something extra to entertain the visitors.'

'Oh. Well...' Like muddy river water reaching the sea, Daphne Stalker found herself subjected to warring forces. A public recital was certainly tempting. She looked round uncertainly, noting the signs of approval. 'Is everyone agreed on that then?'

She consulted her notes.

'Right. Now, gardens – Lady Julia's, Nigella Picket's (if you're sure about it, Nigella?), Mrs Peasmore's, Gerald and ElaineThornway's, The Walled Herb Garden, a cottage garden – possibly Mrs Chitting's. And I'll see if I can persuade Prentice to have his collection of carnivorous plants on display. I'm sure people would find them fascinating, although many will be past their best.'

'I think,' put in Julia hesitantly, 'that you shouldn't rely on Zinnia Peasmore agreeing to take part. As I said earlier, she has expressed... um... reservations about visitors to her garden, in the past. She has a lot of rare things, you know, and there's always the worry about them being damaged...'

Either Daphne Stalker hadn't been listening when they'd discussed the gardens that would be open, or more likely had simply pushed the problem aside. It was a habit of hers at Parish Council meetings. One of her maxims was 'No such word as impossible', and in the face of a formidable organiser people's objections did usually melt away. It was the easiest course.

'Oh I'm sure Mrs Peasmore will open her garden when she knows it's to raise money for the Village Hall,' Daphne declared with certainty. 'Kiln House is our prize garden. Should draw in a lot of people who read her column in that magazine I understand she writes for. Will you ask her, for us?'

'Er... well... no, I'd rather not.' Julia floundered for an excuse. 'I'm happy to try and get Loretta Moss to come for the Flower Arranging Competition, because I know her family. But I think, with Mrs Peasmore, a formal request from you, as this committee's Chairman, would carry more weight.'

This sounded lame and highly improbable to her own ears, but Daphne Stalker had no trouble believing it.

'I'll approach her then,' she said briskly. 'Haven't met her, but Prentice works at Thornways with her son Derek. I'll ask the Thornways too. It would be useful to have the two gardens together, to make it worth the walk to that end of the village.'

A short while later, with disguised gladness Julia ushered the last of her unwanted guests to the front door, and returned to clear the cups off the table.

'You know, Bracken,' she said with a sigh, piling them on to a tray, 'Zinnia's idea of setting up as a bookie or a clairvoyant suddenly has a lot going for it. Beats hosting village meetings any day.'

Chapter Four

A couple of days later, Derek Peasmore was hurrying over what was proving to be not the jolliest of breakfasts. For some reason Veronica had seized on it as an appropriate moment for attack, and was in full flow.

'I think this Whatsisname buying the Pit could be just what your mother needed.'

'Needed!'

'Yes, to make her realise that it's the right time to move.' She put a slice of bread in the toaster, and slid the handle down with unnecessary force. 'I've been saying for years that she should move out of that inconvenient house. It's too big for her, and impossible to keep clean.'

Veronica wasn't convinced that Zinnia actually bothered much in the cleaning department, but her well-meaning attempts to do some herself had been strongly rebuffed. She was shocked and puzzled that anyone would want to live like that, but then she probably never would understand her mother-in-law.

'I think the time has come now, Derek,' she said with the restrained impatience of a headmistress interviewing a problem child's parents. 'You've got to be firm with her, make her face reality.'

'But it's her home,' he protested. 'Mine too, if it comes to that. It was a wonderful place to grow up, and I have very fond memories of it.'

'The trouble with you is you never see the practical side of things,' his wife accused him sharply. 'She can't stay there for ever, can she?'

'Well, no. Perhaps not, but...'

'There you are then.' Picking up a glossy brochure from the worktop, she waved it at him. 'And the great thing is that the timing is just right. I went to the site office yesterday, and got details of all the Sleepy Hollow houses. They're building a group of bungalows, and one of those would be just right for Zinnia, wouldn't it.'

'Oh I don't think she'd ever agree...'

'You've got to persuade her, Derek. It would be best for her in the long run.' Veronica's voice had the earnestness of a missionary bent on converting the happy heathen. Relieving her mother-in-law of the losing struggle against house and work-intensive garden was the right thing to do, she was sure of it.

'But that garden is what she lives for,' he countered weakly, accepting the proffered toast.

Years of experience had taught him there wasn't really any point in arguing with Veronica about his mother, and vice versa. He sighed. They were like a ship and a dockside grinding together, and he was the hapless fender trying to prevent damage. Zinnia regarded his wife's preoccupation with cooking and cleaning as a complete waste of time, while Veronica simply had no inkling of Zinnia's passion for plants and gardening.

It was not a trait he had inherited, he thought, reaching for the butter, which probably made for a more peaceful life. Veronica did their own garden, except for cutting the grass, and liked it to be neat, with rows of colourful bedding plants in the summer, and bulbs in the spring.

Derek spread his toast, mentally comparing his wife's idea of a garden with his mother's wonderful creation. Kiln House always had attracted visits from like-minded friends, and he'd grown up with enthusiastic talk about plants. He realised, in a way that Veronica never would, that to Zinnia this was much more than 'just gardening'. It was visceral.

'All those rare plants,' he objected, 'it's taken her years to collect them.'

'She could take plants with her,' Veronica said, watching with her usual irritation as Derek ignored the spoon, and stuck his knife into the marmalade jar. 'The bungalows all have a bit of land. She'd have fun making a new garden. And it would be so much easier to keep.'

The logic of this last bit was difficult to refute.

'But Kiln House needs so many things doing to it, it wouldn't fetch much. Especially now there's the probability of the Pit being used for tipping. Who'd buy it?'

'Whatsisname...Mike Swathe would.' This was clearly her trump card. 'He'll need a site office, and maybe someone to live there and prevent unauthorised tipping. And, by buying Kiln House he'd gain access from the road, which would mean much less trouble and dust than tipping from the top.'

'Well, it's a thought...'

Veronica recognised the classic slide-away comment, and experienced her habitual exasperation at failing to get him to face up to anything he didn't want to.

'You are impossible,' she said crossly.

Derek gulped the last of his coffee, overtaken by an unusual keenness to depart for work, even though it was early, and he would have liked to finish his breakfast.

'Must go. I thought I'd ...er...call in on Mum on the way.'

This might not have been the wisest excuse.

'Take this brochure, and make her read it,' Veronica threw it at his departing figure, and shouted after him. 'See what she says.'

'Be unrepeatable,' Derek muttered under his breath, heading for the front door just as Matthew came clattering down the stairs.

'Can I have breakfast in peace now, if you sad people have finished arguing?' he greeted his father.

'Yes, be nice to your mother now,' was the coded response, and the two exchanged a glance of understanding.

Matthew bounced into the kitchen. 'And how is my specially favourite mother this fine morning,' he beamed at her.

The frown temporarily left Veronica's face, but of the two men in her life, her son was the most difficult to pin down, and she was not going to be deflected from things that needed to be said, charm or no charm.

'Don't forget that Careers appointment this morning.'

'What Careers appointment?' Matthew had grabbed some bread and was being lavish with the butter.

'I rang and made it last week. I *told* you.'

'No, sorry, can't go. I promised Susie I'd start work on a computerised stock control and labelling system for her. Plants are beginning to arrive already.'

'Oh *Matthew!* You are the limit.'

'You shouldn't try and keep a man from his work, you know', he chided her, straight faced. 'Serious business.'

'But that's just it.' Rising frustration made her blind to the bait, as usual. 'You haven't got a proper job, or likely to the way you're going.. You simply must sort things out, Matthew. If you don't knuckle down and get a place at university, you'll never get anywhere in life. You'll end up like...'

She was going to say 'your father', but stopped herself because it was unfair. True of course, but not a loyal thing to say.

'Mum, when the Heebie Jeebies have girls screaming with lust all round the world, and I'm on my tenth million, I shall tell an incredulous world how my mother kept telling me to "Get a proper job".'

'When will you be able to go, if I set up another appointment with the Careers...?' Her voice tailed away hopelessly, as he rose to go, bearing two slices of bread and marmalade crammed together.

'Bye, thanks for breakfast.' He paused to grab a banana out of the fruit bowl. 'I shall also tell a breathless media that my Mum is the best cook in the world. And you'll have them descending on you in hordes, begging for recipes.'

A defeated Veronica surveyed the remains of breakfast, and mechanically began to clear the table. Men! She sometimes wondered how her life would have been if Matthew had been followed by a sister. A dear, feminine little girl, who would have joined her in the kitchen, delighting in being taught to make cakes and biscuits, and taking her side in family arguments.

Perhaps she hadn't worked things very well. Of course Matthew – the reason she and Derek had married in the first place – hadn't been planned at all.

In the event, neither of them had minded particularly, she remembered, absently putting the marmalade away. It gave Derek an excuse to leave home, and there was no comparing his mother's cooking with hers, a point noted with satisfaction by Veronica, who had made even greater efforts. Not a career-minded girl, she had given up work without much regret, although being a shorthand typist at Thornways had been quite enjoyable. She cleared the china onto the draining board, with a faint smile on her face. There was a friendly atmosphere at the company, and everyone knew everyone else. She'd been greatly struck by the young man taken on as General Manager. He was a protégé of Old Thornway, and she felt proud that he should notice her. He was obviously destined for great things.

She ran hot water into the washing up bowl, and gazed unseeingly out of the window. Twenty years later, Derek was still General Manager at Thornways, at not much more of a salary than he started on, taking inflation into account. Money was tight then, and tight now. The moment had never seemed right to add another child. Especially after she'd set her heart on this house, which took every penny they had.

Mechanically she began washing the plates. Too late to be thinking about daughters now, but money... she had been wondering what she could do about that. A little business would be nice, something she could run from home. Catering for dinner parties, maybe. Perhaps even weddings.

This was a familiar track. She'd thought about it often in the last few months, but somehow that was as far as things got.

The trouble was that she was so busy already, she reflected, rinsing the cutlery. Two mornings a week in term-time were spent helping with the

Infants' Class at the village school. Then on Wednesday's she went to the health club with Elaine Thornway.

As the boss's wife, Elaine could have put on airs, but she never did. In fact you had to feel sorry for her, Veronica thought. She needed encouraging to stick up for herself, and stop Gerry walking all over her. No, it wouldn't be right to leave Elaine in the lurch.

She took a cloth to the table and wiped away the crumbs, and a spot of marmalade that Derek had dropped. Housework used up a lot of time, her train of thought continued. Couldn't let that slip. It'd be awful if her gleaming house ended up like Zinnia's, with cobwebs everywhere and windows you could hardly see out of. And Derek worked hard, she acknowledged. He had the right to live in a nice home and have really good meals cooked for him.

Tipping the water away, Veronica completed the familiar circuit. What was needed was something lucrative to do yet which wouldn't take much time.

Oh well, the solution would come to her at some point.

****

While his wife contemplated the ultimate fantasy – effortless money – Derek found Zinnia in Kiln House kitchen, feeding the cat which was giving a good impression of recent starvation, weaving frantically round her legs.

'Just called in to see how things were going,' he said, kissing her affectionately. 'How's Rosemary settling in?'

'Quite well, I think. She bought a whole load of stuff in Ipswich, including a heater, and that room of hers is like a sauna now.'

Her son thought this unlikely. There were draughts in Kiln House practising for the cyclone Olympics, and none of the windows fitted properly.

Sitting on a chair at the kitchen table, he watched as his mother put down the plate of food, only for Roger to give one sniff, and walk away, tail in air.

'You are a pain,' she informed the cat, severely. 'Can't think why I was ever soft enough to give you asylum.' She opened the back door, and he took the hint. 'Go and catch voles, you useless ingrate,' she called after him.

'And how about the mysterious seeds? Any beanstalks begun popping up yet?' Derek enquired genially.

'No, nothing happening at all.' Zinnia filled the kettle, sounding a touch disappointed. 'Of course it's very early days. But at least some will germinate, I know they will.'

'She goes out three times a day to check. Those seeds will not be *allowed* to fail!'

Coming into the kitchen, Rosemary had caught the end of their conversation. Derek smiled at her, pleased to note that she looked less pinched.

'I'm not staying,' he said, standing up. 'On my way to work. Thought I'd see how you were getting on. And,' he looked at his mother, 'to warn you that you'll be getting a visit from Daphne Stalker.'

'Who's she?' Zinnia plonked the kettle on the Rayburn hotplate, the wet bottom causing a hiss of steam.

'Oh Mum, you must know who she is. Teaches at the primary school, Junior Choir Mistress, Chairman of the Parish Council, she just about runs Haydon these days.'

'I don't have anything to do with the village. They're bores, the lot of them,' Zinnia said dismissively. 'Why does she want to see me? And how do you know about it anyway?'

Derek pulled a face. 'Prentice, her unlovely husband, is in charge of customer care and quality control at Thornways. I've told you about him, remember. Can't stand the man. But he mentioned she was going to ask you about opening your garden for some fund-raising event this summer.'

'Oh that. Huh! If they think I'd agree to have coachloads of ignoramuses tramping all over my precious plants...' retorted Zinnia, with the sweetness of a terrier protecting a bone. 'I shall give her a piece of my mind.'

'Wouldn't that be a good idea though?' Rosemary had been listening with interest.

'Why?'

'Well, if people came and admired the garden, wouldn't that help the fight to keep it? Especially if there was local publicity. You could get visitors to sign a petition against tipping, or something.'

'Hm.' Zinnia considered the merits of this suggestion.

'There's another reason you shouldn't tell Daphne Stalker where to go, in your inimitable fashion,' Derek told her from the door, 'and that's really why I came. Not only is she Chairman of the Parish Council, and you need them on your side. But the ponderous Prentice is now on the County Council. He took Richard Trugglestone's place last year. *And*,' he said with emphasis, 'they are the ones who make the big decisions on waste disposal.'

He caught Rosemary's eye and smiled at her. 'Do you think you could teach my mother to say, "You're welcome. Have a nice day", convincingly?'

****

Derek was still amusing himself with the thought of Zinnia being effusively polite to the ignorant masses, as he drove through the country lanes to Stockleigh. It was certainly preferable to contemplating the increasing problems at Thornways.

Two hours later Gerry Thornway's big BMW nosed out of his driveway next to Kiln House, and took the same route. He saw no reason to get in early. Quite the reverse in fact. Being able to stroll in when you felt like it marked out who was boss.

At thirty-nine, overweight, with an increasingly florid complexion and thinning hair, Gerry Thornway was trying to ignore the face in the mirror these days. It was too much at variance with the mental image of himself. He was, after all, the smart, fast-living Gerald Thornway.

'Any connection with Thornways Therapeutic Teas?' he would be asked at social gatherings. (People always remembered that old slogan, from the happy days when businesses could claim something was good for you, without expensive scientific proof). 'Well yes, actually. It's my company,' he liked telling them airily. With his club ties and bespoke suits, he found it pleasant mixing with other people who had wealth and enjoyed spending it. But the time had come to move on, he had now decided. He should be launching himself into a new field, one where his gifts would be better recognised. And which would make more money.

For there was no denying the problem. Over the last ten years he'd relied on Thornways to fund the building of his modern, lavishly appointed house with landscaped garden, a motor-sailor on the River Orwell, golfing holidays in Bermuda, and a new car every year. And now the funds were drying up as the company faltered. He didn't like the outlook.

His General Manager, Derek Peasmore, wasn't exactly cheering either. The man only ever had bad news, or urgent requests for money to be spent. Replacing the increasingly unreliable packaging machinery was not something that could be contemplated, and as for investing in new products, which Peasmore was always going on about, it was out of the question.

A pheasant was strutting across the road in front of him, but Gerry didn't bother braking. Damn thing would get out of the way, and if it didn't, well that was its look out.

The recent departure of Frank Smiley, his Sales Manager, had been a blessing really, he thought. Saved one salary at any rate. Realising there'd been no bump, he glanced behind with a mixture of regret and justification as the pheasant disappeared into the hedgerow. Gerry could do the Sales job perfectly well himself, along with his own. Life would be more comfortable without Peasmore as well, but now was not the time to give him the sack, regrettably.

He turned on the car radio. *'Everybody's doin' it, doin' it...'* the bouncy refrain made him scowl, and he switched it off again. Everybody was doing it, that was part of the trouble. Herbal teas were becoming more widely accepted by the year, but instead of increasing the company's sales, their popularity had encouraged a lot of competitors into the market Thornways had dominated for so long. Sales were falling, and production costs were rising. It was a recipe for disaster, and he didn't know what to do about it.

But with the sudden opportunity to buy into Stockleigh Golf Club, things had become a lot clearer recently. Of course he was good at managing the family company, but it didn't really use all his abilities, he told himself, and now it needed too much investment. Running a business that was also one of his hobbies would be much more congenial, and more suited to his many talents. He nodded, picturing Gerald Thornway, resplendent in silk tie and blazer, chatting affably at the clubhouse bar with influential members, his charisma causing membership to soar. No comparison with Thornways' utilitarian building on a trading estate, and people perpetually whinging about money.

A tractor with a harrow attachment came into view ahead, reducing his speed to a ridiculous fifteen miles an hour, and Gerry pressed the horn impatiently. These yokels had no business being on the road.

He needed to go through a lot of figures this morning, and do some active thinking. Having already agreed to invest in the Golf Club, now he had to concentrate on selling Thornways quickly, to provide the funds.

Elaine wasn't happy about the decision. 'Your father built it up from nothing,' she'd said reproachfully. 'He would be very upset.' Stupid woman. Did she think he didn't know that? But the old man had been doing something he loved, whereas to Gerry it was a bore. Why should he spend his life carrying on his father's dream?

'Come on, come on!' he yelled in frustration at the tractor driver. The man was being deliberately slow.

No, he'd made up his mind. It was time to sell the company. Clumpings International were the obvious buyers, and he'd already approached them. They'd been cool at first, but this week had shown some interest. What he needed to do now was make Thornways look as good as possible.

He roared past the tractor, causing an oncoming cyclist to take to a gateway for protection. Gerry hardly noticed, preoccupied with the coming day. He would have to tell the most senior employees now, he decided, so that they could put together a favourable profile of the company. Perhaps he could get Peasmore to go through that report of his about possible new food supplement products, and spin it so that they appeared to be in the pipeline, rather than just ideas. Complementary health was the 'in' thing, these days, and Clumpings would probably be very impressed. He smiled to himself. These big conglomerates were all staffed by youngsters just out of university, anyway. They would be easy to string along.

He swung into Thornways' entrance, and cruised across the large car park to the space labelled *Managing Director*. Parking next to that sign never failed to please, it was just a pity that no-one who mattered was able to observe Gerald Thornway arriving in style.

That would all change though, he told himself, adjusting his tie in the mirror. Just as soon as he'd jacked this place in, and become a part-owner of Stockleigh Golf Club.

Chapter Five

A week later, with the heater making her room blessedly warm, Rosemary was composing an e-mail to Bill at the US National Science Foundation Antarctic base in McMurdo.

My computer is all sorted out now. Matthew's friend Ollie, who's some kind of IT guru, got the right piece of equipment for me,, and that cured the problem. (Question: what were computer nerds before computers came on the scene - entomologists?)

It wasn't hard to imagine your ice and blizzards my first week, it was so damn cold here. But suddenly everything is waking up. Blossom on the trees, it's getting warmer, and lighter, and I can't believe how many flowers Zinnia has in her yard (have to remember to call it a garden). It's amazing at this time of year. Seems so early.

Am trying to picture everything closing down for you. And so many people departing, just leaving you 'overwinterers'. Hope you don't feel low. What do they do if the Seasonal Affective Disorder researcher goes down with it too?

I've bought myself a car – how about that! Nothing glamorous, it's eight years old. Derek came with me, and said it was a good buy. Seem's strange driving on the wrong side of the road, and until I get used to using the shift, we won't be going far. But it's really neat, and makes me feel better. More independent..

It's odd not knowing what all the birds are. You would be ashamed of me. Soon the house martins will start arriving from Africa and using the mud nests under the eaves above the back door. Seems they come every *year, and just refresh the old place – like summer homes everywhere. There's a cute little bird already building a nest in the bushy thing outside my bedroom window, which Zinnia says is a dunnock. Mean anything to you? She also said that the Kirtland Warbler I could have sworn I saw in the Pit Garden today must have been a Yellowhammer, or something. Shame. That sure **would** have been one up on you.*

Have decided to set up a project for myself. I'm going to research the history of Zinnia's chalk pit, to help her fight to save it. Apparently it goes back centuries. She's agreed to have the garden open to the public this summer, so we're going to put together a leaflet for visitors. Suffolk County Library is in Ipswich, but the car and I don't feel ready to make that yet, so I'm starting off in the library at Trugglestone Hall tomorrow. Doesn't that sound so 'Agatha Christie'! Her country houses always had libraries. Tell you all about it soon.

****

The following morning, with early mistiness heralding a bright day ahead, Rosemary walked over to Trugglestone Hall. A curve in the drive, and artfully placed trees, meant that the house was hidden from the road, and she had pictured a mansion. So the reality, when she got there, was a bit disappointing. Trugglestone Hall was not particularly large, and lacked any hint of grandeur. The main part of the house had the air of an old and solid farmhouse. But rather ugly wings, clearly built at a later date, had been tacked on to either side. The jarring impression was of a homely farmer's wife incongruously sporting high heels and false eyelashes.

Rosemary hadn't realised there was a second entrance, so was surprised to discover that the drive joined another leading off at right-angles in front of the house, aesthetically demanding precedence, but weedy from lack of traffic. Hesitantly, she approached a large studded door. 'Country people don't use their front doors,' Zinnia had told her firmly, but somehow Rosemary doubted that the Trugglestones fell into this category. And mightn't it be rude to pry round the back in search of a humbler entrance?

A metal lever, presumably attached to a bell inside, seemed to be the only way of announcing her presence, so she pulled it, but heard no distant jangle, nor approaching footsteps. The Trugglestones must abide by country ways after all. Feeling justified now, she went round to the side of the house, and found a green-painted door, with a mail-box, and brass handle, shiny with daily use. Much more promising. Still no electric bell to press, but a metal door knocker determinedly wielded resulted after a few moments in it being opened by a tall, thin, bespectacled man of about forty, wearing brown corduroy trousers and a sloppy jumper, who looked at her enquiringly.

'I'm Rosemary Keel. Susie – Lady Susan said I could come and do some research. In the library,' she told him, awkwardly.

'Ah yes, she said something about that at breakfast.' He gave a friendly smile. 'Susie's just gone out for half an hour, but do come in. I'll show you where everything is. I'm Clive, by the way.'

Sir Clive Trugglestone was not at all the order-barking baronet that Rosemary had imagined but, on reflection, an authoritarian type wouldn't have been right for Susie. Although, glancing at his thinning hair, and rather meek face, as he led her through a large kitchen smelling of casseroles past, she wondered quite what the attraction had been. Perhaps he was just a heck of a good guy. You could forgive them a lot, almost as much as men who made you laugh.

'You're interested in geology, or industrial archaeology, are you?' he asked, ushering her along a corridor lined with large paintings.

'Well no, not really.'

This was difficult. She could hardly say that it was to help save the Pit from the man he'd sold it to.

'We thought it would be nice for visitors to the Pit Garden to understand why it was there. The chalk pit, I mean,' Rosemary told him, rather proud of her tact.

'Good idea,' he said approvingly. 'Lime burning is a part of country life that seems to have been forgotten. It was very important once, you know. And the income from that pit was one of the mainstays of the estate, along with the mill.'

'Why did they stop working it?'

'Well, artificial fertilisers came in, and modern cement. And it just wasn't economic to carry on. But I'm no expert, and I'm sure you'll find all the answers here.'

They had come into a good-sized room that was lined on three sides with books, mostly old and leather-bound, but more modern books occupied quite a few shelves. It was cold, but an electric heater by the central table had been put on at full blast for her benefit.

'My grandfather was interested in the area's history, and I think most of the information you want will be in these books,' Clive indicated one section. 'And here are the Estate Records, which go back a fair way. Look at anything you want, you're very welcome.'

To be back in even a small a library felt both reassuring, and at the same time disconcerting, like returning to a former home and seeing others living there. It carried a claustrophobic whiff of the life she had only just cast off. But she settled herself down at the rather dusty table, found various books that seemed likely to help, and soon became absorbed in her task. She was surprised when Susie stuck her head round the door an hour and a half later, and suggested she take a break and join them for elevenses.

The kitchen, where the family obviously did much of its living, had a distinctly old-fashioned look. Wooden cupboards, whose white paint now had all the freshness of a month-old snowdrift, took up most of one wall, and a dresser and an enormous Aga dominated another. There was a fifties-style double sink under one window, and down the other end of the room resided a large sagging sofa, whose comfy shabbiness invited the weary to take the weight off their legs without guilt, or even removal of footwear. Children's paintings decorated the wall behind it, and a cork notice board was crowded with reminders, advertisements, newspaper cuttings and bills. Down the centre of the room, its bleached surface echoing some of the softly-coloured floor bricks, was a long pine table, at which she was now invited to sit, for a mug of coffee, and biscuits out of a packet.

'I never thought about how stone buildings were built before,' she confessed, appreciating the hot drink and warm kitchen, after the chill library. 'But how on earth did they discover that heating chalk and other limestones led to lime mortar? I mean you don't normally try to burn rocks, do you?'

'You do if you make a stone hearth for a fire,' Clive observed. 'I should think the discovery was entirely accidental, way, way back. And then the process was refined and improved. The Romans made really good lime mortar. That's why their buildings lasted.'

'My problem is that I don't know anything about the countryside,' Rosemary told them. 'This business of putting lime on the fields seems odd. The books just say that it was to improve fertility, but I don't see why. I thought farmers spread animal manure to do that.'

'Well most plants don't like sour, acid soils,' Susie told her. 'They grow better in a neutral, or alkaline soil, and lime helps to tip the balance, and put back what plants and animals take out.' She stirred her coffee. 'We had to study all that stuff about soil structure and acidity on my horticultural course. I could dig out my notes if you like.'

'But surely, your average garden visitor would be far more interested in the social history of the place,' suggested Clive. 'How many men worked there, and what their jobs involved, that sort of thing.'

'Sure. All that stuff,' agreed Rosemary.

'Harry Trench is the person to talk to for local colour,' Clive went on. 'His grandfather was one of the last people to be employed there. When I was little he used to tell me a fascinating story about accidents caused by the quicklime, straight out of the kiln.'

'Oh that'd be perfect.'

'He has one about some farmer who carted it off, taking the risk that it wouldn't rain on the way back. Because if it got wet, the chemical reaction of turning the quicklime into slaked lime would set the carts on fire. I'm sure the old boy exaggerated though.'

'That's great. Who is Harry Trench?'

Clive glanced at Susie, who looked away, pointedly.

'He is...was...the gardener here. Thing is, he's too old really, but we can't, um... persuade him to retire. He lives in the stables cottage. I'm sure he'd be happy to talk to you.'

Rosemary sensed marital undercurrents, and thought it wise to change the subject. 'What about the library when this becomes a conference centre?' she asked, 'Will you let people loose in it? I think some of the books might be quite valuable.'

She didn't like to express her puzzlement that somewhere the size of Trugglestone Hall could be seen as a potential conference centre. But Clive was soon explaining that running his agency had made him realise there was a gap in the market.

'Mostly I just act as a Mister Fixit, if you like,' he told her. 'I match companies with suitable venues for whatever kind of gathering they have in mind – area, size, facilities. Bit like a dating agency really.

But there's one sort of request it's really difficult to fulfil,' he went on. 'When you've got companies who are thinking about a merger, or a joint venture, their first priority is absolute secrecy. But if they meet for exploratory talks at a hotel or a country club, even a college, the place's management and staff get to know, and it leaks into the papers.' Rosemary watched him dunk a biscuit in his coffee, in unconcernedly ill-bred fashion. 'And if they go to a private house, it won't have the facilities they need, fax, ISDN, computers, visual aids. And good catering. We're aiming to provide all that, plus total discretion, in an informal setting.'

'Won't you have the same problem though, with paid staff finding out?'

'No, because we won't have any. Some friends of ours near Cambridge are going to do the catering, and as it will be on a small scale, we can do everything else ourselves,' he explained, biting into his satisfactorily soggy biscuit. 'It's a niche market, but I'm convinced there's enough demand to make it a paying proposition. The first priorities though are to get the house rewired, re-plumbed, and heated properly. As soon as planning permission is through, we can get started.'

'Going to cost an awful lot of money,' Susie added, 'hence the land sales. But this place has to earn its keep, otherwise we'll have to sell up. It's just too large for us. We half thought of putting in for permission to demolish the two nineteenth century wings,' she looked teasingly at Clive, 'built by the infamous Lady Trugglestone the rose is named after.'

'Infamous?'

'Brought the family to ruin,' declared Susie cheerfully, offering the biscuit packet round again.

'How did she manage that?' Rosemary had always thought it would be fun to have colourful ancestry.

'By marrying my great-grandfather and running through his money.' Clive told her. 'Her name was Evelyn, and she was the daughter of an earl, and somewhat 'lively', as they say. With very expensive tastes. Can't think what she saw in him, except that as a besotted husband who wouldn't complain, I suppose he was quite useful.' He took a gulp of his coffee. 'You could get up to all sorts of things as long as you were married in those days, couldn't you. It was only young single women who couldn't so much as be seen alone with a man.'

'She was the one who had the stables moved away from the house, and the two wings built on,' Susie added. 'And then she spent her time in London. She was a celebrated member of the fast set in the naughty nineties. Until the money ran out.'

'But did she like gardening then?' Rosemary couldn't see a connection. 'I mean, to have a rose named after her.'

'No, it was developed by Berrimans nursery, which was just starting up, and they hoped some of her glamour would rub off on the rose.' Susie got up, and went over over to the sink. 'But in fact it never sold very well, because it had a weak neck, which made the flowers droop. And then just before the First World War a climbing version appeared, and of course that was the era of rose pergolas, and Climbing Lady Trugglestone was wonderful for that, because the flowers hung downwards.' She rinsed out her coffee mug, adding, 'It was very popular, and still is with the gardening cognoscenti. We've planted it over the entrance to the Walled Garden, and I've got a lot on order from Berrimans, to sell.'

'So ironically, our one claim to fame is the person who ruined the family,' commented Clive, draining his own cup. 'But she probably did the family a favour in a funny sort of way,' he went on seriously. 'Her son, my grandfather, concentrated on mending the family finances, and he set up a Trust to administer the estate, to stop it ever happening again. So when Susie demands Dior dresses and diamond bracelets for her birthday, I just tell her firmly, "No. The trustees would never agree." She kicks up a fuss of course, but there's nothing she can do about it.'

He put up a hand to catch the dishcloth Susie threw at him, but unfortunately deflected it to land damply on Rosemary's lap.

'Whoops! Sorry,' Susie apologised, retrieving it. 'Time I went. Got to talk to Nigella Picket, about this Gardens Open Day. She's in charge of publicity.'

Rosemary looked questioning.

'Oh, haven't you come across her yet? When you go back, walk down the other drive, which comes out in Mill Lane. Used to be part of the estate, but now there are houses there, and the Pickets live in the one on the end.' Susie's eyes sparkled mischievously. '*Very* keen gardener, she is. And a great fan of your aunt.'

Back in the library, Rosemary broadened her quest, and settled down to skim through A History of Haydon Settleworth, by the Reverend Josiah Ashe. After making notes on his mentions of the Chalk Pit, she flicked through the rest of the leather-bound book, and suddenly stopped.

Boy! she said to herself. Wait till I tell Zinnia about this.

****

Returning to Kiln House at lunch time, Rosemary found a stew slowly simmering on the Rayburn, but no sign of her aunt in the house, nor the immediate garden. As she walked down the ramp in search of her, the mingling scent of flowers was magnified by the still air in the sheltered Pit Garden, and she found Zinnia pulling up ivy, which was trying to throttle a patch of anemones.

'Well, yes, I did know about Haydon's witch,' was the irritatingly calm response to her niece's news. 'She was one of the last women to be tried for witchcraft in Suffolk, I believe. Lived in one of the cottages by the river.'

''Yes, but did you realise she was accused because she used Settlewort to further her wicked aims? Only they weren't wicked at all. According to Josiah Ashe, she was trying to smooth the path of true love.'

'Don't tell me it's an aphrodisiac,' said Zinnia with mild sarcasm. 'That *would* have the world beating a path to our door.'

'No. At least I don't think so. This guy says...' she consulted her notebook. 'Ah, here it is: "Annie Sprigg was noted by the villagers as a 'cunning woman', someone who knew about the power of herbs. They went to her with many ills, and she would give them herbal remedies." '

'Can't see anything wrong with that.' Zinnia had just encountered a stinging nettle amongst the ivy, and was ruefully rubbing a painful hand. 'If I had a dock leaf handy, I'd be applying herbal medicine right now.'

Rosemary ignored the diversion. ' "But on occasions, she would agree to help a villager gain power over someone with whom they were in dispute. She made up a potion, which had to be added to the food of that person, and when it was consumed, they would agree to whatever it was the witch's customer was proposing, or trying to persuade them of." '

'Go on.' Zinnia was sitting back on her heels, and paying more attention.

'Well, the old Reverend is scathing about country people's credulity, but records that at her trial one Peter Huskin accused her of "grievous harme, by bringing to naught his wedding plans". He said Annie Sprigg put a spell on the bride's father, who then went back on an agreement that Huskin could marry his daughter.'

'What's a spell got to do with Settlewort?'

'Are you going to let me finish?' asked Rosemary, sternly.

'It seems the proposed bride wasn't keen on being matched with Peter Huskin, who was one of her father's friends, and past his prime, to put it politely. So she went to Annie Sprigg, and persuaded her to make up a potion of Settlewort, "a very pretious herbe", and when this was given to her old dad, he became putty in her hands. Said she could marry some young guy she'd been having a fling with all along. So it was Settlewort that did the trick, not a spell. Huskin just said that to make her sound more like a witch.'

'Hm,' was Zinnia's response, and a thought struck Rosemary.

'Did you know it was some kind of mind drug?'

'Well, it's a member of the Solanum family, which includes a number of notorious plants like Deadly Nightshade...'

'You mean it's poisonous?' interrupted Rosemary, aghast. 'But surely Annie Sprigg wouldn't have risked giving it to someone. She could have been accused of murder, not just witchcraft.'

'Oh she probably had a good idea what she was doing. These women knew their herbs, and tended to be much more effective than official medicine, which was pretty crude in those days. Besides, not all solanums are poisonous.' Zinnia gave her niece a small smile. 'You're not dead from the potato and tomato salad you ate yesterday, are you?'

She struggled stiffly to her feet, and brushed a twig off her sleeve. 'In answer to your question, I looked up Settlewort in Mrs Grieve's Herbal, which is one of my bibles, and yes, I did know that it had the reputation for being able to affect the mind. I'll show you what it says, when we go in.'

Rosemary was excited by the possibilities that this opened up. 'So we could have every major drug company hammering at the door! You'll make millions, as well as saving the Pit.'

'I think that's called counting your seedlings before they've germinated,' commented Zinnia, who'd been doing exactly that since the seeds' discovery. 'Now where did I put my trowel?'

As if in answer, a small, yellowish bird perched in the JudasTree above their heads gave a loud whistling call.

'That's the bird I thought was a Kirtland Warbler,' remarked Rosemary. 'What did you say it was, a Yellow something?'

'A Yellowhammer.' Zinnia looked up, searchingly. 'Except it isn't. I've no idea what that is, never seen it before.'

The little bird hopped among the leafless branches, obligingly displaying it's yellow breast, black eye-stripe, and black and white wings.

'It does look like a Kirtland Warbler though, I've seen pictures. Bill's always going on about it. It's his life's ambition to spot one.'

Zinnia frowned up at the mystery bird, and commanded, 'Don't you dare eat those buds, whatever you are. I'm hoping that wretched tree is actually going to flower this year. It got burnt by a late frost the last two springs.' She paused. 'What is a Kirtland Warbler?'

'Only one of America's rarest birds. But it couldn't possibly be that, could it? How on earth would it cross the Atlantic? Perhaps it's something exotic over from Europe,' Rosemary suggested, opening her notebook. 'I'll write down it's description anyhow. Have to tell Bill about it. I sometimes think he's more interested in birds than anything else. Dammit.'

****

Bill's e-mails of late had been, it had to be said, rather dull. Not his fault, of course, but she scarcely found his references to workouts in the gym, bowling and table tennis tournaments, of riveting interest. But now his reply sizzled with repressed passion. It was highly likely that she had been mistaken but, he urged, she must get an expert to check out the sighting. Right away.

'Well, there's the Royal Society for the Protection of Birds,' Zinnia suggested. 'They have a reserve at Minsmere, on the Suffolk Coast. Maybe someone could come from there and have a look at it. But I don't suppose they'd be particularly interested, would they?'

She couldn't have been more wrong.

The very next day a bearded young man, armed with camera and impressive-looking binoculars, knocked on the door after breakfast, and Rosemary took him into the Pit Garden to seek the interloper.

'I'm from Michigan, you see,' she explained, as they searched the trees and shrubs for a flash of yellow. 'It's the state's rarest bird, that's how I know about it. And my boyfriend's mad about anything with feathers. His life's ambition is to see a Kirtland Warbler.'

Luckily Rosemary's compatriot, if that's what it was, soon made an appearance, nonchalantly whistling down from a Paulownia, and the young man became visibly energised, as he photographed the little bird, noted down its characteristics, and consulted a printed description. They certainly matched. ' "Spends the summer in north-central Michigan," ' Rosemary read over his shoulder, "and winters in the Bahamas. Reports of vagrancy." '

'What's that mean? That it loses all self-respect, and starts stealing food from other birds?'

She meant it as a joke, but her companion stared at her over his glasses, as if she was a tiresome kid sister tagging along on a date. 'The term means being found hundreds of miles off course,' he informed her stiffly, and went back to scribbling in his notebook.

'So you mean it really could be a Kirtland?' Rosemary had scarcely believed her own identification, it seemed so unlikely. 'Well, what happens now?'

But the young man would not be drawn. 'I'll be reporting back,' he promised, as he got into his car, although whether he meant to the ornithological authorities, or to Rosemary and Zinnia, was left unclear.

Before leaving, he looked about him, assessing the narrowness of the lane, and came out with an odd question.

'Is there anywhere nearby suitable for parking?'

****

Lady Julia Trugglestone noticed something odd was going on when she found, to her irritation, a car partially blocking the entrance to the cottage, as she returned that afternoon. In fact, there were cars parked all down the street, on both sides. Her first thought was that there must be a wedding in the church, or a funeral. But old Mrs Swathe's next door had been the last funeral held, and even though she was a villager born and bred, mourners had scarcely filled the street with their cars. Besides, Julia would have known if such a well-attended ceremony was planned, be it funeral, wedding, or church concert. No, it had to be something else.

She got out, and was wondering whether she could manoeuvre her car very carefully into the restricted space left free, when Daphne Stalker's grey Honda pulled up behind, unable to squeeze past.

'This is atrocious,' she declared, leaning out of the window.

Julia bristled inwardly. Really the woman was getting overbearing these days.

'I'm doing my best to get out of the way,' she replied, with dignity, 'won't keep you a minute.'

'No, not you. This invasion,' Daphne waved her hand at the street full of cars. 'I've been trying to get to Stockleigh, and it's just impossible. They've parked all the way up the lane, and now there's no room for two cars to pass. They're still flooding in, and nobody can move either way. It's complete gridlock.'

'But who are all these people?' Julia was nonplussed.

'Oh haven't you heard? Apparently some particularly rare bird has been seen in the old Chalk Pit, and now all the bird enthusiasts in the country are descending on Haydon. Twitchers, they call them, don't they. Completely daft, if you ask me.'

Julia hadn't asked her, but Daphne Stalker never needed encouragement to bring forth her views.

'I'm going to get this chaos sorted out,' she continued briskly, 'since the police seem conspicuous by their absence.'

'Perhaps they can't get through,' suggested Julia, reasonably. 'After all, they've got to come from Stockleigh themselves.'

But Daphne wasn't listening. Somebody had to do something, and her organising skills would solve this particular village problem. She didn't know what the place would do without her, really.

'That field on the hill has an entrance on to the lane, doesn't it. Could we persuade your son Clive to allow them to use it as a car park, do you think?'

So there were actually some things that escaped the woman's notice, Julia thought, with satisfaction. It gave her an unexpected pleasure to be able to say, 'Well I'm afraid he's recently sold it. You'll have to ask the new owner, Mike Swathe.'

'What, Mrs Swathe's son?'

'Yes. As it happens, I've been given his telephone number, because damp's coming from his mother's cottage and affecting my kitchen wall. If you could just see me into this gap, I'll go in and get it for you,' Julia told her sweetly.

She emerged from the cottage to find Mrs Chitting being instructed about the importance of everyone in the village pulling their weight. As this intolerable invasion just showed, if she, Daphne Stalker, didn't involve herself, nothing would get done.

Knowing Mrs Chitting's views on busybody newcomers, and this one in particular, Julia avoided her eye, and smiled to herself.

'Here's Mike Swathe's telephone number,' she said to Daphne. 'But he works in Stockleigh himself, so if cars are already blocking the road he won't easily be able to get here either. Not that he's likely to bother. He's something of a business tycoon.'

'Well, if he does give permission for car parking in the field, I'll have to find someone in Haydon who'll stand on the gate and organise it.' Daphne Stalker's tone of voice implied that she really couldn't do *everything*, although people seemed to expect her to.

'He'll be wanting to charge for parking, I expect.' Mrs Chitting's plump face, and cherubic expression, belied a worldly wisdom. 'Tell him, if he wants someone to take the money at the gate, Harry Trench might be able to help.' She glanced at Lady Julia. 'He's got a bit of time on his hands these days.'

'What a good idea,' Julia approved warmly, thinking that her daily help's practical intelligence was one of the reasons they'd got on so well for over thirty years. 'He is... used to be, our gardener at the Hall. Tell Mr Swathe he couldn't find anyone more honest and reliable.'

Meanwhile, up at Kiln House, Zinnia was struggling to keep a grip on reality. Earlier in the day, she'd been in the greenhouse, inspecting the pots of Settlewort seed for that still-elusive spark of life, when a blue Transit van had turned into the drive, and disgorged five young men, who clustered round the front door. Probably surveyors or something, she thought, walking down to see what they wanted, noting pagers, and a couple of businesslike telescopes among their array of gear. Surveyors! The word suddenly jangled a warning. That man Swathe must be up to something. Well, she wouldn't be caught napping.

Rosemary was on the doorstep, talking to them, by the time she got there.

'These guys have heard about the Kirtland Warbler,' she said excitedly, 'and want permission to go in the Pit Garden and see it.'

You had to hand it to that Swathe, he had his ear to the ground, Zinnia thought grimly. But she wasn't falling for that sort of subterfuge.

'No,' she said with a stiff little smile, like a film star rebuffing a would-be interviewer. 'I'm afraid not.' And turned back towards the greenhouse.

They looked at each other in disbelief.

'But it's a First!' exclaimed a ginger-haired youth, binoculars festooned with bird rings, 'a Cosmic Mind-F...'

'He means it's never been recorded in Britain before,' hastily interrupted one of his companions, his faded woollen hat covered with badges, 'I can assure your mother there won't be any damage. We won't burn it up, or even be there very long. Just have it, and go.'

It took the combined efforts of Rosemary and Matthew, who was summoned urgently, to persuade Zinnia that this was no cunning ruse thought up by the villainous Swathe. The fact that fourteen more bird enthusiasts arrived in the next twenty minutes was not unhelpful. Money or no money, employing nineteen surveyors to work on one disused chalk pit did seem a trifle extreme.

'But they'll ruin the place,' Zinnia had continued to object, 'trample on my plants, and make a thorough mess. I really can't have dozens of strangers wandering about the garden.'

'A small sacrifice for saving the Pit though, Gran,' Matthew countered.
'How do you mean, save it?'

'Well, old Swathe would hardly be allowed to tip rubbish into the habitat of a very rare bird, would he?'

Completely unaware of the traffic chaos being caused in the village and surrounding lanes, Zinnia was left breathless by the speed and scale of the invasion, as word of a British First spread on pagers, and twitcher hotlines. She retreated to the house, thankful that Rosemary and Matthew were there to take charge.

This, they quickly decided, was not just a great laugh, but a commercial opportunity to be seized.

'An entry charge, I think, don't you?' mused Matthew pleasurably. 'What shall we make it, one pound, two pounds? Five?'

They settled at two pounds, on the grounds that Birders and Twitchers were obsessive, but also impecunious, and a five pound barrier would probably have them attempting to climb down the quarry sides to avoid it.

'Then there'd be bodies littering the place,' commented Rosemary laconically. 'Real messy.'

'*Use of Loo 10p*' Matthew scrawled on a notice by the back door, and while Rosemary stood at the gate taking entrance money, he sped home on his bicycle to raid Veronica's kitchen for refreshments to sell.

By the end of that first day, they had amassed the amazing sum of two hundred and eight pounds, but Zinnia was not the happiest of gardeners.

An apopleptic Gerry Thornway had stormed round, demanding to know why the lane was blocked by cars and scruffy individuals who were all apparently converging on Kiln House. And, as the last of the twitchers melted away with the darkness, Zinnia had done a tour of inspection of her precious garden, and returned to the kitchen quivering with indignation.

'These people,' she said angrily, waving a snapped-off branch of Daphne odora, 'they're philistines. Just look what they've done! And my lovely drift of yellow Asphodeline is trampled down, half the Imperial Fritillaries are broken off, and I don't think the Camassias will flower at all now.' She shook her head in disbelief. 'It's only one little bird, for heaven's sake, hardly of earth shaking significance.'

'They probably think that about your plants,' Rosemary commented, half to herself, but nonetheless feeling sorry for her aunt. The situation was out of her control, and she looked uncertain and apprehensive. Rosemary felt a twinge of guilt at identifying the thing in the first place.

'Sit down by the range, and I'll get you a stiff whisky,' she said kindly.

'Be even worse tomorrow, Gran,' Matthew informed her cheerfully, looking up from his pencilled analysis of the day's takings. 'We've told all the local papers, and I suggested to the BBC and Anglia Television that they might like to send camera crews along to cover it.'

'You've done *what*!' Zinnia was appalled. 'Whatever for?'

'The more publicity you get, the better.' He smiled at her discomfiture. 'Rare wildlife habitat threatened, and all that. What we really need,' he continued speculatively, 'is a breeding pair of Kirtland Warblers. Beats four aces any time.'

He raised his voice for Rosemary's benefit. 'Any volunteers to go down to Felixstowe Docks tomorrow and search for a mate?'

'Say, that's an idea,' she responded evenly, returning with Zinnia's whisky. 'I'll put on my shortest skirt, shall I, and lots of mascara.'

Giving the glass to her bemused aunt, she queried, 'Why Felixstowe Docks?'

'Well I reckon that's where our golden goose came from. You said they winter in the Bahamas. Probably took up residence on a ship, and suddenly found itself transported to the delights of South Suffolk.'

'Bit like me really.' Rosemary warmed her hands on the range. 'Come on Matthew. Get real. We don't have a mouse in a snakepit's chance of finding another one. And these guys migrate anyway, at the end of the summer.'

'So it doesn't even help with saving the Pit?' Zinnia was still trying to get the meaning of the day's events clear in her mind.

'Yeah, course it does,' Matthew assured her breezily. 'We'll feed the thing, and keep it living here all summer, and that'll stop old Thingamybob getting planning permission to tip. And by autumn we'll have sorted something else out. It gives us time.'

****

Haydon Settleworth was used to the odd tourist who admired the picturesque village street, and stopped off for lunch at The Oak, but the influx of twitchers next day was beyond anyone's experience. By lunchtime the pub was thronged with people in distressed-looking anoraks and trainers, and the locals listened in fascination to conversations about being gripped off by dudes, flogging woods and dipping out.

'What's a Penduline Tit?' the landlord enquired saucily of his barmaid, as they raced round, making Herculean efforts to fulfil orders.

'Dunno.' She winked. 'But according to the bloke at the end of the bar, it's been performing well.'

The village store bought in a special supply of crisps, snacks and canned drinks, and still ran out. Even the Antiques shop removed the Closed sign, although no-one was seen to go in.

The police had lined the lane to Stockleigh with cones, to stop people from parking, and Harry Trench was having a happy time marshalling a constant stream of cars into orderly rows, in the field above the Pit.

Quite a few villagers walked up to Kiln House to see what all the fuss was about, and were not best pleased to find themselves relieved of two pounds at the drive entrance, since Rosemary had no idea they were locals. A short, restless-seeming man gave her a piercing look when told there was an entry charge.

'Half's going to charity, and the rest is to put right the wear and tear on the Pit Garden,' she explained, discomfited by his unwavering blue eyes.

'Is it now,' he said softly, and half smiled to himself, as he strode off towards the ramp.

Halfway through the afternoon a television crew arrived, headed by a rather long-faced man in his thirties.

'Hi, I'm Jeremy,' he greeted Rosemary, 'from the BBC, Eastern Region. We understand you're harbouring some exotic bird that's causing great excitement.'

The chasing members of the family being otherwise occupied, Gerry's roaming peacocks had taken advantage of the lull in hostilities in the last two days, and one now gave its loud, keening cry just behind him. He started nervously, and Rosemary saw his sudden expression of doubt.

'No, not that,' she assured him, laughing. 'It's a Kirtland Warbler, little yellow job from the States. Down in the old chalk pit. You'll probably have difficulty filming it though.'

'Oh we thought we'd angle the story on the human interest anyway. You know, hordes of bird watchers descending on a Suffolk country garden. The bird itself is hardly riveting, is it?' He nodded to his camera and sound colleagues. 'We'll go down and cover the bird watchers now, and then we'll need a piece to camera from the garden owner.'

Apprehensive about the vituperative things her aunt might have to say on camera about bird fanatics with large feet, Rosemary went in to warn of the impending interview, but the worries proved unnecessary. She found her busy writing her column for Country Harvest.

'Interview? Tell them to go to hell,' was Zinnia's succinct instruction.

Rosemary was mentally trying out several versions of this refusal, suitably sweetened, when the trio returned.

'You wouldn't believe the scene down there.' Jeremy was clearly amazed. 'Somewhere in the bushes is a poor little bird, and there's this huge semi-circle of twitchers – must be about two hundred of them – all bristling with cameras and telescopes on tripods. Some guy's even set up a refreshment stall. You're right, we didn't see the bird, but we got a great shot of its worshippers. Should make a good last item for the regional news bulletin.'

Rosemary was just telling him that most unfortunately her aunt had walked into a cupboard door only that morning, and was nursing a black eye, so would not, after all, be able to give a television interview, when a young woman with sleekly cropped hair and tight jeans appeared at the gate.

'Oh Jeremy!' she exclaimed loudly, cutting across their conversation. 'Gosh, what are you doing here?'

There was no answering spark of recognition at first, from the recipient of her eager greeting.

'It's Nigella. Nigella Picket. We worked on Blunders Will Never Cease together. Remember. I did the marketing and publicity for the series. What are you doing now?'

With an apologetic glance at Rosemary, Jeremy informed her that he was mainly producing for the BBC, but also working on a series about modern life in the countryside, for an independent company.

'*Really*!' she squealed. 'But that's perfect. You simply *must* include Haydon's Flower Arranging Competition and Gardens Festival in July. We've got Loretta Moss – you know, the famous flower arranger – coming down to visit, lots of things going on, and several interesting gardens. Mine's included, and this one.' She looked around her. 'They're all very different.'

'Well, send me some details...' he suggested, with all the enthusiasm of a strict vegetarian faced with Beef Wellington.

'I was going to send an invitation to the BBC anyway. I'm in charge of publicity, you see.' She smiled flirtatiously. 'Have to keep the old hand in, now I'm a full-time Mum. That's why I've come to see Mrs Peasmore now. I wanted to get a description of her garden, for the leaflets and press releases.'

'We were just going,' her erstwhile colleague lied shamelessly. 'Have to rush back to the studio.' He turned to Rosemary. 'We'll hope to squeeze the item onto tonight's edition of 'Look East'. Sorry to hear about your aunt.'

'I *always* read her column in Country Harvest,' Nigella gushed, as they departed. 'Ever since we moved here I've thought it would be great fun to meet her, and see round the garden. Is it not a good moment?'

'You could say that.' Rosemary thought this would have been obvious, and inwardly winced at the imagined encounter, even if it was one of Zinnia's less acerbic days.

'Tell you what,' she said diplomatically, 'my aunt can put together a suitable description, and I'll bring it down to you in the next day or so. I know nothing about gardening, I'm afraid, but Lady Susan was saying how keen you are, so it would be great to see your garden.'

Nigella Picket smiled proudly, and Rosemary wondered anew at the propensity of marketing and media types to fall for the very arts they practised.

After everyone had gone that evening, Zinnia did a tour of inspection of her beloved garden, and came back looking pale and angry.

'That is *it!*' she said with determination, holding the back door open for Roger who, like her, had been reclaiming his territory. 'I've had bird watchers up to here. From now on,' she informed her grandson, like a judge conveying society's displeasure, 'they are forbidden to set foot in this garden.'

Piece of paper in hand, Rosemary returned to the kitchen from answering the telephone, just in time to catch her aunt's edict.

'Oh, but surely…'

'No-one is coming through that gate, from now on,' Zinnia declared resolutely, 'and if they so much as train their telescopes on the trees, I'll…I'll set the cat on them.'

Matthew had wisely collected all the paper cups and dropped litter, and was now tying up a sack of rubbish, the residue of a decidedly profitable day, due largely to an insatiable demand for Veronica's scones and rock cakes. 'But Gran, you're on to a really good thing,' he objected. 'We've been absolutely coining it in today. Do you know how much I reckon we'll…'

'I don't want any money,' she interrupted him brusquely. 'It would be nice for half to go to a suitable charity, but you and Rosemary have the rest. You've earned it. I just want my garden back.'

'Hang on, what about saving the Pit from being tipped on? I thought you really minded about that.'

But Zinnia had been applying a little logic. 'The whatever-it's-called…bird will still be there,' she told him. 'The only thing that won't be are the hordes of people. They don't have any right to trespass on my garden, and trample it to bits. I'm not having it. Just not.'

Roger had been washing his ears, but at the sound of her raised voice, he paused, and then sneezed, sending a little yellow feather into the air, light as a drifting snowflake, to nestle gently on Rosemary's shoe. She regarded it with idle interest, which gradually deepened to unhappy certainty, like wine on a wedding dress, as its significance sank in.

'Roger!' she said in shocked accusation. 'You wouldn't… You *haven*'t…?'

The others followed her gaze, and thought process.

Becoming aware that all eyes were upon him, the cat ceased washing, and pointedly surveyed his empty feeding dish.

The silence was broken by Zinnia.

'We'll have a look for your favourite tinned mackerel in the larder, my lad,' she said in a changed voice. 'I rather think you may have deserved it.'

Chapter Six

It was not the happiest of coincidences that the new Features Editor of Country Harvest should choose the very next day to visit Haydon Settleworth, and doubly unfortunate that with the fuss over Roger's interest in birds, Rosemary had forgotten to relay this telephoned information to her aunt. The result was that the Zinnia Peasmore he encountered was not quite the one she would have wished to portray.

As feared, early that morning the mangled remains of the Kirtland Warbler had been located, at the foot of a Coronilla glauca, the shrub's mass of yellow flowers echoing the bird's feathers in a perfect colour match. Matthew was then deputed to make known the sad news that the British First from America had pecked the dust.

'We think it must have been next door's cat,' he declared in aggrieved tones down the phone. There didn't seem any need to mention the culprit's recent change of residency.

Word soon winged its way on to the twitchers' communication network, and the result was that just a few people had to be turned away in the morning, and by afternoon Rosemary felt free to go out for a walk. In wonderful solitude, Zinnia was at last able to devote herself to her precious garden.

The trouble was that in the Pit Garden the more she looked, the more damage she discovered, with holes caused by tripods, bruised and crushed plants, and decapitated flowers. Her ire against people obsessed by birds was therefore nicely stoked, when she looked up and spied one apparently walking towards her, camera swinging against his chest, an apologetic smile on his face.

'There didn't seem to be anyone up at the house,' he began, 'so I thought...'

'You should keep up to date,' she interrupted him crustily, firming a loosened plant into the ground with her heel, 'It's all over. You're wasting your time.'

The man's smile changed to puzzlement. 'Sorry?'

'So you should be.' Zinnia's resentment at the cavalier attitude of these strange, bird-mad people now had an outlet. 'You think you can just march into people's gardens, trample on plants, plonk camera tripods down everywhere, and treat the place as if you owned it, without so much as a by-your-leave.'

'I...I don't quite follow you?'

'Look at this place,' she waved her hand angrily. 'It's in a dreadful state. Gardens obviously mean nothing to people like you. You just don't live in the real world.'

Doubt began to set in. 'You are Mrs Peasmore?'

'Yes, and my garden has suffered enough. There's nothing here to interest you now. Please leave.'

Her visitor turned to go, and then stood uncertainly. 'Does this mean that you no longer want to write for us?'

It was Zinnia's turn to be confused. 'Write?'

'Yes. Continue your column for Country Harvest. It's what I've come to talk to you about. You did get my message?'

Zinnia was as practised at exercising charm as a rugby player at sipping sherry but, as she told Rosemary when they were preparing supper, she'd never tried harder than that afternoon, as soon as the visitor's identity had been revealed.

'I apologised profusely, and explained why the garden was looking battered. Told him about the bird watching saga, which he seemed to think was rather amusing,' she said, with indignation. 'And then we discussed the column, over a cup of tea. There weren't any biscuits left to offer him.'

'Why bother coming all this way to see you? What's the matter with the telephone?'

'Oh he's a new broom. Said he wanted to meet all his regular columnists.' Resentfully, she added, 'And sack them.'

Rosemary was chopping onions, but now the knife remained suspended in air.

'He didn't give you the push, did he? Heck, I'm sorry. It's all my fault.'

'Not exactly. But it looks as if I'm being manoeuvred out. I wouldn't care, but the money is a real lifesaver.'

'Manoeuvred out? What does that mean?'

'Well, it was made clear that he doesn't like what I write,' said Zinnia huffily, grinding pepper onto their pork chops. 'Told me it had to be "more relevant to the readers". He's done a survey, apparently, and discovered that the typical readers are fashion conscious young couples, who don't want to spend much time gardening, but expect it to look nice.'

'Not your "proper gardeners" then?' Rosemary teased, tuned in by this time to her aunt's scorn for people who failed to merit the label.

'Hardly.' Zinnia was now lavishly spreading mustard on the meat, and her guest made a mental note to find a large water jug for the table.

'The thing is, I've always written about my experiences in this garden. And the plants of course. Everyone needs to learn what plants there are, and how they like to grow. New gardeners especially.'

This sounded reasonable.

'So what does the guy want you to write instead?'

'Huh! Gardening-Made-Easy, as far as I can see. Lots of glib stuff about how you can transform a garden in one season; make it fashionable, glamorous and easy-care. Be the envy of your friends. All that sort of codswallop.'

'But you could hold your nose and write spiel like that, couldn't you,' suggested Rosemary, tipping the chopped onions into the pan.

'No I could not.' Zinnia's chin jutted uncompromisingly. 'It's a load of rubbish for a start. One of the main pleasures of gardening is that things develop slowly, and you have to be patient. Besides, I can only write about things I know.' She searched the spice rack for garlic granules, and sighed. 'I shall just have to keep doing things my way, and hope the New Broom is swept away before I am. They always get the push in the end. It's just a question of timing.'

****

In the week that followed things settled down, and the sudden invasion by hordes of bird watchers began to be woven into the village's collective memory as just another demonstration of the oddity of outsiders. There was relief that normality had returned, with the exception of those few for whom it had proved a bonanza, although Harry Trench had no regret at casting off his duties as car park attendant. While lucrative, the task had not been without personal sacrifice.

'My poor ole feet ache good tidily,' he complained, 'I was glad to see the inned on it.'

The episode had effectively raised Zinnia Peasmore and her Pit Garden in the village's consciousness, but not in public estimation, and there were a good many grumbles that she should never have allowed access to these peculiar people anyway.

At the beginning of April, a few days after the Great Invasion, planning permission for Susie's commercial Herb Garden and Tea Shop was finally granted, and a willing Rosemary was drafted in to work alongside Matthew in helping to set it up, with the aim of an opening in late May. Matthew worked mainly on the plant and herb garden side, while Rosemary was given responsibility for receiving deliveries, and chasing up the equipment and stock ordered for the tea room and herb-cum-gift shop. She found Susie's enthusiasm infectious, and was gratified to find her own sense and intelligence fully appreciated, so that a genuine friendship began to develop.

In the evenings she would have liked to share with Zinnia each day's progress and problems, but found herself in an awkward position, held back by her aunt's uncharitable view of the Trugglestones, junior and senior. At first Rosemary tried stressing Clive and Susie's real need for money to invest in the Hall, but found Zinnia's mind was closed. There could be no extenuating circumstances. Clive had betrayed her, by selling the Pit, and Julia's behaviour was just as bad.

The difficulty was not helped by the arrival one morning in the second week of April, of an official-looking brown envelope, addressed to The Occupier, Kiln House.

'He's put in for planning permission!' an agitated Zinnia greeted Rosemary on her return that afternoon.

'Planning permission? Who? To do what?'

'That wretched man Swathe. He's applied to use the Pit as a landfill site. He's going to use it to tip rubbish. I *knew* it!'

Derek was summoned when he got home from work, and obligingly came round after supper. His suggestion, as a first step, was a meeting with Mike Swathe to discuss his intentions, but Zinnia wouldn't hear of it.

'I'm certainly not going to crawl to that wretched little man,' she declared resentfully. 'Why hasn't he come to see me?'

Derek knew better than to argue. 'Well, of course you must object strongly to the Council,' he advised, 'but you've got to do it in reasonable terms. Not a torrent of invective.'

Rosemary avoided his eye, suppressing a smile, while Zinnia looked righteous, and ignored the implication.

'What about a petition?' she suggested. 'The village will protest like mad, won't they. I'll talk to Julia about...' She stopped, suddenly remembering that all was not well in that direction.

'Well you should certainly get support from Gerry Thornway. He can't have received this notice from the Council yet, or he'd have been even more impossible at work than usual. He'll hit the roof.' For a moment Derek pleasurably imagined his boss's reaction to a landfill site adjoining his lavishly appointed country residence, before remembering that family interests came first.

'How are your special plant seeds coming on?' he enquired, and she searched his face suspiciously, for signs of amusement, before reluctantly confessing that not a single one had germinated. Yet.

'But growing Settlewort in the Pit is still a wonderful idea,' she added defiantly. 'It can be done, I'm sure of it.'

They talked round her situation for some time, before Derek left, promising to visit Stockleigh Public Library next day in his lunch hour, and seek out the County Council's plan for waste management.

Zinnia went to bed with all sorts of possible actions churning round in her mind, but none of them seemed as promising as getting Settlewort to grow in the Pit. Tomorrow, she decided, before drifting off to sleep, tomorrow she would sow the last of the Settlewort seeds. And *will* them to germinate.

****

A dental appointment in Ipswich used up the morning, so it was not until after a numb and hesitant lunch that Zinnia took the precious box of remaining Settlewort seeds out to the greenhouse, and prepared to plant them. The fact that the original sowings showed no stirrings of life was more disappointing than she cared to admit. Given the care and thought put in to sowing half the seeds, she had fully expected germination by now. Cautiously, she poked at the potting compost of one of the labelled flowerpots. No signs of growth at all, dammit.

Although not competitive in Country Harvest's 'make-your-neighbours-envious' way, she knew herself to be a good gardener. A sound grasp of the technical side was matched by long experience, and an instinctive empathy with plants. Over the years she'd built up a network of equally knowledgeable friends around the country, exchanging plants and information. It would have been useful to consult some of them now, she thought, mentally reviewing them. Basil Berriman could have tapped into his company's expertise, which would have been specially helpful. But with a planned pretence that Settlewort spontaneously appeared in the Pit, approaching anyone was out of the question.

Even though seeds of Mediterranean plants didn't generally need a simulated winter, she still had hopes for the one taken out of the fridge and planted a few days ago. But the thing had better hurry up. It would be just her luck if germination took a year or more. She removed the lid of the box, and regarded the remaining, curiously-shaped seeds with irritation.

'Now you,' she instructed them severely, 'are jolly well going to grow. Do you hear that. My garden depends on it.'

A movement caught her eye, and she looked up to discover one of Gerry's peacocks tugging determinedly at a rooted hebe cutting, while the other was casually trampling seedling salvias underfoot. Damn things!

'Hey!' she shouted, dashing out of the greenhouse, waving a seed catalogue at them threateningly. 'Out! Clear off.'

Her intentions were manifest, but so were theirs. Home was not where they wished to be, and it took some time before Zinnia realised that 'wild goose chase' was a phrase used only because whoever invented it had never encountered errant peacocks. Out of breath and frustrated, she might still have continued her ejection efforts, if large drops of rain had not begun falling, slowly at first, but with increasing vigour, from a menacing black cloud which had crept up unnoticed.

Oh Lord. Buckets. She would have to put buckets under all the roof leaks.

Generally, the cracked and broken tiles could hold off light rain, but the stuff that came down in earnest always managed to find its way down through the ceilings. It had created brown stains, as if a giant in the attic was being careless with the gravy, and with these as guides, placing buckets and bowls to catch the drips was a well-ordered procedure. But by the time they'd all been mustered, the rain was coming down in earnest, accompanied by thunder and lightning, and Zinnia abandoned all thought of seed-sowing until the storm passed over.

But she was fed up with her neighbour's wandering livestock, and decided to say so in stronger terms. Her previous complaints appeared to have had no effect. She picked up the telephone, although Gerry Thornway wouldn't be there of course. It was Elaine's submissive little voice that answered.

'I'm terribly sorry they're being a nuisance,' she sounded embarrassed. 'I'm just going out for the afternoon, but I'll ask Gerry to see if he can find where they're getting through the hedge, and block up the holes with wire when he comes home this evening.'

The rain was still thrumming down. Zinnia went into her study, surveyed the shelves of gardening books, and took out A Modern Herbal by Mrs M Grieve. She turned to the page on Settlewort, and sitting at her desk, read the entry again.

SETTLEWORT (Solanum regale)

Always a scarce plant, even in its native Mediterranean region, the plant is now considered extinct both there and in Britain.

It was originally brought to this country by the Romans, and grew in the southern counties on calcareous soils. Much valued for its medicinal properties, but difficult to cultivate, it is thought to have died out towards the end of the nineteenth century. However, like the Thorn Apple, Settlewort's seeds were renowned for their longevity, and there is a possibility that it may still regenerate somewhere spontaneously, or perhaps be found growing unrecognised in a garden, and for that reason a description is included in this herbal.

Description

Growing to more than four feet in one season, the stalk is thick and sappy, dividing into three or four branches, each of which again branches freely. The leaves are finely lanceolate,, deep green on the upper surface, and grey on the underside. The striking white flowers (deserving of the Latin epithet 'regale', meaning 'outstanding), are produced in cymes in July and Augus, They form shallow cups, about an inch across, with distinctive purple lines dividing each flower into five sections, notched at the outer edge. These are followed by small yellow berries. Old herbalists mention that, like the tomato plant, Settlewort gives off a distinctive aroma, especially when the leaves or stalks are bruised, but in this case pleasing, and reminiscent of peaches. The plant is tender, and thought to be an annual, or possibly a biennial.

History

The Elizabethan herbalists refer to the plant as Settlewort, and make clear that it was a treasured rarity even then. It was highly valued by the Romans as a cure for headaches and fading memory. The plant also had a reputation for affecting the thoughts and conduct of those who had drunk wine to which some juice of this herb had been added, making them suggestible. Plutarch gives a graphic account of the strange effects that followed its use. According to old legends, the plant gained its colloquial name from its role in settling disputes, by making one or both antagonists amenable to a settlement. It is one of the traditional witches' herbs, and in the seventeenth century, when the persecution of so-called witches was at its height, anyone in whose garden Settlewort appeared was immediately an object of suspicion. This fact may well have contributed to its rarity and subsequent extinction.

Why it should have died out in its native Mediterranean is not clear, but the probable reason is simply over-exploitation of a plant that was both sparingly found, and difficult to cultivate.

Medicinal Action and Uses/ Constituents

Many members of the genus solanum contain alkaloids, with varying effects. Since Solanum regale is sadly no longer extant, the properties which caused it to have medicinal and mind-altering properties are not possible to ascertain, but the likelihood is that it was some kind of alkaloid.

Zinnia gazed out at the rain, splashing down with such force that the path outside was covered with a cushion of spray. Maybe she was being irresponsible, it occurred to her, laying the book down on the desk. She now possessed seeds of a plant everyone thought extinct. And not just any plant either. Settlewort was believed to have had important effects on the mind.

From the passage outside came the rhythmic drump, drump of drips finding their way into the bucket, like a piling machine on a distant building site.

If modern chemists got hold of Settlewort, she mused, it was possible they would find it held the cure for scourges like Parkinson's Disease, senile dementia, or Alzheimers. An uncomfortable thought obtruded. What if she, by her determination to grow the plant herself, threw away that chance forever?

With their special expertise, The Royal Botanic Gardens at Kew or the Chelsea Physic Garden would surely stand a better chance of germinating the seed. She rubbed her chin thoughtfully. On the other hand, how could she bear to watch her wonderful garden, the result of years of hard work and devotion, wiped out by some philistine who just saw it as a way to make money? If there was a chance of saving it from destruction, shouldn't she take it?

Zinnia fingered the worn cover of the Herbal, trying to justify in her own mind what she wanted to do, like a burglar protesting that his victim was filthy rich. After all, she thought, if the seed did grow, the world would then have Settlewort again. And if she failed, well, the family were the only ones who knew about the seeds, and they didn't understand their significance. No-one would know what had been missed.

The rain was slackening off now, the sound of thunder becoming just a growl in the distance. She got up to replace Mrs Grieve on the bookshelf, trying to ignore the small voice in her head which was whispering insistently, *But you would.. You would know.*

Remembering an American publication entitled 'Seed Germination Theory and Practice', she began searching for it, but after a few moments gave up, and sat down in defeat.

'Oh sod it,' she said out loud. 'Okay, I'll sow just two more, and Kew can have the rest.'

The sound of the back door closing, and a shout of 'Hi Gran', sent her in to the kitchen, to find Rosemary and Matthew out of breath and laughing, as they took off dripping anoraks.

'Been sent home in disgrace for misbehaving?' she enquired.

'Yeah, it's our Rose,' reported Matthew seriously. 'We just can't stop her sampling the herbal cordials, and smearing perfumes all over herself. The stink set off the smoke alarms in the end.'

There's a power cut that end of the village,' Rosemary explained, and Susie gave us a lift back, so we can use my laptop. We're in the middle of designing a leaflet about the Herb Garden to send to all the tourist information places.'

'Well, I'll be in the greenhouse, if you want me,' Zinnia told them, and went out into a strangely quiet garden, the birds shocked into silence by the storm. The air was heavy with moisture, steady drips from the leaves making a soft background accompaniment to the occasional drum roll of distant thunder.

A few minutes later she was back.

'You didn't shelter in the greenhouse, on your way in, by any chance?' she asked lightly.

Matthew shook his head, his mouth full of biscuit.

'Only... the box of Settlewort seeds was in there, when the rain came on. And now just this box is.' Waving the small cardboard container at them, to demonstrate its emptiness, she was having trouble keeping the agitation out of her voice. 'The seeds have gone!'

Rosemary tried to be reassuring. 'Well nobody would steal them, would they. Especially in the middle of a thunderstorm.'

'That's what you think.' Matthew informed her, straight-faced. 'But we get some seedy types around here. And of course these things are going to lay a golden goose.'

She ignored him. 'Did you perhaps put them in your pocket, without remembering?'

'No, I thought of that. They've just vanished.' Zinnia's dismay was obvious, and obligingly they followed her out into the garden to investigate. But as the trio approached the greenhouse a large avian trespasser hopped down from the workbench, and scurried out of the open door, heading in the direction of home territory.

'Peacocks!' Zinnia exclaimed, an awful realisation slowly dawning. 'It's those ruddy peacocks. They've eaten the Settlewort seed!'

Twenty minutes later they were sitting round the kitchen table over a cup of tea, discussing Zinnia's options, in the light of this new turn of events.

'Education in this country is just shocking,' declared Matthew reproachfully. 'Here I am at the end of my schooling, and no-one has taught me about the digestive system of the peacock.' He ran a hand through his curls in mock despair. 'How am I supposed to face the world, not knowing how long it would take a seed to pass from beak to bum?'

'The things will be digested and destroyed, won't they?' Rosemary didn't see that there was much they could do to retrieve the situation.

'Not necessarily,' Zinnia answered. 'Seeds are usually well protected. Some even have to go through the body of a bird, to germinate. In fact,' she muttered to herself, 'that's about the one thing I didn't try.' She thought for a moment. 'We must make sure anything they deposit is on our side of the hedge.' Her resolve was now setting, like plaster of Paris.

'How are you going to do that?'

'Any volunteers for the peacock kidnapping party?' Matthew joyfully anticipated her reply. 'You may get pecked to death, you may be taken prisoner and never seen again, but these are desperate times. Your country needs you.'

Rosemary looked from one to the other. 'You're not suggesting we go next door and rustle a couple of peacocks, bring them back here and pore over their droppings for several days?' She put on a John McEnroe voice, 'You cannot be serious.'

'Shouldn't take more than a few hours,' Zinnia stated, off-handedly. 'If Matthew had been properly educated, he would know how long. And I don't think it'll be necessary to go and get them. They seem to spend half their time over here anyway. We'll just tempt them over with some food.'

Matthew pursed his lips. 'What do you reckon, Gran. Cornflakes, muesli...?'

'You're nuts, both of you.'

'Nuts? Yes, a good suggestion, our Rose.'

Zinnia frowned. 'Oh Lord, I was forgetting. Because I complained today, Gerry Thornway's going to make the hedge escape-proof this evening, to stop them coming here. We'll have to entice them over right now, before he comes back.'

'I shouldn't worry,' her grandson was laid-back. 'According to Dad, that lazy creep never does anything unless he absolutely has to.'

'Can't take the risk,' she retorted briskly, seizing a packet of porridge oats out of the larder. 'Come on you two, stir yourselves. You're fitter than I am.'

Rosemary and Matthew watched with unease and enjoyment, respectively, as Zinnia crouched by a small gap at the base of the hedge, and made what she evidently thought were enticing noises.

'Kerm along then. Kerm along,' she wheedled, throwing a handful of rolled oats to land on the immaculate lawn just the other side, and then laid a trail through the hedge.

'What's fitness got to do with it?' Rosemary muttered in Matthew's direction.

'Ah well, as soon as Priscilla and Percy Peacock come through the hole, we get 'em with a rugby tackle,' he informed her, an appreciative eye on his grandmother's attempt at enticement, which was akin to a camel fluttering its eyelashes. 'Do they teach rugby across the pond?'

She made a face at him. 'You don't think our presence might be putting them off?' she suggested in a low voice, to her aunt. 'After all, they've probably noticed that none of us has shown great pleasure at their garden visiting up to now.'

'Ah, you haven't observed human nature. Greed overcomes caution, every time. And peacocks have even less sense.'

Despite this belief, Zinnia suggested they went into hiding behind the leathery leaves of a large mahonia, and after what seemed to a chilled Rosemary an awful long time, they were rewarded by the return of the feathered felons.

'Gotcha!' exclaimed Matthew, as the second one squeezed through the hedge, causing the bird to squawk in alarm, and run towards Kiln House, following her mate.

'I'll try and block up the hole, you two herd them into the Pit,' Zinnia instructed, pleased with the whole operation.

Turning to obey orders, Rosemary thought she detected a movement at the upstairs window of the Thornway's house, but when she looked again through the dripping blossom of a cherry tree, there was no-one to be seen.

****

'Don't be surprised if I'm deported as a peacock rustler', she e-mailed Bill that evening, picturing with a certain satisfaction his uncomprehending disapproval. *Zinnia has them captive in the Pit Garden, with a bowl of food in the summer house, and they seem surprisingly happy. At least they've made no attempt to escape, so far. Do you know anyone who's made a study of peacock droppings? Neither do I. So we're about to make a serious contribution to ornithological study. Never say I don't take an interest in your hobby.'*

Rosemary didn't think it necessary to mention the telephone call earlier in the evening, fielded by her aunt.

'Missing?' she'd heard Zinnia exclaim, with simulated surprise. 'Goodness me. They're well known for being great wanderers, though, aren't they.' There was a pause. 'No. No, I haven't. Surprising really, they do come into this garden a lot... Of course I'm sure. I'll let you know if they turn up here. But I expect they'll come home in a day or so.'

Returning to the kitchen, she met her niece's accusing gaze. 'Well they will,' she said blandly, peering into the Rayburn's fuel hopper to check the anthracite level. 'They can go home, oh, let's say tomorrow evening.'

Their feathered guests evidently had other ideas. Before breakfast next morning, Zinnia went out into the garden, moved one of the hurdles that Matthew had placed as a makeshift barrier across the ramp, and walked expectantly down into the Pit Garden.

'Damn things have gone,' she was soon reporting indignantly to Rosemary, who was fixing herself some coffee and toast. 'I don't know how they got out of there. They're supposed to have clipped wings, to stop them flying.'

'Perhaps they can flutter enough to get up into trees. Or over fences,' Rosemary suggested, adding mischievously, 'After all, they're well known for being great wanderers, aren't they?'

Chapter Seven

Rosemary set off for the Walled Herb Garden shortly after breakfast the day after, enjoying a mental image of Zinnia spending hours searching diligently for promising-looking bird droppings, and carefully conveying them to the greenhouse for dissection.

The odd realities of life in Haydon Settleworth were beginning to push back the unhappiness of the past few months, and at last she was feeling more alive. But although the weight of misery was lessening, Rosemary didn't feel inclined to look into the future. Just one day at a time would do fine.

Discovering that her help was welcomed by Susie Trugglestone had been like finding a dry ledge while water lapped all around. Refusing attempts to put it on a financial footing, she insisted that it gave her something to do, which was true. Its unofficial nature also meant there was no obligation to put in hours if she didn't want to, but in fact she was enjoying it very much.

Things were coming on apace now. A little less than three weeks after Rosemary had sat drinking coffee that first day, the builders had finished and cleared up, leaving the converted stable that was to be the Tea Room with a damp-plaster, echoey feeling. This was fading daily, as tables and chairs arrived, with unopened boxes of crockery and kitchen equipment taking up the remaining floor space. On the day she took Rosemary into Ipswich, Susie had spotted some cotton material featuring various herbs, and this had now been made into attractive curtains.

'Totally useless of course,' her ladyship remarked cheerfully, as they clipped them on to the new curtain rails, 'we're never going to be open when it's dark, but they do look good, don't they.'

The adjoining area was for the sale of herb products and souvenirs, and the smell of paint and new wood was rapidly being supplanted by a medley of lavender, sage, bergamot, and pot-pourri, as cases of stuff arrived and were unpacked.

Rosemary was gratified that her opinion had been sought over the selection of goods for the shop, and found herself increasingly interested in this world of herbs and herb products. Clearly Susie was very knowledgeable, but remained clear-eyed about the type of customer they were likely to attract.

'Mostly they'll be coming for something to do,' she had declared practically, as they went through catalogues and sales lists together. She put on an anxious voice, 'What shall we do with Aunt Edna when she comes to visit? I know, we'll take her to the Herb Garden at Haydon Settleworth, they do lovely teas there.' She smiled at Rosemary's expression. 'I don't mind in the least. We'll hope to attract coach parties of old folks on afternoon outings as well. The tea is always much more important than where they go.'

'Don't you want real herb enthusiasts?' Rosemary was surprised.

'Like to, but there aren't enough. If people want to come for the trip and a tea out, that's fine by me. This place is supposed to make money first, and if people learn about herbs as well, that's great.' She paused. 'We hope they'll buy a plant or two, and something from the shop, but the stuff's got to appeal to them. How about these aprons?' She passed the catalogue over to Rosemary for her opinion. 'I'll try and stock some specialist herb products, but I'm afraid the bulk of it will have to be soaps and lavender bags, potpourri, stuff like that, and anything with a herbal motif.'

'And there was me thinking your mission was to spread the word about the wonders of Nature's cures,' Rosemary felt enough at ease now for banter.

Susie laughed. 'We'll have books as well, and maybe a few people will get hooked and come back for more information. These days there's quite a lot of interest in herbs, with the growth of complementary medicine. But I'd rather emphasise their use in cooking, which keeps you well, so you don't need treatment. That's my theory anyhow.'

Pot-grown herbs were now being delivered from various small nurseries, and Matthew was working hard to finish the plant sales area, making it completely level, before laying down weed-proof matting, covering it with gravel, and putting up simple wooden partitions.

Meanwhile, Susie wanted the new arrivals to go in the greenhouse. They would be out of the way there, but also protected if there was a hard frost, since most of them had been grown under cover.

The trouble was there was hardly any room in there, largely filled as it was by big flowerpots of fuchsias, some of them lying on their sides to encourage the rising sap, dahlia tubers, trays of vegetable seedlings and bedding plants, waiting to be planted out.

'What kind of herbs are these, then?' asked Rosemary, puzzled.

'They're not herbs at all. They belong to Harry Trench, and are part of a *big* problem,' Susie said wearily. 'Council planning people, officious hygiene inspectors, Ministry regulations – pfff! They're nothing compared to Trugglestone Hall's home-grown troubles. Honestly, Rosemary, I just don't know what to do about him.'

Rosemary had come across Harry Trench now several times. A small man with a round, wrinkled face, and white, bushy eyebrows above mild eyes, she'd seen him leaving his cottage adjoining what was now going to be the Tea Room and Shop, and had also encountered him in the village, on his way to Lady Julia's cottage, where he was helping with the new garden. He smiled and said good morning, but there hadn't yet been a suitable moment to buttonhole him, and ask about his reminiscences of the Pit when it was working.

'Does he pay rent or something for the use of the greenhouse?' she asked.

'No of *course* not.' The idea was laughable. 'Harry just regards it as his, because it always was. He's been gardener here since the year dot. And my mother-in-law couldn't do much in the way of gardening after she hurt her back in a riding accident, so she just let him get on with it.'

'Why don't you want to keep him on?' Rosemary didn't see the problem. 'Wouldn't he be able to help get this place ready?'

'No,' said Susie flatly. 'He's far too doddery. He'll be seventy next year, and his rheumatism's bad. He's very slow, and it's just time he retired. We've got Berriman's coming in now on a contract basis to do the grass and the hedges.' As she spoke, she attempted to clear some bench space for a batch of newly-arrived hyssop plants. 'Besides,' she added, 'he and I just have completely different ideas about gardening. He wants to have bedding plants round the Hall, and I need to put in perennials and shrubs that will look good all year round. They'll be much less work too.' She brushed off cobwebs, then tried to detach it from her fingers. 'And he's appalled that we won't be growing vegetables and cut flowers here. It used to be the kitchen garden you see.'

'Must have kept him busy, it's quite an area,' commented Rosemary, looking out at the newly-planted beds.

'Well he couldn't manage in the last few years. More than half the place had gone to weeds because he only used part of it. And mostly for his precious fuchsias, and dahlias. Horrible garish things.'

'So you've usurped his territory?' Rosemary was beginning to understand a few things that had puzzled her.

'Well, he's a lovely old boy, and I don't want to upset him, but...' Susie shrugged helplessly. 'The best thing would be for him to retire completely, move out of the stable cottage and have a nice little garden of his own, where he can potter about growing vegetables and fuchsias.'

'And is he refusing to?'

Taking the last flowerpot that Rosemary handed her, Susie wedged it on to the greenhouse bench, and sighed. 'He's not refusing to, because no-one will ask him. And that's the real problem.

We'll leave the door open, I think, now the sun's getting stronger,' she decided, as they left the greenhouse, and went to sort out the rest of the consignment of plants in the yard.

The situation struck Rosemary as silly, and not at all like Susie, whose open and practical attitude was one of the things that was most likeable.

'Why don't you just tell him, tactfully, that it would be best if he retired?' she asked. 'Surely he must realise that things have changed completely.'

'It's just because everything's changed that I can't ask him.' Susie made a wry face. 'I'm already seen as the disastrous new lady of the manor, sweeping tradition out of the door. There was quite a lot of opposition in the village to the idea of having a commercial Herb Garden and, horrors, a Tea Room.' She consulted a delivery form. 'And of course my esteemed mother-in-law is dead against everything we're doing,' she added resentfully. 'She thinks it's all my fault, and that Clive just goes along with whatever I suggest. If I get rid of a beloved family retainer as well, how do you think that will look? I'll have to hire bodyguards.'

Despondently, she brushed a lock of hair out of her face, leaving a peat-coloured smudge across her forehead. 'Now, where did we put that order list?'

****

The morning's conversation had left Susie turning the Harry Trench problem over in her mind. It had to be sorted out, she decided, or at the very least they would have to discuss the whole thing again, instead of skirting round it, as if it was a dog's mess on the pavement, which they'd been doing for some time now.

That evening, after Hazel and Anthea had gone to bed, she waited until Clive was settled down in the Snug, the newspaper open, while he half watched highlights of the afternoon's rugby international. He was looking quite strained these days, she thought anxiously. Like her, he was working flat out, trying to catch and juggle all the balls that seemed to be thrown at him every day. It was a pity to spoil the moment of relaxation, but they'd both been ducking this problem too long.

'Do you really want that on?' she asked him, perching on the armchair opposite. 'Only I want to talk to you.'

'I'll turn the sound down,' he said obligingly, and she controlled a prickle of annoyance, knowing that she still had only part of his attention.

'I know we've talked about this before,' she began, 'but you really are going to have to suggest...tell...Harry that it's time he retired. Half my plant stock is sitting in the yard, when it really needs to be hardened off gradually. But I can't put the stuff in the greenhouse because all Harry's plants are in there.'

'We probably aren't going to have any more really damaging frosts though, are we,' Clive told her comfortingly, his eyes still on the rugby.

'That isn't the point. There's real shortage of space with stock for the shop too. And when we put together that business plan, remember, it envisaged having the use of the cottage, as a stock room upstairs, and an office and pay desk for the plants downstairs.'

'Well, it's early days yet.' He grew animated. 'Oh *yes*! Did you see that? What a fantastic run!'

'But we can't go on as we are,' Susie protested. 'It's not fair on Harry, apart from anything else. He doesn't say so, but I'm sure he must feel very unsettled.'

There was no response.

She pressed on. 'I know he disapproves of everything that's going on to make the Herb Garden, and what with Berriman's doing most of the maintenance up here, he's really lost his job without anyone saying so.'

'Come *on*. Go for it!' Clive yelled at the screen, then glanced at her apologetically. 'Yes, I was listening, and you're absolutely right. But it really has to be you that tells him, Susie. After all, the Herb Garden's your baby, and Berriman's coming in was your idea as well.'

His wife indignantly opened her mouth to protest, and he rushed on. 'I know, I know. I agreed, and it makes much more sense. They do the job in half the time, for less money.'

'They don't cost less if we're keeping Harry on as well, doing nothing,' she pointed out. 'And telling him to go really can't be added to all the other things I'm being blamed for. I'll end up as blackened as the infamous Lady Trugglestone.'

'Evelyn Trugglestone wasn't blackened,' he responded, frowning. 'She was a bad lot altogether. If she hadn't run through all the family money, we wouldn't be having these problems now.' He smiled at her teasingly. 'Four generations later and the lesson is still scorched into us, "Never marry a high roller".'

This could have been construed as less than complimentary, but Susie regarded him fondly, and resisted the temptation to make a barbed comment about his mother looking down on her socially. It wouldn't have helped. Poor Clive was being pulled between the two of them as it was, she reminded herself. He could do without more family strife.

A clash of outlook was the real cause of the frayed relations between herself and Julia, she'd concluded charitably. It was as if they were looking through different lenses. Both she and Clive realised that Trugglestone Hall and estate were struggling on the brink of disaster, in urgent need of change and every penny they they could muster. Julia just didn't see it that way, so it was hardly surprising she resented all the proposed changes.

'You miss Cambridge don't you.' Clive broke into her thoughts.

'Well, it was a different world, wasn't it. Would you like a coffee?'

She went into the kitchen to make it. With a bit of luck the rugby would be over shortly, and then they could talk.

He was right, she reflected, filling the kettle. She did feel the loss of her Cambridge friends, but more than that, she missed the privacy they'd enjoyed there. She'd always known that taking over the running of Trugglestone Hall would mean a complete break with the life they'd built up. She just hadn't pictured it happening so soon.

Their active social life had been fun, with Clive's conference agency giving him links to the colleges. And since he was home-based, even when the children were small she'd been able to manage a part-time job at Berrimans. She spooned in the coffee powder, smiling at the memory. That'd been very rewarding. Invaluable experience, and useful contacts in the nursery trade. It gave her a sense of being a person in her own right too, which contributed to the happiness of their little family unit.

Now problems were confronting them on all sides. But it was no good mourning the life they'd lost, she reflected sensibly. Far better to be positive, and forge ahead.

She made the coffee, and put the mugs on a tray. For one thing, she thought, there was a chance now to make a go of a herb-growing business, something that had only been a fanciful dream up until last year. And she was hoping it would really help the estate finances. Clive was faced with daunting money and other worries, and it was her job to help him. No good adding to them by looking back.

Or feuding with his mother, she told herself, negotiating the kitchen door. He'd been so supportive over her pet venture too, in the teeth of Julia's opposition. But this problem of Harry Trench needed to be sorted out. Clive didn't seem to realise that she really couldn't ask the old boy to retire. It had to come from the Trugglestones themselves, either Clive or Julia.

He leapt up to open the Snug door, and she handed him his mug, then settled into the armchair across the hearth from him. The rugby was just ending.

'I know there's a lot on your plate,' she said sympathetically, 'but couldn't you at least talk to Harry? It would be such a help. You've always got on well with him, haven't you.'

'Old Harry?' Clive turned the television off. 'Of course. He was part of my childhood. If ever I was at a loose end, I could go and help him and Fred Chitting with whatever they were doing.'

'Did they rub along okay, those two?'

'Oh yes. They divided the work between them, but Harry definitely had green fingers, while old Fred was really practical. He could mend just about anything.' He stirred his coffee. 'And with so many things needing doing about the house and estate, Fred ended up doing that virtually full time, and Harry did all the gardening, so they didn't get in each other's way.'

'How come you haven't the slightest idea about growing things now?' Susie asked playfully. 'Brought up at the gardener's knee! You should be the one starting this herb business, not me.'

'I wasn't particularly interested,' he admitted, without regret. 'He did give me a patch of my own in the kitchen garden at one time, but I never really bothered with it. It was much more fun helping Fred Chitting to mend a tractor, or scarf in a new bit of window frame.' He reached over to put the spoon on the tray, thinking back nostalgically. 'I was really cut up when Fred died, you know. He was such a nice chap. We used to talk about all sorts of things. Harry was never much of a one for chatting.'

'Still isn't, is he.' Susie found the gardener's silence rather unnerving. 'I can't make out what goes on in his head, and how much he understands. I know he's a bit deaf, and he gives this impression of being mentally slow, but every so often you wonder if he's more wily than he lets on. Was there ever a Mrs Trench?'

'Good heavens, no. Although I suppose there's no reason why not. My mother says he was walking out with someone called Violet for years, but never popped the question, so she upped and married someone from Ipswich in the end.' He smiled at her. 'And before that apparently there was some girl he adored from afar, but it didn't come to anything. He probably never told her.'

From the hall the grandfather clock struck ten, and Clive remarked reflectively, 'Isn't it odd how there are some characters you simply can't picture as part of a couple? When I was little, there was Mrs Chitting and Fred, and that seemed absolutely right, but Harry Trench was just, well, Harry.'

Susie picked up a log from the basket, and bent down to put it on the fire. 'Is the fact that he's part of your childhood some of the problem?' she asked with understanding.

'Yes, I suppose it is.' He sighed. 'Small boy grows up and sacks faithful family retainer. I don't like that image any more than you like being seen as hard-faced newcomer.'

'Hard-faced!' protested Susie. 'That's a bit strong.'

Clive chuckled. 'Well you know what I mean. To us the things we're doing are essential to modernise the estate, and money is very tight, but I know it doesn't look like that to everyone else.' He paused. 'Actually, it wouldn't save all that much if Harry did go. You know I had a session with the accountants yesterday? Well, along with some other nasty surprises, I've discovered that Dad made no provision for a pension for Harry. But the trustees will need to pay him one. We'll just have to find it from somewhere.'

He gazed into the fire, and went on slowly. 'Come to think of it though, if we could let Harry's cottage, the rent would cover his pension nicely.'

'Oh no,' Susie said firmly, 'you're not pulling that one. I need the cottage, particularly the ground floor rooms, to be the office and plant Pay Desk. We can site the till in the greenhouse to start with, but not as a long term thing.'

'Hm.' Clive privately decided they would have to differ on that. 'You know, aren't we looking at this from the wrong end?'

'How do you mean?'

'Well, we're assuming that Harry wants to continue, and he probably does. But instead of agonising over forcing him to retire, wouldn't it be better to make him keen to move on? What we need to find is something that tempts him out.'

'Somewhere to live that he'll like better than Stable Cottage, for a start,' Susie suggested practically. 'I've asked about a Council house, but there's no hope really. There's already a waiting list several years long of young married couples, and one hardly ever comes up anyway.' She put down her coffee. 'Couldn't your mother get him into one of the village almshouses, she's on the Management Committee isn't she?' adding half to herself, 'One of the many things she wants me to take over.'

He looked at her. 'I'm surprised at you. You know my mother wouldn't dream of using her position to favour anyone.'

'Well if Harry doesn't qualify, I don't know who would. Born and brought up in Haydon, and living in rented accommodation. No need to mention that he doesn't actually pay any rent. And about to be turned out by a heartless landlord. He's the perfect candidate.'

'Yes, you're right,' he admitted, adding reluctantly, 'I'll ask her if there's a vacancy coming up. Or perhaps it would be better to approach Daphne Stalker, she's the Secretary or something. Keep the family out of it.'

'On second thoughts, he wouldn't really want to move into an almshouse though, would he?' Susie concluded regretfully. 'Where would he put his beloved plants?' She couldn't find it in her heart to like fuchsias and dahlias herself, but no gardener should be separated from the objects of his passion. Particularly if there wasn't much else in his life.

A whimsical idea struck her. 'I know. Couldn't we find his lost love? Maybe she adored him as well, and it broke her heart that he didn't respond. Perhaps she married a rich man, and is now a lonely widow,' she suggested laughingly, 'with an enormous conservatory, and a garden that's just crying out for fuchsias.'

Looking across at her, freckled nose crinkling as it always did when she laughed, Clive marvelled again at how lucky he'd been to find her. He couldn't imagine what it must be like to go through life alone. Especially when you got old.

'Listen, I've had a thought,' he said slowly. 'And if you ever try to pin it on me, I shall flatly deny having anything to do with it.'

Susie raised her eyebrows at him humorously.

'What about pairing him off with Mrs Chitting? She's always been good to him. I remember when Fred was alive, she used to take him pies and things all the time. She has him round for meals several times a week now, according to my mother, and he does bits and bobs in her garden in return. She has her own cottage, and she's a wonderful cook. What more could a man want?'

'You old romantic, you!' she came to sit on the arm of his chair, and tweaked his hair affectionately.

'It's not romantic at all. Very practical. And solves your problem at a stroke.'

'Just one teeny difficulty,' she told him. 'How is this miracle to be accomplished? After all they have known each other for donkeys years, and romance hasn't blossomed yet. Or were you planning to dress up as Cupid and fire a few arrows?'

'Oh the matchmaking's down to you,' he said airily. 'Shouldn't be difficult, should it.'

'What am I supposed to do? Send bouquets of roses and pretend they came from old Harry?'

'Just exercise a little witchcraft. What have you got a whole garden of herbs for? Bound to be an aphrodisiac amongst them, surely. Slip it into their tea, and ...' He looked up at her expressively.

'If I was growing an aphrodisiac, husband dear, we'd be raking in the money,' Susie informed him levelly. 'Anyway, don't you think I'd be trying it out on you?'

A log on the fire slipped and crackled into flames, the orange light lending a glow to her face. Clive reached up and stroked her cheek, a glint in his eye.

'I think you'll find that won't be necessary', he said meaningfully. 'Come here.'

Chapter Eight

'Marry the old boy off!' Rosemary exclaimed the following morning. 'Say, that's neat, but...' She looked at Susie as if she'd suggested pairing a giraffe and a gerbil, not realising she wasn't really serious. 'Who is this Mrs Chitting anyway?'

'My mother-in-law's cook-cum-cleaner-cum-everything-else when she was at the Hall, and a really decent sort,' Susie explained. 'She did offer to stay on for us, but I think she was just being kind, and it's not what I wanted anyway.'

Matthew had taken the day off to do a computing job for a friend, and the two women were unpacking cutlery and china for theTea Room, piling them on the worktops ready to be washed and put away.

'I asked her to help cook and serve in the Tea Room instead, and she seemed happy about that. Even if we don't have many visitors to start with, we're going to need all hands on deck for the Open Gardens Day in July. Oh bother, this one's chipped.' She examined the cup she'd been unwrapping, and put it to one side. 'That's going to be a real bonus for us,' she went on enthusiastically, reaching into the box for another. 'Should bring visitors pouring in to the Herb Garden. And we'll be doing the Teas for it, of course.'

'Have you decided on the official opening day for the Herb Garden?' asked Rosemary, trying to wrench her way into a box of cutlery that was bound with swathes of brown sticky tape. 'You'll need to have got over all the teething problems before the Open Gardens Day, won't you.'

'I thought the beginning of June at the latest, or mid-May if we're ready in time. Heavens, that's not far off now is it.'

Time did seem to be galloping past. With so much needing doing at the Walled Herb Garden, Rosemary had done little else for the past few days, and was feeling guilty that she'd got no further with producing an information leaflet about the Pit Garden for Zinnia. A visit to the County Library in Ipswich was necessary, and although more confident about driving her car now, she was still worried about negotiating a town. But the thing also needed to be leavened with local colour and anecdotes, and talking about Harry Trench reminded her of Clive's suggestion that she speak to the old boy.

'He's quite difficult to pin down these days,' Susie told her. 'Although he's still officially employed by the estate, he spends a lot of time helping my mother-in-law with her new garden, and he's apparently working on Mrs Chitting's as well.'

'I'd like to meet her too. Where does she live?'

'Oh, just along from here, in the end riverside cottage. Her garden's included in the Gardens Open Day, you must go and have a look. Harry's going to fill it with his fuchsias, and the bedding plants in the greenhouse. I expect it'll be very, er, colourful.'

'So he and she are already being flung together quite a lot are they?' Rosemary kept a straight face.

'Oh getting them together isn't the problem,' Susie smiled. 'It's making them view each other in a romantic light. Clive says I should use witchcraft, and let's face it, you would need something pretty powerful to see Harry Trench in any kind of rosy glow, wouldn't you.'

'How about the trick Shakespeare used in As You Like It?' suggested Rosemary, laying the knives out in bundles of ten for easy checking, 'Telling each in turn that the other one had the hots for them.'

They looked at each other, and giggled. 'Oh dear, we shouldn't laugh,' Susie declared, without any great contrition. 'We'll be old ourselves one day.'

'Sure, but there's old age, and old age,' observed Rosemary sagely. 'Some people manage to make it a golden time. And you can behave really badly, and get away with it,' she added jocularly.

'You aren't aiming to be a sweet old lady then?'

'Well, I think it's usual to be a sweet young lady first, so that's a non-starter.' She folded the box flat, and tossed it on to the pile of cardboard. 'You need to plan for old age though, don't you. Not pretend it isn't happening, like your Harry. Or my aunt for that matter.'

Susie considered. 'But isn't it often the need to fight that keeps them going?'

'Sheer cussedness, you mean?' Rosemary delved into the packing case for a large box of spoons, and resumed battle with the sticky tape. 'Yeah, perhaps. Zinnia just refuses to acknowledge that age has crept up on her. You have to admire her spirit, but it doesn't solve any problems. It would make sense for her to move to a smaller house and garden, but she won't hear of it. Which is why she wants me to do this leaflet.'

She shot a cautious glance at Lady Susan Trugglestone, and decided to continue. 'Did you know that the new owner of the Pit has applied for permission to tip garbage in it?'

'No!' Susie was shocked. 'I can't believe it.'

'You can see why the Trugglestone name is mud.'

'Oh dear. Clive thought it was a very good deal, which the trustees would have been silly not to accept. But there was no mention of tipping. Swathe said he would put in for planning permission, but that was supposed to be for a house on the field.'

'What sort of guy is he?' Rosemary had been speculating on the man's character for some time, but her aunt refused even to talk about him.

'I've never met him. Julia has though. They're about the same age, so I think she knew him when they were children.' She tried to be reassuring. 'I'm sure he wouldn't despoil the village. He was brought up here.'

'Zinnia's also hopping mad that no-one told her what was going on.'

'Yes, I'm very sorry about that,' Susie said slowly, running some water into the sink. 'I think the whole thing was a bit rushed. As I understand it, Swathe's offer came out of the blue, and he was in a hurry for some reason. And I think Clive just funked telling your aunt in the end. She's definitely owed an apology.'

By the end of the morning all the china and cutlery had been unpacked, washed, and put away. It was really a bit soon to be doing all that, but as a result packing cases no longer cluttered up the tea room, which seemed a wonderful step forward. By nervous experimentation, they discovered how to tame the large and gleaming water heater, which gurgled and hissed at them like a dragon who'd unwisely matched ginger wine with chicken vindaloo. Then they celebrated by making themselves coffee.

Whilst drinking it, they discussed the best placing for the tables and chairs, and then tried out different layouts. It needed a compromise between looking good, and fitting in as many people as possible. When they'd settled on the right arrangement, Rosemary weaved among the tables, carrying a tray, bending down to the empty chairs with obsequious murmurings of, 'But of course, madam.' 'Decaffeinated? Certainly.' 'Muffin not hot enough? I'll put that right *immediately*.'

'You have got high-falutin ideas of our customers,' Susie told her laughingly. 'Lot of learning to do.'

One table they laid with a tablecloth, plates, cups and cutlery, just for the pleasure of seeing what it looked like, and stood back to admire their handiwork.

'Suddenly it's all coming together, isn't it,' Susie sounded like a child anticipating Christmas. 'Oh I do hope it's a success.'

She had to rush off to see a supplier in the afternoon, so Rosemary sauntered back through the village. She enjoyed her walks to and from The Herb Garden, and was rather disappointed if it was raining and Susie ran her home in the car. Today white, fluffy clouds were chasing each other skittishly across the sky, like spring lambs, the sun benignly overseeing their play. Making a mockery of its name, some late-flowering blackthorn still frothed with bright blossom in the hedges, and there was a smell of damp earth. In the gardens sturdy hyacinths clustered together, like gorgeously dressed soldiers gossiping in groups.

It was interesting to note the different designs and styles of the gardens that she passed. Zinnia maintained that you could tell the character of a person by their garden, but when pressed on this, it appeared that the only people with well-rounded characters were those whose gardens were full of perennial plants, artistically arranged. Like hers, in fact.

Everyone else was damned. The owners of excessively neat plots, with everything clipped and restrained, were clearly unimaginative, control freaks. Had there been anyone in Haydon embracing contemporary sculpture amidst a design-orientated, flowerless garden, Zinnia would immediately have labelled them cold and severe. By contrast, a jumble of flowers, every space crammed with a little bit of this and a little bit of that, indicated a disorganised owner with an impulsive nature and untidy mind. Probably warm-hearted though, Zinnia was prepared to concede. Gardeners who were essentially collectors of one type of plant, didn't escape criticism either. Obsessive, was her dismissive comment.

'You don't think all that might be a trifle simplistic?' Rosemary had ventured, bravely. But Zinnia's views were too certain to be questioned.

'You see if I'm not right,' she said firmly. 'A garden gives its owner's personality away like nothing else.'

Mostly, Rosemary decided, Zinnia's dogmatic prejudices didn't apply to the gardens of Haydon Settleworth, since they were neither in one category nor another, just kind of messy. But she did find herself imagining the occupants of each house according to their gardens nonetheless.

The back gardens of the riverside cottages went down to the water, but on the roadside each had a small plot which, she noted, were all treated differently. A couple of people had paved or concreted them over, to make less work, while some had a small patch of grass. She could picture her aunt's scathing glance. 'Useless. Are they going to sit on it? It's just there because they think you must have a lawn. If they think at all.'

Several were bright with spring bulbs and clumps of primroses, and despite herself, Rosemary felt she would be more likely to warm to the occupants of these houses than the owners of the concrete. In one of the flowery gardens a small bush covered in pink flowers gave off an exquisite scent, the petals warmed in the sun. The perfume wafted after her, and as she stood at the end of the row, Rosemary looked back up the street, admiring the way each cottage was individual – tiled roofs at varying heights and angles, windows at different levels. Some had had porches added on, and individuality was also established by their assortment of different coloured facades. Yet together they made such a pleasing whole. Like a family photograph, she reflected.

'They understood about proportions then, didn't they?'

She hadn't noticed an elegantly dressed woman emerge from the front door of the last cottage, but her architectural scrutiny had obviously been observed.

'I just love the way they look as if they've been here for ever,' she explained. Damn, caught out gawping like a tourist.

'You must be Zinnia's niece from America,' the woman responded warmly, noting her trans-Atlantic accent. 'How nice to meet you, I'm Julia Trugglestone.'

Rosemary was taken aback. Of course, she ought to have remembered that this was where Susie's mother-in-law had gone to live, but even so, she would never have connected this slight, delicate-looking woman with the disapproving ogre she had pictured.

'These were weavers' cottages, as I expect you know,' the ogre continued pleasantly. 'Come and see inside. Have you got time for a cup of tea? I'm dying to hear about Zinnia's trial by bird enthusiasts. Haydon's never known such a stir.'

Rosemary found herself ushered into a low-beamed room, with a large inglenook fireplace on one side. A fire was laid in the grate, but any warmth it might have given was evidently redundant, radiators having already raised the temperature to a luxurious level. A comfortable-looking sofa and armchairs covered in a flowered print invited relaxation, plump cushions echoing the subtle grey-green of the carpet. Antique tables, a desk and a chest of drawers whose brass handles gleamed from hours of devotion, gave the room a graciousness that somehow married perfectly with the cottage atmosphere. Small original paintings and drawings hung on the walls, between the beams, horses and hunting being the predominant subjects, and from the corner came the slow tick of an old clock, certain of its place.

'Oh what a lovely room,' she exclaimed with unquestionable sincerity.

'You should have seen the place a few months ago,' Lady Julia told her, smiling at the evident admiration. 'Re-wiring, central heating, new plumbing, I thought the builders would never finish. And now I'm really in, it's wonderful.' She opened the door of the dining room, where a handsome sideboard showed off silver tankards, and a set of intricately-decorated plates, while in the centre the polished table's rich, dark shine reflected the light from the window.

'Come and see my little kitchen. I hardly dare cook in it.'

Rosemary followed her into a modern kitchen, with a gleaming hob and wall-mounted oven inset into the units, which ran round three sides of the room. A pine table and chairs occupied the remaining corner by the window.

'When I'm sitting here in the morning doing the crossword, it's a great temptation just to gaze at the view.' Julia indicated the kitchen window, and Rosemary found herself looking over a terraced garden down to the river, the green meadow beyond dotted with mature trees, their bare branches an intricate tracery. It was crossed by the second driveway to Trugglestone Hall, although the gate was out of sight, and along the river twisted willows leaned over the water, as if searching for something lost. Covered now with delicate green, their lower branches were muddy, and clogged with detritus from winter floods. At the other side of the wide valley, the low hills were patterned with woods and fields, and a tractor crawled over a ploughed field, like a sleepy bumblebee.

'That is some view! If I lived here I'd spend all my time looking out of the window.' The peace and gentleness of the river landscape were really speaking to Rosemary, who had somehow not thought about what outlook the row of cottages enjoyed on the far side. 'Is that a heron?'

With slow gravity, the long-legged fisherman was wading along the shallows by the far bank, stopping every few moments to gaze intently into the water.

'Yes, doesn't he look like an old man in a grey morning suit. It seems to be a favourite fishing ground. I spend ages watching him. Do you mind China tea?'

Rosemary sat in the chair nearest the window, absorbing the view, while Lady Julia made a pot of tea, and searched for a sugar bowl.

'There are so many cupboards I don't know where anything is,' she remarked lightly. 'I sometimes wonder what the original occupants of this cottage would think if they could see it now. They wouldn't believe the things we take for granted.'

They might be surprised to find a lady of quality living in it at all, Rosemary thought, noting the well-cut jacket, and expensive looking shoes.

'I love the way nothing's straight. When was this place built?' she asked, looking up at the ceiling beams. 'And why were there weavers here?'

'It's about four hundred and fifty years old,' Julia told her, pouring boiling water into the teapot. 'The whole area was the centre of the wool trade then – the industrial area of its time – and these cottages would have housed weavers who worked from home. This is two knocked into one. Most of them are now, of course. Originally they would have been quite small. But they've always been workman's cottages, so I feel rather guilty moving in.'

'What's wrong with that?'

'Well, there are hardly any what I call proper village people left in these cottages now. The old lady next door was Haydon born and bred, but she's just died. And Mrs Chitting at Spring Cottage, at the other end, is certainly a real village person, but even she's moving to one of those horrible bungalows that are going up. They all seem to want modern houses. And of course these cottages fetch a lot of money now.'

'I'm not surprised. I'd love to live here.' As she spoke, Rosemary was suddenly aware that it was true. This cottage combined all the things she subconsciously yearned for in a place to call her own. Security and cosiness, individuality and inspiration. The revelation was a surprise, and would need thinking about, but now she found herself gently quizzed about Zinnia and the bird saga. In between sips of tea, she launched into an amusing account of the episode, starting with her own identification of the Kirtland Warbler, and Zinnia's prickly relations with the bird enthusiasts. But she began to realise that the drift of the questioning was about her aunt, not the events.

This was difficult ground, and Rosemary wasn't confident of avoiding the marshy bits. That there'd been a rift between Julia and Zinnia over the sale of the Pit Garden was no secret, but she didn't know the details. She also had a feeling her aunt was minded to patch things up now, but any attempt to assist the process was likely to be seen as interference. And would probably backfire anyway. All in all, the fact that Zinnia was agitated and upset by the sale of her beloved Pit Garden was probably best glossed over.

'She's concentrating on repairing all the damage,' Rosemary said carefully, 'and getting the garden ready for the Open Gardens Day in the summer.' This seemed a safe sidetrack. 'I never figured she'd agree to open the garden, but she thought it might...'

Oh rats, we were back to fighting to save the Pit Garden.

She was rescued by the telephone ringing, which, with apologies, Julia went into the sitting room to answer. Rosemary gazed out of the window. She could see very little of the garden from there, but clearly there was much renewal going on. An appealing brown and white Springer spaniel wandered into sight, nosing among some bags of gravel, and she could see a tweed cap bobbing up and down, obviously belonging to someone working on a lower terrace. Aha, perhaps this was the elusive Harry Trench.

She could hear Julia Trugglestone's side of the telephone conversation perfectly well, and was faced with a visitor's dilemma. To listen, or not to listen. At the beginning, she let the words flow over her. But the fact that the talk was about teas for the Open Gardens Day gradually registered, and flicked her attention switch.

The call ended, and she searched guiltily for something to be absorbed in, to show she hadn't listened to a thing. She fixed her attention on an old photograph of Haydon, depicting the row of weavers' cottages, with a pony and trap outside, and small children in smocks playing in the dusty street. But it wasn't necessary.

'Dear me, why does village life never run smoothly?' Julia exclaimed with mild exasperation, returning to the kitchen. 'I thought we'd got the Village Hall booked ages ago for the day before the Gardens and Flower Festival, so everything can be set up for the Teas, and suddenly the Haydon Players are complaining they're supposed to be having a rehearsal there that day.' She sighed resignedly. 'I've just been given the task of smoothing ruffled feathers.'

'The Teas are going to be served at the village hall?' Rosemary tried not to sound surprised, although this was going to be news to Susie.

'Oh yes, the W.I have undertaken to produce all the food, and provide the er, manpower.' Julia smiled at her visitor, but realised there was no answering amusement at her choice of words. 'The Women's Institute,' she explained, 'still the bedrock of village life. Although a lot of young women with jobs don't want to join, these days. Including my daughter-in-law, Susan. Have you met her? Too busy, they say, and I suppose they have a point.'

Rosemary felt it would be impolite, like bringing up politics at a party, to explain how she had been helping Susie at the Walled Herb Garden. It was a project not known to be close to her hostess's heart.

'I was wondering,' she said, hoping the turning of the conversation would go unnoticed 'if that was Harry Trench working in your garden. Apparently his grandfather worked in the chalk pit behind my aunt's house, and I'm doing a bit of research into its history. Is there any chance you could introduce me?'

'Yes of course. Although you might find him a bit difficult to understand. He's fairly deaf, and slow, and,' her hostess paused, 'simple, in the nicest sense of the word. He's not too good with strangers either. You'll have to be patient.'

She glanced out of the window to see if the bobbing cap was still there. 'We'll go down now, and you can meet him. I'd like you to see the garden anyway. Come and tell me what you think.'

Rosemary wondered if the English upper classes were trained in subtle flattery, or if it came with the genes. Lady Julia couldn't possibly want her opinion on the new garden, but with her natural, easy manner managed to make her guest feel valued, overcoming in-built scepticism. It was like being praised by a favourite teacher.

Opening the door into the garden unleashed a display of joyous enthusiasm by the brown and white dog observed from the window.

'This is Bracken. Unfortunately she's got far too much energy,' Julia explained apologetically. 'She was my husband's gun dog, and now she misses the exercise. Bracken, *sit*!'

Impressively, the Springer spaniel did as it was told. 'Now behave yourself.' The tone was one that expected obedience, and Rosemary found herself wondering what it would be like to be in disagreement with its owner. Best avoided probably.

'The garden had to be remodelled,' Julia was saying, 'because it was all steep little steps, which I'm not very good at. Berrimans have altered the terraces, and put in ramps, or else wider, easier steps. And here by the house they've made raised beds, so that I don't have to bend down. Basil Berriman is supervising the planting. I expect you'll meet him at Zinnia's.'

'I don't know anything about gardening', Rosemary told her, 'but I think this is lovely.'

She did too. Instead of gazing at the view from the kitchen window, on fine days you would be able to have meals on the little, south-facing patio, tucked in beside the cottage, and quite private. Birds would sing, and with the scent of flowers and that tranquil outlook it would be your own private paradise. Hold hard girl, she told herself brusquely. Be asking directions to the Yellow Brick Road next.

Lady Julia led the way down some shallow steps to the terrace below, fielding her stick, Bracken forming a delighted escort. Harry Trench was planting out young violas, in a circular bed at the foot of a weeping pear. He wore an old tweed jacket, and a cap that had once been patterned, but had long since settled into a camouflaging dinge. Bushy white eyebrows overhung faded blue eyes, and his face was the colour of a plum just beginning to ripen, with the nose about three days ahead.. Stiffly, he straightened up as they approached, and gave them an enquiring half smile.

'Harry, this is Rosemary, Mrs Peasmore's niece from America.'

The old boy looked at her and nodded in greeting, as Julia continued in a slightly raised voice, pronouncing each word clearly. 'She was hoping to talk to you about when the chalk pit was still being used. Your grandfather worked there, didn't he.'

'Tha's right.'

Harry didn't seem to be an interviewer's delight.

'I can come and talk to you when it's more convenient,' Rosemary told him, interpreting this terse reply as an unwillingness to respond.

'I should strike while the iron is hot,' Julia advised her in a low tone. 'He just takes his time, that's all.' Raising her voice, she said encouragingly, 'I have to go and get a letter in the post, but I'm sure Harry can tell you something about it.' Turning to him, she obligingly primed the pump. 'How many men did you say used to work there?'

'Well now,' he considered slowly, as she gave a conspiratorial smile to Rosemary, and quietly retreated up the steps, with the dog, 'that'd be about ten.'

'Ten! Whatever did they all do?'

'That were a busy place, y'see,' he responded, ignoring the question. 'Lime were important in them days.'

He went back to his viola planting, as Rosemary settled herself on a step, wishing she'd brought a notebook to record the historical revelations about to be divulged.

'The cottages hereabouts is all lime-washed, and they alus wants it for the fields,' he offered, after a few moments. 'Farmers, builders, plasterers, they all come for the lime.'

'So it was just used locally?' she prompted.

He appeared not to have heard, and went on with his work for almost a minute.

'Most of it go down to Ipswich,' he finally divulged. 'Them owd carts carries the coal up for the kilns, and takes the lime back. Course, that were slaked lime.'

Silence resumed.

'And what did your grandfather do?' Rosemary tried.

He took another plant from the tray, and closed his hand round it protectively. After a while, like a windscreen wiper switched to intermittent, he continued.

'Tha's the kilns he worked on mos'ly. Skilled job, that were.' He made a hole for the viola, and firmed it into the brown earth. 'You 'as to get them roots down, y'see,' he explained. 'Saves on the waterin'.'

This wasn't exactly the flow of useful information she'd hoped for. It was disappointing, like expecting a luscious looking orange to be full of juice, only to find it dry and pippy. But perhaps she wasn't pressing from the best angle.

'So the chalk went into the brick kilns,' she said encouragingly. 'And they fired them with coal. Then what happened?'

She watched while he put in another plant, unhurriedly.

'Well then you has quick lime. Properly got a temper on it, that have.' He sniffed, and the large dewdrop that had been forming on his nose disappeared. 'Ain't no use till you puts water on it, but a man have to know what he's a'doin'.'

'Oh yes, wasn't there some tale about a farmer whose cart exploded?'

The chance to tell a favourite story finally caused a break in the planting. 'That were an owd boy by the name of Charlie Bricett,' recalled Harry, sitting back. 'Took his stuff from the wrong pile, he did. And when they towd him, he 'ouldn't unload it. Said as how he knew it 'ouldn't rain. Course, halfway to Stowmarket this grut owd tempest come up, and it wholly pour.' He chuckled. 'Next thing he knew, that cart was took on fire. Well, he unhitched that owd horse and runned. Fair frit, he was.'

This was more like it. But the burst of loquacity seemed to have exhausted the old boy's powers of communication. His attention reverted to the violas, and further gentle probing failed to elicit anything else that she could use for background information. Rosemary was anyway fast coming to the conclusion that Harry's knowledge of the Pit was more limited than she'd hoped. Just a few things gleaned from his grandfather, and that was it. But she had another tack to try.

'The village is named after Settlewort, isn't it? Did you ever hear any stories about it growing in the Pit?'

This wasn't interesting enough to give him pause, and he carefully separated two plants from the tray, and laid one down whilst dealing with the other.

'Blist if I know,' he said finally. 'Never heard tell on it. But tha's distinct, ain't it.'

Oh *yes*! Rosemary couldn't believe her luck. Here was someone who evidently knew what Settlewort looked like - she'd struck gold. Boy, was Zinnia going to be pleased with her.

'You've seen it growing?' she asked, having no trouble now with the raised voice his deafness required.

Harry went on working. 'Course not,' and there was a flat tone to his voice. 'Nobody have. Stands t'reason - tha's distinct. Like that owd Do-do.'

'Do-do,' she repeated, 'the bird?' Suddenly understanding and disappointment coincided. 'Oh you mean it's *extinct*.'

'Like I said. Folks 'ouldn't know what that looked like anyways.' He pushed up his cap, and considered. 'Tha's like one of them 'erbs as they make such a fuss of nowadays, ain't it.'

The drip was reforming, and Rosemary regarded it with uneasy fascination.

'Erbs is all right in their place,' he volunteered. 'Nice bit of parsley with the fish of a Friday, but where's the point of growin' a garden full of the things?'

Aha, so we'd got round to the Walled Herb Garden, thought Rosemary. Although, according to Susie, he must think of it as his garden still. Perhaps this was an opportunity to do some peace-making. "American separates warring factions and draws up a deal", and all that. But how to start?

'It's lovely soil in the Walled Garden at Trugglestone Hall,' she said cleverly, recycling one of Susie's remarks. 'What did you do to make it so good?'

For the first time, Harry stopped and looked at her. He had a calm and gentle gaze that made him seem almost child-like, despite his age.

'Tha's muck and compost. You got to have muck to make good moulds,' he said with satisfaction. 'I ain't ever bin one for fertlizas, but there's not many what know how to make a proper compost heap nowadays.' As an afterthought he added, 'I bin tellin' young Lady. She went to Horticulcher College, but they don't larn yer nothin' there.'

Rosemary debated how to put the next question.

'What do you think about the Walled Garden being made into a herb garden?'

'You should a seen them owd fooshas what growd there. And dahlias. Lady, she say she ain't never seen such blooms. Big as cabbages, some on 'em.'

Perhaps he hadn't heard the question. Another angle was worth a try.

'I saw your fuchsias in the greenhouse,' she said encouragingly. 'Where will you grow them this year, with the Walled Garden full of herbs?'

He turned the now empty seedtray upside down, and tapped it clean.

'They's all goin' in Daisy Chitting's. That'll be the best little owd garden in Haydon, come Open Day,' he told her, adding with something approaching animation. 'Talk about colour – that'll wholly cheer folks. I ask Lady if she want some here, but that Mr Berriman, he's plannin' the plantin'.' There was a pause. 'He found me a job though.'

'A job? Aren't you going to retire?'

'No, I ain't retirin'. Got to keep busy.' Harry put his tools to one side and creakily carried a full watering can to the newly-planted bed. 'Lady, she wants me to help here, and there's Daisy Chitting's. And Mr Berriman, he say how the gentleman next to your aunt is looking for a body to do his garden.'

'What, Gerry Thornway?' Rosemary couldn't keep the surprise out of her voice, and then she added mischievously, 'Perhaps you could grow fuchsias in his garden.'

Harry shook his head, and the dewdrop leaped joyously to nourish the violas. 'Mr Berriman was a sayin' his company make the garden for the gentleman two year ago, and only thing he wants is grass and heathers and trees. Them conifers.' His tone implied a lack of enthusiasm, like a wife referring to her husband's train set. 'But he like it to look tidy, and seems he haven't the time to do it hisself.'

He was watering each viola carefully, ensuring the can's contents were not wasted. It was a slow and painstaking task. 'Master Clive, and young Lady, they don't have no time neither,' he added. 'But Berrimans is agoin' to do the grass and hedges up at The Hall. It's a rum ol' do.'

'Do you mind?' Rosemary asked, and then rather wished she hadn't. Of course Harry minded, and it wasn't fair to stir up his hurt feelings.

'Spect they'll larn,' he said, with the tolerance of an old fox watching cubs muff their first rabbit chase. 'Tha's not everythin' you can do by them machines.' He paused to reflect. 'Mind you, me rumatics din't half give me jip when I 'as to do them hedges. Happen it's best. That 'ont be the same with Lady gone, anyways.' He put the can down and felt in his jacket pocket for a handkerchief. 'I alus 'as me little owd cottage, and me fooshas.' He gave his nose a half-hearted blow, and added simply, 'Long as I 'as me home and me plants, what more do a man want?'

Chapter Nine

Surprisingly, in Kiln House's garden the hole in the hedge had been repaired on the Thornway's side, or at least rendered impassable with wire netting. Nevertheless on the grounds that the speed of peacock digestion was somewhat uncertain, for a few days after their abortive kidnap, Zinnia had laid enticing trails of porridge oats from various places in the hedge where it seemed a determined intruder might squeeze through. But they were keeping their distance. Perhaps, she reflected wryly, incarceration was a useful deterrent that should have been tried before.

Zinnia's inspections of the seed-sown pots, had now dwindled to once a day, and the eagerness had worn off. She wouldn't have admitted it, but hope had rather faded of seeing any indication of life heaving up through the compost. But she searched the soil of the Pit Garden itself most days, and weeded there with the care and delicacy of a fashion model posing for a gardening catalogue. The extra time all this took was irritating, especially as she was determined that the Pit Garden was going to look the best it ever had for the Gardens Open Day. With a bit of luck, villagers and visitors would be so horrified at Swathe's plans for tipping, the resulting outcry would stop him in his tracks.

As the hopeful excitement about the Settlewort seeds died down, and with it, any chance of using the plant to save the Pit Garden, she mulled over the prospects of gathering together opposition in the village. This seemed a promising course of action, however she was going to need Julia's help.

But Zinnia still felt too raw to go knocking on the cottage door, offering peace overtures. Julia's silence, when she had clearly known about the sale of the Pit Garden, seemed a betrayal of their long friendship that would remain, like a stain on the floor, long after the cause was cleared up.

Potting up cuttings in the greenhouse a week after Rosemary's encounter with Harry Trench, Zinnia considered the situation. It was true that her friend disapproved of just about everything Clive was doing, now he'd taken over running the Trugglestone Estate, but then why did she let him get away with it? She firmed a young salvia into the compost, trying to be understanding, a state of mind that came as naturally as swimming to an eagle. Julia was hidebound by this stupid aristocrats' convention that the older generation just stood aside when the younger ones took charge, that's what it was.

But surely she would offer her help in marshalling opposition to the Pit Garden becoming a tip, now that it no longer belonged to the estate. Through her various committees and activities, Julia was acquainted with just about everyone in the locality.

Not that Zinnia didn't know a fair few people of course, she told herself, sprinkling grit on the top. You could hardly live in a village for over forty years without getting to know most of the families round about, but having Julia's advice and help would be very welcome.

Accordingly, an hour later, Zinnia coaxed her bad-tempered old Vauxhall into life, and drove down to the village to intercept the itinerant fish man when he parked his van, as he did every Friday morning, outside the village hall. A contrite visit to Julia's cottage might be out of the question, but an apparently chance meeting while standing in a sociable little queue, well, that was different.

She didn't normally have to dance attendance on the fish man since he called at Kiln House about lunch time, on his way to Stockleigh. Indeed she'd been avoiding the village lately, precisely because she might have encountered Julia. Now, having parked the car, she joined a cluster of women awaiting the fish man's arrival, and suggesting to each other reasons why he was late. They eyed the newcomer with curiosity, while Zinnia ignored them.

A plump woman in an ankle-length skirt was giving it as her belief that he must have been caught in those road works on the way from Stowmarket. Causing havoc with everyone who travelled from that direction, they were. Another, her frizzy blond hair tied with a shocking pink ribbon exactly matching the stain round the mouth of her lolly-sucking toddler, suggested he might have had a flat tyre, her husband had had a puncture on that road only the other day. Zinnia's opinions about the banality of everyday conversation in Haydon were steadily reinforced as she listened, whilst indulging in studied ignorance of Julia Trugglestone's approach. Out of the corner of her eye she noticed her hesitate, seeing who was there, then join the group. Casually, Zinnia turned and smiled warmly.

'Oh hello Julia,' she said. 'I'm glad to see you. I was splitting up clumps of snowdrops yesterday, and thought you might want some for your new garden. They're really best planted in the green. I wondered if there was anything else you'd like as well, while it's still transplanting weather.'

Julia Trugglestone looked surprised, and then relieved, knowing a peace token when it was offered. She nodded to the other customers, and gave Zinnia a delighted smile.

'That's very kind, yes I'd love some,' she said, diplomatically forgetting the large snowdrop clumps Harry had dug up from the Hall garden.

'I wanted to talk to you as well about organising a petition in the village against the proposal to tip in the Pit.' Zinnia was choosing her words with care. 'There's bound to be a lot of opposition to it.'

'Is that the old chalk pit up on the way to Stockleigh?' the large woman enquired, quite oblivious to having butted in. 'Best thing they could do with it, I'd say. It's so dangerous, with that footpath right near the edge.'

The frizzy-haired blonde agreed. 'I'd be worried about my Shane if it's still there when he's old enough to go out with his friends. That boy who fell in last month isn't out of plaster yet, is he? Saw his mother collecting him from school yesterday.'

Zinnia was taken aback, both at the rudeness of the interruptions, and the opinions expressed. With an effort she attempted a condescending smile, and voice of kindly reason. 'But Haydon surely wouldn't put up with the noise, and the traffic. There'd be hundreds of lorries.'

'It's well away from the houses though, and the lorries wouldn't have to come through the village, would they?' A thin woman in dark-rimmed spectacles had joined in. 'They'd come down the Stockleigh road, which is going to be widened anyway.'

There was nodding agreement, and she added, 'I've joined a pressure group fighting against setting up incinerators to burn rubbish. They spew out dioxin and all sorts of nasties. And one of our arguments is that they haven't used all the conventional sites yet.'

The impromptu focus group was suddenly halted by the arrival of the fish van, weighty environmental matters immediately giving way to such considerations as the availability of mackerel, and whether four small plaice fillets would be better than three large ones.

But Zinnia had been rather shocked at the unexpected reaction. It was as if she'd been about to set foot on a lawn, only to discover it was actually green duckweed floating on water. Still, she didn't know any of these women, they must be newcomers to Haydon. The proper villagers, people like herself who'd lived in the place for decades, they would be up in arms about the fate of the old chalk pit, surely.

Julia Trugglestone had wisely refrained from joining in the discussion, and Zinnia waited while she bought her fish, intending to walk back to the cottage with her. Then they could have a long, relaxed talk over a cup of coffee, both pleased that good relations had been restored. They'd sketch out a plan of how to raise local awareness and marshal resistance to this preposterous idea of filling in the Pit, and Zinnia would go home warmed with renewed hope and friendship.

'Met your niece, the other day, I expect she told you,' Julia said, as Zinnia fell into step beside her. 'I hope you're treating the poor girl properly. Let's face it, rural Suffolk must be a bit of a culture shock for an American, not to mention the, uh, special circumstances of Kiln House.'

It was nice to be on teasing terms again. 'Doing her the world of good,' Zinnia retorted cheerfully. 'Leaking ceilings, cold bedrooms, plain cooking – giving her a whole new perspective on life.'

They had reached Julia's front door.

'I'm looking forward to seeing how your garden's getting on,' Zinnia said, 'and I'd like to discuss with you how to start a petition against this ridiculous tipping proposal of Swathe's.'

'Unfortunately it's a really bad moment,' Julia sounded agitated. 'Sorry, but I'm expecting someone any minute. Love to have a nice long chat some other time.'

This wasn't like Julia, usually so relaxed and, well, gracious.

'I'll just have a peek at your garden, then,' Zinnia suggested, slightly nettled. 'Basil was telling me how pleased he was with it. And of course I'll go as soon as your visitor arrives.'

'No. Not today, actually.' She seemed to be struggling for an excuse. 'The, um, patio paving stones have just been cemented in,' she said hurriedly. 'They can't be walked on till tomorrow. Look Zinnia, I'm really sorry to rush, but I'll give you a ring, and we'll arrange some other time.'

As Julia opened the front door, her companion was left standing by the gate like an archbishop turned away by St Peter. Zinnia Peasmore, she said to herself indignantly, you have just been given the brush off, and no mistake.

She turned and began walking to the car, resentment rising with every step. It hadn't been easy, swallowing her pride, and making the first gesture of reconciliation, and now it had been thrown back in her face. Her company had been spurned in favour of some...hold on a minute, what visitor was Julia expecting? Or was that just a fiction?

Reaching her car, she looked back up the street, and saw a green Range Rover pull up outside Julia's cottage. A man got out, and marched confidently up to the front door. Zinnia stared. Maybe Julia had an admirer. Oh ho, a secret lover! That did put a different complexion on things. Perhaps she had been a bit quick to judge, under those circumstances. But who was he? The car meant nothing to her, and she was too far away to see the face. Yet there was something about that purposeful stride...

Intrigued, she manoeuvred the car from its parking space, and drove slowly out of the village, dredging her memory for clues. She was halfway home when the right synapse fired, and she almost collided with an oncoming car at the shock of the realisation. 'That was no visitor,' she exclaimed out loud, in stunned anger. 'Hell's teeth! That was Mike Swathe!'

Julia was still shaken with the effort of averting an explosive meeting. Oh dear, she wasn't good at this lying game, Zinnia was bound to have seen through her excuses, and been hurt. But what else could she have done?

She was putting the fish in the fridge when a thunderous knocking on the front door made her jump. Pull yourself together woman, she told herself sternly, wiping her hands hurriedly, and patting her hair on the way to the front door.

A small man stood on the doorstep, dressed in jeans and a casual top. The short, wavy hair was still discernibly ginger, and his startlingly blue eyes seemed to bore into hers.

'Oh, good heavens... how good of you to come,' she greeted the visitor, trying to regain her usual poise.

He said nothing, but regarded her steadily, a look of wry interrogation on his face.

'I told your secretary there was no need to bother you,' she plunged on, awkwardly. 'My builder just wanted access to your mother's cottage to find out where the damp was coming from.'

'We'd better have a look then, hadn't we,' he said, holding the gate open for her while he reached in his pocket for a key.

'I was sorry to hear about your mother,' Julia told him, filling the silence as he turned the key in the neighbouring front door. 'She was a great character.'

'Is that polite speak for cantankerous old besom?' he enquired, putting his shoulder to the swollen door, which gave reluctantly.

She opened her mouth to protest, then caught his eye. 'Yes, I suppose it is,' she admitted, laughing, and followed him inside. 'Other people's parents are 'interesting characters', aren't they, whereas one's own are just embarrassing when they behave badly.'

'I can't imagine yours ever behaving less than perfectly – your mother especially,' he remarked, pushing the half-drawn curtains back to let more light through the dusty windows.

'Well she did get a bit peculiar towards the end,' Julia admitted, with a small smile. 'Kept accusing people of whispering about her, and stealing her purse. And my father wouldn't believe there was anything wrong with his driving. He terrified the life out of everyone...'

They were walking through a small, beamed room, empty of furniture, and musty with stale air. Mike Swathe paused and looked round. 'Don't tell me he was still driving his old Alvis? That was a lovely machine.'

'Yes, wasn't it,' she responded warmly. 'I always felt really grand, when I was small, rushing through the lanes in that. No he had to sell it, and get an automatic. But then of course his hearing went, and his judgement. It was a miracle he died in his bed.'

They'd gone through into a small kitchen, where the mustiness was overlaid with the clinging smell of damp, although there was no obvious effect on the walls. She gave an involuntary little shudder, as he pulled open a cupboard door beneath the sink, and peered in.

'I think we've homed in on the problem,' he announced. 'The seal on the u-bend is leaking. Water's probably been seeping into this cupboard for months, no wonder the wall's affected.' He rubbed the pipe with his hand, and it came away wet and blackened. 'The water was supposed to have been turned off. Can't think why it isn't.' He reached further into the cupboard, seeking the mains stopcock. 'I'll get a plumber to sort it out straight away. And tell your builder, anything that needs to be done your side, he can send the bill to me.'

Julia was looking about her with curiosity. There were reminders of her own cottage in the layout of the rooms, but her cosy home contrasted starkly with this dank and dirty place, echoing with abandoned emptiness. She had difficulty imagining it transformed into a welcoming home.

'What are you going to do with this cottage?' she asked, watching as he tried to turn off the stopcock. 'Spring is always a good time to sell.'

'Haven't decided yet.' His voice from inside the cupboard was muffled. 'Might even come and live in it myself.'

'Oh surely not!' Julia was taken by surprise.

He sat back on his heels and looked at her mockingly. 'Not the right kind of neighbour, eh?'

'Good heavens no, I didn't mean that.' she said, flustered. She was about to say she'd thought he was going to build in the field above the chalk pit. But talk about his intentions for Zinnia's Pit Garden and the field above were pencilled in for later, over a friendly cup of coffee in her sitting room. She thought quickly. 'It's just that I understood you had a lovely house by the golf course at Stockleigh.'

'Going to sell it. My wife and I are getting divorced,' he informed her tersely, and resumed battle with the stopcock.

'Oh dear, I'm sorry.' She didn't seem to be handling things with her usual aplomb.

'Don't be. It's just tidying things up,' the voice from the cupboard assured her. 'Doreen's always preferred our house in Spain. She's decided to stay there permanently, that's all. The children have left now, and the house is too big for me. Rather have another racehorse anyway.'

'You've got racehorses!'

'One,' he corrected her, finally terminating his efforts, and straightening up. 'What I really need is a bucket to catch the drip just for the moment. There might be one in the shed.'

'You always did love horses,' Julia recalled fondly. 'Remember Misty?'

'The little grey pony?' He was searching in a drawer for the back door key.

'Yes. It was a nightmare trying to get her shod. Until you started work at the blacksmiths. I don't know what you did to her, but she used to relax and look all dreamy.'

'Mm,' he agreed off-handedly. 'If it'd been my business, I'd have charged extra for the magic touch.'

'Is that what you do these days,' she suggested playfully, 'invoice your customers for the charm?'

He turned and looked at her, before trying a key in the door. 'Not much call for charm in waste disposal,' he commented. 'Although I am thinking of...'

Unlocked, the back door suddenly swung open, and a draught, even colder than the room, rushed in. Julia shivered.

'Look, you go back in the warm,' he told her. 'I'll just search for a bucket, but anyway we've discovered what the problem is. It needs a plumber. And I'll drop this key through your letterbox, so the builder can have a look if he wants to.'

'But you'll come in for a cup of coffee or something?'

'No, I don't think so.' He was making no attempt to be sociable.

'Oh, do come. I'd like you to see what's been done with my cottage.' Julia smiled at him, trying her hardest. 'Especially if you're thinking of moving in here. I'll go and put the kettle on.'

And before he could refuse again, she turned and made her way out of the front door.

Two minutes later she was back, to find him placing a misshapen, galvanised bucket in the under-sink cupboard. He looked up at her enquiringly.

'I, um... I seem to have locked myself out,' she said in embarrassment.

He stood up, leaned back against the draining board and took in her discomfiture. 'Dear me,' he said slowly, his face expressionless. 'No minions to let you in, then.'

Julia, who had been intending to pop up the road to borrow Mrs Chitting's key, instantly changed her mind.

'Of course not,' she said crossly. 'I'll have to ring my son, and ask him to bring his key. Can I use the phone in here?'

'No, sorry, it's cut off. I'll run you over there.'

Julia flinched inwardly at the thought of cruising up to Trugglestone Hall in a Range Rover chauffeured by Mike Swathe. No way Zinnia wouldn't get to hear about that. And she could picture her daughter-in-law's reaction only too well.

He was watching her face.

'I wouldn't dream of putting you to all that trouble,' she told him, trying to recover her equanimity, 'I'll just walk up the road and phone from a friend's house.'

'No need.' He produced a mobile phone from his pocket, and handed it to her. 'Use this.'

Reluctantly she took it, and regarded the rows of buttons with apprehension. For a moment she hesitated between honesty and the desire not to seem foolish, like a leaf between competing whirlpools. But there was no help for it.

'I'm afraid I don't know how to use one,' she confessed awkwardly.

This time there was a definite twitch of the lips.

'You're enjoying this!' she accused him.

'Can't think what gave you that idea?' He reached for the phone. 'What's the number? I'll get it for you.'

Julia wondered if he would cause her the embarrassment of waiting till Clive answered, and telling him his mother wanted to speak to him. But as soon as it was ringing, he handed her the phone, told her which button to press, and left the room.

A minute or so later, she found him lounging against the Range Rover, examining the cottage's roof tiles.

'That was kind of you,' she said, returning the mobile. 'My son's coming straight down with a key.'

'Well, I'll just lock up and then I'll be off,' he told her briskly. 'Thank you for the invitation to coffee. Some other time perhaps.'

And as she watched him drive off, Julia was left in the street feeling more disconcerted than a shampooed cat.

****

After breakfast the next morning, Zinnia descended on her son and daughter-in-law. She found Veronica in the kitchen, baking cakes for the school Bring and Buy sale that afternoon, while Derek was removing the letterbox from the back door.

'The postman's promised to deliver severed fingers and a threat to sue, if we don't fix up a less aggressive letterbox,' Derek explained to his mother, as she arrived. 'To what do we owe this unexpected pleasure?'

'I've come to consult you both,' Zinnia announced, sitting herself down at the kitchen table, without waiting to be asked. 'I'm hoping to stir up resistance in the village to this ridiculous tipping proposal, but there doesn't seem to be much support for a fight, judging by what I heard yesterday. What do you think?'

'People don't really seem to care,' Veronica told her, searching for one of her recipe books. 'It's too far out of the village to affect it, and I think families with children are quite pleased at the idea of it being filled in.'

'But household rubbish!' protested Zinnia. 'Smells, and rats and seagulls – surely they can't be happy about the prospect?'

'He won't get permission for that,' Derek assured her. 'The word is that he's put in for household rubbish, knowing that the Council won't grant it, but then they'll be more likely to agree to infilling with rubble. And that's what he really wants.' He paused in his battle to prise off the resisting letterbox. 'I've been asking around - apparently he's a wily old devil, Mike Swathe.'

'Oh.' Zinnia considered. 'But that doesn't alter the fact that I've got to try and organise local resistance.'

'Well Gerry Thornway's property will be affected as well, so he's your best ally,' suggested Derek, 'although it pains me to say it. What happened when you went to see him?'

'He's never there. I've been three times now,' Zinnia told him. 'You don't think he's avoiding me do you?'

'You should be so lucky,' her son said heavily. 'He's being unbearable at work.'

'Anyway,' she returned to the subject, 'I need your help to draw up a list of people who can be briefed to make a fuss.'

'Julia Trugglestone is the person for that surely, she knows everyone,' Derek suggested. 'Couldn't you use it as an excuse to put an end to your cold war?'

'*No, I could not!*' Zinnia declared, with a fierceness that caused Veronica and Derek to exchange questioning glances.

'Thinking about it yesterday, I've made a start.' She pulled out of her pocket a folded brown envelope, on the back of which were a number of names. 'There are the Fazeleys of course. Remember the dust Monica Fazeley kicked up about using the field next to them for a motor-cross track. She'd be just the person to help run this campaign, I think.'

'Yes, she would,' agreed Derek, 'if she hadn't gone down to live with her daughter in deepest Dorset. Poor woman,' he added, leaving the recipient of his sympathy unclear.

'What happened to her husband then? What was his name?'

Derek couldn't resist. 'Well, he'd always suffered from chronic nagging, you know,' he said in a confidential voice. 'It just turned nasty one night. He was rushed into hospital of course, but they couldn't save him.'

His mother wasn't listening.

'And then I thought Colonel Dowty. Wasn't he responsible for getting the village sign made, when nobody else could be bothered?'

'That's because no-one else's son stood to profit from the contract to make it,' Veronica remarked, breaking eggs expertly into a bowl. 'There was a bit of a stink about that, and he suddenly thought Harrogate air would suit him better. Nice family live in that house now, the wife plays the organ in church, and helps out with me at the school.'

'Well, I've got the woman who plays the organ down on my list.' Zinnia was puzzled. 'I thought it was Marjorie Morlop. Has she stopped doing it?'

'Depends what you mean by 'it'.' Derek had removed the old letter box, and peered through the hole at them. 'You know she went a bit peculiar.'

'No. What sort of peculiar?'

'Took to lurking in Mill Lane making lewd suggestions to lone men. Poor old Harry Trench refused to cycle home that way after a while, and lots of people complained to the vicar.'

'But he wouldn't hear a word against her, would he,' Veronica reached into a cupboard for the sugar. 'People said he was taking Christian forgiveness a bit far, but the fact was he didn't want to lose his organist.'

'Then she made the mistake of showing her knickers to the vicar after choir practice one evening,' Derek added with enjoyment, trying to wrench the new letterbox from its shrink wrapping.

'Good heavens, I didn't know any of this.' Zinnia felt rather cheated. 'What's happened to her?'

'Gone to live in sheltered housing in Stockleigh,' he informed her. 'Livens up the place no end.'

'Oh dear. Well what about the people who live in that Victorian house near the school. They used to take you swimming Derek, with their son. You remember.'

'Mm.' He was holding the new letterbox against the door, and measuring. 'Went to live in Cyprus several years ago. They let the house. I don't know who's there now, people only seem to stay about six months.'

Zinnia consulted her list, but with less confidence. 'There was that young couple who took one of the new houses in Mill Lane a few years ago. He was trying to start a local branch of that environmental group, Lovers of the Earth, wasn't he.'

'Friends of the Earth,' corrected Veronica, taking a break from beating the cake mixture.

'No, I think Mum had it right, actually,' Derek remarked, inserting a bit into his electric drill. 'It developed into something of a wife-swapping party, that group, and things got a touch acrimonious.' He paused. 'Why don't we have wife-swapping parties?'

Veronica gave him one of her looks.

Zinnia began to feel like a Channel swimmer battling an unfavourable tide. 'Well what about the Birkins? Now they're stalwarts of Haydon, if anyone is. They were here before we were.'

'She's in a nursing home, he's got the DT's,' Veronica shouted, above the whine of the drill, which suddenly ceased.

'The family are already circling,' added Derek blowing sawdust out of the screw hole he'd just made. 'That place will fetch a packet.'

Veronica looked on with annoyance. She'd gone to the trouble of providing him with a dustpan and brush. Why couldn't he use it? But her irritation was tempered by the slow realisation that her mother-in-law was perfectly illustrating the force of Veronica's own argument of the need to move out of Kiln House. This could be a major breakthrough.

'Let's have a look at that list,' she said lightly. 'Hm. I don't think there's anybody on it who'd be any use to you. Just about everyone's either died or moved away.'

'Great advertisement for country living,' commented Derek cheerfully, lining up the second screw hole. Veronica frowned at him.

'The thing is, Haydon has moved on. Surprising what a turnover of people there is. And of course it's not easy to stay up with village happenings when you live so much on the edge of the place,' she said, keeping her voice bright, like a teacher encouraging a timid child on its first day. 'But if you were to live actually in the village, and become more involved…'

'If you mean move into one of those awful modern boxes,' interrupted Zinnia sharply, 'I've told you before, the answer is no. Absolutely not. And frankly, the idea of helping to organise the Old People's Mystery Tour, and the Under-Fives' Christmas Party, curls me up. It's just not me.'

She stood up, folding her envelope and shoved it into her anorak pocket. 'Well, I'll leave you to your Saturday morning labours, and get back to mine.'

Derek pushed the door wide open, and stood aside to let her through. 'Don't worry Mum,' he murmured with a wink, as she passed, 'they wouldn't let you near the Under-Fives' Christmas Party.'

****

Zinnia returned to Kiln House in a bad mood. Rosemary had gone off early to play the tourist, and experience the delights of Cambridge, so she had the day completely to herself. A cold wind that had rattled the windows all night was dropping, and the sun was coaxing that indefinable smell from the damp earth that gladdens the heart of every gardener in spring.

But Zinnia remained ungladdened. She was beginning to feel alone and beleaguered, as if lost on a moor with the sun going down. It had been a genuine shock to discover that there was no local support against tipping in the Pit Garden, and bewildering to find that just about all the people she thought she knew had somehow moved on. I've lived in Haydon for fifty-two years, she thought defiantly, it's *my* village. And yet apparently she had become irrelevant to its present inhabitants, most of whom appeared not even to be aware of her existence.

This was depressing enough, but with no local support, and without Julia, whom she wasn't prepared even to think about at the moment, common sense told her that she'd probably lost any chance of winning a fight for the Pit Garden. Zinnia wasn't one to give up, but it did cross her mind that perhaps she was getting old. The world was changing, leaving her behind, and it was not a comfortable thought.

Gloomily, she mixed up a can of weedkiller. The cat was safely snoozing in the kitchen, and conditions were perfect for giving the paths their spring dose, which would hopefully kill off everything and keep them clear for at least four months. It was a job she disliked, but just at the moment it matched her mood. She was on to her second can full, and applying it to the path by the greenhouse, when an unusual-looking seedling caught her eye, its deep green leaves gleaming with the wetness of the weedkiller that had just drenched it.

That's a funny looking tomato seedling, she thought casually, and a second later had flung down the watering can, which landed on her foot. Ignoring the pain, she made for the outside tap at a hobbling run that would have earned marks for style in any three-legged race. Scrabbling to connect the hose, she turned the tap full on, and pulled the gushing hose back up to the path by the greenhouse. Subjecting the little plant to another deluge, she examined it anxiously. Whilst there was certainly a slight resemblance to a tomato plant, even as it bowed under the stream of water, she could detect that the characteristics were different, and it did look a bit like the plant she had been shown as a little girl. At least as far as she could remember.

How could you have been so lax? she reproached herself. That path should have been inspected first for any interesting seedlings. Suppose this is Settlewort, and you've just weedkilled it out of existence? You're a fool, Zinnia Peasemore.

The question was, how long would it take to dilute the weedkiller to harmlessness, always supposing that the plant hadn't absorbed a lethal dose straight away? About five minutes, she reckoned. After eight, she left the hose running, and limped back to turn off the tap. Returning to the soggy seedling, she contemplated how best to dig it up, but reluctantly came to the conclusion that this was just about impossible. The thing was growing out of a crack that had formed in the concrete step on which the greenhouse partly rested. She would have had to demolish the whole structure.

But, it occurred to her, if one Settlewort seed had germinated without her noticing, perhaps others had as well. And it *was* Settlewort, it just had to be. For the rest of the morning she hobbled round the garden, bent double, examining the ground yard by yard, with the diligence of a detective searching a scene of crime.

When Rosemary returned from Cambridge in the evening, it was to discover Zinnia, suffering from serious backache, and nursing one swollen foot in a slipper, but full of elation, which had completely ousted her earlier gloom. Rosemary was bursting to relive her experiences of the beauties and car parking nightmares of Cambridge, but clearly these stood no chance against her aunt's far more important news that there were not one, not two, but *three* Settlewort seedlings growing in the garden.

'In the Pit Garden?' Rosemary enquired, giving up on the idea of recounting her day to an interested and receptive audience.

'Well no, it's a pity, that,' her aunt conceded. 'One's growing out of a step, one is entangled with the roots of the Mount Etna Broom near the garage, but the third one was just in among the primroses. And that,' she added triumphantly, 'has now been transplanted. I dug it up very carefully, and it's in a large pot, safely in the greenhouse. Eureka!'

'You mean when it's bigger you're going to transfer it into the Pit Garden, and try and fool the authorities that it was growing there all the time?'

Zinnia sounded surprised, 'Did you expect me to do anything else?'

'Of course not,' Rosemary shook her head laughingly, 'Silly me.'

Chapter Ten

'Oh here you are, I might have known.' Rosemary poked her head round the greenhouse door several days later, glowing from her early morning walk. She was getting to know all the footpaths round about, and was surprised at the pleasure walking gave her, each day discovering some new sign of the countryside's spring awakening. Today the sun was shining from a cloudless sky, and on the way to the greenhouse she had stood entranced beneath the lime tree, while a thrush gave a concert from its topmost branch. Its joyous notes made contact with something inside her which had been crushed, and was now slowly unfolding, like a trampled seedling.

'What a wonderful morning,' she remarked cheerily. 'Just came to remind you, I won't be back till late this evening.'

Her aunt looked vaguely questioning.

'You know, I'm going with Clive and Susie to a party in Cambridge. I told you.'

'Oh yes. Have you seen how the Settlewort has grown!' There was no mistaking where her interest lay.

Responding to the April sunshine fingering the greenhouse roof earlier each day, the plant was now twice the size. As if it was a favourite child, it contrasted markedly with the ill-treated young sibling growing out of the greenhouse step. Perhaps not surprising in the circumstances.

'If you'd been bathed in poison, drenched in cold water, and only had old rubble for food, you might not be a picture of health either,' he aunt had observed sagely. The one beside the garage seemed to be struggling a bit too, but the plant she had potted up was giving her a daily thrill with its evident zest for life. It was becoming almost bushy, as it put out more elegantly divided leaves, with a contrasting grey-green underside.

'Come on my beauty,' Zinnia encouraged it now, as she did several times a day, 'you just don't know how special you are.'

'You don't *know* that it's Settlewort,' Rosemary commented, leaning against the door, and unwisely re-opening a running disagreement. 'How can you be certain?'

'Of course it is,' retorted Zinnia impatiently. 'I've told you before, the leaves exactly match the description in Mrs Grieve's Herbal, and it's definitely the same plant that appeared in the bomb crater during the war. Everyone said that was Settlewort.'

'But no expert came and looked at it then, did they? You said yourself. Why don't you get someone down to identify it now? Then you'll have proof.'

'Can't possibly do that,' her aunt was dismissive. 'The whole idea is that it's supposed to suddenly reappear in the Pit Garden. If some bod from Kew finds it sitting in my greenhouse, with a couple more near the house, what good will that do? Anyway, nobody really knows what the thing is supposed to look like.'

'I thought you said Kew Gardens might have a dried specimen somewhere?'

'Mm.' Zinnia was having a battle with herself about that. Part of her wasn't at all sure it would be a good thing for her precious Settlewort plant to be compared with a dried specimen from the past. Suppose it turned out to be something quite different? Didn't bear thinking about.

'Well, why not just plant it out in the Pit Garden right now?,' Rosemary persisted. 'Surely, the smaller it is when you put it there, the more convincing it will look?'

'Can't do that either,' Zinnia responded, resuming her watering. 'Not until it's certain there won't be any more frosts. They're worse in the Pit than up here too, because the cold air collects in the bottom.'

She was not in fact in a position to plant out anything, since her foot had swelled badly, and was causing her considerable pain. Initially dismissing the family's pressure to go and see the doctor, she was now beginning to wonder if that mightn't perhaps be sensible. But not today. She had a column waiting to be written for Country Harvest. At least it would give her the opportunity to sit with her foot up, and if Rosemary was going to be back late, she could go to bed really early, without inviting comment.

'Have a nice time,' she told her now. 'It's an awfully long way to go for a party.'

'Well, they've got lots of friends in Cambridge. Isn't it great of them to get me invited though?' She laughed. 'Susie thinks I'm leading too quiet a life.'

****

Halfway through the morning, Rosemary was beginning to see Susie's point, as she found herself repetitively repotting a batch of recently delivered hyssop and lavender. Susie maintained that even with the price of compost and pots, the task was worth doing. Bigger plants were healthier, she said, and needed less watering. Also you could charge more for a larger unit, which was not unimportant. She'd demonstrated what needed doing, and warned that it was a boring job.

It was, but while working Rosemary used the time to think through the problem of identifying this plant that her aunt was convinced was Settlewort. The difficulty lay in not arousing anyone's curiosity too soon. It was rather like the difficult situation faced by lone inventors, hesitating over applying for a patent, which might then expose their idea to unscrupulous exploitation.

Surely, she reflected, firming a hyssop plant into its new pot, if Settlewort had been an important herb once, it would have been mentioned quite a lot, in old books. The question was, where would you find these books now?

Later in the morning, with all the plants looking good in their new, more expensive pots, she sought out Susie in the office, up at the Hall.

'Well, I've got quite a few,' Susie suggested, when Rosemary casually enquired about old herbals. 'Not the originals of course, but modern or nineteenth century reprints. Why the sudden interest?'

'She's training to be a witch, didn't you know?' Matthew looked up from the computer screen. 'Got all interested when she found out about Haydon's very own wicked witch. No frog is safe at Kiln House now, and as for the cat...'

'Turn you into a toad, if you don't watch out,' Rosemary threatened him, realising that actually this was quite a good cover line.

'I'm just interested in the herbs that witches used, especially...er...hallucinatory and mind-bending substances,' she told Susie. 'We had the so-called witches of Salem, as you know, and now they think the girls' visions might have been caused by a type of fungus growing on the food. It's fascinating.'

'Well, you're welcome to look at whatever you want,' Susie said, indicating the bookshelf, 'those are the ones that would probably be most informative. Matthew, old son, how are you getting on with that catalogue? The printer is pressing me to give him a date, but...'

The telephone interrupted. 'Yes, be right with you,' she informed the caller, and grabbing a notebook, rushed out.

Matthew looked up. 'Hallucinatory drugs, eh? Ho, ho! I shall have to come and eat at Kiln House more often.'

'No, silly,' Rosemary told him, surveying the book titles. 'I'm really trying to find out about Settlewort for Zinnia. That plant in the pot is growing nicely. Ah, this is the book Zinnia can't find,' she said, selecting Gerard's Herbal. 'She was turning the place upside down for it the other night.'

Sitting down at the desk, she consulted the index. 'Here it is,' she said with satisfaction, and turned to the page.

'*The root is of a mean bignesse,*' she read, '*divided into two or three parts, and full of strings. The stalke is thicke, fat and green of color, full of spongeous pith, and is divided into sundry branches, set with smooth and narrowe leaves, most pleasing to the eies, for everie leafe resembleth a faire and comely feather.*'

'I'd better write this down,' she told Matthew, 'chuck over some of that paper.'

'*The floures are white, bell-fashion, yet doe hold up their heads, wherein doth consist much beauty, being divided into five sections with curious blue lines. The whole plant is of a most pleasant sweet smell, somewhat stuffing the head. It is greene all Summer long, and a great part of Autumne, and floureth in the warmest days. Which beeing past there succeed faire berries of the bignesse of a small nut, green, but yellow when ripe. It will continue flourishing till the frost overtake the plant, at what time it perisheth. It farre exceedeth my skill to describe the beauty and excellencie of this rare plant, and I thinke the pensil of the most curious painter will be at a stay, when he shall come.'*

'So, as soon as the thing flowers, we'll know for certain that it's really Settlewort,' she announced triumphantly, as she finished writing this down. 'They sound really distinctive. Do you think I need to copy it all?'

But her librarian's instinct for thoroughness prevailed. After all, something she didn't consider interesting might turn out to be important.

These herbes doe grow of themselves for the most part, in desart and untilled places, among rubbish and old walls, she noted, *Whose seeds I received of the right honourable the Lord Edward Zouch; which he brought from Constantinope, and of his liberalitie did bestow them upon me, as also many other rare and strange seeds. Notwithstanding, it joyeth not to grow in my Garden, by reason that the seeds sprang not to life.*

Wait till Zinnia hears that, she thought, she'll be really pleased with herself for succeeding with the plant when he failed.

Under the heading *'Vertues,'* she read, *The Apothecaries keepe the Latine name Solanum regale, but we of England call it Settlewort. The leaves hereof are a remedie for the paine of head called the Megram or Migram, that hath bin of long continuance. It provoketh sleepe and asswageth paine, and some have reported that it prevaileth against the falling sickness and phrensies. A knowne experience came from Canterbury, where Mistresse Parker a merchants wife there being most grievously taken with the phrensies, and not finding ease or cure in any other thing, by this found helpe and was perfectly cured when all hope was past, by the report of Mr William Ram publique Notari of the said towne.*

'What do you think the 'phrensies' was?' she asked rhetorically. 'Could it have been epilepsy? Oh wait a minute, this is for you Matthew, *"They that have seene the proof hereof, have credibly reported that it purgeth the brain from gross and slimie humors."* Gross and slimey – that's you to a T, better start putting the leaves in your salad immediately.'

She'd caught his attention. 'Go on,' he said, 'what else is it supposed to do?'

'Well, there's a bit of historical stuff... *"Mithridates the great was famous for his knowledge herein, as Plutarch noteth. Nicander in his Geoponicks beleeveth that the Grecians did call it Panakeiodora, being the gift of the goddess Panakeia."* Oh, this is better,' she raised her voice:- *"There is a conserve made of the leaves and sugar, good for many things, and especially for the head-ache. The same is ministred with great successe unto such as are become peevish."* '

She looked across at him, a smile hovering. 'Would you say that described Zinnia at all?'

' *"There is no other herbe to be found, whereof so small a quantity will do so much good,"* ' she continued. ' *"But he that will know more concerning the making, difference, choise and use of this herbe, let him read Pena, where he shall finde many excellent secrets worth the noticing of those which would know how to use such rare and excellent medicine. There have beene many ridiculous tales brought up of this plant, whether of old wives, or some runnagate surgeons or Physicke-mongers I know not. All of which dreames and old wives tales you shall henceforth cast out of your bookes and memory, knowing this, that they are all and every part of them false and most untrue, that it gives power over them that take it."* '

'Power over them that take it, eh,' Matthew repeated slowly.

'No, he says it *doesn't* do that. That's only an old wives tale. So it's no good you slipping it into girls' drinks to make them susceptible to your charms.'

'Don't need to,' he claimed, with a smile and a modest shrug.

Rosemary could believe it. She'd heard about Matthew's 'girlies', as they were disparagingly referred to by his mother, who couldn't work out the attraction he exerted over the local talent. But then she didn't appear to understand her son at all.

'Is it mentioned in other books?' he asked.

'Well there's Mrs Grieve's Herbal,' Rosemary told him, getting it out and showing him the entry. 'Look, she mentions its mind-bending capabilities, or reputation for it anyway. But I don't need to take notes on that, because Zinnia's got it already. Ah, Culpeper's Complete Herbal and English Physician, that sounds hopeful.'

She opened the book, and soon found the right page.

'Yes, here we are. *"The root of Settlewort is outwardly brown, and within white, sharpe in taste, wherewith is mingled a superficiall sweetnesse. From this root riseth up a fat, thick and straight stem of two cubits high, but tender and soft, whereon are placed in most pleasing order very faire leaves, like to the willow, but far passing it in comelinesse. The faire and beautifull floures come forth of long toothed cups, white, of the form of a bell, or like the floures of the great Withwinde that rampeth in hedges, but altogether greater and wider in the mouth, sharpe cornered at the brimmes. Each floure divideth it selfe into five parts by divers lines, blew in colour. Then doe come yellow berries, of a sweet taste at the first, but after of too strong savor, growing together in clusters like burnished coral, wherein is contained the seed. It bringeth new floures from July unto October in infinite number, yea even untill the frosts doe cause the whole plant to perish. It recovereth it self againe of his own seed. It comes from seed in one yeare to beare both floures and seed. It delighteth to grow, as Palladius saith, in rough and craggy places, and in a leane soil where no moisture is. Myself have seen it flourishing in the ruines of an old bricke-kilne by Colchester, in the ground of Mr George Sayer, called Miles End, and at Haydon in the County of Suffolk. It groweth also upon the end of Blacke heath neere London, and upon barren hills and untoiled places in the County of Kent."*

'How about that!' exclaimed Rosemary excitedly. 'It mentions Haydon.'

Her eyes skipped down the page. 'This is real neat.'

'Why, what does it say?'

' *"It doth helpe the panting and passion of the heart, prevaileth against giddinesse, turning or swimming of the braine. It purifieth the bloud, and,"* she read quickly, 'this is the important bit – *"makes young wenches look faire and cherry-like."* '

She pretended to simper at her cousin, who screwed up his face sceptically, and looked her up and down.

'Packs a *helluva* punch then, does it?' and he ducked, as she threw a biro at him.

'They obviously thought highly of it, but you have to take what these herbalists say with spoonfuls of salt, don't you,' Rosemary commented, retrieving the spent missile. 'I mean, listen to this:- *"Settlewort comforteth the braine, the memories, the inward senses, and restoreth speech unto them that are possessed with the dumbe palsie."* Hardly sounds likely, does it, whatever the 'dumb palsie' is. Ah, this is better…'

Matthew had ceased any pretence at working, and now stood looking over her shoulder.

' *"Being a most pretious remedie,"'* he read, in an exaggeratedly yokel accent, ' *"this is the herbe which Tiberius the Emperour commanded to bee conveied unto him from the island of Aiphysos, as Pliny reporteth. It prolongeth life, quickeneth all the senses, and doth not only preserve the memory, but also recovereth it when it is lost. Settlewort hath such force and power, in strengthening of the heart and stirring the instruments of the senses, that it is most effectuall, not only inwardly taken to the quantity of a little spoonful, but also outwardly applied. It is cherished everie where it joyeth to grow."* '

'Man, this stuff sounds as if it's a real mind blower.' His eyes danced. 'I wonder how the HJ's would play if we were all high on it.'

Rosemary regarded him severely. 'Don't even think about it,' she said, like a traffic warden, parking ticket at the ready. 'But the way I figure it,' she added slowly, 'the medical drug companies would give their eye teeth to get hold of something like this.'

She could see the riposte coming, and cut him short. 'Okay, so drug companies don't have teeth. But they sure have a deal of money.'

They looked at each other, as he sat down again at the computer.

'If this really is Settlewort – the only plants of it left in the world – well, it's kind of scary to think about it.' Her voice was serious. 'And we have to handle the situation very carefully. So no telling anyone, and no fooling around. Okay?'

Matthew assumed the practised innocence of a child surreptitiously feeding the dog under the table.

'As if I would,' he said.

****

Rosemary had brought several dresses over with her, and to date they had hung forlornly in the closet, while she wore trousers and thick pullovers like everyone else. No point in freezing to death, even if you looked good whilst expiring. But a party, in beautiful Cambridge, with friends of the Trugglestones, well that did seem to call for a raising of the sartorial standard.

Accordingly, she had chosen a fitted, low-necked dress of cobalt blue, with short sleeves, which she'd worn a couple of times in the States, and felt really good in. But sitting in the back of the Trugglestone's old Volvo, she was beginning to wonder if she wasn't a little overdressed – for the occasion, if not for the temperature. Clive wore slacks and a thin jersey, under a blazer jacket, and Susie had on smarter trousers than her usual grubby jeans, but to the casual eye her attire did not immediately shout 'party'.

As they drove along the dual carriageway towards Cambridge, Susie was discussing the launch of The Walled Herb Garden.

'The key to success is publicity, but what can I do to grab the attention of the local media? I don't want just a little mention. What's needed is a big splash.'

'How about Rosemary posing nude except for a few sprigs of lavender, in the middle of the garden?' suggested Clive blandly, his concentration appearing to be on a lorry threatening to swing out in front of them.

The proposed model was somewhat taken aback, and avoided looking in the the mirror in case she should catch his eye. She'd always assumed he was rather shy and earnest.

'No, she'd get sunburn, and sue us,' Susie responded evenly. 'But you're right, I do need some kind of gimmick. Preferably more in keeping with the aims of the place. A pot of Silphion would do nicely.'

'What's that?'

'Only joking,' Susie half turned to talk to their passenger. 'Silphion is the legendary lost herb of Roman times. It grew in Cyrenaica, which is part of Libya now I think, and there was a thriving trade in it in ancient Greece and Rome. We know what it looked like, because it was depicted on coins. It was that important. But the plant just seems to have been driven to extinction.'

'But why didn't people grow it commercially?' Rosemary was puzzled. 'Surely, if you can sell something, then it's worth growing fields of it?'

'You'd think so, wouldn't you. But perhaps that's a modern way of looking at things. After all, we had Settlewort growing here in Haydon, and that was allowed to die out as well.'

A thought struck her. 'Now that'd be really good as an opening ploy.'

'What, a display of Settlewort?' Clive glanced at her fondly.

'I wish,' she retorted. 'And if your ancestors had been a bit more conservation minded, maybe we could have. But we could link the Walled Garden to the Lost Herb of Haydon Settleworth – you know, the new place of herbs in the home of the Lost Herb. It's the sort of angle feature editors like to latch on to.'

'What do you think?' she looked over to the back seat, but Rosemary had gone rather quiet. 'You know about Settlewort, don't you? In fact, did I see you'd been making some notes on it this afternoon?'

'Um. Yes. It...it was one of the herbs witches were supposed to have used, wasn't it. I'm kind of interested in that side of it, as I said.'

Rosemary fidgeted uncomfortably, not sounding particularly convincing, and Susie looked at her curiously.

'Well, there's someone coming this evening you might enjoy talking to, in that case. Simon and I did our horticultural training together, and we were both interested in herbs. But he's gone into the medicinal side of things. Working for one of the big drug companies now, I believe.'

****

The party was being held in a family house on the outskirts of Cambridge, the home of a married couple who were evidently great friends of Clive and Susie. In fact their hostess was, with another girlfriend, going to do the catering for Trugglestone Hall when it began its new life as an exclusive and very private conference centre.

'So the party grub should be good,' Susie assured Rosemary, who was suddenly feeling nervous and gauche, confronted by about forty people, a large proportion of whom clearly knew each other. They were almost all older than she was, it seemed, and married, with children, judging from overheard snatches in which schools loomed large.

Susie kept her protégé by her side, and worked hard at introducing her to the various people she talked to, trying to include her in their conversations, which Rosemary appreciated. But she never had been any good at the social thing. A one to one conversation in relaxed circumstances was okay, but getting to know someone on a superficial basis, exchanging banalities in a crowd of noisy people, no, she couldn't cut it.

She was feeling inadequate, and guilty at letting her benefactor down, when Susie spotted a fair-haired man, and towed Rosemary across the room to greet him.

'Simon, how lovely to see you!' she exclaimed. 'I want to talk to you later, and catch up on all your news, but first I want you to meet Rosemary Keel, who's over from the States, and being a wonderful help with setting up my new project. She's quite the expert in witch's herbs, especially Settlewort. Isn't that right?'

'Well, no, not really,' Rosemary muttered uncomfortably, but Susie was already slipping away, and she was left facing a man of about thirty-five, whose nose was meant to be snub, but somehow had a bump in the middle, as if the designer had had second thoughts halfway through. The face was at that interesting stage where youth is merging into maturity, and his brown eyes looked at Rosemary questioningly from behind rather trendy glasses.

'You've been dumped on,' she told him candidly. 'I don't fit in – I'm not married, can't make small talk, and I sure as heck don't care about schools.'

'That makes two of us then,' he assured her, laughing.

'And parties mean party clothes, where I come from, so I feel decidedly overdressed as well.'

His eye dwelt on her low neckline. 'Overdressed?' he mused. 'Well, if you say so.'

Rosemary kicked herself for falling into that one, and attempted to drag the conversation back to party norms.

'Susie said you worked for one of the drug companies, is that right?'

'Not exactly. I'm working on a project that's partly funded by a group of drug companies, and partly by the World Health Organisation, with Kew Botanic Garden. We're taking a close look at the scientific properties of herbs that have been traditionally used for healing in cultures all over the world.'

'Sounds fascinating,' Rosemary told him, and meant it. 'But why now? It's the sort of thing you assume was done years ago.'

'You would think so, wouldn't you. But drugs companies have traditionally rubbished anything to do with plants that have healing properties. Do you fancy some food, I'm starving?'

They made their way to the next room, where an inviting array of buffet food had been laid on a large table, and queued up behind similarly-minded guests.

'Why would drugs companies do that?' she asked, puzzled. 'Despise plants, I mean. You'd think they'd have rushed to find out what made these things work.'

'Not enough money in it,' he said succinctly. 'You can't patent a plant, or a plant extract, that's the trouble. And to market anything as a medicine, you have to carry out extensive clinical trials, which costs a bomb. Then, as soon as you launch your product, all your competitors say "Thanks, pal", and market their own versions.'

He picked up a plate and surveyed the first inviting dish. 'Do you reckon that's as good as it looks?'

With plates piled high, they made their way to the other room, and found a quiet corner.

'Well why,' Rosemary enquired, between mouthfuls of an extremely tasty chicken and mushroom risotto, 'are drug companies employing you to look at natural cures now?'

'Swing of the pendulum really. There's increasing dissatisfaction with sophisticated drugs that have so many side effects they often create more problems than they solve. And health food shops have taken off like nobody's business. People like the idea of plant-based preventions and cures, especially as they don't have to go passively to a doctor and ask for them.' He sampled some salmon mousse and looked at her plate. 'You really missed out on this, it's fantastic.'

'So are the big drug companies interested now?'

'They're less sceptical, but some of the smaller companies have decided it's an area worth exploring, with an eye to food supplements, and that's why this project's been put together. They're mostly biochemists on the team. I just supply the horticultural and herbal stuff.'

'But where do you start? I mean how do you know what to look for?'

'Well, I'm working at Kew at the moment, going through old herbals, and the journals of explorers and botanists who recorded what they found in various parts of the world, and their uses by the native populations. It makes you think. There's a tree found growing just on the Greek island of Chios, which produces a gum that appears to cure stomach ulcers. They're doing tests at the moment.'

He paused, fork in the air. 'You know it's amazing what we've ignored. We're so arrogant. For centuries the Neem tree has been used in India for curing all sorts of skin problems, and the West is only just waking up to what valuable compounds its leaves contain. And that's just one traditionally used plant, out of scores out there. Part of the team are going out to India at the end of the summer. I'm looking forward to it.'

Rosemary was just waking up to the fact that Simon might be an extremely useful source of information.

'Supposing you found a valuable plant, but it was very scarce, what would you do then?' she asked casually.

'Depends why it was scarce, I suppose. But if it had great potential, these days you can get plants micro-propagated, which makes hundreds of tiny plants grow from just a few cells. But you'd have to be careful not to effectively steal a plant from its native country. We're very strict about that. It's essential these places benefit from their native flora.'

He laid his fork down with regret. 'I'm afraid I'm going back for seconds, how about you?'

Rosemary overcame temptation, and declined, and in his absence pondered how best to use this lucky meeting to advantage. He was rather nice, and clearly exactly the right person to be able to pronounce on Settlewort – it's true identity, and what should be done with it, if it really was a medicinal plant that had been thought extinct.

But he was also completely the wrong person to blab to prematurely. Zinnia would never forgive her if she failed to save her beloved Pit Garden just because Rosemary had caused a team to race down from Kew, before her aunt had got Settlewort growing in the Pit itself.

Watch it girl, she told herself sternly.

Simon returned from the food sortie with almost as much as before.

'You'll never manage those delicious looking desserts,' Rosemary reproached him mildly.

He laughed. 'You want to bet?'

'My aunt's a keen gardener,' she said carefully, 'and she's got this plant she thinks is something rather special, but she's not sure. Would there be a dried specimen at Kew that she could compare it with?'

'Bound to be.' He was tackling the second plateful with undiminished enjoyment. 'The Herbarium contains thousands and thousands of dried plant samples, from all over the world. It's an amazing place. She could send me a sample, if you like, and I'll check it for her. What is it? At least what does she think it is?'

'Oh, um…I don't know,' her voice was suddenly defensive. 'I'm not great on gardening.'

'What was all that about you and witches' herbs then?'

'Oh, nothing really. Susie was just laying it on thick.' Rosemary played for time, searching for a convincing change of subject. 'When I was a child I had a real bad sting from poison ivy. That plant sure has a well-stocked armoury. Must be able to cure something! Has anybody ever analysed it?'

Chapter Eleven

As April turned into May, the opening day of the Walled Herb Garden and Tea Room seemed to be racing up, and Susie blessed the good fortune that had provided her with two invaluable helpers. Rosemary was happy to do whatever was asked, she was good with people on the telephone, and made an excellent sounding board for ideas. She still refused to take a penny in payment for her help, which was a financial bonus, but made Susie feel somewhat uncomfortable. Matthew, meanwhile, invaluably managed to combine strong and cheerful labour with computer knowledge that she wouldn't have known where else to obtain, even if they could have afforded some consultant's fees. He was currently teaching her how to use the stock control system he had designed specially.

'Eventually, when you've got a computer terminal at the plant till, and in the tea shop, you'll just type in the code on the price label, and the system will do it all for you', he explained, having made her sit at the keyboard in the office, and do a practice day's takings. 'Until then, you'll just have to list all the codes, and type them in every evening.'

'You're a wonder,' she told him gratefully, still tentative about computer systems of any kind.

'That's what they all say,' he grinned at her.

'You ought to be able to make good money out of all this know-how,' she remarked. 'Although goodness knows where you picked it up.'

'Oh just natural talent,' he responded modestly. 'I wish you'd talk to my mother. I'm hardly through the door before she's on at me about going to university. It's a total waste of time.'

'What, going to university, or her trying to persuade you?'

He left the question unanswered. 'Some kind of distraction would get her off my back,' he mused. 'You don't need a cook, do you? She's brilliant. Mind-blowing scones. Your Tea Room would get four Michelin stars straight off.'

Susie laughed. 'Well, it's very kind of you to offer your mother's services, but I've already arranged for Mrs Chitting to do the cakes and scones. And in any case we're not opening till Whitsun.' A thought struck her. 'There is one thing though – but I don't suppose she'd be interested.'

'Of course she will.'

His confidence about her wishes was amusing, but doubtless based on sound psychiatry. Susie had yet to meet his parents, but could imagine Matthew in persuasive mode would be hard to resist. He had the exuberance of a dancing reflected light on the ceiling.

'Well, I was thinking of selling speciality jams in the shop, based on old recipes,' she said. 'And obviously they'd have to be thoroughly tested first. I was going to try them out myself, but...' She shrugged helplessly. Time was passing disconcertingly fast.

'If your mother was interested in having a go, it really would be a help. I came across a seventeenth century recipe using Betony leaves only yesterday', and she searched on the untidy desk, locating an old envelope on which she'd scribbled it down.

'Great idea!' he said, taking the recipe, and putting it in his pocket.

'Shall I go and see your mother about it?'

'No, leave it to me,' Matthew assured her happily, aware that the sight of his unassuming and scruffily-dressed employer was unlikely to impress Veronica, whereas his own account of Lady Susan Trugglestone's crying need for culinary expertise would have instant effect.

****

At the time that Matthew was insouciantly offering his mother's services as cook, she was volunteering his to Zinnia. Veronica had called in at Kiln House to see if her mother-in-law would like any shopping done in Ipswich, and had found her attempting to light a fire in the sitting room, although she was supposed to be resting her foot which was still swollen and painful.

It had been a five-bucket night, with heavy rain finding its way through the roof, and into the necessary plastic receptacles. There was a pervasive dampness in the atmosphere, which Zinnia had thought a roaring fire might help to dispel, but Veronica found her in a room full of smoke, the fire exhibiting the flickering will to live of a man who's just written off a friend's vintage Rolls Royce.

'It's just not drawing properly', she lamented, brushing a black hand across her face. 'I think there must be something blocking the chimney. Perhaps some bird's trying to build a nest in the top, although I can't see anything from outside.'

As she spoke a trickle of loosened soot descended on the struggling flame, and spread its dusty darkness over the hearth rug.

Veronica regarded the mess with horror, instinctively recoiling, lest a speck of it sully her polished shoes.

'Matthew can come over when he's had his tea', she said in the kindly, organising tone much heard in old people's homes. 'He'll sweep the chimney for you.'

This was unselfish of her, since she would then have to cope with his filthy clothes, but Veronica was not one to shirk her duties as a daughter-in-law.

'No, no, he'll enjoy it', she said, dismissing Zinnia's unconvincing protestations. 'I'll send him round this afternoon.'

****

Surprisingly, she had no difficulty in persuading Matthew to do this good deed for his grandmother. This was partly due to the fact that she had just fallen for his carefully placed blandishments about her culinary skills.

'I told Lady Trugglestone what a wonderful cook you are, Mum,' he informed her, not without truth. 'She's just desperate to find someone who would be able to follow these difficult old recipes, and make speciality jams for the Tea Shop.'

'Well, I don't know that I'd be able to...' his mother began diffidently, but with a pleased expression.

'It'd be a great opening for you, Mum. If they're a success, maybe you could start a little business. And of course when Trugglestone Hall becomes an exclusive conference centre, there'll be all sorts of influential people staying there.'

He let that sink in.

'She found this recipe in an old book,' he went on casually, taking the piece of paper out of his pocket. "Conserve of Betony After the Italian Way, from the cook to Queen Henrietta Maria 1655". Sounds great. And I've brought some Betony leaves home. I was sure you would be able to follow the instructions. Lady Trugglestone was thrilled.'

****

Derek had picked up a bargain set of chimney brushes some years ago at a farm sale, but as Veronica had long since insisted that their own fireplaces be converted to gas fires, the implements now resided at Kiln House.

Matthew had helped his father to sweep the chimney before, and was rather pleased to be able to conduct the operation himself, with Rosemary as his uncomprehending assistant.

'You'll need old clothes,' he warned her, but she had nothing suitably decrepit, so after a few minutes reappeared wearing a cast-off raincoat of Zinnia's, and a pair of her corduroy gardening trousers, too big round the waist. He snorted with laughter at the sight.

'You see,' he informed her, as she made a face at him, 'we can teach you Yanks a thing or two about fashion. Now, your task is to hold this sheet over the fireplace, while I push the brushes up. Then all the soot will fall into the fireplace.'

'All?' queried his grandmother, coming in from the kitchen, and catching this last.

'Don't worry, Gran,' he assured her confidently, attaching the brush to the first handle section. 'We'll have this chimney clear faster than you can say, "Is there no end to the man's talents?" Just you watch.'

Unfortunately, there was a snag. Or rather some kind of blockage. Avalanches of acrid soot cascaded into the fireplace, overcoming the sheet held to the chimney breast by Rosemary, with the ease of a deer leaping an allotment fence. Zinnia came to her assistance, but little clouds still curled their way into the room, black as a ring master's moustache. The amateur sweep struggled to push the brush all the way up, but was meeting with stubborn resistance.

'If it's a bird's nest,' he panted, 'it's some bird!'

'There's hardly any soot coming down now, I can hold the sheet. Why don't you go outside and yell if you can see the brush at the top,' suggested Zinnia, after a while.

Obediently, Rosemary went out into the garden, and gazed up at the chimney. Wisps of black drifted upwards from the brick top, but of the brush there was no sign. She was just about to convey this information, when there was a grating sound, and half a chimney pot shot upwards, and descended in a graceful arc into the garden, leaving the brush waving triumphantly in the air.

She set off in search of the projectile, thinking up a suitable tease about the elusive Lesser Potted Phoenix Bird, whose nest this must be, when she suddenly stopped in her tracks, aghast.

It was a sober Rosemary who joined the jubilant sweep and his grandmother.

'I just gave the thing a twist, and phoom!, it suddenly went,' he explained in exhilaration, unscrewing the handle, section by section. 'Did you see what was causing the blockage, our Rose? What happened to it?'

'Um. Not really,' she said slowly. 'It sailed off into the garden somewhere.'

'I'll make a cup of tea,' announced Zinnia, 'we all deserve it.'

'Matthew, you're a murderer,' Rosemary hissed at him, as they heard sounds of the kettle being filled in the kitchen. 'You'd better come and look.'

Quietly they exited through the front door, and she led him towards the garage. There, beneath the delicate tracery of the Mount Etna Broom, lay a broken chimney pot, and beside it, stretched out on the ground, one of the precious Settlewort plants, snapped off at the base.

Matthew surveyed the scene. 'Whoops,' he said.

'I'll whoops you. What are we going to tell Zinnia?' demanded Rosemary. 'She's setting so much store by this damn plant.'

'We don't need to say anything', he decided. 'I'll remove the evidence, and she probably won't notice for days, specially with her bad foot.'

'But she's going to find out eventually. What do we tell her then?'

Matthew picked up the broken plant, and hefted it in his hand thoughtfully. Then he smiled brightly at his cousin.

'Oh, you'll think of something.'

****

He came home the next evening to find a small jar of greeny-coloured jam on the kitchen work-top, and his mother in an unusually good mood.

'I had to scale the recipe down,' she told him, rolling out some pastry. 'It said one pound of leaves, and three pounds of sugar, but of course those Betony leaves you brought didn't weigh anything like that. The stalks were quite heavy, and perhaps I should have used those as well, but I thought it was best to stick exactly to the recipe.'

'Stalks?' queried Matthew, raiding the flapjack tin in the larder. 'Now would I bring my esteemed mother anything but the best produce from Trugglestone Hall? They didn't have any stalks.'

'Yes, they did,' she insisted, adding a bit more flour to the board. 'Thick, sappy things. And the juice had a clingy smell too, quite nice though, rather like peaches.'

The flapjack that had been raised to her son's mouth slowly descended. He looked searchingly at his mother, unconcernedly cutting out the pastry to fit the top of a pie dish. She never teased. He went over to the fridge, and opened the door, with the wariness of a mongoose anticipating a snake. There, at the back of the bottom shelf was the little bag of Betony leaves that Susie had sent him home with the day before. And in the salad compartment, where he had hurriedly placed the stricken Settlewort plant, were now only lettuce, cucumber, and tomatoes.

He sat down at the kitchen table, a curious expression on his face.

'What, um... what was the Betony jam like?' he asked casually.

'Oh I didn't taste it,' his mother smiled at him. 'But we can try it this evening. There was a bit left over, so I made a small sponge cake and spread it in the middle. I thought we could have it as dessert. Lady Trugglestone will want to know what we think of the special jam, won't she?'

****

It was a pity that two hours later his mother's sunny mood should have been dissipated by the telephone call from Suffolk College, and the atmosphere was already laden by the time the family sat down to their evening meal. Veronica held back until they were just finishing the steak and kidney pie, then went in for the attack.

'According to the Examinations Manager, or whatever he called himself,' she said, like counsel opening for the prosecution, 'you haven't entered for any of the 'A' levels you're supposed to be taking, Matthew. You've just been pretending to work for them, when you weren't turning up at college even one day a week. You've been deceiving us.'

'Deceive you? Now would I?' her son responded lightly, scooping the last bit of mashed potato onto his fork. 'You just assumed that's where I was going, and it seemed a shame to disillusion you. Anyway, you should be pleased. I won't be able to fail them now, will I?'

Veronica regarded him with exasperation. 'But we agreed that you should retake them. And you could pass exams easily if you put even a tiny effort into it. You just can't be bothered, can you?'

'But Mum, what's the use of knowing all about Poor Law Reforms, or that alfalfa is a staple crop of Chile? It's hardly going to impress a future employer, is it?'

'What's alfalfa?' Derek unwisely wanted to know, pushing his emptied plate away.

Matthew grinned at him. 'Search me.'

Veronica glared at them both. 'The point is – and I shouldn't have to spell this out – you need a university degree to get anywhere today. And you can't get a place without 'A' levels. To say nothing of the fact that you've been misleading us.'

She gathered up the plates angrily, and took them into the kitchen, while Derek tried to remove a small gravy stain on the tablecloth, with his handkerchief. He wanted to keep out of this if at all possible.

'You know I was telling you about the Millennium Bug,' Matthew called towards the door. 'Every business in the country will have to have its computers checked to make sure they're not going to go haywire when the date flicks over to 2000. They're only just waking up to the problem now. But it'll be an absolute bonanza for the next three years. I could make zillions out of it. Not if I'm slaving away at some poxy university though, learning stuff that was out of date years ago.'

'That's all very well,' his mother said, returning with the jam-filled sponge cake on a plate. 'But you have to think about the long-term. Having a university degree will be something to fall back on. You never know what will happen in the future. Your father's worried about Thornways at the moment, and what he'd do if it folds, largely because he's got no qualifications. Isn't that right, Derek?'

'Mm,' he muttered unwillingly.

The sight of the cake, risen to perfection, green jam oozing from its moist-looking centre took the edge off Veronica's temper, as the satisfying results of her cooking always did.

'Now,' she announced in a somewhat mollified tone, sinking a knife into its centre, 'I want to know what you think about this.'

She passed a generous wedge on a plate to Derek. 'This has a special jam in it,' she told him self-importantly, 'made from one of Lady Trugglestone's herbal recipes.'

He sniffed it curiously. 'Smells as if it's got peaches in it.'

Matthew eyed the cake with uncharacteristic mistrust. 'I think I'll give it a miss this time', he said slowly. 'That steak and kidney pie was brilliant, but it's really filled me up.'

His mother looked pained. 'Oh but you must have some. Lady Trugglestone will want to know if you liked it,' and she cut a slice for him, leaving the last portion for herself.

As soon as he could, Matthew escaped to the kitchen. His offer of doing the washing up had surprised Veronica, but it was useful to have him out of the room while she tackled Derek. She wanted to make sure he would back her up in insisting that their wayward son didn't toss aside his future. He simply must not be allowed to squander his talents, as his father had. Pressure would have to be applied, and it was no good if they didn't present a united parental front.

Matthew could hear their raised voices as he dawdled over the washing up. The potato masher, he discovered, made a brilliant multiple-bubble dispenser, when you dipped it in soapy water, and then blew.

He might have won the skirmish over supper, but his mother was clearly regrouping for another assault. She just couldn't see things his way, that was the trouble. She was completely obsessed by the idea that you didn't get anywhere unless you had a degree.

The iridescent bubbles jostled each other in their upward scramble, then drifted slowly around the kitchen, each bursting with a moist little phut. Veronica's immaculately wiped worktop was soon dotted with small wet patches, like mermaid's kisses.

What was the point of always harping on about The Future? Matthew reflected. Life was a laugh right now. It was good fun working for Susie, and more and more people were ringing him up wanting computer advice. He didn't charge them much, they were usually friends of friends. But he could make quite a lot of money that way.

He lowered the potato masher into the washing up bowl and stirred it about in the water, as a thought obtruded: What if they were only asking him because they didn't have to pay much? He shrugged off the idea.

The HJ's were getting more bookings now, as well. Even if they didn't get a record contract – and of course they soon would – there was good dosh to be had from live gigs. It was a pity that Pete would be leaving in a few months to go to Birmingham University, but they would find another drummer. Bound to. And Josh's parents were emigrating to Canada next year, but he probably wasn't going to go with them. Yeah, the HJ's would be going strong for years.

A picture edged into his unwilling brain of himself at thirty – God, *ancient* – playing guitar at the twenty-first birthday of some well-off student at Cambridge. It was not a happy image, and he brushed it away.

He blew on the potato masher, but, with time and grease, the washing up liquid had lost the strength to create firm bubbles. One formed feebly, and burst in his face, stinging his eyes.

Surveying the dirty saucepans, he decided to give them a miss. Well, he couldn't be expected to do everything. When he had a place of his own he would invent throw-away saucepans. That wouldn't be for a while though, he had to admit. You needed to be rolling in it to afford a house. Unless you shared. Pete was going to live with four other students in Birmingham, he had it all fixed up. Idly, Matthew imagined life without parental influence at all. Parties, laid back drinking sessions, late night jamming. Man, that'd be brilliant.

He sighed, and swished the water round the bowl. How did people get like his parents? I mean you couldn't imagine them being young and funky, could you? If there was one thing he'd promise himself, it was that he wouldn't end up like his father – at the mercy of his boss and his wife.

The water gurgled away, and Matthew tried to ignore a small but insistent thought. Isn't that just what your mother is saying? it argued. That a degree would make sure you don't get trapped like your father?

The warring voices from the sitting room had quietened to a murmur as he dried his hands. He was relieved, then suddenly a little concerned. The Settlewort jam hadn't had any effect on him, he felt fine, but Derek had had a bigger slice of cake. It was obviously a load of hooey that the stuff did anything at all, but he ought to check that his father was okay, all the same.

It was letting himself in for further skirmishing. He knew perfectly well what the subject of the heated debate had been, and that Veronica was regrouping for further battle. His father would appear tense and morose, with a beaten look about him, while his mother would be tight-lipped and determined.

So as he poked his head round the sitting room door, he was unprepared for the sight of his parents companionably sitting on the settee together. Derek was outstretched, leaning back in a relaxed pose, with his hands behind his head. Veronica, legs tucked beneath her, was nestling into the cushions, an uncharacteristically benign expression on her face.

Matthew gaped. It was like discovering a Tyrannosaurus Rex being kittenish.

'Wondered if you'd like some coffee,' he enquired cautiously.

'Ah, we've been talking about you,' his mother said pleasantly. 'Come and sit down.'

'Your father and I have been discussing this university thing. And we realise that perhaps we have been a bit rigid in our thinking.'

Matthew glanced at Derek, who had largely sided with his son all along, but received no answering acknowledgement.

'This computer stuff,' Veronica went on, 'it does seem to move very fast, so perhaps you're right that university courses are not at the, er, cutting edge.' She was pleased with that phrase, it sounded knowledgeably sophisticated. 'If you want to do something in computers, than perhaps a degree is not as important as it would be in other things.'

Sitting opposite his parents, Matthew looked from one to the other, for once completely stalled. Especially as a few minutes ago he had privately conceded that ending up at university might just have things going for it.

'But it would be no bad thing for you to put together some kind of career map,' his father added mildly. 'Perhaps you could discuss that with the college, and then us, so we can see if there's anything we can do to help.'

'Although Bill Gates didn't seem to need much help, did he?' Veronica giggled. 'The Matthew Peasmore Corporation', she pretended to write it in the air. 'Sounds good, doesn't it. Our son, the multi-millionaire.'

'Are you, um...are you feeling all right?' enquired the disconcerted subject of her pipe dream.

'Just fine,' Veronica told him, giving a roguish sideways look at Derek. 'Absolutely terrific.'

****

'It was gross,' Matthew recounted to Rosemary the next day, as they treated themselves to the privacy of a pub lunch in the village. 'They were behaving like Romeo and Juliet. At their age! You should have seen them. It was just sad.'

'Really?' she commented drily. 'Didn't Juliet take some potion and go into a coma? Matthew how *could* you let them eat that stuff? You didn't know what effect it would have.'

'Well, in all that Herbal guff you read out, there was nothing about causing any harm, was there?'

'But we only think it's Settlewort. There's no proof,' Rosemary reminded him. 'You could have poisoned them.'

'Don't forget I had some myself,' protested Matthew defensively. He neglected to mention that this had not been entirely voluntary.

'And?'

'And what?'

Just then their ploughman's lunches arrived, brought to the table by Mrs Chitting's granddaughter, Tracy, who worked part-time at The Oak. Matthew gave her an appreciative look, and she sparkled back at him flirtatiously. Rosemary observed the body language with a mixture of empathy and scepticism, like a recent initiate into the realities of Father Christmas watching younger siblings lay out their stockings.

'I meant,' she went on firmly, opening the foil of her butter portion, 'how did it make you feel?'

'Oh, didn't have any effect on me,' he began breezily, but caught her eye. 'Well okay, it might have done. A bit.' And between mouthfuls of bread and cheese, he recounted how after supper he had reluctantly come round to the drift of his mother's argument, whereas before he had completely dismissed any idea of going to university.

'Kind of strange really,' he reflected, 'because I can't remember now why it seemed a good idea, it just did.'

'So you don't agree with her now?'

'God no. It'd be a complete waste of time. And money.' He waved his knife airily. 'By the time all that sad lecture fodder start looking for a job, I'll be halfway to my first million.'

'Wait a minute,' Rosemary fingered a slice of tomato thoughtfully, 'let me get this straight. After eating that Settlewort jam, you came round to your parents' way of thinking. And they saw your point of view, and you all felt kind of mellow. Is that right?'

'Sort of, yeah.'

'Only now the effect's worn off, you're back in your entrenched positions?'

'I suppose so. Why are you looking like that?'

'Jeez, it really works!' her face was animated. 'Don't you see, that plant just has to be Settlewort! Remember, that's what it was supposed to do – why it got its name.'

Her raised voice had caused a couple of people standing at the bar to glance their way curiously, and she looked round self-consciously.

'The thing is,' she continued quietly, edging her chair closer to the table, 'what are we going to do now?'

'Dose my Mum with it every day?' ventured Matthew, hopefully.

'Well, you'll certainly have to tell her what really happened.' Rosemary ignored his suggestion, while privately sympathising.

'Oh no,' he protested. 'I was just going to buy some gooseberry jam or something, and swap it for the jar Mum made. She won't taste it, so she won't know.'

'What about Susie? She's trying to find special stock for the shop. Gooseberry jam bought in a supermarket hardly fills the bill, does it?'

Matthew fidgeted, folding the butter foil into little wands, and pressing them smooth.

'And Zinnia,' Rosemary continued relentlessly, 'who's going to tell her that one of her precious Settlewort plants just met its jam maker?'

They looked at each other, and simultaneously declared, 'You are!'

Chapter Twelve

The following day her aunt received Rosemary's account of the Settlewort jam saga with distress, but even Zinnia could see there was little point in being angry. After all, the chimney pot's unerring aim could hardly be blamed on anyone. And there were still two plants left.

'But if anyone touches those,' she said fiercely, 'I'll twist their ears off. Why on earth didn't you tell me what had happened though? I could have tried to take cuttings from it.'

Rosemary was peeling the potatoes for their evening meal, while Zinnia sat at the kitchen table trimming broccoli spears into a saucepan. Roger the Lodger stretched somnolently in his cardboard box beside the stove, not even bothering to monitor the surrounding activity. Vegetable preparations were decidedly unpromising.

'I reckon it's better that we've found out what effect Settlewort has on people.' Rosemary looked up from pulling wedged skins out of the potato peeler. 'After all, you wouldn't have taken a chance like that, would you? Made people eat it, I mean.'

Her aunt didn't answer. She was thinking.

'So where's the jar of Settlewort jam now?' she enquired casually.

'In Veronica's kitchen, I think. Matthew 'forgot' to take it to Susie this morning. We decided he should tell his mother what happened, and ask her to make the proper Betony recipe tomorrow.

'I see.'

Zinnia limped over to the sink, and Rosemary stood aside while she ran cold water onto the broccoli spears. 'Well, I'll ask her if she'll bring it over tomorrow. After all, it was my Settlewort plant. I rather think It's my jam.' She plonked the saucepan on the draining board, with a secretive little smile, like a dieter with chocolate cake hidden behind the sofa.

'What are you going to do with it?' a suspicious Rosemary demanded.

'Oh, nothing much,' she shrugged, sweeping the broccoli leaves and stalks from the kitchen table, with her hands.

'I sure won't be eating in this house if you're going to be spooning that stuff into the food,' her niece informed her firmly. 'It'd be like living with Lucrezia Borgia.'

'Lucrezia Borgia went around poisoning people,' Zinnia retorted. 'Jam made from Settlewort isn't going to poison anyone. Besides, I wouldn't waste it on you.'

Cutting up the potatoes, Rosemary absorbed this information. 'Did you have someone else in mind?' she enquired apprehensively, wondering if she shouldn't nip round to Matthew's house now, and destroy the wretched stuff.

'Well, I was just thinking,' Zinnia smiled sweetly, 'that it was about time I had a talk with that Swathe man, who's bought the Pit. See if he can be persuaded to drop this awful idea of filling it with rubbish.'

'That's hardly likely, is it?' commented Rosemary, who wasn't connecting too well.

'Can't do any harm to discuss his plans though, can it?' Her aunt's tone was deceptively light. 'In fact, I rather thought I might invite him here for tea.'

****

The revelation that he had consumed jam made from one of the rarest plants on earth did not, in the event, make much impact on Derek. He had other things on his mind. Gerry Thornway chose the very next day to announce that negotiations had been going on for the sale of Thornways to Clumpings International – in fact the process was now well advanced – and the news caused consternation within the small company. Derek had kept the unhappy secret for some time, and now, as, as General Manager, had a duty to uphold his boss's line. The sale would supposedly be good for the firm, and open up opportunities for investment and expansion – all that guff. But he didn't believe a word of it. Neither, he suspected, would Prentice Stalker.

Derek regarded Prentice as a cold fish, humourless and pedantic. But with Frank Smiley, the Marketing Manager gone, and Gerry Thornway wearing both the Finance and Managing Director hats, and firmly in Clumping's pocket, there was now an urgent need to put their frosty relations into the microwave.

He approached Prentice Stalker's office somewhat reluctantly. The man was obsessed with carnivorous plants, and had a large collection at home, some of which he brought to the office. They lined the windowsill, glowered from the tops of filing cabinets, and squatted malignly on the desk. Derek found their sinister shapes strange and threatening. What's more, they stank. The stagnant water the pots stood in gave the office a stale, rotting smell that turned his stomach. Mind you, he reflected walking along the corridor, it was quite a good method of speeding people on their way. No-one was likely to linger, chatting idly, when they were gasping for fresh, wholesome air. Perhaps he could adopt a similar strategy for keeping Gerry Thornway out of his own office.

He frowned at the thought of his unloved boss. Smarmy git. And now he was selling the company his father had worked so hard to build up, and everyone would be abandoned to the scrap heap, in all probability. Well, he wouldn't accept that without a fight, and he might as well try and recruit Prentice Stalker to the resistance. He knocked on the door, and repressed a smile at a sudden thought. Perhaps the man could set his plants on the Clumpings people. That'd be enough to scare anyone away.

After they'd finished discussing a customer complaint, Derek broached the subject he'd really come about.

'Clumpings are just going to take over the Thomways brand name, and close this place down, aren't they?' he declared gloomily. 'You and I and all the workforce will be out of a job.'

'Well, I don't know that it's as bad as that,' Prentice countered, in his rather supercilious manner.. He was a thin, upright man, with short, greying hair, and wire-rimmed spectacles. His wide, brainy-looking forehead and clipped beard made his face appear triangular, and he gave the impression of being preoccupied with more important matters whenever you wanted to speak to him. Matthew, on one of his holiday work sessions at Thomways, had nicknamed him the Mad Professor. At fifty-four, Prentice Stalker would probably not find it easier to get another local job than he would himself, Derek reflected, and tried to feel sorry about that. After all, they had a battle to fight together.

'You didn't know Old Man Thornway, did you,' he said, sitting on the edge of Prentice's desk, and trying to ignore the gaping throat of an obscene looking plant at his elbow. 'But he'd never have done this to the people who'd worked loyally for him, however bad things got. He'd rather have given the company to them.'

'Some of the older ones have been saying much the same, this morning,' Prentice agreed, as he got up and adjusted the blind, protecting the plants on the windowsill from strong sunshine.

'Several people have asked me if we couldn't organise a Buy-out, and run the company ourselves,' Derek said slowly. 'It's a possibility that we should at least look at, don't you agree?'

'Hm.' Prentice stroked his beard and considered. He had, with some dismay, come to the same conclusion about his future work prospects as

Derek, and didn't relish the idea of being the only member of the County Council who was on the Unemployed Register. On the other hand, he'd never regarded his job as anything other than a regrettable necessity. The idea of flinging himself into a company, determined to make it succeed and grow, held no appeal. It would mean long hours of work, which would take him away from his beloved plants, for one thing. Might even scupper his dearest ambition, of being invited to become a committee member by the Royal Horticultural Society. They expected you to be available for committee meetings, and things like judging. He could just see himself as a judge at the Chelsea Flower Show.

'It would be a non-starter if it involved putting in large amounts of capital,' he objected cautiously. 'Daphne would never agree to anything like that.'

'Well I don't have any money anyway,' Derek told him frankly. 'But I was talking to someone at a Vintage Tractor Rally last summer who'd been involved in a Management Buy Out, and he found a venture capitalist who was prepared to put up the money, in return for shares. He was very pleased by the outcome. Although he did say he'd never worked so hard in his life.'

Their discussion finally bore fruit to the extent that by the time Derek emerged, his clothes smelling dankly, they had agreed to contact a venture capital company, and see where that led. But Derek was unconvinced that Prentice Stalker was a pillar on which much could be built. To be honest, he wasn't sure that he himself was much better. Running the production side of Thornways from day to day was not a problem, but he had no experience of company finance, or the higher profile role of managing director.

He glanced across the large car park on his way back to his own office. It was underused space, and he smiled wryly, remembering how Old Man Thornway had refused to sell any of it for development, when the company had hit a bad patch. 'We can expand on to it ourselves one day,' he'd said optimistically. 'Far more use to us as growth potential, than a few thousand in the bank.' The company had been very dear to the man's heart.

Derek's eye fell on Gerry Thornway's gleaming new car. Goodness knows how much money the Old Man's son had taken out of the company to fund his lavish lifestyle. They would have to bring in a Finance guy. Gerry should never have tried to do it himself, despite his accountancy training. And probably the venture capital people would want to put in their own man as Managing Director. As long as they got on okay, Derek wouldn't mind. He wasn't at all sure that he was chief executive material.

Veronica, that evening, had no such doubts. She was thrilled with the idea of a Management Buy Out, when Derek discussed it with her. The thought of being the Managing Director's wife appealed no end.

'Of *course* you must go for it,' she urged him excitedly. 'You're the one running that place as it is. I've always said you never got the credit you deserve.'

Derek couldn't recall her coming out with quite this form of words.

'Do you think Gerry consulted Elaine about all this?' Veronica went on. 'She hasn't said anything on our Health Club mornings.'

'You mustn't breathe a word to her at this stage about the chance of a Management Buy Out,' instructed Derek, wondering whether secrecy was going to be possible. 'It's really important that we don't say anything until we're further down the line.'

'I always knew you should have been Managing Director,' Veronica told him proudly, gratified to think that her choice of husband had been proved right after all.

'It' s only an outside possibility,' he warned. 'There's so little time to get anything organised. And Gerry's told us that Clumpings' people will be crawling all over the place, doing due diligence, so we'll have to spend hours getting all sorts of information for them. How on earth am I going to do that, and organise an MBO, and run the place all at the same time?'

'What's due... whatever you said?' Veronica asked suspiciously.

'Due diligence? It just means that they'll be examining the books and asking enough questions to get a picture of exactly what state the business is in.' A thought struck him. 'I wonder what line Gerry has spun them?'

The day after, it became clear that Gerry Thornway had been exercising his imagination where quite a few things about the business were concerned, whilst glossing over inconvenient little facts, like investment, cash-flow, and profits.

'I told them you had several new products in the pipeline,' he declared airily, having called Derek into his lavishly appointed office.

'But we haven't,' he protested. 'That's part of the...' he was going to say 'trouble', but there was no point in irritating his boss, who never liked him pointing out that Thornways was not going splendidly under its illustrious Managing Director.

Gerry had moved on anyway. Flicking into motion one of the executive toys on his desk, he interrupted. 'So I want you to polish up that Feasibility Report you did, on diversifying into the health food market. Cut out all that stuff about new machinery, staff and investment. They don't need to know that. Oh, and Peasmore,' he leaned back imperiously in his black leather chair, the lock of hair trained over his bald patch shifting insecurely, 'You will of course want to be helpful to the Clumpings due diligence people, but not too helpful, eh.'

Derek felt like a tin can, with steam rollers approaching from two directions. 'Now I know what they mean by a fall guy,' he thought gloomily, a few minutes later, waiting for the coffee dispenser to part with a slopped-over cup of brown gunge. 'If I spin Clumpings along to please Gerry, they'll sack me as soon as they take over. But if I tell them like it is, and they back out, Gerry will give me the boot.'

Taking a sip of the coffee, he swore as he burnt his tongue, and not just at the pain. He wouldn't let these people walk all over him, he promised himself. This idea of organising a Management Buy Out – they really would give it a go. He retreated to his office and shut the door. Being independent, and able to run Thornways properly, was suddenly gaining in attraction.

****

Next afternoon Gerry Thornway decided to visit Lady Susan Trugglestone. The sales team divided most areas of the country between them, but Frank Smiley had covered Suffolk himself. Not replacing his Sales Director meant that the home patch had had to manage on its own of late, since you could hardly expect the Managing Director to waste time visiting customers.

Lady Trugglestone was rather different, he thought to himself, enjoying the powerful revs of his car, as he backed out of his special parking space. He had yet to meet her, although he remembered Clive, from the year above him at Greshams School. Unfortunately, efforts to remind Clive Trugglestone and other ex-pupils in the area that they had great memories of a shared educational journey, somehow met with collective amnesia. It nettled him. Even though Thornways was a well-known name, he got the impression these people looked down on him as 'trade'. Well, that was going to change, he told himself, swinging the car round a tight bend and accelerating along the narrow road. When he'd sold Thornways and was part owner of Stockleigh Golf Club, they would be more than happy to socialise with him in the bar.

Clive and his wife had unfortunately not been free on the two occasions in the past few months he'd sent invitations to dinner. But Elaine had told him about the Walled Herb Garden and Tea Shop that the new Lady Trugglestone was due to open soon, and he felt it would be remiss of him not to introduce himself. The place was going to be included in the Gardens Open Day, as was his own garden, he thought smugly. He would drop that into the conversation. And of course she would be doing a roaring trade in teas.

Approaching the village at almost twice the speed limit, he glanced at his reflection in the rear view mirror. Lady Trugglestone could hardly fail to appreciate Gerald Thornway himself coming to talk to her about Thornways' famous herbal teas, he told himself. She must be aware of the range already, of course, but perhaps she just hadn't thought about stocking them. It would be pleasing too, to be able to mention her name casually to the Clumpings people:- 'As I was saying to Lady Trugglestone, one of our most enthusiastic local customers, only the other day...'

Knowing Lady Julia, he expected the new mistress of Trugglestone Hall to be on similarly elegant lines, and was taken aback to discover that his aristocratic potential customer was, tousle-haired and muddy, helping to set up an automatic irrigation system in the plant sales area.

'It s just dribbling out of the nozzles,' she was calling to Rosemary and Matthew, as he appeared. 'Have you got the water turned up full?'

What happened next was, according to an innocently wide-eyed Matthew later, entirely accidental. A snail, partially blocking the main pipe, happened to get dislodged just at the moment Gerry introduced himself to Susie. The result was that as he stood between her and one of the dribbling spray nozzles, it suddenly burst into life, and he received the wetting spray full in the back.

The ensuing kerfuffle entirely spoilt his planned approach. Matthew and Rosemary clutched each other helplessly, and disappeared from sight, while Susie, apologising profusely, brought him into the Tea Room, to try and dry his jacket.

Normally she would have brushed aside his visit with the polite coolness that she was learning people accepted from titled ladies. But under the circumstances, a glass of lemon cordial and some smoothing of ruffled feathers seemed called for, plus a slightly gentler refusal of Thornways' wares.

'You see people just want a good old cuppa tea,' she explained, tearing off several sheets of paper towel, 'and that's what they're going to get. Nothing fancy.'

'But I'm sure you'll want to stock Thornways' Herbal Teas on the shelves, as a product they can buy in the shop.' Sitting at one of the tables, Gerry tried to sound urbane, but was feeling undignified minus his jacket, like a zebra without its stripes.

'Well, the thing is,' Susie wanted to be diplomatic, 'Thornways Teas are so well known, aren't they. And awfully good of course. You must be very proud of the firm.'

Completely pervious to flattery, a pleased expression crossed her visitor's face.

'But we can all go into a supermarket and buy them,' she continued, laying his wet jacket down on a neighbouring table. 'I rather wanted to stock more unusual stuff, that people couldn't easily get anywhere else. Things like herb pillows, tinctures and natural dyeing kits.'

She was pressing the paper towels onto the material to soak up the moisture, when there was a knock at the door.

'In fact,' she said, going to open it, 'I'm thinking of creating a range of herb-based jams, that will really be unique.'

On the doorstep stood a rather plump woman, wearing a smart turquoise suit, with carefully matched blouse and earrings, and holding a small jar, decoratively labelled 'Betony Jam'.

'Good heavens,' exclaimed Susie. 'You must be Matthew's mother. How nice to of you to come. And what a coincidence. I was just telling Mr Thornway here, about the herbal jams we want to try out for the shop. Do you two know each other?'

Veronica found herself ushered into a large, low-ceilinged room, set about with chairs and tables, at one of which sat her husband's boss, in his shirtsleeves, glaring at her. And could this mud-spattered, freckle-faced woman really be the new Lady Trugglestone, up to now only glimpsed at a distance in the village, or driving past in her car? Disappointment, and confusion at finding them inexplicably in each other's company rendered Veronica's brain, never incisive, incapable of coherent thought.

At Susie's invitation she sat down, putting the jar down on the table in front of her.

'I haven't tasted this one, but the Settlewort jam was delicious,' she twittered nervously, like a budgerigar on fast forward.

'What did you say?' Susie paused, while getting another glass out of a cupboard.

'The Settlewort jam. I expect Matthew told you all about how I made it by mistake. So silly of me.' She gave a little laugh. 'But he put it in the fridge, you see, and I thought it was for that old recipe you sent him home with. It made a very nice jam though.'

Glass in hand, Susie stared at her.

'Matthew had some *Settlewort!*' she said incredulously. 'You can't mean it.'

Gerry was becoming increasingly impatient. First of all his dignity had been upset by the water spraying episode, and now his manager's wife had the impertinence to hijack his sales pitch, just when he had the customer in the palm of his hand.

'Whatever it was, it can't have been very important,' he cut in brusquely, and gave a dismissive nod to Veronica. 'Lady Trugglestone and I were just talking about stock for the Tea Shop.'

'Settlewort. Not important!' Susie rounded on him. 'That's a bit thick, coming from someone who sells herbal teas. Don't you know it was one of the most interesting herbs ever known?' And it's supposed to have been extinct for over a century.'

She turned urgently to Veronica. 'How on earth does Matthew know what it looks like? *Matthew,* of all people! And where did he find it growing? I must go and see.'

'Oh my mother-in-law's a very keen gardener,' began Veronica, but warning voices were beginning to overlay her pleasure at being the centre of attention. She remembered the chaos of the bird watchers' invasion, and, oh dear, that Zinnia was going to pretend Settlewort had spontaneously appeared in The Pit.

'Of course it might not be Settlewort,' she stammered, trying to backtrack. 'Probably isn't, in fact. But, er, the Betony jam, I hope it's what you wanted.'

Suddenly keen to leave, she got up and headed for the door. 'I won't stay,' she said hurriedly, 'but I'd be very pleased to try out any other recipes for you, Lady Trugglestone.'

'Won't you have a glass of lemonade or something,' Susie urged, 'I'd like to hear more about...'

'No thank you, I can see you're busy,' Veronica gave a weak smile. 'Very nice to meet you.'

'Now,' Gerry tried to recover his genial tone, as she closed the door, 'we were just talking about teas for your shop, weren't we. And of course, teas for the Gardens Festival. My garden has been chosen for that, you know.'

'Really,' said Susie distantly. 'Actually we're not now doing the official Teas for that. The W.I. are going to do them in the Village Hall. I suggest you talk to Daphne Stalker about it, if you want them to offer Thornways Teas.'

She picked up his jacket, now less sodden, but not as dry as she could have made it, given the inclination, and handed it to him.

Her meaning was clear, even to Gerry.

'But what about stocking our herbal teas in the shop?' he tried, grimacing as the dampness chilled his back.

'Well perhaps you would leave me some literature about them, and a price list,' she suggested smoothly, walking him to the door. 'It was good of you to call, Mr Thornway.'

She stood there, after he'd left, her head in a whirl. Settlewort! Matthew had somehow found some Settlewort. It couldn't be true. Then she remembered Rosemary's sudden interest in the herb. What were those two up to? And why hadn't they confided in her – she, who was specialising in herbs. She felt betrayed, and it was hurtful.

Taking the glass off the table, she went through to the kitchen to wash it, trying to collect her thoughts.

Settlewort reappeared! Somewhere in the village. Could it really have happened? she asked herself, imagining the stir it would make in the herb world. And, she suddenly realised with a thrill, what a boost it would give to the Walled Herb Garden, if she could grow some plants of it. Talk about a publicity coup – you couldn't ask for anything better.

Hold on, a thought struck as she dried her hands, what if there was only one, and Matthew had picked it? Oh that just didn't bear thinking about. But then, she reasoned, Matthew wouldn't go round picking wild flowers. The whole thing simply didn't make sense.

Head up determinedly, she stepped onto the newly gravelled path outside the Tea Room, and went in search of her helpers.

She found them attempting to monitor on the meter the amount of water used by the sprinkler system. Rosemary looked rather guilty, while Matthew was evidently pleased with himself.

'Because of you,' Susie sounded like a teacher taking detentions, 'I have had to be unnaturally polite to Geny Thomway. And,' she looked from one to the other severely, 'you stand accused of the even more serious charge of withholding vital information. What's this about Settlewort reappearing?'

She saw them look at each other.

'I want to hear all about it, or it's the dungeons for you both.'

'Trugglestone Hall hasn't got any dungeons,' Matthew aimed a disarming smile at her, in vain.

'We'll dig some,' she said grimly. 'Come on. Tell me.'

****

Gerry Thornway smarted with indignation as he drove home. The Managing Director of Thornways had taken the trouble to call on a prospective customer, and been given the brush off. What was it she'd said? 'That's a bit thick, coming from someone who sells herbal teas.' *Sells herbal teas!* He, the owner of a famous company, had first been humiliated by her staff, and then treated like a two-a-penny salesman.

Didn't she know he wasn't supposed to be genned up on detail like that? She wasn't talking to some underling after all. That sort of thing was what he employed staff for.

He turned into his drive, and pulled up outside the house with a scrunch of flying stones.

Susan Trugglestone knew about herbs though, he suddenly thought to himself, and something had made her excited enough to turf him out. Just when he was gaining her confidence. He tapped the leather steering wheel with his fingers. Settlewort, she'd said. 'One of the most interesting herbs ever known.'

The peahen wandered across the grass towards his car. He watched it, with his thoughts elsewhere. If Thornways could get a supply of the stuff, it occurred to him, and have plans for making Settlewort herbal tea, that would impress the Clumpings people no end. A unique product. Hah! They'd love that.

But how to set about it? Where was this herb, for a start, and what was so special about it? He frowned as he reached across for his coat. His general manager's wife had somehow got hold of the stuff, although she obviously didn't realise it was anything special. He could just ask Peasmore about it. But there was a rumour that he was trying to organise a management buyout. He'd never liked the man, and now he was not to be trusted with confidential information.

Gerry swung open the door, almost decapitating the bird, which squawked and scuttled off in alarm. He would put Prentice Stalker on to the problem, he decided, pointing the central locking fob at the car. He could easily look up whatever was in books, and the man was keen on plants as well, so it would seem natural for him to be asking about some new and interesting plant in the village.

With careful handling, he concluded with satisfaction, this afternoon's visit might just turn into a trump card, which he could use to screw a much better price for the company out of Clumpings.

He gave a lordly wave to Harry Trench, who was sweeping the lawn with the slow, and steady sureness of a closing lock gate. He gave no sign of noticing.

Pleased with his own astuteness, Gerry went in to change and fetch his golf clubs.

Chapter Thirteen

Two days later, Daphne Stalker was having husband trouble, and it was making her short-tempered. So much of the village's affairs ended up on her shoulders, it was unfair of Prentice to be adding to them, she thought with annoyance, running a hand distractedly over her neatly cropped grey hair. And it wasn't like him to be intransigent, where her plans were concerned. She dumped her music books down on the piano top, and decided to tackle him about it this evening. Get him to see reason. Meanwhile, her disciplined side instructed, better concentrate on this afternoon's Junior Choir practice.

'As you know,' she said, peering over her glasses at the assembled children, standing in various states of boredom round the piano, 'the choir is going to be singing several traditional country songs at the village's Gardens and Flower Festival, in July.'

A small girl, overburdened with a large brace on her teeth, put up her hand. 'Mrs Stalker, my Mum says we'd look ever so nice dressed as milkmaids.'

A ripple of derision passed along the row of boys at the back, and Daphne moved swiftly to quash that one. 'I think it would look neater if you were all in your school uniforms, Angelica,' she said firmly. 'Nothing to stop you dressing up as a milkmaid for the Fancy Dress, of course. Now, we're going to sing a mix of songs everyone knows, and ones that are less famil...'

Her words were drowned out by a sudden tattoo of stamping feet, from the Cubs' meeting in a screened-off section the other end of the hall. An arcane ritual of some sort, no doubt, she thought with irritation. There could be no better illustration of how badly they needed this new hall the village was raising money for.

'We'll start off with *Barbara Allen*,' she informed her choristers briskly, 'everyone likes that.'

'I don't, it's stupid,' a bristle-haired boy muttered audibly, and sullenly declined to join in, preferring to poke his finger into the ribs of the girl in front of him in time to the music, until Daphne broke off in exasperation.

'Dennis, that's enough, leave Sharon alone.' She tried flattery. 'You've got a very good voice, let's hear it.'

'My Mum'd kill me if I told her to make my bed, like what it says in the song,' he objected truculently. 'I have to make me own, or she shouts at me.'

Daphne experienced a certain sympathy with the woman in question. But music teachers were, like estate agents, supposed to remain positive at all times.

She handed him a spare copy of "Sing Together!" 'I tell you what,' her voice remained level, 'look through this, and you can choose a song for us,' and she was gratified when he sat down at the side of the hall, flicking through the pages with apparent interest. Men were only grown-up boys, she allowed herself to reflect fleetingly. She would manage Prentice in just the same way.

The choir had negotiated its way uneventfully, if a little reedily, through *Early One Morning, Bobby Shafto* and *Donkey Riding*, by the time she summoned the absentee chorister.

'What have you found for us to sing?' she enquired, and was pleasantly surprised to be handed the book open at a song entitled *The Shepherdess*.

'That one looks good, Miss,' he requested, and gave her an unexpected little smile.

'Right, page twenty-eight everyone,' she instructed, quickly scanning through the music of a song that was new to her, and gave them an encouraging nod with the first notes.

'*A shepherdess was watching,*' the children began hesitantly.

'Then the chorus,' she called, '*Ding-dong, ding-dong, ting-a-ling, ding dong*". Nice and strong. You're supposed to be bells.'

What an odd choice Dennis had made.

'*Her flock the whole day long, ding-dong, her flock the whole day long.*'

You'd think it would have been something stirring like *Hearts of Oak*, or *The British Grenadiers*. Out of the corner of her eye, Daphne Stalker could see Dennis whispering to the boy next to him, but decided against remarking on it, as the rest of the choir moved on to the cheese the shepherdess made one morning, ding-dong.

'Third verse,' she called, giving the back row a hard look over her glasses.

'*Her pussy-cat lay winking, Ding-dong, ding-dong, ting-a-ling, ding dong.*'

At that moment there was a deafening cheer from the Cubs, just as the boys at the back collapsed in a fit of noisy sniggering.

Daphne ran her eye over the remaining verses, and hastily decided that the hall clock was probably several minutes slow.

'Well, that's all we've got time for now,' she announced in considerable annoyance, as the choir broke up in disarray. 'Next week we'll have to start working hard on our songs for the recital...' but her voice was drowned out by the sound of chairs being stacked, and another joyous shout from the other end of the room.

****

'We've just got to raise this money for the new hall,' she told Prentice sharply, a couple of hours later, 'it's so important. And the Millennium Commission won't budge on the conditions. We have to match their grant by October, or we don't get it at all.'

He'd been run to ground, unsurprisingly, in the larger of his two greenhouses. She stood inside the door while he carefully filled up one of the growing trays with a watering can, the fetid smell of stagnant water beginning to explore the air, like a rat checking for danger.

'Well, I'm sure the money will come rolling in,' he told her, with no evident enthusiasm.

'Yes, but we need all the gardens to be open, Prentice. And,' she added cogently, 'your carnivorous plant collection was going to be one of the big draws. Lots of people have never seen plants like that before.'

'You know me, Daphne,' he responded loftily. 'If I do a thing, I do it properly.'

He squeezed past her to the water butt outside, and stood while the can refilled. 'It should be a learning process,' he insisted. 'I'd want to do all sorts of information panels, about where each plant came from, for instance, a bit about its history, its habitat, how to grow it and propagate it.' He turned off the stopcock, and carried the full watering can inside. 'And I just won't have time to concentrate on exhibiting them as they should be shown. You know how important the County Council work is. And then you've roped me into being Treasurer of the Open Gardens Day.' There was a hint of rebellion in his voice..

'Yes, but...'

'Plus this Management Buyout thing is going to take up so much time,' he interrupted her, reaching for another plant tray. 'I spent the whole of this morning getting a mass of figures together. These Venture Capitalists talk a completely different language – Mezzanine Finance, Bimbos and Comfort Factors – Derek and I haven't a clue what they're on about.'

'It's not going to happen though, is it,' his wife addressed his stooping back

'What?'

'This buying Gerry out... you haven't a hope in hell.'

He straightened up, and looked at her for the first time. 'Possibly not,' he conceded reluctantly. 'Gerry Thornway hasn't said he won't sell to us if we got the finance together, but it's clear he'd much rather do a deal with Clumpings. Quick and easy, and he can swagger off and buy into Stockleigh Golf Club. Mind you,' he resumed his watering, 'the Clumpings people are making some rather unhappy noises at the moment. They insist on turning over stones, and then don't like what they find underneath.' He gave a wry smile.

'So you've suddenly decided not to open the garden because of this nonsense about a Management Buy Out. Which isn't going to come off, and you aren't suited to anyway.' Her tone reflected the resentment she felt at the undermining of her own efforts, like a hostess whose husband has just revealed that the much-praised dinner was entirely bought in. 'Working all the hours God gave to run your own company. It's just not your style, is it. Be honest.'

He didn't reply.

'Prentice, you must see how embarrassing this is for me.' She knew she was treading a fine line between being reproachful, and outright scolding, which might have had a detrimental effect.

'It's been quite a struggle to get some of the owners to open their gardens,' she complained. 'And now you've dropped this bombshell about our own garden not being included. It's going to make me look so hypocritical.'

'I won't have time to do it properly,' he repeated obstinately, picking some dead leaves off the plant he had just adjusted to summer growing conditions. 'As befits someone who might be asked to join an RHS Floral Committee. None of your amateur stuff.'

Daphne regarded him calculatingly, an alternative line of attack beginning to form.

'You do realise,' she said slowly, 'that Loretta Moss is coming to judge the Flower Arrangement Competition.'

'So?'

'Well, she's a big noise in the horticultural world. We were lucky to get her. And,' she added, hoping it was true, 'she has a lot of influence with the top brass of the Royal Horticultural Society, I believe.' There was no indication that he was listening, but she ploughed on.

'Mrs Moss is bound to be impressed if you displayed your plant collection the way you want to. You'd have the chance to talk to her, and I'm sure she'd remember you when they're thinking about appointing people to the floral committees.'

There was silence.

'This proposed Management Buy Out, Prentice,' she went on persuasively, 'it's a complete waste of time, you know it is. Why don't you concentrate on what you really want? You won't get on that RHS Committee by being half-hearted about it.'

He took Sarracenia 'Sultry Maid' from the shelf above the workbench, and stood its pot in the tray of stagnant water.

'Well, okay,' he said at last, without looking at her. 'You're probably right. And,' he added thoughtfully, fingering one of its leaves, 'it so happens there might soon be another thing in my favour at the RHS. Gerry Thornway has asked me to investigate some report that Settlewort – you know the thing the village is named after – has reappeared here. Now if I could exhibit *that* at one of the RHS shows, they'd certainly sit up and take notice.'

He turned to her questioningly. 'You haven't heard anything about where it might be growing, have you?'

****

Who was it said, "Reality is where you are"? It's so true, Rosemary began her e-mail to Bill the following Monday. *I know that you must be facing unimaginable cold, ice and wind, but the trouble is it's just that – unimaginable to me.*

First few days into May, and here everything is growing like crazy. Yesterday Zinnia took me to see a Bluebell Wood.. I guess it's no good describing a breathtaking carpet of blue stretching as far as the eye could see, because your reality is a numbing whiteness. But it gave me a real buzz. ('Where d'ya get ya thrills from, lady? Blue flowers in woods, huh? Get a life.')

There's not so much for me to do now for Susie. She's just about ready to open, although it's still too early to plant some things out. In case of late frosts, they're still in the greenhouse, now that old Harry Trench has been persuaded to remove all his stuff out of there to Mrs Chitting's garden. I suggested The Herb Garden ought to open early, but Susie wants to wait until the date announced in the leaflets and press release, and then have a Grand Opening.

She had high hopes of being able to use Settlewort as a tie-in to the opening, when she first found out about it, but Zinnia soon put her right on that. Wouldn't even let her see the plant. Jeez, that was awkward. I owe both of them a lot, and suddenly felt the need to go for a long walk. (I'm so fit now, you wouldn't believe.)

I like her mum-in-law, Lady Julia too, and both Susie and Zinnia are hardly on speaking terms with the poor woman. Julia disapproves of converting the stables to a Tea Room, and reckons Susie ought to go on producing children till she has a boy to inherit the title (what is it with these people!). Also, Susie seems to think her dear mother-in-law used her influence to get the official Teas for the Gardens Festival based in the Village Hall, instead of at the Walled Herb Garden, just to spite her. I'm sure that can't be right. (Whaddya mean − "Blessed are the peace makers?" I'm sure as hell keeping out of it.)

Zinnia's feud with Julia seems to concern selling the Pit Garden to a guy named Mike Swathe. That Odious Little Man, she calls him. So far the OLM has resisted pressing invitations to come to tea at Kiln House and discuss things. Wise, I'd say. She's fixing to put Settlewort jam on his scones, and have him eating out of her hand. As it were. Ye gods, where would that leave me? 'So, Miss Keel, you don't deny that you knew the deceased was going to be given this plant-based substance by your aunt...'

Would you still marry a convict?

If your imagination has managed to adjust, and now sees me gambolling with cute lambs across green grass in the sunshine... forget it. If there's one thing that riles these country Brits, it must be seeing someone with not enough to do. Leastways, Julia Trugglestone has asked me to take on something that'll soak up a deal of time. She's a big cheese in the organisation of this Gardens and Flower Festival thing, and says the publicity side of it wasn't being handled 'as well as it might be'. (They're so polite these aristos. Especially when they're sticking the knife in.) And boy, is she smart at making a body feel good. By the time she was through telling me what a capable, reliable, and resourceful Publicity

Officer I'd be, I was wondering why the White House hadn't come head-hunting years ago.

So now I've been given the task of teaming up with Nigella Picket, the one who 'wasn't handling it...etc'. Should be interesting. Persuading businesses to advertise in the programme, making contact with television and local radio, printing leaflets, getting the press on board. The organisers are desperate to make a splash with this Festival thing, and raise a lot of money. I'd sure like to help, it sounds fun. But only if I can get on okay with this Nigella person. Am searching for the key to my Tact Store, before going to see her tomorrow. I already met her a couple of times, and reckon I'm going to need it. Wish me luck.

****

It took Rosemary some time next day to work out why Nigella Picket was not in the least offended by having her drafted in to help with Publicity. At first she thought Julia Trugglestone's diplomacy must have reached superhuman levels, but slowly the truth dawned on her. Nigella's supreme self confidence was not only impervious to criticism, she simply failed to perceive any.

The sun was shining gloriously, promising one of those hot days of late Spring which have young mothers rushing to don bikinis in the garden, while the older generation swelter in their vests, muttering about May being a treacherous month. Rosemary had sensibly put on layers, several of which had been peeled off by the time she reached the village. She leant on the bridge for a moment to enjoy the gurgling water and the last of the gentle mistiness over the water meadows. Walking up Mill Lane, with the river on one side, and the small estate of houses on the other, apprehensively she practised insincere-sounding reasons why she might have been asked to help. But in the event there was no need.

Nigella, out in the garden, had evidently been watching the lane, and bounded to greet her at the gate, her blonde-streaked bob an advertisement for Ipswich's most expensive hairdresser. Figure-hugging jeans had not yet given way to shorts, but her patterned pink shirt had been tied in a neat bow at the front, leaving two-inches of midriff in homage to the sun.

'*Wonderful* timing,' she exclaimed animatedly, 'Angelica's at school, and I've just dropped Miles off at Playgroup, so we've got the morning to ourselves.'

Rosemary opened her mouth, but the flow carried on.

'I'm so pleased Lady Julia has asked you. We're going to have *such* fun! I'll show you all I've been doing, but first you *must* come and do a tour of the garden. It was raining when you brought your aunt's garden description here, back in March, do you remember?'

Rosemary did. Also having to smooth down an outraged Zinnia, after she'd read Nigella Picket's resulting summary of the garden at Kiln House, for the publicity material. 'This bears no resemblance to my description! None at all,' her aunt had spluttered. 'She's gone overboard about "famous columnist for Country Harvest", and all that, and then made it sound as if the garden's just an overgrown quarry.'

Zinnia's indignation was not helped by the glowing terms in which the Picket's own garden was described. Rosemary couldn't recall being struck by anything particularly noteworthy on her brief previous visit, so was now curious to see what all the hyperbole was about.

'We bought the end house, because it had the largest plot,' Nigella was rushing to tell her, as they stood on the drive. 'And then I persuaded Toby to buy extra land from the Trugglestones, so now our garden stretches behind the other houses. Come and see, I'm dying to show you all that we've done in just two years.'

She led the way round the garage to an area at the side of the house, fronting the access road from Mill Lane. Wallflowers and red and yellow polyanthus, going over now, were partnered with scarlet tulips, making a splash of colour in the borders, not altogether complementing a stridently pink flowering cherry. A double Kerria japonica was challenging a yellow 'Canary Bird' rose arching over the central path, which was made of roundels of wood, set in the grass. And along the edges of the beds multi-coloured pansies were just getting into their stride.

'This is the Cottage Garden,' said Nigella proudly. 'I think it's *very* important not to lose sight of the history of gardening in this country, don't you?'

'I'm afraid I don't know much about it,' Rosemary confessed truthfully, unable to put her finger on why this self-conscious effort somehow lacked the appeal of some of the front gardens she passed in the village.

The area was bordered on one side by a beech hedge, with an arch in the middle, through which she was now invited to follow her hostess, down a grass path between lines of a prickly shrub, covered with small orange flowers.

'Our Berberis Walk,' she was informed. 'Isn't it fun? I got the idea for it in a magazine. Of course I'd love to have a Laburnum Walk, with purple alliums underneath, like that famous one. But we can't have poisonous seeds with small children.'

'They've got a wonderful sandpit though', she indicated an area next to the house, 'they play in it such a lot. It's made to look like a little beach, with all the right plants and everything.'

'Oh,' said Rosemary. She had assumed it was for the convenience of local cats, having spied, out of the window, one making good use of it on her earlier visit.

'The beach leads on to the Mediterranean Garden – all those grey-leaved plants you can see, outside the conservatory. Of course that was one of the first things we did, build a conservatory. We practically *live* in there,' Nigella enthused.

'And on this side is my Foliage Garden,' she indicated a narrow strip bordering Mill Lane, where four clipped box balls, under planted with a black, strap-leaved plant, stood guard over a large bush of startling yellow leaves. 'That's Choisya 'Sundance'. Isn't it wonderful? I saw it on Berriman's stand at Chelsea last year, and just *had* to have it. And,' she pointed to a column of sacking and bubble-wrap, trussed with green twine, 'I'm going to get Toby to help me unwrap the tree fern this weekend, now the weather's changed. There's this firm importing them from New Zealand now. Not cheap of course, but *such* fun.'

They had reached the end of the Berberis Walk, and encountered the statue of a woman minimally but strategically draped, gazing vacantly in the direction of a purple wooden seat, set against the hedge, a log basket, painted the same colour, placed artlessly alongside.

'Venus,' stated Nigella, seeing her visitor's doubtful glance. 'Goddess of Love, of course,' she smirked.

'I should have known.'

Nigella warmed to her visitor's humility. Educating people about the art of gardening was what it was all about.

'She forms an important part of the axis to the garden,' she explained. 'The end of the Berberis Walk, and then,' they turned right and began walking along a path made of round cobbles, cemented in, 'she forms a focal point for the Stream Garden, as well.'

Beside the path was a little runnel of water that began in a container filled with large pebbles, and disappeared a few yards away. Along its narrow banks purple heads of the Drumhead Primula battled for territory with crimson candelabra primulas, and a colony of skunk cabbage was lying in wait at the end.

'Of course we can't have a pond, because of the children, but Toby fixed up a hidden pump and a liner to make this wonderful stream. Doesn't it look realistic?'

Her visitor left the question unanswered, but Nigella evidently didn't need one.

'I'm dying to have a Monet-style bridge over it,' she confided, 'and Toby has promised to order one next time he makes a killing on some shares.'

They were now in a strip of land behind the gardens of other houses. 'We've only had this bit a year,' she said, 'so it's all rather new. But I've just finished the Japanese garden, and I'm so pleased with it.' She waved at an area on the right, where hostas were emerging from raked gravel surrounding a large rock, beside which was a clump of bamboo, and a weeping maple, just coming into leaf. Azaleas and a miniature pine were growing in oriental-looking pots, beside a rather concrete-looking stone lantern. The area was fenced off with woven matting, which awaited the first gale with the sagging resignation of a goat pegged out to bait a tiger.

'And of course I just *adore* grasses.' On the far side of the matting, Nigella had laid out a horseshoe-shaped bed with clumps of vegetation, green shoots now emanating from last season's untidy, straw-coloured foliage. 'This is the Grasses Garden,' she announced proudly, 'I bought a Collection last spring, and they're doing very well. That quaking grass is seeding beautifully.

Now I wasn't sure what to do with this last area,' Nigella took her visitor into her confidence, as they progressed to where the path finished. 'I had thought of a Wild Garden, or a White Garden, but I think that's a bit passé now, don't you?'

'I'm the wrong person to be asking,' Rosemary reminded her. 'Gardening's a closed book to me.'

'But you can tell me what you think about having a Trompe d'Oeil at the end,' Nigella exclaimed encouragingly. It's so *important* to have surprises, isn't it. And I thought perhaps a little plastered wall along the back, with a painting on it of a path between herbaceous borders, stretching into the distance.'

Rosemary gave a quick glance at her hostess to ensure she wasn't teasing, but there was no mistaking the earnest pleasure with which Nigella was seeing this device in her mind's eye.

'Or possibly a gazebo would look nice. We'll have to look at the costs. But that's long-term of course,' she added. 'For the Big Day in July, I've decided on a Red and Green Garden at the end here.'

'Oh.' Rosemary was suddenly reminded of an unfortunate red and green outfit she'd bought years ago in a benighted moment, which had made her feel like the apple offered to Snow White by the wicked stepmother. But realising that a positive comment was expected, she added tactfully, 'An unusual combination, red and green.'

'*Just* what I thought,' Nigella was gratified at her visitor's discernment. 'And the strange thing is,' she added happily, 'no-one's done it before. I've put in packets of red nasturtiums, bought scarlet Verbena, some of those dwarf red dahlias, and lots of Alchemilla mollis.'

****

'No-one plants red and green gardens,' snorted Zinnia, on hearing an account of the morning, 'for the simple reason that it looks horrible.'

'And she's going to give every visitor a little map, done on the computer,' Rosemary informed her with enjoyment. 'All the so-called Gardens will be marked on it, plus plant lists, and Before and After photographs scanned in. She has it all planned. You'll need to do something to compete,' she added teasingly.

'I shall do no such thing.' Her aunt's disdain was obvious. 'But from what you say, the village will be lucky to get any visitors at all. And that won't help to help save the Pit. It's no good that Picket woman sending out press releases, or whatever, and expecting national television to take an interest. I thought she'd be concentrating on drumming up local support.'

'Well, things were successfully nudged in that direction,' Rosemary reassured her, modestly. 'We're going to talk to local businesses about advertising in the programme, and I undertook to produce a flyer on the computer, which we can have printed for local distribution. And of course I'll need your help to draw up a list of people and places to receive it.'

'You can have all the help you want,' Zinnia assured her gloomily. 'At least it's a chance to whip up public resistance about the tipping. I'm getting absolutely nowhere with Gerry Thornway.' Frogspawn's got nothing on that man. Every time I try to get hold of him, he slips through my fingers.'

'Doesn't make sense.' Rosemary was puzzled. 'His property'll be affected too, won't it? You think he'd be hollering like crazy.'

'Well he isn't,' Zinnia said shortly. 'And apparently doesn't want to. I can't understand it.'

Chapter Fourteen

It was five-thirty in the morning, as Mike Swathe drove towards Newmarket the following day. He had turned off the dual carriageway, and was making his way along minor roads, and through sleeping villages. No point in arriving early, and besides, he wanted time to think.

The trees, like fashionable women at a party, ensured they were all subtly different in their new, green attire. Grass on the verge was on the move, and lacy tablecloths of Stitchwort stretched out under the hedges, as if inviting wayside picnics. He caught occasional glimpses of little crowds of cowslips on the banks, and the early morning air was cool and fresh. Passing through a village lined with parked cars, he had to draw in to give room to an oncoming post van. And as the car brushed against an overhanging lilac, a faint scent wafted through the air ducts.

It never failed. The lilac tree outside his bedroom window in Haydon had always signalled the coming of summer. And now that scent took him straight back to childhood. Perhaps, he thought, the smell of dusty, hot tarmac, or the distinctive roar of a double decker bus, had the same effect on people brought up in towns. But somehow he doubted it. The smells of the countryside were special. He smiled nostalgically, remembering the buzzing of the bees' nest in the roof above his bed. Occasionally they swarmed, formed a living cloud, and left for a new life. As he had himself.

Country boy makes good. That's how the world would sum up his life, he reflected, glancing round with appreciation at the solid comforts of the Range Rover's interior. 'Uneducated and poor, Michael Swathe built up his waste disposal business by sheer hard work and native wit,' his obituary would say in the local paper. 'A life to be proud of', he would like to add. Except, that... well, the arrival of divorce papers yesterday had sounded a harsh note. They both knew it was the sensible thing to do, no more than throwing out food that had gone off. And Doreen wanted it.

It could hardly be put down in the Success column though. Not his fault, he told himself, steering the car round a bend, but honesty overrode the self-deception. Perhaps he needn't have worked as if it was the only thing that mattered, he admitted unwillingly. He could have set aside more time for the family, and tried to understand what she wanted. If you ever could understand women.

The body of a fox lay in the road ahead, its rust-coloured coat glowing in the rays of the low sun, like a little patch of autumn. He slowed down to make sure the wheels didn't spoil its still beauty. Sixty-five next birthday, the sight of death reminded him uncomfortably. An old codger, even if he didn't feel it.

And Eddie was getting restless. He'd watched his elder son this last year or two, and knew what was in his mind. If the old man didn't move over soon, and let him run the business, he would leave and set up on his own. That sixty-fifth birthday had been the planned landmark for handing over the reins, but a few things had happened lately which were making him wonder if he shouldn't bring it forward.

The great thing was that he had the premises now for setting up his new business. Doing that deal to buy the car park from Thornways had been a steal, he thought with satisfaction. Such an arrogant fool, Gerry Thornway. Unlike his dad.

Mike Swathe smiled to himself, remembering Old Man Thornway with respect and affection. It had been good of him to offer support and encouragement to a young lad from the village with nothing going for him but ambition and energy. And the provision of land so that he could set up in business at the back of Thornways had been a godsend. Collecting scrap metal from the blacksmith and local farms hadn't made much to start with, and he'd been grateful for Thornway's generously low rent, and later, after diversifying into skip hire, a reasonable sale price.

Now that fool of a son was letting it all go. He shook his head at the thought of Gerry Thornway's bovine stupidity. They'd agreed a deal involving most of the adjacent car park, in exchange for a ridiculously low sum, and a strip of his garden that the Golf Club had always wanted tossed in. And I'm selling the house anyway, he thought with amused scorn. As a bonus, enough of the deal was left hanging in the balance to ensure Gerry didn't dare squeak in protest about tipping in the chalk pit right next to his house. Mike Swathe chuckled. There was nothing quite like the buzz of putting one over on people, especially if, like Gerry, they clearly thought they were superior.

He wondered where Old Man Thornway had gone wrong. His own sons could both go down in the Success column of his life. He caught sight of some baby rabbits feeding on the verge, but they seemed unperturbed as the car passed, made confident by parental example and past experience. Eddie and he didn't agree on the future direction of Swathe's Environmental Services though, he reflected. They had fierce arguments about it, and his son had been especially scathing about that purchase of the old chalk pit from Clive Trugglestone. Waste of money, Eddie reckoned. He saw the future in chemical disposal. But he would make a good job of running the company all the same. He had nouse, did Eddie.

And Ian, well, the lad was bright. University, and now he was doing well in one of these big food companies, he thought proudly. They were both chips off the old block, in their own ways. He must find a way to help Ian, to balance Eddie taking over Swathes.

Passing a farmyard, he caught a glimpse of a hay bailer, brought out for an overhaul before its early summer duties. Having grown-up children made you conscious of the fact that you were moving inexorably up the conveyor belt of life, he thought. That, and having the older generation die off.

He'd found the recent death of his mother unexpectedly disorientating, but not in the conventional way. When newspapers said of some famous family that 'they'd never been close,' you knew it was a euphemism. But did that cover caustic dislike, he wondered, peering at a signpost almost illegible with green mould. He glanced up the road thus indicated, and decided against it. Must be the next turning he needed.

What he'd needed when he was young, was for his mother to be proud of him. With a father who hadn't come back from the war, he'd taken on the role of being the family provider, determined to show that he could look after her. And he had. Been successful and made more money than she could have dreamed of. It had been his mother's choice to stay in that old cottage. She wouldn't move, or let him change anything. Kept the money he gave her, and just put it in her Post Office account. Miserable old bat. Never once, had she even said, 'Well done, son.' And now she never would.

At the thought, bitterness stirred. But his mother was only part of it. There'd been other reasons for avoiding Haydon all these years.

The vibrant countryside was giving him no pleasure now, as he drove almost automatically, his face set and tense.

Seeing Julia again had affected him more than he wanted to admit, and he was angry with himself. It was a weakness. Besides, all that was behind him now. Years ago. He wasn't good enough for her, she'd made that clear, and he'd spent his life proving her wrong.

Now he was the one with the money and the good life. Able to buy Trugglestone land because the family needed money. That was sweet, and he should be rubbing it in triumphantly, and leave things at that. Not getting knots in his stomach just looking at her.

He swore, suddenly conscious of having passed the road he wanted, and looked for a drive or a field entrance in which to turn. That's what happens when you let a bloody woman distract you, he told himself angrily.

Round the next corner was a house with paddock and tennis court, and he smiled grimly as he reversed into its gravelled entrance, and drove back down the road. Tennis courts. Oh yes, they said it all.

Julia, and her friend Zinnia were invited to tennis parties up at Kiln House. No-one ever thought of asking him. The Swathes were not the right sort of family. He and Julia got on fine away from everyone else, though. As he thought about her, his expression softened. Their shared love of horses was the spark that started the friendship. But socially, they might as well have been in different worlds.

Julia had tried to get him invited to a tennis party once, he remembered, looking back down the years. And that Zinnia friend of hers had made sure it didn't happen.

Back at the junction, he consulted a map, and took the other road.

That tennis court was still there, in the old chalk pit. He'd seen it the day he joined the ranks of bird watchers. And it was going to give him great pleasure to bury it for ever under tons of building spoil. That would teach Zinnia Peasmore not to look down on Mike Swathe.

A couple of crows, feeding on a road kill, flew off just in time to avoid a similar fate. Intelligent birds, crows, he acknowledged grudgingly, watching them flap away. Lived by their own rules, and didn't give a damn about anyone. A good attitude.

It was satisfying to think of that Zinnia woman getting het up about the pit's future. Her repeated invitations to come to tea and talk about his plans for tipping, he'd found vaguely amusing. Tea! What did she think he did all day?

On the other hand... He had an unexpected thought. What if she didn't remember he was the village boy she'd been so snooty about? That was important. He wanted her to know what a mistake she'd made. And, it suddenly occurred to him, he might rather enjoy himself. A picture of Zinnia, grovelling and humbled, began to form pleasurably in his mind. Yes, perhaps he might make the time to go to tea at Kiln House, after all.

The untidy hedgerows on his left had given way now to white painted post and rail fencing, and he turned off the road towards a Georgian-style house next to the neat, low buildings that made up his trainer's racing stables. He parked the car, and strode confidently into the yard, which bustled with activity as the horses were saddled up.

He sniffed appreciatively, the freshness of the air mingling with the reassuring smell of horse, leather and stable.

'You couldn't have picked a better morning to watch them ride out,' the trainer greeted him, as they shook hands. He liked Mike Swathe. Not many of his owners had the same feel for horses that Swathe clearly did, and the man didn't put on airs and try to patronise him.

'No Nannicking's on great form, he's moving a treat just now. You see.'

And Mike Swathe relaxed, and prepared for the treat.

****

Zinnia was exultant. '*Yes*, he's coming. I've got him,' she exclaimed, a few days later, putting down the phone in triumph.

'Don't tell me, you've finally found someone to fix the roof,' Rosemary guessed with teasing sarcasm, passing through the hall.

'No of course not.' Her aunt feigned bravado. 'Nothing wrong with the roof...except when it really pours. And that's not often. No, it's Mike Swathe. He's agreed to come and discuss his plans for tipping in the Pit.'

'Brave guy,' commented Rosemary, picking up the post from the doormat and handing it Zinnia. 'But I can't see what that gains. He's bought a big hole in the ground to fill in – at least that's how he views it.

And to you it's a precious garden that's taken years to create. No room for compromise there. What are you going to do? Set on him and bury the body, or convert him to gardening in one hour flat?'

'Well I'll show him round of course.' To Zinnia, people who had no feel for plants and gardens went through life blindfolded, and it was only fair, one's duty in fact, to point this out.

'Show him round his own property?'

'Well, he doesn't have any means of access does he?' That was her one ace in a weak hand, with Settlewort the joker. 'And the garden's looking really good at the moment. Basil Berriman's promised to come and photograph it, if he gets a moment off from his Chelsea duties. By next week quite a few of the shrub roses should be out in the Pit, as well. Even a philistine like Mike Swathe will have to admit that it's not just any old hole in the ground.'

They had gone through into the kitchen, and Zinnia sat down at the table to open her post, while Rosemary succumbed to Roger's ingratiating affection, and fetched a tin of cat food from the larder.

'And there will of course be scones for tea,' her aunt continued in a light tone, 'liberally spread with Settlewort jam.'

Pausing in her search for the tin opener, Rosemary closed her eyes and grimaced in dismay. 'Oh you're kidding. You can't administer stuff like that to someone. You'll end up in jail.'

'Nonsense,' Zinnia ripped open a letter, slipping the envelope into the table drawer to add to the pile of free jotting paper. 'Three members of my family have eaten it, with no ill effects.'

'But he might have a reaction to it.'

'I hope he does.' The missive she'd been reading was sent sailing in the direction of a cardboard box in the corner, already overflowing with assorted paper. 'Why do charities spend so much money sending out biros with begging letters? There can't be a household in the country that doesn't have dozens of the things lurking in corners, quietly breeding.'

'What do you mean, you hope he has a reaction?' demanded Rosemary. 'Is that an admission of murderous intent?'

'Mm.' Zinnia was now absorbed in the complexities of her Water Rate Demand.

After a moment she looked up. 'You know very well why Settlewort got its name. It was supposed to settle people's arguments. Make their minds open to reasoning, and understand other points of view. I just think a few scones spread with the jam might help Mike Swathe realise that tipping in the Pit Garden would be an act of complete vandalism. Nothing wrong with that.'

'Oh sure.'

The tin opener was putting up considerable resistance, Rosemary having given up looking for the one that worked. 'And what about you?' she asked, as a beguiling thought struck her, 'suppose you end up seeing things his way?'

'I shan't be having any.'

Roger watched with impatience as his meal server paused in her duties. 'This whole thing is crazy,' she said. 'That plant probably does have mind-bending properties, but it needs to be scientifically tested. We shouldn't mess with it.'

Her aunt was trying to get the new biro to work, and appeared not to be listening.

'It's a great idea to make out that you found Settlewort growing in the Pit Garden,' persisted Rosemary, 'and save the place that way.'

'That's Plan A,' Zinnia commented, tearing an unfranked stamp off an envelope. 'But all good generals have a back-up plan.'

'And administering the stuff to old Swathe is Plan B, is it? Well, I think it's far too risky. Besides, I can't see what good it would do if it did change his mind.'

'How do you mean?'

'Well according to Matthew the effect was only temporary. So even if your jam scones made the guy think it was the Garden of Eden, he's going to go back to seeing it as a profitable hole in the ground, after a while.'

Zinnia rubbed her chin thoughtfully. 'You're right, that is a problem. What I need is some kind of agreement, saying that he won't use it for tipping, and get him to sign it.'

'Yes, yes, your food is coming,' Rosemary assured the cat, spooning the stuff on to his saucer. 'Well, I don't want anything to do with it. Suppose the poor man just happens to have a heart attack on the premises? Your defence isn't going to be helped by the fact that you can't stand him, is it?' A thought struck her. 'You said he used to live in Haydon. Have you always been like a couple of street kids, duking it out?'

Zinnia was perusing a newly-opened catalogue. 'I think I must be getting old,' she remarked, shaking her head. 'Would you believe they're selling a gadget in here for making the ears of Alsation puppies stand up straight?'

She put the catalogue down, and gazed out of the window. 'No, actually I hardly knew him. He was a year younger, and that matters a lot when you're teenagers, doesn't it. He had ginger hair, with these really piercing, blue eyes, and a chippy attitude, even then. Julia was friendly with him, because she had a pony, and he was always hanging round the blacksmiths, offering to measure their inside legs, or whatever horses have done. He left school and got a job there, as I remember, just before we moved away.'

'Dad said you went to… was it Hampshire?'

'Yes, my family were only here for three years, we never seemed to stay in one place long. I didn't want to go, of course. I was having great fun. Julia and I used to get invited to the Peasmore's terrific tennis parties, here at Kiln House. At least we thought they were wonderful.'

'So why the venom?' Rosemary was washing catfood off the spoon, as Roger hunkered down to his long-awaited meal.

'Well…' Zinnia paused, and then decided on frankness. 'Julia tried to get him included in the tennis parties. In fact she was quite sweet on him, I think. And I, um…' She hesitated. 'I told her mother, who disapproved of him anyway. He didn't come from the right sort of family, you see. It seemed important in those days,' she added defensively, 'not like things are now. Anyway, she spoke to Mrs Peasmore, and…that was that.'

Rosemary mulled over this information as she walked to the towel on the back of the door, and dried her hands. 'You were *jealous*!' she accused.

'Mm… I'm not proud of it,' Zinnia was fiddling with the biro, 'but I was at a silly age. As you might expect, there was definite hostility after that. But by the time I got married and came to live here, he'd moved to Stockleigh and started up in business. There were often snippets about him in the local paper. He's made a fortune. And now,' she added bitterly, 'he's bought my wonderful Pit Garden and wants to destroy it. So you see, I'm going to need all the help that Settlewort jam can give, to get the better of him.'

Rosemary did see. But she also felt a certain sympathy for Mike Swathe. Julia was attractive now, but she must have been really lovely when she was young.

'I still don't think you should do it,' she insisted. 'When's he coming? I shall make myself very scarce.'

'Tuesday afternoon,' her aunt informed her, getting up. 'And,' she added with a small smile, reading her niece's mind with accuracy, 'don't bother looking in the larder for the Settlewort jam, because it's not there any longer. Bad luck.'

****

It was the second Tuesday in the month, and that meant the Haydon Voluntary Services Committee meeting this afternoon. Why, Julia Trugglestone wondered wearily, unlocking the door into the garden, did committee meetings always have to take place on the nicest days? Light clouds were drifting slowly from the west, with the patches of blue sky between them getting bigger and joining, as if in happy alliance. Stepping onto her little patio, she turned her face gratefully to the sun. It would have been just the afternoon for a gentle walk along the valley. The poor dog deserved some proper exercise, and it would have done her good too. She sighed. Damn all committees.

Bracken bounded eagerly down to the bottom of the garden, tail waving, and Julia followed slowly, taking care on the flights of steps still in shadow, where dampness lingered like bad memories. She sat down on the seat by the river, while Bracken investigated an interesting rustle in the rushes. Sunshine sparked a miriad lights on the water, and from downstream came the hooc-rooc of a moorhen, as it chugged across from the far bank.

This, she told herself, is idyllic. Why do I feel so...so restless? She looked up at the house, pretty, and ideal for her needs. Old Mrs Swathe's adjoining cottage stared back at her blankly, its dirty windows and greening plasterwork a stark contrast to her own newly-painted property, like a matted street cur next to a pampered pooch. The water seepage had been fixed now, but something would have to be done about that cottage soon. Despite resolving not to think about it any more, she pictured again the inside, and her brief encounter with Mike Swathe. That was more than three weeks ago, but like a tongue exploring a new filling, she kept going back to it.

Why wouldn't he accept her invitation to come in? Had he been unable to forgive, even though it was all so long ago? Bracken came for affection, and she stroked the dog's head absently. Seeing him again had been such a trigger for all sorts of memories. Surely chatting about the old days would have been enjoyable for both of them.

Cautiously, she allowed herself to picture him. The years didn't seem to have had much effect. His hair was nearly grey, but those blue eyes of his retained that unnerving directness. When the young Mike Swathe had looked straight at you and smiled, she recalled, it seemed almost like a thrilling conspiracy between the two of you.

Why had he been unsmiling, curt almost? Was he still so bitter?

'You are behaving like a silly, adolescent girl,' she told herself out loud, and at the sound of her voice Bracken looked up, ears cocked.

'I'm afraid that you and I will be spending the afternoon at the vicarage,' she informed the dog resignedly, getting up, and starting back up to the house, 'instead of enjoying the sunshine and going for a nice... oops, mustn't say the W-word, or you'll get the wrong idea.'

Well at least this committee meeting was one of the more worthwhile ones. They would be discussing which organisations were going to have stalls at the Gardens and Flower Festival, and where. But that was bound to cause trouble, with everyone wanting the best sites. She did have an ally though. Mrs Chitting's daughter, Carol, was a committee member, and she would help to smooth things along. Nice girl, efficient too. The

Brownies had really flourished since she'd taken them over, and just about all the girls of that age in Haydon had joined now. It's what village life was about – keeping the young and the old happy.

That doesn't include you, Julia Trugglestone, she told herself severely. You're aren't old yet, and you're not supposed to be happy.

Reaching the top terrace she became aware of the telephone ringing, and hurried the last few steps to reach in and pick up the receiver.

'Oh I *am* sorry,' she despised herself for the apparent sincerity in her voice. 'Yes, next Tuesday will be fine. I do hope he's better soon.'

She put down the phone. 'Most unfortunately the vicar has gone down with a temperature,' she reported to Bracken seriously, and then ruffled the dog's fur with delight. 'So it looks as if you and I really can go for a w... pedestrian journey, this afternoon. It'll make us both feel better.'

****

Zinnia was going to be on her best behaviour. The term 'charm offensive' covered the situation, she felt, as she prepared to take Mike Swathe on a tour of the Pit Garden. It was her child, her creation, the fruit of decades of hard work. She would outwit this man who only wanted to destroy it.

The thought that the place was not actually hers to show was ignored, like an irrevocably stained garment best left in the bottom of the laundry basket.

'Be nice to him,' Rosemary had urged. 'He'll see that it's beautiful anyway, but make him realise how much the place means to you. And *be pleasant.*'

He arrived exactly on time, and they were both polite, but wary as a pair of stiff-legged dogs sizing each other up.

As they walked down the ramp, the sound of a tractor in a nearby field faded away, and the Pit seemed to enfold them in its still and secret world.

'At first I didn't know what to do with the place,' Zinnia told him. 'It was terribly overgrown. I started by cutting down a lot of trees and clearing the brambles round the tennis court and the pond. And the garden sort of grew from there.'

They were walking round the perimeter path, a patch of blue Corydalis flexuosa lapping the edge, enjoying the shade cast by the steep side. 'This little beauty has only recently been collected, in China', she remarked, bending down to finger its ferny leaves. 'We like to think we've discovered all the plants of the world, but of course we haven't.'

Scent drifted deliciously down from an early-flowering honeysuckle, colonising the tree above, while its neighbour sheltered a Clematis alpina, the many-petalled flowers starring the tree like a galaxy. They walked through a large colony of Solomon's Seal, the bowed heads bearing their creamy bellflowers in elegant submission. 'A British wild flower,' she told him. 'It really loves the conditions here. Surprising what a vast number of plants do.'

Mike Swathe was looking about him in surprise. You got no idea of the size of the place peering down from the top, nor had he when it had been thronged with birdwatchers wielding tripods as offensive weapons.

'This place is huge,' he said. 'And when you think it was created by men without modern tools, it gives some idea how long it must have been worked.'

Zinnia shot a glance at him, unsure whether this remark showed a sense of history, or merely satisfaction at the Pit's capacity for rubbish tipping.

Tactfully, she turned off the perimeter path before they reached the tennis court. In any case round the back of the court had become rather overgrown, with ivy and brambles encroaching faster than she could clear them.

Instead she took him across the centre of the garden, past an area where purple alliums held sway. Their large heads, like an elegant cathedral, seemed to challenge the supports that held them aloft. At their feet Dicentra 'Langtrees' formed a drift of grey-tinted leaves, each heart-shaped, creamy flower delicately tinged with pink.

'The man whose garden this plant is named after, gave it to me,' Zinnia told him, seeing no harm in establishing her gardening world credentials. 'Such a wonderful plant.'

They were approaching the pond, and her visitor looked puzzled.

'How can you have a pond in chalk?' he asked.

'Well just here they'd got down to the clay underneath,' she explained, 'but in any case it's got a concrete lining. That was cracked to start with, and I had to mend it.'

The golden globes of double Marsh Marigolds, packed with countless glossy petals, were mirrored in the still water, wriggling tadpoles occasionally causing the reflection to oscillate gently.

'They look like the Kingcups that grew by Haydon bridge. I fell in once, trying to pick some,' he volunteered, neatly reminding her who he was, in case she had forgotten. It also fulfilled his strategy of polite urbanity. To start with anyway. When she got to the begging bit, he could rub her nose in the situation.

'Yes, it's the double form,' she acknowledged. 'There are quite a few double forms of wild flowers in cultivation, and I always picture little old cottage women finding them and transplanting them into their gardens.'

Realising that this could be interpreted as condescension towards a boy who grew up in one of Haydon's 'little old cottages', Zinnia glanced at him apprehensively, and moved on, and they joined the perimeter path at the back of the Pit. Here the edge towered above them at an impressive height, the line between the field soil, and the chalk clearly visible. South-facing, the quarry face had proved a congenial home for cliff-loving plants like wallflowers, thrift and cascading, white Anthemis daisies, which had seeded themselves into its crevices. Zinnia had piled soil on to the lowest ledges, on which to grow choicer things, so that the garden seemed to flow up the sides.

Spires of almost black flowers rose impressively from layers of horizontal leaves, at the foot of the cliff, and she turned up one of the bell-shaped blooms to show off its dusky beauty. 'A fritillary from the Middle East,' she remarked. 'The books say that it needs deep, rich soil, but,' she gave a half smile, ' I'm careful not to tell mine, so they make do with what's here.'

Mike Swathe found himself unwillingly impressed as the escorted tour round the Pit Garden continued. The woman was not the bitchy snob of his imagination, and clearly she had put in years of work, and succeeded in creating something remarkable. Foolish to do it on land she didn't own though. His land now.

'Is there anything left of the old lime kilns?' he asked, genuinely interested, 'I'd like to see where they were.'

****

Rosemary was inwardly railing at the unfairness of life, as she took the footpath across the fields and down towards the river. If you were meant to choose right from wrong, the least it could do was make clear which was which.

Disloyalty to her aunt, who was family, and who had made her welcome these past few weeks – well, that was clearly wrong. But shouldn't she also stop Zinnia feeding that damn Settlewort stuff to an unsuspecting guest? Who knows what effect it might have? You could argue she had a duty of care not only to a stranger, but also to protect her aunt from her own lack of judgement.

That Swathe guy would be arriving about now, she thought uneasily, swinging along the path which crossed a field of growing corn, tall enough now for the breeze to be rippling it like green water. The unfortunate thing was she could see the situation clearly from both sides.

Approaching the stile at the end, she became aware of someone walking along the river path, and soon recognised the accompanying dog, and slightly stiff gait of Lady Julia Trugglestone. As she saw who it was, relief flooded through her. Of *course!* Exactly the right person to consult.

Except it would mean telling somebody else about Settlewort, before it was safely planted in the Pit. Oh, what the heck...

'Leave it to me, I'll sort it out,' Julia told her firmly, after Rosemary had unburdened herself of the whole dilemma. 'Come on Bracken.' And she set off up the cornfield path at a considerably quickened pace, leaving Rosemary hoping that Mike Swathe had turned up late, or that the tour of the Pit Garden was taking a good long time.

****

'The fact is, Mrs Peasmore, this country is fast running out of places to put its waste.'

They had made their way back to the house, and Mike Swathe was now sitting at the table, an inviting plate of scones, spread with what appeared to be gooseberry jam, in front of him. He looked about, taking in the shabbiness of the untidy kitchen, his eye lingering with interest on the primrose painting. Both were aware that, like a tin roof in a tornado, their covering of politeness was in imminent danger of being ripped away.

'People produce far too much rubbish,' Zinnia retorted righteously. 'If everyone had compost heaps, and didn't buy convenience food with all that packaging, there'd be no problem. I have difficulty finding enough to fill even one bag for the dustman every three weeks.'

'Very laudable. But you do expect it to be collected, don't you? And if you had some building work done, or an area of concrete broken up to make more garden, you'd soon complain if the builder didn't take away the spoil. Where do you think it goes?'

'I don't see why they can't use that sort of stuff for road building, or something.' Zinnia reached for the tea caddy, pleased that she had taken the trouble to anticipate the question earlier, and think of an answer.

'Do you know of any roads being built round here?'

She didn't reply. The Rayburn, never at its best in the afternoon, was taking its time over boiling the kettle. She willed it on, cursing herself for not getting her electric kettle mended. It would look suspicious to press the scones on Swathe before pouring him a cup of tea.

'I'm afraid tipping in the old chalk pit is simply not negotiable,' he told her, seeing no point in pussy-footing around any longer. 'Permission for infill with building spoil is likely to be granted at the next Council meeting.'

'But does a beautiful garden mean *nothing* to you?'

'What you've achieved is most impressive. But business isn't about sentiment, Mrs Peasmore. And that is not, of course, your land.'

He said it with emphasis. She was absolutely in his hands, he wanted her to be quite clear about it.

'Officially, you are trespassing every time you go down that ramp.'

'What!'

She filled the teapot, her hands shaking, certain that he was enjoying the situation.

Mike Swathe had fully intended to forbid her from going on his land in future. It would have been a crushing blow to inflict, and entirely within his rights. But seeing the beauty of the place, made against such odds, and hearing the way she talked about it, had changed his mind. As they went round the garden he had, somewhat grudgingly, recognised in her a fighting spirit. That was a quality he respected, and it didn't deserve humiliation.

'Tipping won't start for some time,' he continued, watching her put milk in the cups, 'so you have my permission to carry on gardening there for the time being. And of course you can remove all the plants you wish to save.'

The condescending arrogance of the man! Zinnia wanted to throw him out of the house. But that was hardly going to help. The agreement she had drawn up for him to sign was in her pocket. She had to stick to the plan.

'I made some scones specially,' she said tight-lipped, handing him his scarcely brewed tea, just as there came a knock on the back door.

Without waiting for a response, Julia Trugglestone rushed in. She was out of breath, grass pollen powdered her skirt, and strands of hair were escaping from her normally neat chignon.

'Zinnia, I was just passing, and there's something about the Gardens Festival I wanted to ask you... Oh, sorry, I didn't realise you had a visitor,' she tailed off – implausibly, unless Range Rovers possessed an unpublicised ability to camouflage themselves.

At the other side of the room the black, whiskery face of Roger the Lodger had appeared at the open window. Now he jumped to the floor, a mouse grasped triumphantly in his jaws, its shrill squeaking indicating a degree of unhappiness about the situation.

'Damn cat!' Zinnia exploded in exasperation, and menaced him with arms flailing. 'Out, take it *out!*'

She opened the back door wide, and Bracken, hurt at being left outside, responded to the invitation, and bounded joyously into the room. Instantly the cat did an about turn and, fur on end, streaked across the room towards the window, like a turbo-charged toilet brush, just as Julia surreptitiously leaned forward and tipped the plate of scones off the table. Then, grabbing wildly, and appearing to lose her balance, she fell, and ended up laid out, as if she was a bar club brawler, amongst the ruined scones and broken china.

Helped to a chair, she was trembling, and full of apologies.

'Oh dear. I'm terribly sorry, so stupid of me. I... I tripped over the cat. Just didn't see it.'

Bracken, at first startled by the crash, now proceeded to consume the thoughtfully provided jam scones, while her mistress protested that she was perfectly okay. This was open to question however, as she was clearly bruised and shaken, and blood was trickling from a cut on her leg.

'I'll take her home,' Mike Swathe informed Zinnia shortly, and, ignoring Julia's protestations, proceeded to assist her to the car.

'You,' he pointed at the accompanying Bracken. '*In!*'

Surprised at the tone of authority, the dog obediently leapt into the back. And as the car turned out of the drive, an angry and emotionally bruised Zinnia was left contemplating the ruins of Plan B.

****

'I'm sorry to be such a nuisance,' Julia apologised, smoothing back her hair with a hand that was still unsteady. 'Should have brought my stick. I forgot it, and then thought I could manage without. Just vanity really.'

'Why do you need one?'

'Oh it's my back.' She shrugged dismissively. 'A riding accident. Years ago.'

He said nothing, and after a moment she added, 'You know, it wasn't what it did to me physically that I minded so much. You get used to that. The worst thing was not being able to ride again, having to sell the horses, and go past those empty stables every day.' She paused, and continued resentfully, 'Well that problem's solved now anyway.'

'Because you don't have to pass them any more?'

'No, because my dear daughter-in-law has converted them into a Herb Shop and Tea Room.' Her tone was bitter.

'Sensible girl,' he commented approvingly. 'No point in having assets lying around earning nothing. From what I gather, the scheme stands a good chance of being a success.'

This was not at all what Julia wanted to hear, and she had relapsed into indignant silence by the time they stopped outside her front door. She expected him to come round and help her out, but he made no move, and she looked at him.

'I'm waiting,' he told her.

'For what?'

'To be invited in. After all, I never did get a chance to drink my cup of tea at Kiln House nor, I might add, taste some very tempting looking jam scones.'

'Oh, yes.' The recollection seemed to fluster her. 'Yes, of course, you must come in.'

This wasn't at all how things ought to be. She was feeling very shaken, her back was aching, the leg hurt, and her clothes were covered in crumbs and sticky jam. She wanted to sink into a hot bath and close her eyes, not play hostess to a man who upset her equilibrium in so many ways.

But once inside, it was he who took charge.

'You sit down,' he told her, indicating her favourite armchair. 'Before anything else, we'd better get that leg seen to.'

'No really, it's fine,' she protested feebly.

'Needs cleaning up, and a plaster put on it,' he insisted. 'Where will I find those? In the bathroom? And arnica is the best thing for that bruising. Have you got any?'

How did he know about arnica? she wondered, collapsing gratefully into the chair, after letting Bracken into the garden. Oh yes, of course. You rubbed arnica into horses' sprains, she remembered, hoping the pain in her leg was just bruising, and not a more serious sprain.

What a fool, she scolded herself. It was supposed to be a theatrical little stumble, not a fall, full-length on the floor.

Returning with a tube of arnica cream, scissors, a bowl of warm water and tissues, Mike Swathe made as if to attend to her leg, but she protested, 'I can manage perfectly well, thank you.' Really, the man was treating her like a child.

He brought a stool for the leg to rest on, and she bent forward, then gave a little gasp of pain and sank back into her chair.

'Change of mind?' he enquired drily, and without permission cut off the torn tight below the knee, and began cleaning blood, dirt and jam from the cut.

He was taking a lot for granted, Julia thought, with slight annoyance, but then she relaxed. It made a nice change to be cared for.

After a few moments, without glancing up, he asked, 'Why did you do it?'

'Do what?'

'Knock over those scones.'

'Oh…well, I just wasn't expecting the cat to…' her voice faltered, in the face of his challenging look.

'Julia. I saw what happened,' he said with slow deliberation. 'Why did you tip those scones on the floor? Were they poisoned?'

'No, of *course* not!'

Tiredly, she tried to think of some feasible explanation, but failed. And you couldn't fool this man. His eyes, as unsettling as a wolf's, missed nothing.

'Well… you see,' she confessed haltingly, not looking at him, 'Zinnia had got hold of some stuff which is supposed to make people more, um, open to persuasion. It was in the jam.'

'Was it now.'

Anger and amusement struggled for supremacy, as he took this in, then both gave way to a more insistent question.

'But why did you try and stop her? She's your friend. Don't you want to help her fight for the garden?'

'Yes, of course I do.' She looked at him pleadingly. 'She really loves that garden, you know. It's taken her years to make, and it's wonderful. And to ruin it by dumping rubbish there! Couldn't you reconsider?'

He ignored her request, patting the leg dry with a tissue, and said quietly, 'So why do it, Julia? You could have been badly hurt.'

She looked away uncomfortably, not knowing what to say. A pigeon perched on the chimney pot cooed rhythmically, the sound echoing down the flue, emphasising the quietness in the room. The whole thing seemed rather an overreaction now, and she was feeling foolish, like a prefect caught out in some silly misdemeanour

'This stuff,' she told him, 'it's completely untested. 'I was…' she hesitated, anticipating a snide comment. 'I was afraid you might come to some harm.'

There was silence for a few moments, a sprinkle of soot raining down as the pigeon flew off.

Julia had put herself at serious risk. For *him*. As Mike Swathe absorbed the implications of this amazing piece of information, he felt a curious lightening inside, as if a shaft of sunlight had broken through to his soul

Peeling the protective plastic from a plaster, he pressed it firmly over the cut. 'That should do,' he said, straightening up. 'Now what about this arnica?'

'If you think you're going to give me a body massage with that stuff, you're in for a grave disappointment,' she responded, with spirit. 'I'll apply it myself, thank you very much.'

He picked up the bowl and spent tissues, and headed towards the kitchen, lips twitching.

'Just so long as you do,' he said over his shoulder, with mock severity. 'Need to be fit by Saturday.'

'Why, what happens on Saturday?'

At the doorway, he turned as she struggled unsteadily out of the chair, and gave her a long, slow smile. 'You're coming to the races, with me.'

Chapter Fifteen

Zinnia cleared up the plate and scone debris, seething with anger. She swept the china pieces into a dustpan with exaggerated swipes of the brush. Damn cat, damn Swathe, damn, *damn*! I nearly had him.

But she was not in the habit of deluding herself. Oh come off it, a sarcastic voice in her mind broke through, as she cleared up. He would never have fallen for signing anything. He hasn't made all that money by being gullible, and her anger abated slowly as rationality began to assert itself. Zinnia put great store by reason, it was one of her watchwords. That, and common sense.

Going out to tip the sweepings into the bin, her eye was taken by the late afternoon sun as it caught the burgeoning branches of Rose 'Moonlight'. One of the earliest roses, it was smothering a dead elm stump at the top of the ramp, and before long the delicately scented sprays would give her much pleasure. But next year would it be covered in dust from tipping in the Pit below?

Bloody man! Just her luck to have him in the area, she reflected morosely, shutting the dustbin lid. How many people would want to buy a huge hole in the ground? As Rosemary correctly remarked, that's what he reckoned to have bought. Only it had a squatter in it.

Trespassing, every time she went down that ramp. That's what he'd said. And she'd felt so angry he'd nearly had tea thrown in his face. But now, as she ran hot water into the sink, unwillingly Zinnia admitted it was something she'd known all along. One of the reasons she hadn't made much attempt to meet Swathe face to face before, was that it seemed better to lie low, and carry on as if there'd been no change of ownership. The possibility that he would stand on his rights, if she challenged him, was a risk she'd been unwilling to take, prior to the hatching of Plan B. Now her mind went back over their conversation.

Why hadn't he forbidden her to go there?

She added washing up liquid to the water, and carried the bowl to the messy floor, a frown on her face. He could have fenced it off, and crowed over her. There was no doubt he remembered her, and he was hardly likely to have forgotten how she'd behaved towards him all those years ago.

With a cloth she wiped up the sticky patches of jam, or what Bracken had left of them, but her mind was not on the task. It was as if someone had given the kaleidoscope a slight twist, and now there was a whole new picture to take in. Something had changed unexpectedly. What was it?

She tore off sheets of kitchen paper, and started to rub the floor dry.

In meeting the enemy who had dominated her mind all these weeks, Zinnia had been surprised to encounter not a monster, but a direct and focussed man, who in other circumstances she might quite have liked. He clearly had an enquiring mind, and his brisk, no nonsense attitude to life was not that far away from her own. Moreover, she reflected, he had refrained from grinding her into the ground, when he must have been tempted to do just that.

She picked up the bowl, and as the soapy water gurgled away down the sink, all at once she knew what it was that had changed. She and Mike Swathe might still be antagonists, still diametrically opposed in their aims, but, she suddenly realised, that was all. The hate that had sustained her over the weeks had gone.

But in its place grew a creeping despair.

****

Rosemary found her down in the Pit Garden, planting out rooted salvia cuttings, and was immediately given a paper bag, and put to work collecting hellebore seeds, while hearing about the afternoon's shenanigans with carefully underplayed interest.

'Ruddy cat!' Zinnia declared, with theatrical resentment. 'After all I've done for that animal, and it spends its time sabotaging my efforts. Hamlet was right:- "How sharper than a serpent's sting it is to have a thankless cat!"'

'Tooth actually. And wasn't it King Lear? I didn't know he had a cat,' Rosemary smiled at her, but there was no response. 'You can hardly blame Roger,' she added soothingly, 'after all if some menacing beast came bounding in, you'd make a quick exit, wouldn't you. I hope Lady Julia wasn't badly hurt.'

'No, I don't think so. Just shaken. I'll ring her tomorrow. You know,' the trowel paused in mid air as her aunt considered, 'there's something odd about the whole thing. Julia and I have been keeping our distance for weeks, and then suddenly she comes breezing in, supposedly wanting to say something about...'

'What about this Swathe guy?' Rosemary interrupted quickly, anxious to deflect that train of thought, 'didn't speaking to him help any? Surely he liked the garden?'

'I think he did, surprisingly enough. But that isn't going to shift him. The worst of it is, he's right. This place doesn't belong to me. He owns it.' She added in a voice that was despairing, 'I have about as much chance of defeating him and the County Council as a flea trying to steer an elephant.'

She knocked a plant out of its pot, and proceeded to plant it, her face hidden. 'I'm just a foolish old woman,' she stated bleakly, 'fighting against impossible odds. For a garden that nobody cares about, except me.' Reaching for another plant, mechanically she began excavating a receiving hole. 'I don't know why I'm planting these,' she shrugged resignedly, 'What's the point?'

'You haven't been at that jam yourself, have you?'

This raised a faint smile. 'No, just had a dose of reality.'

Rosemary was concerned. She'd never seen her aunt this low before, and it could be said to be all her fault. As a result of her well-meant interference, she reflected guiltily, Lady Julia had been hurt, and Zinnia was thoroughly depressed. Sure did a great job there, gal.

'Do you want all these seeds?' she enquired doubtfully. 'There seem to be an awful lot of them.'

'Yes, it's one of my favourite hellebores, a really dark one that flowers early,' Zinnia told her. 'It wouldn't survive a move, so I'd like all the seeds I can get.'

Oh dear. More pessimism.

Hesitantly, Rosemary decided perhaps the time had come to voice thoughts she had been keeping to herself up to now, fearing a likely explosion.

'Don't get mad at me for saying this,' she said, mentally covering herself with a shield, 'but I figure... well, wouldn't you really be better off selling up, and buying a cottage in the village? With a nice garden,' she emphasised hurriedly. 'What about one of those ones by the river? Lady Julia just loves hers.'

'Yes.'

It was unclear to what the affirmative response applied.

Zinnia sat back, and regarded her niece steadily. She looked tired, and her eyes were blank. 'Part of me knows you're right, although I hate to admit it. Especially with Veronica going on at me to move. The plain fact is,' she said wearily, 'I won't be able to keep this garden up much longer. Being laid up with a bad foot brought that home. It doesn't have a future, even if we do manage to stop the tipping, and...and the new owner gave his permission.'

Rosemary didn't know what to say. She felt as if she'd lit a rocket and stood well back, only to have it merely fizz and topple over. But this change of mind opened up all sorts of positive possibilities.

'That cottage next to Lady Julia's is probably going to go on the market, wouldn't that be very suit...' She stopped, suddenly remembering who the owner was.

'It's no good you finding 'suitable places',' Zinnia told her, all the life gone out of her voice, 'no good at all.'

'Why not?'

Zinnia firmed the last of the salvias into the soil, and stacked the empty pots together, then she looked up, her face sagging. 'Who do you think would buy a house with an industrial tip just behind it? No-one.' She added bitterly, 'I've got to stay in Kiln House and watch them destroy this garden day by day.'

It was upsetting to see her usually ebullient aunt so miserable. And there was no denying the logic either. Rosemary reproached herself for not looking at the full scenario before. They weren't just fighting to save the Pit Garden. If tipping took place, it would be a much bigger disaster.

'It ain't gonna happen,' she said with sudden determination. 'We won't let it. Why don't you come to the summer house and sit down.'

She was a good girl, a great support, Zinnia thought warmly, realising for the first time that she would miss Rosemary's company when she went back to the States.

A robin flew down to inspect the new plantings for displaced worms, as they made their way to the summer house and sat down on the encircling bench. The intoxicating scent of a strategically planted Viburnum carlesii enveloped them, and Rosemary patted her aunt's arm.

'Don't forget you still have a real ace,' she said encouragingly, 'Settlewort trumps everything! As soon as it's growing in the Pit, all sorts of people will have to sit up and take notice, won't they. And they sure won't allow it to be buried in rubble. Why don't you plant it out right now?'

'Well, it's a toss up between the risk of a frost, and the need to get the plant well enough rooted to pass inspection. Although it's hardly likely that anyone would be taken in.'

A tide of greyness had enveloped her like a sea fret, and the idea of pretending that Settlewort had appeared spontaneously in the Pit now seemed just another unreality to fool herself with.

She shrugged. 'Maybe it's not even worth doing.'

'It sure is.' Rosemary felt like a relay runner, taking over the baton from a runner who had flagged dramatically. 'I discovered the seeds, remember. You can't duck out now. It'll be a gas.'

Zinnia smiled tolerantly at the optimism of youth, forgetting that she had shared it until this afternoon. 'You wouldn't be encouraging me in a huge deception, by any chance?'

'You bet. Do you know where you're going to plant it?'

'Well I thought one of the lower ledges would be best. It would explain the short root system, and seems a likely place for it to have regenerated naturally. I used soil from the Pit to fill the pot, so at least that will look right.' She paused, gloom now fighting the renewal of optimism her niece was working towards. 'Trouble is, it'll have real experts examining it, and if I'm found out, my reputation's finished.'

'If anyone can carry it off, you can,' Rosemary assured her loyally, as they spotted Derek's solid figure at the top of the ramp, evidently in search of them.

'Over here!' Zinnia called to him, then continued musingly, 'We're probably not going to get any more frosts now, and perhaps I could protect it. But Basil Berriman's coming tomorrow to do some photographing. He'd be bound to spot it, and the fact that it had just been put in. So it would be best to plant it as soon as he's gone.'

'You look as if you're concocting some deadly plot,' Derek teased as he approached, adding in a thick Russian accent, 'Come to ze summer house vhere we can talk freely. Unless ze bees are bugged,' and he wiggled his eyebrows. 'I've come to bring you good news, and bad news. Which do you want first?'

'The good news,' Rosemary told him emphatically, wondering if there was any way of deflecting the bad until her aunt's morale had at least emerged from Intensive Care.

'Okay. I've finally persuaded Prentice Stalker to get off his arse and do something about the Pit.' He leant against the twisted trunks of a ceanothus, and a shower of tiny blue petals descended, incongruously decorating his brindling hair. His face looked tired and strained, but he added jokingly, 'No use rubbing shoulders with a member of the County Council, if you can't put him to work on a local problem. Got to have some compensation for the man being a pompous prig.'

'Is he on the Planning Committee or something?'

'No, he's just your bog standard Council Member, but he should be able to ask pertinent questions,' Derek assured his mother. 'Anyway, he's going to come and look at the place on Friday, and I said you'd put him straight on whatever facts and figures he wants. He likes plants by the way.'

'Does he?' Haydon and District's representative on the County Council was immediately boosted several notches in Zinnia's estimation.

'Yeah. But only man-eating ones.'

'You're kidding!'

Well okay, it might be flies,' Derek conceded, enjoying Rosemary's look of alarm, 'but they stink. And don't ever turn your back on them.'

'What's the bad news?' Zinnia enquired.

'How's the Management Buyout coming along?' Rosemary interrupted swiftly, seeking to postpone further gloom for as long as possible.

'Not wonderful,' he admitted ruefully. 'Well, actually, work's a nightmare at the moment. It's like one of those dramas where things get more and more frantic, and you only watch because you know it'll be okay in the end. Only I don't see how it can come right. Clumpings' people are crawling all over the place asking stupid questions, and Prentice and I have been trying to put together a four-year Business Plan, and a Feasibility Assessment for our Venture Capitalists. But frankly I can't see it coming to anything,'

'Why not? Surely you can run the place?' Zinnia's own bout of defeatism was conveniently forgotten, and she didn't like the sound of surrender without a fight.

'That's not the problem,' her son informed her wearily. 'To stand any chance of success, management buyouts need absolute commitment, and it looks as if Prentice is just going through the motions. To be honest, I'm out of my depth myself.'

The robin flew up into the ceanothus and chirruped conversationally above him, dislodging another shower of petals on to Derek's shoulder. 'You wouldn't believe the load of gibberish these Venture Capitalists come out with,' he told them. 'The Clumpings people are just as bad. And they keep going on about Thornways' USP. Gerry's stringing them a line about that, something chronic.'

'What's a USP?' asked Rosemary.

'UniqueSelling Proposition. And that's part of the bad news I've come to tell you. Gerry's making out that Thornways is on the track of something really special to add to the herbal tea range. Something so valuable, anyone who bought the company would wipe the floor with the competition.'

'If it was that good, he wouldn't be selling, surely?'

He gave Rosemary an approving smile. 'They don't appear to have your sceptical turn of mind,' he said. 'At least not yet.'

'You've lost me,' Zinnia was getting impatient. 'I can't see why this is bad news.'

'Because,' said Derek, rather apprehensively, 'the special plant he's talking about is Settlewort.'

'*Settlewort!*'

'He's somehow found out it's growing in the village again.'

'How *could* he?' His mother was aghast. Her mind whirled round the people who knew. Only family, except...

'It's that Susan Trugglestone!' she said with fury. 'Must be.'

'No, it isn't. I mean, it couldn't be,' Rosemary leapt to her defence. 'She promised not to tell a soul, and I know she'd keep her word. Truly.'

Family relations would hardly be enhanced by Zinnia realising that her unloved daughter-in-law was the gabby little bird who'd carelessly informed Susie about Settlewort, in Gerry's presence.

Rosemary had valiently taken the blame for that herself. She'd apologised to Zinnia, saying that her own persistent interest and requests for information had aroused her friend's suspicions.

'Perhaps Gerry overheard us talking about it when we were in the garden,' she suggested. 'Or,' she made an attempt at distracting levity, 'Roger the Lodger is actually a secret agent, planted by Gerry Thornway.'

'Hm.' Her aunt was adjusting her thoughts to the new situation. 'I don't know how he found out, but actually, it doesn't make any difference, does it? Gerry Thornway knowing, I mean. In fact it could be no bad thing, if he gets people in the herbal tea field jumping up and down about it. All helps with the publicity.'

'After you've got it safely growing in the Pit, yes,' Derek said meaningly. 'But there's something else I came to warn you about. Gerry wouldn't know a rose from a raspberry, but he's set Prentice Stalker on the trail. I've told Prentice if he finds some Settlewort, not to tell Gerry. If anyone's going to make use of it, it should be us, when we've completed the Management Buyout. So I suppose it'd be a good test of his loyalty,' he added thoughtfully.

'Would it be valuable to you?' asked Zinnia.

'I'll say. Long term of course. You'd have to have lots of tests to ensure safety, and its beneficial effects, and it would need to be grown commercially. So a good many hurdles to get over. But while Thornways was the only firm selling it, yeah, it'd be a gold mine. Imagine the market for something that made people feel conciliatory – warring couples, business meetings, Northern Ireland! Anyway,' he gave a tired sigh, 'when our esteemed County Councillor comes here he'll probably ask you about it. And he'll have his eyes peeled.'

'He won't know what Settlewort looks like, surely?' Rosemary had a mental picture of a human bloodhound, nostrils flared and eyes darting everywhere.

'Prentice will have made it his business to know exactly what he's looking for.'

'It's not a problem,' announced Zinnia equably. 'We'll just move the pot into the house. He won't catch so much as a sniff of it.'

'Don't forget the one growing in the greenhouse step though,' her niece reminded her. 'What can you do about that?'

'Ah yes, that is a bit tricky. I was thinking up something to tell Basil Berriman if he remarked on it. But that won't do if Gerry's scout knows what to look for.'

Being presented with a new obstacle surprisingly cheered Zinnia up, as her mind tackled the problem.

'Any good at sketching, Rosemary?' she asked thoughtfully. 'You know I think there's a particularly good view of the garden to be had from the greenhouse step. We'll have to find you a stool to sit on. A tall one that would cover the Settlewort nicely.'

****

'It's very good of you to bother, Basil,' Zinnia thanked him, the following morning, 'especially with Chelsea coming up in two weeks.'

'Glad of an excuse to get away, to tell you the truth,' he told her, reaching into the car for camera and tripod. 'Everyone gets so frantic at this stage. Plants being waltzed out of tunnels and into cold houses because they're coming on too fast, or coaxed into flower with extra heat and light. The public have no idea what an effort it all is.'

'But the stand's your special baby this year. It'll be exciting seeing it all come to fruition, won't it?'

He gestured to Heaven. 'Well they won't let me interfere with the actual staging of it next week, of course, that's down to the show team. But the theme of conserving rare plants was an inspiration. So worthy!' His chubby face beamed. 'And between you and me, being the advisor on what to exhibit has raised my stock considerably. Helps them to forget I'm not the right sort of Berriman.'

'What do you mean, not the right sort?'

'Well my side of the family are okay to employ, but we're not deemed to have management potential,' he winked saucily. 'I would have liked to come up with one real pearl of a plant though for Chelsea, something that would get everyone talking. Just to show them. Too late to find one now, of course.'

'Yes,' Zinnia agreed blandly, leading the way down the ramp into the Pit Garden.

It was a pity more Settlewort hadn't germinated. She would have liked to help Basil, and caused a stir at Chelsea, but the one precious plant in a pot was safely hidden in her bedroom, and was going to stay there until after he'd gone. He was a dear friend, but the fewer people who knew about the impending deception, the better.

'Have you got the right film in for the blue of the ceanothus?' she asked. 'It's looking quite good, don't you think?'

'My dear Zinnia, you are a master of understatement,' he exclaimed, glancing round with knowledgeable appreciation. 'The place is looking just wonderful, the best ever. If I'd created a garden like this, I could die happy. You must let me bring Maurice to see it. He's getting obsessed with his vegetables now, you know. He's already got a potager, and now he wants to plant them in my borders. It's too bad of him.'

After nearly an hour, in which Basil took photographs, while chatting animatedly about plants and mutual gardening friends, they made their way up again.

'How are you getting on with those elusive Tropaeolum azureum seeds we shared last autumn?' he enquired.

Zinnia opened her mouth to answer, but Basil in full flow had the unstoppability of ground elder.

'I can't wait to behold this legendary blue nasturtium,' he enthused, 'and mine have actually germinated. A major triumph. You know what I'm like with seeds! But some of them are looking decidedly *outré*, and one has to suspect a little hanky panky somewhere along the line. Do let me have a look at yours, to compare.'

He was taking the path to the greenhouse as he spoke, with Zinnia beside him, rehearsing her explanation, if he should comment, of the inhabitant of the cracked step.

There was no 'if' about it, as she should have known.

He stopped, a few feet from the greenhouse. 'Now *what* is that? Just the sort of thing my dreadful sister is always after for her flower arranging.'

The Settlewort plant had gathered strength with the warming of the weather, and was now about knee high, producing its slender, willow-like foliage with exuberance. The grey of the undersides made an attractive contrast to the deep, glossy green above, as its elegant leaves stirred in the slight breeze.

'No, don't tell me, let me guess,' Basil instructed, looking it up and down like a customs officer searching for signs of guilt. 'Hm, not a willow, I think, the stalk's too sappy. Could be some sort of epilobium perhaps, although that leaf looks a bit like Solanum laciniatum...'

Time to interrupt, thought Zinnia.

'It's just something exotic that's germinated from the birdseed next door's peacocks are fed on,' she told him carelessly, walking ahead and opening the greenhouse door invitingly. 'They've been a thorough nuisance with their invasions this spring. I'm probably going to pull it up, in case it seeds all over the place, and the thing's in the way in any case. Now, here are the blue nasturtium seedlings. Do they look the same as yours?'

They emerged after exhausting the delights of the greenhouse, with Basil clutching various treasures in small pots that had been bestowed on him. From the other side of the hedge came the harsh cry of a peacock.

'How is our friend Gerald Thornway?' he enquired. 'Do you know, his was the only garden I've ever not wanted to do. He was determined to have such *awful* things, all conifers, and heathers. On chalk, I ask you!' He gestured with pot-laden hands. 'We had to put in a liner and special ericaceous soil, in those horrible, curvy island beds. And I just knew he'd go round boasting about it being designed by Basil Berriman, with me cringing in a corner.'

Zinnia smiled. 'Apparently he's thrilled that his garden's included in this Gardens Festival thing. You should be honoured. Two out of the seven gardens are going to be your creations.'

'I *am* pleased with Lady Julia's,' he admitted modestly, 'but of course it's such a wonderful site. I asked if I could call in on her this morning. In fact I must fly...Oh, now isn't that exquisite!'

His eye had been caught by a group of blue and white miniature irises, nestling beside the greenhouse.

'It suffers under the name of 'Knick-Knack,' Zinnia told him, shaking her head at the ways of the iris world. 'I'll be dividing it up later, would you like some?'

'Oh thank you, yes. Even Maurice couldn't fail to be charmed,' he exclaimed, putting down his plant trophies, and unfolding the camera tripod again. 'I simply must take it. Such a wonderful shot!'

Zinnia watched with good-humoured affection, as he crouched down and adjusted the camera to bring them into focus. 'No, we need to get the whole group in,' he announced, and moved backwards. There was a crunching sound, as his heel collided with the Settlewort on the step, and her smile froze. Basil looked round, and removed the broken plant from underfoot.

'Well, that saved you the trouble of pulling it up,' he remarked brightly, 'although I think you were being unduly harsh. It might have been fun to grow on, and see what it turned into.' He sniffed. 'Extraordinary scent, like...what do you think?'

Zinnia looked as if a hornet was exploring down her neck, and didn't answer.

'...*Peaches*, that's what it is.' He frowned. 'I remember reading about something that smelt of peaches, when I was mugging up about threatened and extinct plants.' He examined the leaves with renewed interest, then put down the broken stalk, and turned his attention back to the camera. 'I'll try and remember to look it up for you,' he told her obligingly. Studying the irises through the viewfinder, he made some adjustments to the camera, then clicked the shutter.

'Must instruct my sister to sow birdseed, if she's looking for unusual things for her flower arrangements,' he remarked jovially, straightening up. 'No telling what might appear.'

As soon as he'd gone, Zinnia urgently set about taking cuttings from the wilting casualty, but they drooped reproachfully, like a beaten puppy, and she had little hope of their survival. She put the pot and its dejected inhabitants into the propagator, then examined the base of the Settlewort plant, still protruding from the cracked step. Aromatic sap had ceased oozing from it, and the thing stood a chance of regenerating, she decided. Not that it was any use to her there, except as a source of seeds and cuttings, but as one of only two plants in the world, it deserved dedicated treatment .

She retrieved its precious sibling from her bedroom, the whole room now fruitily aromatic, and carried the pot down to the greenhouse. Bigger, and more lax in growth than its fissure-dwelling companion, the plant was branching, and developing fast.

Brushing her hand lightly across the leaves, she set it down on the bench. 'Now listen, you have a duty to perform. Look after me, and I'll make you famous,' she told the plant, oblivious of the fact that the reverse was just as valid.

****

Rosemary was becoming more adventurous with her car now, and had gone off to explore the delights of Norwich for the day. Zinnia could have done with her help, that afternoon, as she struggled to roll the big terracotta urns out of the garage. They had stood either side of the front porch, every summer, for as long as anyone could remember, and Zinnia always planted them up, to brighten the front of the house. Panting and cross, she finally admitted defeat, and telephoned Veronica to see if Matthew's assistance might be available.

'He was doing a computer job for someone in Ipswich this morning,' her daughter-in-law informed her. 'Should be back soon. I'll ask him to come round.'

He duly appeared not long after. 'Hi Gran,' he greeted her cheerfully. 'Mum said you wanted some gardening advice. Now, the important thing is to get to know your plants,' he instructed, in an accurate imitation of her own voice, 'and what conditions they like…' He swerved, laughing, as she made as if to spank him.

'You're a cheeky young varmint,' she told him affectionately. 'Come on, make yourself useful, and help me get these urns to the front door.'

They were halfway there with the second one, when a stranger appeared, walking up the drive. Matthew noticed him first. 'Why's the Mad Professor coming to see you?' he asked.

'Who?'

'You know, the guy Dad works with, Prentice Stalker.'

'*What*!' Zinnia was aghast. 'He's not supposed to be coming until Friday. Matthew, you know what the Settlewort plant looks like don't you? Take it out of the greenhouse,' she commanded urgently, 'and hide it! I'll take him round the Pit Garden while you do that. He mustn't see it. And can you find a flowerpot or something to put on the greenhouse step?'

Prentice Stalker was pleased with the idea of arranging to visit on one day, but in fact coming earlier, unannounced. It was a tactic he'd read about in a book about intelligence agents, and just at the moment he felt like one. Gerald Thornway had entrusted him with finding where Settlewort was growing, and he felt sure he could succeed if anyone could. Not that he'd known what the thing was, until he began investigating in books, but with knowledge came a sense of destiny. He, Prentice Stalker, would find this plant, and take it to one of the Royal Horticultural Society shows. It would be a sensation, and so would he. The RHS would feel bound to invite him onto one of its Floral Committees after that, maybe even the Council. All he had to do was find it.

Gerry Thornway had patently been away the day brains were given out, whereas Prentice had been very much in attendance. He questioned his boss closely. How had it come to Gerry's notice that Settlewort existed, let alone that it had reappeared? Derek's wife knew, it transpired, but had clammed up, and would not divulge anything more, even to her friend Elaine Thornway. Derek must therefore know something about the plant, but he was pretending not to. Odd. What, Prentice wondered, did he have to gain by keeping such a thing secret? Especially when they were supposedly working together on this Management Buyout thing.

And then Derek had talked to him about the threat to the disused chalk pit at the back of his old home, stressing that his mother was a dedicated gardener. And Prentice began to wonder. Settlewort liked calcareous soils, the books said. A chalk pit would be just the place where it might regenerate.

He greeted Zinnia with the slightly patronising urbanity that seemed appropriate for a County Councillor.

'I don't know that I can change Council policy,' he said in a tone which implied they would certainly listen if he tried, 'we can but see.'

He asked all sorts of questions, as they went round the Pit Garden, and Zinnia found him a slightly uncomfortable companion. He was, she discovered, the author of a turgid article on carnivorous plants that had recently appeared in the RHS Journal, but he resented the fact that they had rejected several other offerings. They found common ground, however, in shared apprehension about ignorant visitors to their respective gardens for the Gardens Festival. And even more in unprincipled people who knew only too well what they were doing, and might come armed with trowels, and capacious bags. But she was keenly aware that his own insistence on seeing every inch of the Pit was not just in the line of public duty.

The garden was interesting, Prentice thought, but sloppy and haphazard. She obviously didn't study one group of plants in depth, which was what he found so enjoyable. And she professed to know nothing about Settlewort. He introduced it as a topic, but the ball was hit into the conversational net with casual indifference.

By the end of the conducted tour, he had satisfied himself that the plant was not growing anywhere in the Pit Garden. This was disappointing, but something was preoccupying him. When he'd shaken hands with Derek's mother, his nostrils had caught a faint smell, which it took him till halfway round the Pit to identify. Peaches, he suddenly realised. It was the scent of peaches.

'I wonder if I could see the rest of your garden,' he asked, as they came up the ramp, 'that is if you've got the time to show me round.'

Zinnia was torn between gratification and suspicion, but nevertheless gave him a quick conducted tour. Clearly he wasn't interested in talking about plants like normal gardening friends, yet he wanted to see it all. She smiled grimly to herself, whilst affecting polite affability. She knew exactly what he was after, and there was satisfaction in getting the better of someone who was confident of outwitting her.

Nevertheless she intended giving the greenhouse a miss. Matthew could be trusted to have removed the Settlewort in its pot, but she'd suddenly remembered about the cuttings in the propagator. Her visitor was unlikely to spot them, but even so...

As they came near, he peered with intense interest at the plants inside, before his eye was caught by an upturned wastepaper basket adorning the step. At the same time, he caught a faint whiff of the peachy smell.

'That's an interesting garden ornament,' he said with forced jollity, pointing to the step.

'Slug bait,' declared Zinnia, who never used the stuff. 'You put it underneath, and the slimy little beggars go for it, but the birds can't. Well, that's about it, I'm afraid, nothing special in the greenhouse.'

She walked him firmly past.

'It was good of you to come, Mr Stalker,' she said in terminating tones, as they approached the house. 'You can see why I'm so determined that the Pit shouldn't even be considered for tipping. I'd be very grateful for anything you could do to help.'

She escorted him to the gate with a quiet sense of triumph, and, noting that Matthew had obligingly placed the second terracotta urn outside the front door, went in, to find him sleepily relaxed in the chair by the range, Roger the Lodger purring on his knee.

'Thank you for doing that,' she smiled at him, 'lucky you were here. Why the wastepaper basket though?'

'What do you mean "wastepaper basket", he said in a hurt voice. 'I'll have you know, that was High Art. Signifies the interweaving strands of the world, and the emptiness of most people's lives. Should win the Turner Art Prize.' He turfed the cat off his knee. 'I'm starving, do you feed your slave labour, Gran?'

Over a large slice of Veronica's famously moist fruit cake and a cup of tea, Zinnia was regaled with his group's latest doings.

'And we're angling to be one of the support bands at a pop concert in Ipswich in a couple of months,' he informed her with enthusiasm, 'That'd be brilliant! Oh, and guess what – the Heebie Jeebies have been booked to play at Haydon's Garden Festival. Apparently some of the old fogies wanted Morris Dancers instead. *Morris Dancers!* Is that sad, or what?'

Zinnia watched his animated face with a faint smile. Youth was like a plant in bud, she reflected, so much promise that you knew what followed might disappoint. Derek had been like that once.

'We'll blow 'em away,' her grandson declared happily. 'Oh yeah, that reminds me. Why have you put the bellows in the porch? It's to ward off unwanted callers, isn't it.' He leapt to his feet in a menacing stance, pulled an imaginary cowboy hat over his eyes and growled, 'One step nearer and I'll blow you to blazes!'

Her eyes twinkled at him. 'Might just try that on the next Bible bashers who come wasting my time. No, it's just that Rosemary noticed it was infested with woodworm, so the thing was better out of the house. I'll get some stuff to treat it. What were you doing in the front porch anyway?'

'It's where I hid the Settlewort.'

'Good thinking,' she said approvingly. 'Would you mind putting it back in the greenhouse before you go, though. The thing's growing so fast the pot's getting quite heavy. And watch where you're walking, won't you,' she added warningly, as he made to go, 'it's the only one in the world now.'

She was clearing the mugs off the table when he returned a few moments later. 'That was quick,' she remarked.

'It's not there,' he said uncertainly.

'What?'

'Your Settlewort plant. It's gone.'

'I'm not falling for that one, Matthew,' she said with a touch of acidity. 'Far too obvious.'

'No, really. I put it in the front door porch, like I told you. And...it's vanished! Come and see.'

Five minutes later, and Zinnia still couldn't take it in. She'd been quite fierce with Matthew, sure that this was one of his jokes, but he had indignantly protested his innocence, and she was now inclined to believe him. Not only was he uncharacteristically subdued, but his story was backed up by the faint smell of peaches now hanging about the front porch, and a few crumbs of soil where he'd set the pot down, out of sight of any casual passer by.

'The Mad Professor must have made off with it,' suggested Matthew, as she looked about her with the disbelieving expression of a cat whose mouse has inexplicably legged it.

'No, I saw him to the gate, empty-handed.'

'He could have crept back though, couldn't he, while we were in the kitchen.'

'But how would he have known it was there? He did ask about Settlewort, but I headed him off. And the greenhouse was what he was interested in. Hell's teeth!' a thought struck her, 'I wonder if the cuttings have gone.'

She hurried off to check, and while pleased to find them undisturbed, was dismayed to note their limp and unpromising state. If there was a will to live, they were having trouble locating it.

She returned to find Matthew fishing in the kitchen table drawer for a biro and an old envelope.

'Crime report,' he explained. 'We need to record exactly what happened, when, and who the suspects are. Then we check their whereabouts at the time.' He was beginning to enjoy the situation.

'Of course, I should have rung the police immediately, and reported one plant in a pot missing in mysterious circumstances,' retorted his grandmother sarcastically. 'They'd have been round here like a shot.'

He was unperturbed. 'This column's for people who actually knew you had Settlewort, and here's where we put anyone who would have liked to get their mitts on it. The Mad Professor goes in both. Who else?'

Zinnia sighed, and sat down at the table. 'Oh all right,' she humoured him. 'Basil Berriman goes in the second column. He'd love to have it for his Chelsea stand, and he did see the one in the step this morning. But he didn't realise what it was. Gerry Thornway goes in both categories, but he wouldn't know what to take.' Her face darkened. 'And I tell you who else fits, your friend Susan Trugglestone. It would be just perfect as the centrepiece for the opening of her Herb Garden. When's that? Whitsun Bank Holiday isn't it?'

'Oh come on Gran, there's no way she'd do anything like that. Anyway, she could hardly display the thing, could she, so there'd be no point.'

'She needs to be put down,' she instructed him firmly, just as Rosemary, tired but pleased with her day out, came through the back door.

'Someone outlived her useful life?' she enquired cheerily. 'Euthanasia's a bit strong though, wouldn't a rest home be adequate?'

The day's events having been recounted to her, she went with them to inspect the scene of crime, and immediately noticed something odd that had escaped the others.

'He's taken the bellows as well.'

'What?'

'That thing for blowing the fire. You asked me to put it in here yesterday. And now it's gone.'

Zinnia paused to consider the state of mind of someone making off with a large, odoriferous plant under one arm, and a wormy, fire-encouraging device in the other, but gave up. The only thing that mattered was to track down the Settlewort.

'Well, never mind that,' she said, leading the way back to the kitchen. 'I'm sorry to say that I think your friend Susan Trugglestone is at the bottom of this.'

But Rosemary sided with Matthew, in giving Susie a character reference.

'You don't know her properly, that's the trouble,' she told her aunt. 'Tell you what, why don't we go down and see her right now. You can tell her about the thing being stolen, and she can keep her ear to the ground. She knows all sorts of herbie people. And you can talk to her, and see for yourself how nice she is.'

****

'I don't know what Julia's complaining about,' Zinnia remarked the next day at breakfast. 'The way she talks you'd think her son had married some low class harridan determined to bring the family to its knees.'

'Oh I'm sure she doesn't.' Rosemary hid a smile. She'd enjoyed seeing Susie win Zinnia over yesterday, as they did a tour of the Walled Herb Garden. Like strangers discovering they were from the same village, each had recognised a 'proper gardener', thrown off polite constraint, and talked enthusiastically about plants, leaving Rosemary feeling excluded from a club whose members spoke a foreign language. Zinnia had promised to propagate for Susie some grey-leaved Greek herb, which she thought would sell well, and had come home with a rather special origanum.

Susie had been incredulous, and very sympathetic about the Settlewort's disappearance.

'How would anyone have known about it? she wanted to know.

'Or where Matthew had hidden it,' agreed Zinnia. 'I just can't understand it.'

Now, their breakfast coffee was getting cold as she and Rosemary discussed what courses of action were open to them. The disappearance of her only weapon against losing the Pit Garden had left Zinnia with heavy stones in her stomach, but she was determined not to give up and let a thief triumph over her, especially when she had a strong suspicion who the culprit was.

'I think an inspection of that man's greenhouses is called for,' she declared. Prentice Stalker had already acquired 'That Man' status. 'And after all he said about people who steal plants,' she added, half to herself.

'He's hardly going to put it anywhere so obvious though. It'll be in the house. But when he gives it to Gerry Thornway, Derek will hear about it, won't he?'

The snap of the letter box could be heard from the hall, and Rosemary got up to fetch the day's crop of bills, news of free gifts, and unbeatable credit card offers. Zinnia often didn't bother to pick these missives off the mat, and there was a pile of such assorted mail beneath that day's deliveries.

Putting the proper letters on her aunt's side plate, she sifted through the rest. Throwing out junk mail without even opening it went against her librarian's training.

'Open them and keep the envelopes for scrap paper,' Zinnia instructed, holding down the handle of the toaster, which was otherwise liable to abandon its duties peremptorily, like a guard dog scenting a rat. ' They're always useful.'

'There's a flyer here about a local window-cleaning business.'

'Oh yes.'

It could have been promoting sparkly nail varnish for all the enthusiasm elicited, which came as no surprise. Zinnia maintained that after they'd been left about three years, windows didn't actually get any dirtier. That you could still see out of Kiln House, except when the sun shone on the dust, tended to support her argument.

'And this one's asking if you've got any jumble or produce for the Brownies' stall at the Gardens Festival.'

'I could probably find something.' Zinnia peered at the stiffening bread. 'Lots of stuff in the garage we could offload. I thought you might like to turn the place out some time.'

'Oh yeah?' her niece sounded about as keen as a foreign guest offered the sheep's eye at a feast, then added with relief, 'Too late, Collection Day was yesterday. How long do you leave this stuff on the mat?'

Zinnia let go the handle and removed her toast, without replying. Rosemary was reading on, with heightened interest.

'Listen to this.' She read from the flyer, ' *"All saleable objects welcome. If you won't be at home, please leave things out for our collector. Anything you can offer will be gratefully received."'*

'Well, you can turn out the garage this morning, if you like, instead of coming into Stockleigh with me. They'll be pleased to receive things right up to the Gardens day, I'm sure. Yesterday wasn't a deadline.'

'But they came to collect yesterday.'

The girl was being unusually obtuse, Zinnia thought impatiently, as she sat down and began spreading her toast. Perhaps you couldn't expect Americans to adapt to the slow pace of English village life. 'Well, we'll take stuff down to them, instead,' she said with kindly finality.

'And,' Rosemary looked at her aunt meaningly, and continued with steady insistence, 'they collected what you'd kindly put out - *a pot plant, and a pair of bellows.*'

Chapter Sixteen

Rosemary drove down to the village after breakfast smiling to herself. Seeing the relief on Zinnia's face as the implications of her surmising sank in, had been like watching the sun come out.

'Of *course*! I knew it couldn't be a gardener,' she beamed, her mutterings about Prentice Stalker conveniently forgotten, 'they just don't do things like that. All we've got to do is find out who's collecting the stuff for their stall, and tell them it was all a mistake.' Then her face fell. 'But I've got this wretched eye test this morning. Booked it ages ago.' She looked hopefully at Rosemary. 'Could you possibly...'

'Sure. What are the Brownies exactly? It might be as well to know.'

'Oh small girls prancing round, tying themselves in knots, and singing "Dib, Dib, Dib". Or is that the Cubs? Julia will know.'

Rosemary was lost. 'Does she have something to do with them then?'

'No, but she'll tell you who does. She always knows that sort of thing.'

It was a pity to be taking the car, instead of walking down to the village on such a beautiful morning, but she would need to transport the precious Settlewort home. On her walks Rosemary had watched the daily awakening of the countryside, inwardly cheering it on. The leaves of the horse chestnut tree in the lane had struggled free almost overnight it seemed, first hanging with the limpness of damp tee-shirts, now they were flamboyant candle holders.

The road verges frothed with what Zinnia called Queen Anne's Lace, hawthorn blossom billowed from every hedge, and the medley of different greens made you long to be an artist. The lambs she passed every day had become strong and rebellious, boisterously playing King of the Castle on the mound near the water trough.

She slowed down to wave at them, then laughed at herself. What would Bill say, if he could see her? She imagined the lecture he'd give her on the limitations of a sheep's brain, and the absurdity of thinking about such animals in anything but a strictly economic way. He wouldn't realise, she reflected sadly, how the unfurling beauty of the Spring was soothing to her heart; how she felt at home here, as if the village, the river and the countryside were making her welcome, telling her life was lovely, come on in.

She parked outside the church. There was a dull burr from a lawnmower in the graveyard behind, and she sniffed appreciatively at the smell of cut grass. Why didn't some company bottle it as a perfume? It'd be a riot on the subway.

Lady Julia opened the door to her with pleasure. She had a small plaster on her leg, but her eyes were bright, and she was very smiley. For one who'd taken a considerable tumble, her sprightliness was unexpected, thought Rosemary, but then HRT was surprisingly good these days.

Anxious enquiries about her welfare were swept aside.

'Just fine,' she said. 'Zinnia rang yesterday to ask if I was all right. She didn't suspect anything, did she? Only relations have been a bit, er, strained for a while.'

'No. You've missed your vocation', Rosemary assured her, bending to reciprocate Bracken's welcome, 'should have been a secret agent. Thank you for helping me out of a dilemma.'

'We can't talk about That Plant,' Julia warned her in a low voice, 'because Mrs Chitting's here this morning.'

'Actually I've come to ask you if you know who runs the Brownies.' And Rosemary related the happenings of the day before, or at least the mistaken collection of a plant very dear to her aunt, the Only One She Had.

'Ah.' Julia nodded, with conspiratorial understanding, and led the way into the dining room, where a large, grey-haired woman was polishing the brass handles of an antique sideboard.

'This is Rosemary, Zinnia Peasmore's niece.' She turned to her visitor. 'Mrs Chitting very kindly came to help me out temporarily when I had my riding accident – must be thirty years ago. And she's been my Rock ever since.'

'I've heard a lot about you, and your wonderful cakes', Rosemary smiled at her. 'We're both going to be helping at the Tea Room when the Herb Garden opens...'

She glanced uncertainly at Lady Julia. Why did she never think before she spoke!

'I can't pretend to approve of the project, but now it's done I wish it well,' Julia assured her, not altogether convincingly. 'It's Mrs Chitting's daughter, Carol, who's in charge of the Brownies. It seems there's been a slight mix up,' she explained, 'someone went off with a plant they thought Mrs Peasmore had put out for collection yesterday.'

'Do it have long, frondy leaves, and a sort of fruity smell?' Mrs Chitting wanted to know. 'Ah well, you're in luck. Carol didn't know what to do with something like that, so she give it me to look after. Harry Trench have took quite a shine to it.'

They arranged that Rosemary would call for the plant, and she duly approached Mrs Chitting's evocatively-named Spring Cottage later that morning, looking about her at the small front garden. It had caught her eye before, gay with bright colours. Short-stalked, double daisies, that would have you falling asleep playing 'He loves me, He loves me not', there were so many petals, beamed from the path edge, along with the gentle, hazy blue of forget-me-nots. On either side of the central path were little patches of lawn, which Zinnia would have been scathing about, and pink tulips were partnered with blue grape hyacinths in beds beneath the cottage windows. Beside the front door grew a large bush of rosemary, it's flowers humming with happy bees. As she brushed against the leaves, its fresh, invigorating aroma filled the air.

It wasn't Zinnia's sort of gardening, Rosemary thought, looking about her, but it had a certain charm nonetheless.

As if symbolising a social distance, Julia and Mrs Chitting both lived in the end cottages of the row that made up most of the village street on that side. But of the two, Mrs Chitting's was the more attractive from the outside, thought Rosemary, stepping back to admire the charming asymmetry of its lines, its huge chimney and the small dormer windows in the lichen-mottled roof. These old houses were like ancient oak trees – you couldn't imagine them ever not being exactly as they looked today.

Daisy Chitting came to the door. She had the large figure and plump face that tends to be called 'comfortable', especially by those with scant chance of being slim. She was the lynchpin of her family, with children and grandchildren living nearby, and this, plus a placid, unquestioning nature, had given her an inner contentment with life. It showed in her benign expression, which was framed by iron-grey hair, neatly permed, and she wore floral dresses of ample proportions, with, or without, a cardigan, signalling the season. Despite today's cold breeze it was, according to this clothing indicator, officially summer.

She greeted the visitor warmly, ushering her in. The front door led directly into a large room, with enormous wooden beams traversing the ceiling. Expecting the tasteful elegance of Julia Trugglestone's home, Rosemary was rather taken aback to find that Mrs Chitting's love of floral patterns extended to carpets, curtains, and three piece suite, and she evidently had a weakness for ornaments too. Where Julia had a welcoming fire, with its warm, faintly smoky scent, here the big inglenook fireplace at the end had been boarded across, and housed a modern gas heater. But the room had fine proportions, and she could imagine how good it would look, stripped of clutter and sympathetically furnished.

'Sorry about the mistake. I put the plant through here,' Mrs Chitting told her, leading the way to a smaller room at the back. 'That looked as how it needed a nice sunny windowsill.'

Leading to the kitchen, and evidently used as some kind of utility area, this room was dominated by a big bay window, looking out over the river. The broad windowsill was crowded with plants in pots, reaching to the light, and in the middle, joining in the melee, was the precious Settlewort, evidently unharmed. Like the greenery, Rosemary was irresistibly drawn to the window, and she peered out over the plants. The house being situated on a slight bend, you could see upriver towards the trees which hid Trugglestone Hall, and down as far as the bridge. In the meadow opposite, rooks squirled and flapped above nests that punctuated the big trees like smudgy full stops, and on the river bank a group of dun coloured cattle were jostling for position at a favourite drinking area.

'What a great view!' exclaimed Rosemary. 'If I lived here I'd spend all my time looking out of this window.'

'Yes, I shall properly miss it.'

'I didn't know you were moving.' In fact, she now remembered, Lady Julia had said something about it.

'Just across the road. I've got one of them nice little bungalows, just being built in Sleepy Hollow. That'll be much more convenient than this old place. Warm and easy to clean.'

Rosemary couldn't imagine anyone wanting to swap this atmospheric cottage for a modern box.

'But looks as if that's lost now, unless I can sell this house quick,' Mrs Chitting continued regretfully, looking in a cupboard for a plastic carrier bag in which to encase the plant's pot. 'The people buying this, they pulled out sudden. Seems they've been let down over their own house in London.'

Rosemary was experiencing that strange feeling of having heard all this before, in a dream, or a previous existence.

'Could I...' she hesitated. 'Would you mind if... I looked round the house? It's such a wonderful old building,' she added lamely.

She followed the floral dress, as they went upstairs, the stairs and landing not enhanced by a busy red carpet and rose-infested wallpaper, into a large bedroom with a window overlooking the road. The modern units on either side of the bed argued with the ambience of the beamed walls and ceiling, but Rosemary pictured the room furnished with antique furniture. Maybe even a four poster bed.

'Likely they would have used this room for weaving, but I don't know why they needed such a high ceiling,' Mrs Chitting remarked, then showed Rosemary the bathroom, and a second, smaller bedroom.

'Where are the dormer windows that you can see from outside?' she asked, puzzled, as they stood on the landing.

In answer, Mrs Chitting opened what appeared to be a cupboard door, revealing a flight of steep stairs that led upward to a second floor.

'You have a look yourself,' she said kindly. 'Stairs are a bit much for me. I'll be down in the kitchen.'

Rosemary found herself in a narrow room which ran the length of the building, up in the roof, It was cluttered with boxes, suitcases and bags of clothes and blankets. A plastic Christmas tree leaned tiredly against two rusty paraffin heaters, and an old-fashioned looking television formed a modern still-life with a paint-spattered stepladder and rolls of wallpaper. Evidently the place had long been used as a dump room.

A dispassionate eye would have noted the lack of power points and heating, plus a patch of damp on the ceiling, all indicating a need for considerable spending, but Rosemary saw only a wonderful den.   The walls sloped inwards, towards a ceiling that was low, with businesslike beams as braces. Light came from dormer windows which, on one side, looked out over what remained of the Dower House garden, and the Sleepy Hollow development. Rosemary wondered which of the newly finished bungalows was Mrs Chitting's ideal home. Then, like someone saving the most exciting looking letter till last, she finally allowed herself to take in the view from the other window, out over the river.

As she gazed, besotted, a movement below caught her eye, and she noticed the terraced garden for the first time, and in it a figure in an ancient cap digging. She needed to check out the garden, she suddenly remembered, for the leaflet she was helping Nigella produce for the Gardens Festival. It had been crowded out of her thoughts by the events of the past couple of days.

Slowly she descended the top stairs, shutting the door at the foot with a smile. It gave such a sense of cosiness. Why didn't all stairs have doors?

She had an odd feeling in her stomach, as if she had fallen in love. The rosiness of the wallpaper on the landing now perfectly reflected her state of mind, and she went down to see Mrs Chitting in the kitchen with her heart singing.

****

You are stir crazy, Rosemary told herself dazedly, driving back to Kiln House, the Settlewort plant wedged firmly behind the passenger seat. You go to collect a plant, and end up agreeing to buy a cottage! It's a deal of money. Don't pretend it isn't. And what use is a place in England? You're going back to the States in a few months. What a dumb thing to do!

She had followed her heart, now her bemused head had some catching up to do, and she flinched inwardly at the prospect of facing Zinnia's disbelief, without having concocted some kind of rational framework. Hardly registering, she turned left past the church, and parked the car by the bridge, where the riverbank footpath joined the road. Negotiating the kissing gate, she sat on the grassy bank, and tried to marshal her thoughts.

Zinnia could live in it! Yes, that was it. She had bought a cottage for her aunt. Oh yeah? a sarcastic voice in her head objected, and how's she going to feel about it? She wants to stay at Kiln House, right? And even if she didn't, she couldn't accept the gift of a house. Zinnia's got pride, lots of it.

Rosemary pulled off some plantain heads, and rolled them in her fingers. Well, how about charging rent for the place? Yes, that could work. A low rent that Zinnia could afford. Unwillingly, she pictured her aunt writing her out a cheque once a month, paying it into Rosemary's bank account, and asking her to have some builder come and fix a rotting window, or renew a floorboard. No, no, that didn't seem right either. It would probably poison their relationship. She'd grown fond of her cussed old aunt these last few weeks, and had a feeling it went both ways. That was something too valuable to chuck away. She doesn't want to leave Kiln House anyhow, she reminded herself. And if I try and persuade her to move, I'll just sound like Veronica.

She flung the plantain heads into the water, and a swan, recognising signs of largesse, paddled up expectantly. His more cautious mate, in charge of four fluffy cygnets, held back.

'Sorry, haven't got anything for you,' Rosemary apologised to him. 'A house maybe? Four hundred years old, charming river views.'

But what was the point of agreeing to buy that lovely cottage, if she was just going to give it away, or rent it out?

She watched, as a water vole swam jerkily through the floating weed upstream, then disappeared into a hole in the far bank. I don't want anyone else to have it, she admitted quietly to herself. I want to live there.

Well you can't, her rational self ruled harshly. When you go see the real estate guy this afternoon, just tell him you've changed your mind. It was all a mistake. Buy Mrs Chitting a big bunch of flowers, and apologise.

The swan gave up on her, and cruised off huffily to join his family. A cloud moved over the sun, and the chill breeze ruffled the water with added strength. She shivered, and suddenly felt very alone. Dad would have been the one to consult. Not, of course, that she'd have had money to buy a weavers' cottage in England, if he'd still been around. But he would have known how she felt. He used to say that a life with no room for romance was like a journey where the driver never lifted his eyes from the road. You got there okay, but you sure as hell missed a lot.

Bill's reaction would be patronising incomprehension. Oh heck, she didn't want to think about that.

The cold dampness of the ground had seeped through her jeans, a stone was making its presence felt, and now her tummy rumbled, demanding lunch. Quit dithering gal, she told herself, practically. Decision time... Okay. I'll buy it – as an investment, if nothing else. And Bill doesn't need to be told. Zinnia will hear about it anyway, so she does.

An ant had climbed the steep hill of her shoe, and was looking around, waving its legs. Considerately, Rosemary waited until it scurried down again, then got up, brushed herself off, and went back to the car, just as the sun came out.

****

Next day Rosemary found in Susie a warm and friendly confidant.

'Wonderful!' she exclaimed, on hearing the news, 'everyone needs somewhere that's really their own.'

'That's just it! It's such an odd sensation, not having a base. Makes me feel kind of lost.' It was a relief that someone seemed to understand. Zinnia certainly hadn't.

'And you can come over for months at a time.'

'Oh I don't think Bill would be happy about that,' admitted Rosemary reluctantly, and Susie gave her a quizzical look. This fiancé of hers sounded about as exciting as polystyrene padding.

'So what are you going to do with it?'

'That's the question you're not supposed to ask until I've thought of an answer myself.' She gave a self-deprecating little smile. 'It was a gut thing really. I just knew I'd always regret not going for it. But I've told my aunt it's an investment.'

'I didn't know you were a Rich Bitch,' Susie teased.

'Haven't got used to the idea myself,' responded Rosemary cheerfully. 'But it's not the sort of filthy lucre that'll keep me in asses' milk baths and golden ear trumpets. I'll still have to work. Just enables me to take a while deciding what to do.'

'And means you can splash out on the odd cottage! I hope you're allowing enough to do it up. That place will soak up money, you know.'

They were having a blitz on the greenhouse, Harry Trench having cleared out the last of his fuchsias, dahlias, and bedding plant seedlings the day before. He was busy planting them in Mrs Chitting's back garden, where they were going to make a 'proper show', for its day of glory. In their absence the place's space, and scruffiness, was suddenly revealed. Susie wanted people to pay for their plants at one end of the greenhouse, while the remaining area would be for tender and easily damaged plants, decorative pots, and garden sundries which people might feel the impulse to buy, but which wouldn't fit into the main shop.

'It's not ideal,' she said, as they pulled out grass and groundsel from beneath the work benches that ran along both sides. 'The original plan was to knock through into Harry Trench's cottage, but...' she shrugged resignedly. She hadn't given up on the battle to get him to move out, but was meeting passive resistance on all fronts. 'Trouble is this will be far too hot in midsummer, but at least we can make it a pleasant place to be if it's a cold, damp day.'

'I feel a bit like that about Spring Cottage,' confided Rosemary. 'It's kind of a refuge, a place to be warm and safe in. That's dumb isn't it.'

'Well you could be struggling for the warm bit,' Susie suggested with a smile, 'those old places are not exactly hermetically sealed. I rather thought you'd discovered that at your aunt's house. How did she take the news, by the way?'

'She thinks I'm crazy. And she didn't know about the money either, so we've got some adjusting to do. Is this a weed?' Rosemary sought guidance, and Susie nodded. 'But right now she's so pleased to have her precious Settlewort back that everything else is taking a back seat. She's going to plant it in the Pit Garden today. Do you think she has a hope of fooling anyone?'

'Into believing it's regenerated in the place naturally, you mean?' Susie considered. 'Well, no-one alive today has ever seen it growing. It'll be a sensation in the herb world! And botanists are going to be knocked out by it reappearing. They won't have any reason to suspect subterfuge, will they? Unless of course they come and talk to me.' Her blue eyes danced. 'What price my silence?'

'The price of newspaper headlines,' retorted Rosemary gamely, using her foot to flatten the earth. '"Aristocratic Family in Blackmail Scandal."'

'Mm. What about a few plants of it, as soon as you've got some to spare?' Susie suggested, less playfully. 'That'd really get this place going with a sizzle.'

By mid afternoon all the weeds had gone, gravel had been spread along both sides, the work benches swept, and there was a pleasing smell of fresh paint, where they had started on the doors. Tired out and dirty, the two women surveyed the transformation with satisfaction.

'All we need now is some wet days,' Rosemary observed teasingly. 'You'll have visitors flocking to set up home in here.'

'Oh don't,' groaned Susie. 'I'm getting so nervous about the place opening as it is. Only ten days to go now. What if it pours with rain? What if nobody comes?'

****

Susie had reckoned that Whitsun Bank Holiday weekend would be a smart time for the opening of the Walled Herb Garden. No-one likes admitting to just staying at home and cutting the grass, she said, and if relatives come to visit, well you have to take them somewhere. Besides, relief at the end of the General Election campaign would make everyone feel like going out.

She'd been lavish with the advertising in area newspapers, had managed to wangle an interview on local radio, and have the garden listed on Things To Do Over the Holiday Weekend on the BBC's Look East programme. Zinnia had been consulted about whether it could publicised as The Herb Garden In The Home Of The Lost Herb, and they decided that the more publicity about Settlewort, the better. It would be helpful to both of them. Susie had also cheerfully exploited people's snobbery, making sure that her name was linked to the attraction.

'If they want to see it just because it's Lady Trugglestone's Herb Garden, that's their problem,' she told Clive, after Julia had remonstrated with him over the publicity. 'I don't mind why they come, just as long as they arrive and spend their cash. We're doing it for money we badly need, after all.'

The day dawned exactly to order, warm but cloudy, with the threat of light showers. 'Cold enough to keep 'em off the beach,' observed a pleased Susie, 'but not so bad that they opt to stay at home.'

Rosemary had offered to do whatever was necessary, and had been deputed to help in the Tea Room, with Mrs Chitting. Susie's daughters, Hazel and Anthea, were also keen to be included, but at eight and ten, were considered too young to do any waitressing. So they were to be mostly behind the scenes, slicing cakes and making sure the place didn't run out of clean cups, plates and saucers. The posies of flowers on each table had been their handiwork, and although Susie might have preferred more of a herbal theme, the little arrangements of Campion, ox-eye daisies, Granny's Bonnets, pinks and London Pride, picked from the Hall garden, had a simple charm. The girls thought their grandmother might like flowers from her garden to be included, and had to be subtly dissuaded from raiding it. In fact Julia was pointedly ignoring the opening, and had arranged to be away for the day. She seemed to be going out rather a lot, lately.

Clive had volunteered to organise parking in the field next to the Garden, a low profile job which suited his talents, he said. Also, if he was extra obliging, and touched his cap to the visitors, there was a chance of cleaning up on tips.

'You reckon?' Susie parried affectionately. 'Well, in the unlikely event that someone does slip twenty pence into your hot little hand, you'll be expected to share it with the rest of the staff, you know.'

Matthew was helping out on the plant sales, assisted, for kindness' sake, by Harry Trench, and they would be available to help anyone loading heavy purchases into cars. (Susie had hopes of selling several expensive bay trees in pots). In fact the Peasmore family were well represented, since Susie had reluctantly accepted Veronica's offer of helping Rosemary and Mrs Chitting in the Tea Room.

The woman was obviously dying to be included, and she had certainly been a great help in formulating the herbal spreads that it was hoped would be a special feature. Trial and error with old recipes, and some that Veronica had suggested herself, had resulted in three which passed the family-and-helpers taste test – Sweet Cicely and Pear, Sage and Apple, and Betony Preserve (with the right ingredients this time). If they were a success, the plan was to expand the range, but for now they had been put in small glass jars, lids fancily adorned with gingham, the attractive labels designed and run off by Rosemary, on her laptop computer. Veronica was thrilled with the result of her culinary efforts. Her eyes kept straying to the rows of jars, like a young girl who can't resist admiring her first pair of stylish shoes.

She had expended much thought on what to wear, covering her bed with tried, and rejected, outfits, before finally deciding on a pink and beige dress, with a full skirt and frilled neckline, in which, Rosemary couldn't help thinking, she was faintly reminiscent of a coffee and strawberry flavoured sundae. In return, Veronica regarded Rosemary's jeans and shirt with disdain. Surely the girl should have tried harder. And as for the other woman who was helping, that Mrs Chitting, the less said about her voluminous floral dress, the better. Still, Lady Trugglestone was paying her of course, whereas she and Rosemary were volunteering their services. This assumed superiority of volunteers over paid staff conveniently ignored Matthew's position. He was a student, which didn't count.

The fact that the Herb Garden was relying on so much temporary help was not unnoticed by Rosemary, who had queried it.

'Shouldn't you be employing people in the village?' she suggested to Susie. 'After all, what will you do when we've all gone?'

You reckon I'm penny pinching, do you? Susie laughed, and cut short her protestations. 'Yes, you're right. But we daren't take on anyone else until there's some idea what the demand will be. I haven't a clue whether a hundred people will turn up today, or ten. Let's take bets on it.'

Rosemary guessed forty-five, but her number was trampled underfoot by the arrival in the first half hour of a coach-load of old age pensioners from Ipswich.

'We're on a Mystery Tour, dear,' an over made-up woman informed Clive, as they disembarked from the coach. He looked blank. 'You buy your ticket, and you don't know where you're going,' she explained to what was evidently a simple countryman, 'it's ever such fun. What's this place? I hope there's somewhere nice for tea.'

Matthew's cherished stock control system soon had to be abandoned, in the interests of speeding up plant purchases at the till. In any case he and Harry Trench were kept busy helping people carry things to their cars, so that it was largely Susie manning the till, at the same time as trying to answer people's questions. Apprised of the problem, Rosemary telephoned Zinnia, who obligingly drove down to help with the horticultural advice.

'They asked such inane questions,' she confided to Rosemary later. 'The most usual one was, "Is this a herb?" It's a Herb Garden, for heaven's sake.'

But she proved surprisingly good at giving practical information, and making the plants interesting. Susie could undoubtedly have talked at length on their medicinal and culinary uses, but Zinnia soon attracted a group, entertained by such descriptions as the beautiful blue chicory flowers being used as a reliable clock, and why the Victorians dubbed Salvia sclarea 'Hot Housemaid.' And several people bought Climbing Lady Trugglestone roses after Zinnia had thoroughly recommended it, telling them deliciously scurrilous stories about its namesake, which the present one couldn't possibly have related. Hearing her, Susie fought off a faint feeling of jealousy, and managed instead to be grateful for all the plant sales that resulted.

With the label 'Lady Susan Trugglestone' pinned to her chest, she herself was not only busy at the till, but had to deal politely with that curious element who seemed keen to strike up a conversation just because they'd encountered a titled being.

Perhaps Julia had been right, she concluded ruefully, and the advertising should be toned down on the 'Lady' bit.

A good many of Haydon's inhabitants strolled along during the afternoon. Having observed the activity over the last few months, curiosity impelled them to see what it had all been in aid of. Zinnia spotted Prentice and Daphne Stalker, and edged behind a Witch Hazel as she watched their progress round the Walled Garden. He seemed to be taking a closer interest in the herbs than might have been expected from someone obsessed with quite another kind of plant. Daphne was no doubt making sure that nothing was being done which might fall outside the planning permission that had been granted. According to Rosemary, she had been a stone in Susie's shoe, and disapproved of the whole enterprise. Far too commercial for a quiet little village.

Nigella Picket arrived, with husband Toby and fractious small daughter in tow. Angelica proceeded to make a nuisance of herself, attempting to climb into large terracotta pots in order to hide and annoy her parents. Nigella hardly noticed. She was busy showing off her knowledge of those plants she knew, speaking to Toby, but sufficiently loudly to impress those around that they had an expert in their midst.

'*Wonderful* to have a really good place to buy plants, in the village,' she gushed to Susie, paying for an Eau de Cologne Mint. 'I shan't be able to resist coming every week.'

Only a certain proportion of visitors were taking any interest in the Herb Garden. The rest were sampling the Herb Shop and Tea Room, and chat among the Mystery Tour pensioners largely seemed to consist of previous trips, and the quality of the fare at various destinations. Two couples, ensconced at a table by the kitchen door, were evidently veterans of such outings.

'Remember when they took us to Ely?' one of the women, in a striped cardigan recalled. 'Lots of places for tea there. Spoilt for choice, we were. Ron went up and down deciding which made the best lardy cake, didn't you love. Never had time for the cathedral.'

'I reckoned we'd be going to Flatford again,' he remarked, 'with that Billy Lott's cottage. Lovely cup of tea that were.'

'Not like that Vineyard place last summer,' one of their companions remarked. 'All they had was wine. What's the good of that?'

Rosemary wondered how the Herb Garden at Haydon Settleworth was scoring in their ratings, and intended asking them, but when she did have a moment, it was to find they had departed, their coach heading off for some other mysterious attraction.

This gave them a breathing space, but the supply of cakes was beginning to be a concern.

'I did what Lady Susan asked,' Mrs Chitting said, both pleased and anxious at the speed at which her cakes were disappearing. 'She knew the visitors'd like that soft coffee cake, so I done plenty of that, and the chocolate brownies. But they won't last at this rate, will they?'

The Tea Room staff surveyed the depleted stocks anxiously.

'Me and Anthea could go down to the village shop and buy some biscuits and stuff,' Hazel volunteered, with admirable practicality.

'No need to do that,' Veronica told her. There was a note of satisfaction in her voice, like a train announcer with news that normal service has been resumed. 'We can use the cakes I've been making for the Cricket Club tea tomorrow. I can easily make some more tonight,' she added, with self-conscious nobility, and went off to fetch them.

Gerry Thornway had returned from a two-week golfing holiday in Bermuda the day before, and was not averse to showing off his tan. The opening of the Walled Herb Garden by a friend of his, Lady Susan Trugglestone, was also, he felt, an event at which he should make an appearance, and therefore drove down, nattily dressed in blazer and chinos, halfway through the afternoon. He had parked where the attendant indicated, before realising who the spare figure in kneed trousers was.

'How's it going then Clive?' he called, making a detour on his way to the gate, intending to slap his old school contemporary on the back, but Clive succeeded in keeping a car between them. 'Your missus roped in all the family, has she?'

Clive managed a faint smile. 'I didn't know you were interested in gardening.'

'My garden's been chosen for the Festival in July, you know. Thought I'd see what the competition was,' Gerry informed him matily.

Veronica spotted her husband's boss emerge from the car parking field just as she was carrying the Cricket Tea cakes, carefully stacked in a plastic storage box, the short distance from her house. Her first reaction was one of pleasure. To be found being so essential to Lady Trugglestone would be gratifying. But then she remembered their last encounter and her pace slowed, like a nervous horse sensing a threat ahead. She put the box down, pretending to adjust the contents, and only after he had entered the Walled Herb Garden and there was no chance of their paths crossing, did she carry the cakes into the Tea Room.

'Gerry Thornway's here,' she remarked with assumed casualness to Rosemary, as they unpacked the cakes. 'He didn't see me though.'

She was wrong.

Prentice Stalker had concluded, and reported to his boss before he went on holiday, that Settlewort probably *was* growing in the village again, and that Zinnia Peasmore was almost certainly involved. Admittedly he had drawn a blank in her garden, and in the rest of the village, but he was sure the whole family knew more than they were letting on. Both Gerry and Prentice had then separately tried talking to Derek about it, but he had seen them off without trouble, remarking caustically that if they hadn't anything better than some mythical herb to think about, at such a frantically busy time, then he certainly had.

Gerry didn't feel up to tackling Zinnia herself, especially as he had no wish to encounter her. But Derek's wife was another matter, he thought, walking round the Herb Garden. Seeing her outside reminded him - Elaine had said something about her friend Veronica helping with the Teas, and he nodded to himself. Every great tactician took advantage of circumstances, and this surely presented an opportunity. If she was caught on her own, there was a good chance she could be either flattered or bullied into telling him what he wanted to know. Needed to know, in fact. Clumpings were making increasingly unhappy noises, he'd discovered on his return. The sale of Thornways was now looking a good deal less certain, unless he could come up with some reason why the buyer should overlook its rocky financial situation. Settlewort would be just the trump card he needed. If it really was in the village, he must be able to get hold of it.

Completing his quick tour of the Walled Garden, ostentatiously greeting Lady Susan Trugglestone like a dear family friend, Gerry came in, looked round the Herb Shop, then sat down at a table by the window. Mrs Chitting went to take his order, but he waved her away. 'I'll wait till Mrs Peasmore's free,' he said imperiously. 'I want to talk to her.'

'That gentleman over there,' Mrs Chitting informed Veronica good humouredly, 'seems he wants you to serve him.'

Rosemary was busy in the Herb Shop, explaining how to use the herbal dye kits to a bespectacled young man already wearing a sludge green shirt, and shorts that may once have been brown.

There was no help for it, and Veronica put her chin up, and headed bravely for the window table. But halfway there a thought damaged her resolve. Gerry wouldn't know she was just helping out her friend Lady Trugglestone. He would think she had taken on waitressing as a job!

But he was very chummy, and exuded joviality. 'Nice to see the place opening at last, isn't it,' he said.

'Oh yes,' she rushed to dispel the waitress image, 'I've been helping Lady Trugglestone develop the herbal preserves. She wants to make quite a feature of them.'

'They sound delicious, I'll have to try some on my scones,' he said, spreading bonhomie thickly. 'You're interested in herbs, aren't you?'

'Yes. Well, that is…just in cooking, you know.' She fidgeted nervously with her note pad.

'I'd like to know more about that Settlewort, you were talking about last time we met.' He gave her a patronising smile. 'Why don't you sit down.'

'Oh no, really.' Gratification at being inveigled by her husband's boss vied with suspicion, and the fear that she would say the wrong thing. 'I'll just take your order,' she stammered, 'we're very busy.'

In fact, they were now experiencing something of a lull, as people who had made it their afternoon's outing departed, and those calling in on their way home from some other attraction had yet to arrive. In the Walled Garden Susie was telling Zinnia what a wonderful asset she had been.

'I don't know what we'd have done without you,' she said gratefully. 'Do go and have a cup of tea and something to eat, I'm sure you must need it.'

Zinnia accepted the invitation, and made her way to the Tea Room, realising suddenly that she was quite tired, although exhilarated. She had rather enjoyed her role, playing to the audience like an old pro. Plants were endlessly fascinating to her, but she found people, and youngsters especially, needed to be hooked by anecdotes, legends, or quaint historical and botanical facts. In fact this habit of linking her horticultural knowledge to so many other subjects was one of the things that made her gardening columns enjoyable to read.

She went into the Shop area, noting that Rosemary was serving, and looked around with interest, raising her eyebrows at some of the stock. Aprons and tablemats were not her thing, let alone ones lavishly decorated with herbs, but doubtless they would sell well.

From the Teas area came a murmur of conversation, most of it indistinguishable, but clearly through the babble, to her astonishment, she distinctly heard the word 'Settlewort', and what's more, it was a voice she recognised. Unobtrusively she perused the customers, quickly spotting it's owner sitting at a table by the window. And serving Gerry Thornway with tea and a scone was her daughter-in-law, looking about as happy as a rabbit marked out by a fox.

'You've got time to come and sit down now, I'm sure,' he wheedled, 'or perhaps I could come into the kitchen. Lady Susan wouldn't mind. Especially as it's a herb I want to talk about,' he added genially.

'Is this seat free?' Zinnia sped smoothly to the rescue, noting with satisfaction the look of grateful relief on Veronica's face. 'Good heavens Gerald, it comes to something when neighbours only meet when they bump into each other out for tea. You are an elusive man! Been trying to catch up with you for weeks.'

Gerry's face was a treat. From being the predator, he was now the trapped. But his discomfort was lessened when he realised, with surprise, that Zinnia didn't seem bent on talking about opposition to tipping in the Pit.

'Herbs are such interesting plants, aren't they,' she said conversationally. 'I've just acquired one I'm thrilled about.'

Gerry's hunted expression changed to one of hopeful interest.

'A new one?' he prompted.

'Well, not new of course. All medicinal plants are very old, as you know. But I never expected to be able to grow it.'

She smiled at him brightly. 'Do you want all that pot of tea, or might I cadge some of it?'

'Yes of course,' he said effusively, 'I'll ask for an extra cup.'

At last he could be getting somewhere. He flicked a bit of fluff off his sleeve, trying to look coolly casual. Just had to play the old girl along carefully.

'This herb,' he continued off-handedly, after a warily intrigued Veronica had brought another cup, 'What's it called, and, er, how many are you growing?'

'Oh goodness, just the one. It was an amazing piece of luck to come by it,' Zinnia told him, conveniently ignoring the first question. 'That's why I'm being so careful with it. At the moment I'm keeping the thing in a large pot in the greenhouse. I haven't any idea how tender it is, and you never know with these late frosts, do you.'

Enjoying herself now, she poured the tea, tiredness forgotten.

'But fairly shortly I'll put the pot outside, where I can see it from the kitchen window. Don't want to miss seeing it develop. According to the books it's rather beautiful. Not many herbs are, are they?'

Taking a sip of her tea, she paused while Gerry's brain processed this information.

'Do you have much to do with the herbs that your company uses?' she enquired guilelessly. 'I suppose it would be useful to visit your suppliers, for instance, and see the way the plants are grown.'

'This herb,' he said, brushing aside her enquiry, 'the thing you've only got one of – what does it do?'

'Oh powerful stuff, I believe. The Romans used it a lot.' Zinnia's evasive answer was worthy of a politician. 'Don't think I'd want to take it. And speaking of "taking it", I shall be putting it well out of the way on the Open Day. It pains me to say it, but plants have been known to go missing. What are you going to do about security?'

Rosemary was passing their table on her way back to the kitchen, and Zinnia gestured her over. 'I don't think you've met my niece from America,' she said easily. 'Rosemary this is Gerald Thornway.'

Gerry gave no sign of remembering her from the back-wetting incident at the Walled Garden a few weeks back, as he rose to shake hands.

'They're his peacocks you can hear from next door.'

'Yes, sorry about the peacocks,' Gerry mumbled, still standing. 'They don't come over now, I hope.'

'Not any more, no,' Zinnia's tone was dry. 'Can't think why. You haven't been putting the evil eye on them, have you Rosemary?'

'Maybe they were spooked by getting into the Pit Garden a while back,' Rosemary suggested with a sweet smile, 'and, er, not being able to find their way out.'

'Ah, yes, the Pit. Gerald, we need to talk…'

'Another time, I'm afraid I must be off,' Gerry cut Zinnia short. His tête-à-tête with her had proved surprisingly useful, but the Pit, and why he was not joining in her fight was the last thing he wanted to talk about.

'Derek's right. Swathe must have nobbled him somehow,' Zinnia remarked, unperturbed, watching him depart. 'Oh dear, he's left his scone. Shame to waste it,' and she reached across for the plate.

'You know I *have* enjoyed myself this afternoon,' she confided to Rosemary, who left her happily consuming her neighbour's tea with the satisfied expression of one who's just handed some sharp-clawed puppy a balloon to play with.

****

In Mrs Chitting, Rosemary found a steady, hard-working and obliging colleague. Susie had only asked her to stay until five-thirty, when the tea room closed, but unexpectedly there was a last minute rush, and neither she nor Rosemary was willing to leave the place until everything had been properly cleared and put away. Veronica had gone off to make some more cakes for the Cricket Club tea, Clive had cashed up and taken the girls back to the Hall, and Susie was still coping with lingering customers in the Walled Garden, so they tackled the task on their own.

'You must find it awkward, helping both Lady Julia and Lady Susan,' Rosemary remarked, unsure whether she could call them Julia and Susie in such circumstances. She put down a pile of plates and cups to be washed. 'I mean they don't get on, do they?'

'Lot worse when they was both living at the Hall, it were,' said Mrs Chitting placidly. 'Been better since Lady have her own place. And the last week or so she's been happy as I've ever seen her. That's dropped years off her, that has.'

'Summer makes everybody feel better, doesn't it.' Rosemary was aware of this in the lightening of her own mood.

'Not the weather. She's took up with a friend.' Mrs Chitting sounded cautious. 'Can't say as I'd have chosen him, but he certainly have a way with her. Took her to the races, and the theatre. She's gone to London today with him.'

This was intriguing news.

'Hey that's great! She's such a nice person.' Rosemary went to collect more things from the Tea Room. 'I must tell Zinnia,' she called back. 'Is she likely to know the lucky man?'

Mrs Chitting was fishing in a teapot for a fugitive teabag. 'Reckon she will,' she said, and there was a long pause. 'It's that Mike Swathe.'

'No kidding!'

Rosemary put the tray down with a crash on the worktop, misjudging the distance. 'Wow. Better not tell my aunt then. Hardly going to make things better between them, is it?'

She was thinking, as she unloaded the tray. 'Zinnia said they all knew each other when they were young. Were you living in Haydon then?'

'Lived here all my life,' she said simply. 'But he's older, and I were only about twelve when he went away.' She put Rosemary's load of plates and saucers in the water. 'Seems he couldn't wait to leave the village.'

'And he never came back?'

'Not to live. Can't say as I blame him. Sour as a bullace, old Mrs Swathe were. He couldn't do nothing right.'

'But you don't like him?' Rosemary was hunting in the cupboards for a dustpan and brush.

'I just want Lady to be happy.' Mrs Chitting paused, to let the drips pour off a plate before putting it in the rack. 'She've been through bad times. It were a shock, Sir Richard dying like that. My Fred now, he were ill for almost a year, so that weren't the same.'

A thought occurred to Rosemary as she swept crumbs off the chairs. Perhaps she could help Susie in her so far fruitless struggle over Harry Trench's cottage.

'It must be strange, living on your own after all those years together,' she said delicately, 'don't you ever think it would be nice to get married again, and have a man about the house. Someone to cook for and look after?'

Unbidden, Zinnia's horrified face at any such suggestion came to mind, and she suppressed a smile.

Mrs Chitting chuckled. 'Old Harry Trench, he have the same idea. Me and Fred always used to have him in, seeing as how he were on his own. Now he does the garden for me, and I cook him his tea most days.'

'Can I borrow that cloth to wipe the tables?' Rosemary asked, and, temporarily halted, Mrs Chitting stood at the sink, gazing out of the window. 'Wouldn't have felt right though, having another man in the cottage. Not in Fred's place.'

'But you'll be moving to your new home soon,' Rosemary called, encouragingly. 'It'll be a whole new start.'

'Yes,' was the pensive reply. 'Yes, that will.'

Chapter Seventeen

By the end of the first week in June, a fortnight after being carefully planted out, the Settlewort was beginning to look at home in its new surroundings. Zinnia had chosen one of the south-facing ledges about four foot from the ground, and carefully chipped away at the chalk to form a deeper pocket of soil for its roots. Cunningly, she had then planted a grey-leaved deadnettle as a companion, and already this was rooting its way along the ledge. The plan was for it to grow over the base of the Settlewort, making it look as though the plant had germinated there, pushing its way through the groundcover.

About two and a half feet tall now, the plant on which all her hopes were fastened had thickened up and branched, the top surface of the glossy, willow-like leaves gleaming in the midday sun, contrasting attractively with the greyish underside. Zinnia paid it visits two or three times a day, as restlessly anxious as a mother leaving her offspring at nursery school for the first time.

'I just don't know how much to water it,' she confessed to Rosemary, and tended to see-saw between giving it a little every day, and administering a soaking once every three or four days. Obligingly, the plant continued to flourish under both regimes, but of developing buds there was no sign.

This was disappointing.

'What if it doesn't flower at all?' asked Rosemary, going to call her aunt in for supper, and finding her standing in front of it. 'You said that's what would really clinch its identification.'

'Well, we're only a week into June, so it's early days. The books say it doesn't flower until July, but... yes, you're right, it is a worry. I want to be able to announce that it's growing in the Pit as soon as it looks natural.'

'Surely the answer is to get some expert you trust to identify it. How about that Simon Forb? The guy I met at Susie's party. If we sent him a few leaves, he could check it at Kew. He's working there.'

'No.' Zinnia was adamant. 'I'm not letting anyone have bits of it. And in any case, he'd head straight down here, and the plant's not ready for that. When the experts do come and give it the once over, it's got to look really convincing and well established.'

She brushed away from the Settlewort some paulownia flowers, now being shed in a rain of regretful mauve from the nearby tree. Their scent still lingered, but was now being conquered by waves of intoxicating fragrance from a large philadelphus behind the summer house. It seemed to be fighting it out with a neighbouring kolkwitzia as to which could bear the most flowers, and as the two women walked up the ramp to the house, the scent of Sweet Rocket, self-seeded copiously around the Pit, wafted up to them, mingling deliciously with the early roses. The burgeoning of the garden had been a revelation to Rosemary, who was overwhelmed by the colour, beauty and scent. The thought of it being buried under tons of rubble just didn't bear thinking about.

'Well, how about you taking some leaves down to Kew yourself,' she suggested, taking the savoury rice out of the warming oven, 'and checking them against a dried example. You could write and say you were interested in Settlewort because of its association with the village.'

'Mm.' Clearly this didn't evoke enthusiasm. 'I'm not really happy about leaving the premises for that long. I don't trust Gerry or that Stalker man one inch.'

Truth to tell, she found the whole idea of the trip rather daunting as well, but there was no need to admit it. Her face suddenly cleared. 'But you could.'

'Could what?'

'Take a leaf down to the Herbarium at Kew, and compare it with a dried specimen. How about asking your friend if he can arrange a visit? Then none of the powers that be are likely to start asking awkward questions.'

'Well...' Rosemary was doubtful, sharply aware of her horticultural limitations.

'You could stay a couple of nights,' Zinnia encouraged her, 'it's about time you got away from the village, and sampled the great metropolis. It's a different world.' She gave a faint smile. 'Up there they think we Suffolk bumpkins are still pointing at planes.'

****

The following week Rosemary found herself on a broad expanse of grass outside the main gate of Kew Gardens, and very inclined to point at planes, as they loured enormously overhead, with their landing wheels down, on their way into Heathrow. Hard to believe that not so long ago she had been sitting in one of those things, apprehensively looking down at London, and wondering what she was letting herself in for. A trip to the Royal Botanical Gardens to consult their Herbarium about a plant considered extinct? No chance. Yet here she was, having made an early start, negotiated the train from Ipswich, and then rather apprehensively taken the Tube across London. Now she needed to discover the entrance to the Herbarium and Library.

The brick-built building was large and had a dignity of age and design. She found her way to the Reception Desk, and signed the Visitors Book, while the receptionist rang for Simon, who duly appeared.

'Good to see you again,' he greeted her with casual friendliness. 'Look, I'll show you where you can leave your stuff,' he indicated her overnight bag, 'and then we'll go into the Herbarium. I've told the staff I'll sort you out.'

That done, she followed him into a large room divided into window bays, each containing a table. The walls were lined with three layers of white-painted cupboards, five double-doors deep, bearing brass bracketed labels announcing mysteries such as "113.01 Convulaceae", which might have meant something to her aunt, but could have been in Sanskrit for all they conveyed to Rosemary. The middle of the room was taken up with a large island of wooden cabinets, while at first and second floor level were galleries, evidently packed with more records and plant samples.

'Say, this is like something out of Dickens,' exclaimed Rosemary, gazing round.

'Well, I'm not sure he had computers,' Simon commented, waving towards a monitor on one of the tables, 'but Kew Herbarium was certainly established in his day. I find it fascinating, reading the accounts of people who collected plants, maybe a hundred and fifty years ago, and there, in front of you, is the dried specimen they're describing. It's like being a time traveller.'

He led her over to a bay, and opened one of the cupboards.

'It's Solanum regale, you want to look at, isn't it? I'm not quite clear why though.'

Rosemary was well-rehearsed. 'Well we're having this Gardens Festival in the village next month, and Haydon Settleworth is named after Settlewort, so my aunt thought we ought to mug up on it. I'm helping with the publicity, you see.'

'Uh huh.' Simon's tone was light. 'Would that be the aunt who's this plant she thinks is rather special, and wants to identify? You were telling me, at the party, remember?'

Oh rats, he had a good memory. 'Er... yes. How stupid, I should have brought it with me. We didn't think.' This hardly established herself and Zinnia as the dynamic duo. 'And of course, I'm interested in the herbs witches used,' she rushed on, anxious to distract. 'I was reading about someone in Haydon who was tried for witchcraft. Actually she was just trying to help some poor girl marry the right man.'

'Ah, love potions,' said Simon amiably, lifting a book like an enormous photograph album onto the table. 'Tricky things, those. Now, have you ever consulted Herbarium specimens before, or do you need me to show you what's what?'

A few minutes later, she was fully instructed in the rules and niceties of examining dried plant specimens, and Simon made to go. 'I'll call back and see how you're getting on in a while,' he said encouragingly. 'And I thought we could go to a pub across the green for lunch. You'll need a breath of fresh air by then.'

Rosemary was left sitting at the table, notebook at the ready, the book of pressed specimens in front of her. Gingerly she opened it, turned to a page labelled *Solanum regale*, and found herself staring at the willow-like fronds of Settlewort. The vibrant green of the top surface was faded with desiccation and age, but the contrast with the grey underside was still clearly evident. She looked about her cautiously, then reached down for her handbag, and brought out the clear plastic covering from a greetings card. Putting it on the table, she carefully removed the leaf which Zinnia, with the wincing reluctance of a child compelled to pull out a hanging milk tooth, had cut early that morning. A faint smell of peaches invaded the air, and clung to her fingers, as she laid the leaf on the table, and compared the two. There was no mistaking – they were the same.

Unseen on the first floor gallery opposite, Simon watched her, nodded thoughtfully, and then went back to his work.

Painstakingly, Rosemary copied into her notebook everything that she thought might be useful. "*Stamens exserted, inserted in throat of corolla-tube, anthers connivent, in an ovoid column, dehiscing by two terminal pores*" was as clear as a legal document to her, but perhaps it would mean more to Zinnia. Although she had her doubts.

The pressed specimen had apparently been collected in 1875 from wasteland around Dartford, and showed a white (now grey) flower, with the circumference of an egg cup. It was divided into five segments by purple lines, and she could imagine the blooms would be very attractive on a plant. Also pretty distinctive. Certainly she had never seen anything like them. And the seed... with a thrill of recognition, she realised that, even crushed flat for a hundred and twenty-two years, the Solanum's brown seed had the curious butt shape of the ones she had discovered in that little box.

After copying down everything that seemed relevant, Rosemary gazed out of the window at a depressing flat roof, and was wondering which unsympathetic member of staff was in charge of the dying spider plants in pots on the sill, when Simon came back. She was glad to see him, and very ready for the bar food offered by the Coach and Horses across the other side of the green.

Several people greeted him, as they came in and sat at a table in the corner.

'Tends to be the lunchtime oasis for a lot of the researchers,' he explained, and went to the bar with their order.

'Now, tell me about Susie's Herb Garden effort. She's just opened it hasn't she,' he suggested, sitting down again. Glad of a nice, safe subject, Rosemary launched into an account of the opening weekend, including overheard customer remarks, which she rather enjoyed telling, although there wasn't much listener reaction. Prompted, she told him about the village, and how relaxed and at home she felt there, and about Zinnia, battling to save her garden.

'I can't bear to think of it all being destroyed,' she said, 'it's just wonderful.'

'Hm. A chalk pit,' he said musingly. 'Didn't know there was any chalk in Suffolk. I must look at a geological map. And come down and see it. Susie clearly needs me to tell her where she's going wrong with that herb place, and it would be nice to see you in your Suffolk habitat as well. How about next week?'

'Ah, well...I think next week might be a bit soon,' Rosemary was suddenly on the defensive. 'That is, I'll have to ask my aunt.'

'Doesn't she allow visitors? I thought she was opening it to the public?'

'Well, yes. No. I mean...she's very particular about...it only being seen at its best. In fact, she doesn't like people at all really.' Rosemary could hear herself becoming more implausible by the second.

'I see.' Simon took a slow pull at his beer. 'Well, I'll come and visit Susie, and then present myself at your aunt's abode, shall I, and ask if she'll let me in I? Be on my best behaviour.'

He seemed irritatingly determined. She opened her mouth to object, and then gave up.

'Pity really,' he added, and she looked at him questioningly.

'If Settlewort had still been growing in your village, I could have asked you to slip some in her tea or something. Put your knowledge of witchcraft herbs into practice. Isn't that what it was supposed to do? Soften people up?'

'I think our food's ready. They're waving at you from the bar,' Rosemary told him, uncomfortably.

She was saved from more awkward conversation when he returned, by the arrival of three of his colleagues, whom Simon introduced as part of the team going out to India in a few weeks' time. They drew chairs up to the table, and although she asked a few questions, mostly she just listened as the chat flowed back and forth. Much of it was over her head, but the forthcoming trip did sound fascinating just the same.

****

I guess there doesn't have to be a thousand mile distance to feel you're in a separate part of the universe, Rosemary e-mailed to Bill a few days later. *Haydon and London might as well be different worlds. I wasn't prepared for the crowds of people somehow, half of them rushing around like it was Sale time at Mace's, and throngs of tourists milling about with maps. I hid mine, and consulted it furtively in doorways. No use asking anyone for directions. They all turn out to be from Munich, or Milan, or Milwaukee.*

Don't think I make a good tourist, you would be ashamed of me. Sure I saw Buckingham Palace and the Houses of Parliament, watched people taking photos of other people feeding pigeons in Trafalgar Square, and walked along Piccadilly. Did the gallery bit too. But shopping in Oxford Street – well what's so great about it?

Then, at Derek's suggestion, I went to the Science Museum. Oh boy, what a great place! Could have spent a whole week in there, it was just wonderful.

She hardly mentioned Simon. Well it didn't seem necessary, except to say that he was a friend of Susie's who had been her entrée to the Herbarium, and was coming down to Haydon the following week, and might call in to see the Pit Garden while he was there.

She and Zinnia had chewed over what to do about this.

'You can hardly refuse to let him come round,' Rosemary argued, having been detailed to pull out seedy forget-me-nots in the bed by the back door, while her aunt cut off spent aquilegias. Roger the Lodger sat on the step in the sun, casually overseeing their labours. 'I already made myself sound ridiculous by implying you don't welcome visitors.'

'I don't,' said Zinnia shortly, 'in fact...'

'I know, I know, only "proper gardeners",' Rosemary cut in teasingly. 'But I'd say this guy was a real gift. Not only does his work involve medicinal plants, but he's got exactly the right connections. He can have Settlewort identified properly, and then get the Kew people all excited, so they kick up a fuss about the tipping, and put a stop to it.'

'Mm.' Zinnia considered, while she dumped a load of aquilegias in the wheelbarrow. 'But it's too soon. The plant doesn't look quite natural enough yet. I really don't want anyone questioning the fact that it grew there of its own accord. Another couple of weeks and it would be fine.'

Gathering up an armful of forget-me-nots, Rosemary took them towards the barrow, Roger trying to decide whether to pounce on a trailing piece. 'See, I don't reckon you have much choice,' she insisted. 'Who are you going to ask to come down here and identify it, otherwise?. Someone smelling a rat is a risk you'll just have to take. And don't forget, Simon seems determined to come, whether you want him to or not.'

Her aunt gave her a searching look. 'Is he? You wouldn't be the attraction, by any chance?'

'Oh sure,' Rosemary laughed dismissively. But secretly she found it a not unpleasant thought.

****

The following Thursday Susie was pleased to be able to show the Walled Herb Garden to a knowledgeable friend.

'Pity you didn't see it before, though,' she lamented, giving him a tour of the place in drizzling rain. 'It was a sea of weeds. The old gardener here had taken over part of it for his precious fuchsias and things, but the rest of it had been let go. We've been working frantically to get it ready.'

'I hear you were almost knocked over in the rush at the opening weekend,' he commented, pinching a lemon balm leaf and sniffing appreciatively, 'how's it been since then?'

'Well, we're only opening at weekends for the moment. And actually the response has been very pleasing. I've now got a couple of women from the village to come in and serve teas, and man the shop. I wasn't sure the takings would warrant paid staff at first.'

'Ah yes, I heard you deployed the redoubtable Rosemary on voluntary waitressing duties.'

Susie was unlocking the shop, before ushering him in. 'Now you're not to mock,' she told him severely. 'Okay, so some of the stuff is a bit chi-chi, but it sells, that's the main thing. People *like* pot-pourri jars.'

Giving a cursory look round, he picked up a leaflet by the till. '*The Walled Herb Garden at Haydon Settleworth, – Home of the Lost Herb*,' he read aloud. 'I always said you should have been in marketing. That's Solanum regale you're referring to, I presume.' He raised his eyebrows at her. 'A bit of artistic licence there. It did grow in other places, didn't it.'

He put it down, and examined the titles of books on one of the shelves. Susie looked at him curiously.

'Simon, why exactly are you here? I mean, it's lovely to see you, and show you what I'm doing. But it's a Thursday. Why aren't you busy searching out what makes fakirs rise, or whatever you're doing at the moment?'

'Just thought I'd take a day's holiday, and come down and see how you peasants live,' he said, adding casually, 'and I'm going to see this Pit Garden of Rosemary's Dragon Aunt. She was telling me about it. Sounds fascinating.'

Enlightenment slowly dawned. 'Oh, it's *Rosemary* you've come to see!' exclaimed Susie. 'Why didn't you say so?'

He took out a book, and flipped through the pages without responding.

'Now you're not to mess her around,' Susie warned him. 'She's a sweet girl, I'm very fond of her. *And* she's got a fiancé in Antarctica. He sounds a complete dork, but...' she shrugged.

'Yes, she told me about him.' He put back the book, and continued scanning the titles.

'Seriously Simon, she's had a tough time recently, and I wouldn't like to see her get hurt.'

He turned round. 'You can quit the Mother Hen act,' he gave her a bland smile. 'I think you'll find she'll be quite safe.'

By the time Simon arrived at Kiln House that afternoon, the rain had ceased, leaving a damp, warm atmosphere, and the steady dripping of moisture from the trees.

Zinnia had decided she wanted to sum him up, whilst touring the garden. Only if he passed muster was she prepared to trust him. But she was pleasantly surprised to find that he had a great deal of knowledge, and not just about medicinal plants. Also he seemed interested in how the garden had evolved, and her choice of plants.

'We lived on the Sussex Downs when I was a child,' he told her, 'and I always marvelled at the number of flowers thriving on what seemed like pure chalk. How did you decide what to grow?'

Rosemary was included in the group, if barely in the conversation, as they progressed round the Pit Garden. She felt irrelevant, and somewhat nettled, like a girl bringing the new boyfriend home, only to have him chumming up with her mother and discussing recipes. Trailing behind them she found her eyes drawn to the nape of Simon's neck. What was it about a man's youthful neck that was so attractive, she wondered. And did they know? Judging by the off-putting display of chest hair and pectorals on beaches, probably not. Mind you, it might be rather difficult to flaunt the back of your neck. She smiled at the thought, but found she still had the yen to stroke Simon's blonde hair and neck. Cool it, she told herself sternly. You've been starved of male company, that's all it is.

Zinnia's plan had been to avoid the far section of the perimeter path, but obviously their visitor must have passed whatever devious horticultural tests had been set, for now she turned right at the pond, past a large white abutilon, and a spread of yellow spires standing smartly to attention.

'A friend gave me the seed of that verbascum,' she told him, 'but he didn't know its name. It's a very good one, perennial, and doesn't seed badly.' She spotted a yellow and black caterpillar, and picked it off with annoyance. 'You have to keep a close eye on these little beggars, or they strip it to shreds.'

Simon made polite noises, but clearly his attention was elsewhere. From yards away he had spotted the solanum growing on the ledge, and couldn't take his eyes off it as they approached. Zinnia noticed him staring, smiled to herself, and decided to do away with the teasing, as she stopped in front of it.

The dead-nettle had made good progress, and was at least partially covering the base of the plant, although not yet providing complete cover. Moisture clung to the fronded leaves of the Settlewort like drop diamonds, and the smell of damp earth rose to mingle with a faint scent of peaches as the sun broke through and fingered the plant warmly.

'Now, this is what I need identifying,' she said, her voice a mixture of pride and apprehension. 'It's a solanum, isn't it. Do you think it could be…?'

Rosemary watched Simon's expression. He stood as if at a shrine. By now he had memorised every description in Kew's library and herbarium concerning Solanum regale, and felt certain that this striking plant just couldn't be anything else. If so, he was standing before one of the most important medicinal plants of the ancient world, something that was thought extinct and had miraculously reappeared. It was momentous. And wouldn't do his career any harm at all.

He took off his glasses and peered at the plant, then put them on again. 'Very interesting,' he said eventually, trying to keep the excitement out of his voice. 'Certainly looks like a solanum. I'd need to take some leaves back to Kew to be certain what it was,' and he stepped towards it.

'Absolutely not,' Zinnia told him, peremptorily.

She decided to put her cards on the table. Well some of them anyhow.

'Now let's not mess about,' she said firmly. 'We're pretty sure the thing is Settlewort. Rosemary did take one leaf up to Kew, and it matched the sample there.'

'Yes, I wondered about her interest', he admitted, glancing at Rosemary for the first time, 'especially when she said you had a very special plant you wanted to identify.'

'What we need,' Zinnia went on, 'is official identification. And then wheels must be put in motion to stop the company that's bought this Pit from using it for tipping. They've already got permission from the County Council. Would you be able to help?'

'Well…yes, I think so,' he said earnestly. 'That is, I'll speak to people at Kew, and see what we can do. When did you first notice it?' A thought struck him. 'And are there any more?'

'Not that I know of,' Zinnia appeared not to have heard the first question. 'But they could possibly be germinating all round the Pit. Maybe conditions are just right this year or something. I'm keeping my eyes peeled.'

Rosemary sent her aunt a look of fond exasperation. She was laying it on a bit thick. The man wasn't a fool.

But Simon was too exhilarated to look for any seams in the tale, as he quickly reviewed who to speak to as soon as he got back.

'They are going to need some leaves, you know,' he informed Zinnia, cautiously fingering one, and savouring the fruity aroma. 'For identification. No-one's just going to take my word for it.'

'You can have *one*,' she told him grudgingly, reaching into her pocket for secateurs. 'And if that isn't enough, you can tell the bods at Kew that they'll just have to come down and see it for themselves.'

****

They rather expected to hear from Simon in the next few days, but there followed a frustrating silence.

Zinnia brooded mistrustfully on whether she should have let anyone have a leaf of her one precious plant, which she was now guarding fiercely. Any visitor found wandering round to the back, having gained no response at the front door, discovered, like a fly on a spider's web, that the owner was immediately alerted. Kiln House was too far out of the village for the usual charity collections, but distance was merely one of God's tests to those intent on preaching His message. A couple of fresh-faced American evangelists were somewhat taken aback to find their mission encountering such stony ground, while the electricity meter reader she surprised checking that there was no external meter, reckoned that he preferred protective dogs any day, and decided to request a change of route.

The plant by the garage had never recovered from the crushing embrace of the chimney pot, the second, which had flourished so promisingly in the cracked greenhouse step, was now a crushed and blackened stump, and the cuttings taken from it had not found life to their liking either. So all Zinnia's hopes rested on the one survivor.

'In a way that's good,' Rosemary assured her. 'After all if there is only one in the world, it's unthinkable to destroy where it's growing.'

She had much to distract her from Zinnia's problems, as she continued to help Susie, whilst becoming more involved with the organisation and publicity drive for the Gardens Festival. She particularly enjoyed contact with local business people, approached to advertise in the programme cum entry ticket. They were warm and friendly, and she was pleased to be accepted as part of the village.

There was also the purchase of Mrs Chitting's cottage. She'd engaged Zinnia's solicitor, who she now suspected had been a snail in a previous incarnation. A very good snail, of course, to have made the leap of life forms, but she was finding his mollusc-like progress decidedly irritating.

With those antecedents, why couldn't he have become an artists' model, or a sentry outside Buckingham Palace?

There was no particular reason for hurry, since Mrs Chitting's bungalow purchase seemed to be going just as slowly, but Rosemary felt impatient just the same. She managed to prise her aunt away from guard duties, and eagerly took her to see the house and garden, with it's owner's permission.

'Well,' said Zinnia without obvious enthusiasm, after looking round the house, and ruefully noting that it was in better shape than her own, 'hope you know what you're doing.'

But the garden evoked a much more favourable reaction. Like Julia's, it sloped down to the river in three terraces. The top one, behind the cottage, Harry Trench had planted out with his beloved fuchsias, and an array of antirrhinums, lobelia and petunias, which were already making a bright show. African Marigolds and pelargoniums lit the way along the path at the side of the house, and large-flowered fuchsias, in plastic tubs, were just breaking into flower at the top of the steps.

On the second level, he was growing vegetables and soft fruit in orderly rows, while the bottom terrace by the river was largely grass, with rows of dahlias making strong growth in a bed. But what gave Spring Cottage its name was the clear water that bubbled up into a stone trough, from the foot of a wall on the second level. Someone had built a concrete channel for it, and here and there it disappeared into large sections of pipe as it made its way down to the river.

'What a waste!' Zinnia exclaimed, standing on the river bank, looking up. 'I've always wanted a stream. And think what could be done with this! You could make a series of ponds, and waterfalls, and little runnels with damp-loving plants. It would be just wonderful! And these retaining walls are positively crying out for things growing against them, and in them, and plants draping down from above.'

'You think the garden might need a bit of a change then?' suggested Rosemary, dead-pan. 'Only I sure don't know what to do.'

'Hm,' Zinnia sounded cautious. The cry of 'You must tell me what to do with my garden!' was a familiar one, always uttered by non-gardeners who could be guaranteed not to follow her suggestions, or if they did, would make a complete dog's dinner through lack of interest and empathy. 'It'd be a lot of hard work, and maybe you'd have to get landscapers in to build the ponds and stream bed. But,' her voice was gaining in enthusiasm as a gardener's instincts took hold, 'I could give you plants, and suggest where to put them. It's an ideal size, and has the potential to be simply lovely.'

Harry Trench's bent-backed figure hove into view on the top terrace, as they began to make their way up. With his earth-coloured tweed cap and faded jacket, which he seemed to wear all year round, he blended into the background, like a thrush on the ground, and it was movement you noticed rather than the outline. He stood up, critically assessing the straightness of a row of newly-planted petunias.

'How are you Harry? We've been admiring your vegetables,' Zinnia lied shamelessly.

'Fair to midlin',' he touched his cap, and nodded in greeting. 'Them beans is looking good, and the taters,' he agreed immodestly. 'You 'ont grow a good tater in these parts without you give 'em a good bit o' compost.'

'Yes, I was noticing your compost heap,' she told him, adding, truthfully this time, 'it looked wonderful stuff.'

They were duly given an escorted tour of all his fuchsias and other treasures in the garden near the house, Harry being 'partial to a bit o'colour', as he remarked, with understatement. Inadvertently, Rosemary brushed against a pelargonium, and enquired what was making the pungent smell. Zinnia pointed out the culprit, and it was then that Harry dropped the explosive.

'That ol' plant you was a-growin',' he said to her, when they were about to make polite leaving overtures, 'the one as have that there fruity pong. Do it have a name?'

Zinnia looked startled. 'You mean the plant in a pot that was put out for the Brownies' stall by mistake? Um...no. At least, I don't know what it is. Why?' she added guardedly. 'Are you interested in it?'

Harry bent over to pull out a bit of chickweed. 'That gentleman, Mr Thornway, as lives next to you, I do 'is garden of a Tuesday,' he informed her, straightening up slowly. 'Asked me what it was, he did. He have it coming up all over the place.'

****

Zinnia's skin was too weather beaten to go ashen, but she looked decidedly sick as they returned home.

'Why didn't I think of that,' she berated herself, sinking onto a chair at the kitchen table. 'Of course. Most of the peacock's droppings would have been deposited over there.'

Rosemary filled the kettle from the tap, judging that a cup of tea should be administered. 'I wonder how many plants there are in his garden?' she said. '"All over the place" might mean ten, or, I don't know... a hundred.'

'No it couldn't.' Zinnia's brain had been active. 'After all, there were only thirty-two seeds in that box, weren't there. I sowed half, and they did nothing. Then later the peacocks ate the rest, and as a result of their, um, enforced holiday over here, three seeds germinated. If only the ruddy birds hadn't escaped...'

'Oh I see, that means there could only be, er, thirteen plants over there, and that's if they all germinated.'

Zinnia shook her head gloomily. 'Yes, but three or thirteen, it still scuppers our plan to save the Pit Garden. It's no longer Settlewort's special habitat, is it?' She paused, and then declared forcefully, 'We've just got to get those plants out of Gerry's garden!. But how?'

Opening the tin of teabags, Rosemary could see what was coming. 'Oh no,' she warned, 'you sure as hell aren't getting me in on the act. I draw the line at stealing.'

'Well it wouldn't exactly be stealing, would it,' her aunt's voice was persuasive. 'It isn't as if he wants the things, does he? Just wondered what they were.'

'You bet he would if he knew what the plant was.'

They looked at each other, the delicious irony of the situation suddenly appealing to their sense of humour.

'Oh it's wonderful. There's Gerry virtually importuning poor Veronica at the Herb Garden,' said Zinnia, her voice breaking up, 'chasing her for information about a plant for Thornways...'

'And all the time he's got it growing in his own garden!' Rosemary put the teapot on the table with a hand that was shaking. 'Don't that beat all,' she said in a southern drawl, and they collapsed into giggles.

'Oh dear,' Zinnia was the first to recover, feeling better already. 'No, we've got to think about this situation seriously. Apart from anything else, what's going to happen when Simon gets the botanical Powers That Be jumping up and down about saving the chalk pit habitat of this unique plant – and it turns out there are plenty more in an ordinary garden next door? We'd look complete fools. And his career would be ruined.'

This thought hadn't occurred to Rosemary, and was immediately sobering. She couldn't let that happen to Simon.

'Well, let's consider the options,' she suggested seriously, pouring the tea. 'One, you could dig them up at dead of night. And I stress the word "you". Or two, you could kill them. Spray them with weedkiller or something. But that's only if your conscience would allow you to destroy something so rare and valuable...'

She passed a mug across the table with raised eyebrows and disapproving expression, but her aunt's face was giving nothing away.

A third option occurred. 'Or perhaps you could tell Gerry they were very poisonous plants, so that he turfs them out.'

'I don't think that would work,' Zinnia reflected, stirring her tea. 'If it came from me, he'd be bound to suspect something. But maybe if we told Harry, he'd inform Gerry they were deadly poisonous.'

'Better still, why don't you let Harry in on the secret, then he could dig them up… '

'Encourage him to steal from his employer!' Zinnia affected shock. 'Really, I'm surprised at you. No, I don't think telling Harry anything is a good idea. He looks simple and childlike, but you just don't know how much he understands. Besides, I wouldn't feel comfortable deceiving the old boy.' She took a sip. 'I suppose the first thing to do is take a look at these plants. How many there are, where, and how easy it would be to dig them up. Now, when could we do that?'

'We? You aren't roping me into this you know.'

Zinnia smiled. 'You're rejecting the Lookout's job then? You're so incurious,' she teased. 'Wouldn't you like to view the great Gerald Thornway's garden?'

'I already did,' retorted Rosemary. 'Went round all the gardens that are going to be open for the Gardens Festival, when I was composing that flyer, remember. His wife, Elaine, let me look round. Not that the place was exciting. Nigella had to write the description in the end, because I couldn't make it sound interesting.'

'Now there's a thought,' said Zinnia, and Rosemary looked at her with suspicion. 'Elaine and Veronica are chummy, and I've remembered they go to a Health Club in Stockleigh on Wednesday mornings. Goodness knows what goes on in a Health Club,' she commented disparagingly. 'It could be a cover for a bordello, for all I know.' There was a pause, while she pictured her uptight daughter-in-law, and the mousy Elaine, and then shook her head with slight regret. 'No. At least this one couldn't. Anyway, Gerry'll be at work, she'll be healthing it up in Stockleigh, and it's the ideal time for us to go on a little light trespassing.'

'You,' corrected Rosemary, taking her mug to the sink. 'I shall make sure I'm some place else.'

****

She didn't have to try particularly hard, since two days later Susie was anxious for her help at the Herb Garden. Matthew's elaborate stock control system was not going according to plan, and it was plain that the numbers of plants in the garden and greenhouse fell short of what the computer was listing. Probably some had been lost to theft, but the biggest discrepancy, Susie reckoned, was simply down to not entering the sales properly.

'My fault,' she admitted, 'but the trouble is, when we're busy and there's a queue of people, you just want to process each sale as quickly as possible. And I really do need to know what the true stock position is, so I can order more stuff, apart from anything else.'

As they went round the sales area together, the sun kept peeping out from behind grey clouds, becoming shy, and retreating again, like a teenager trying to flirt for the first time. Susie counted the plants, while Rosemary wrote the number down, compared it to the figure on the computer printout, and came up with the shortfall.

The successful launch of the Walled Herb Garden, and its continuing popularity, had been a great relief to Susie. Unfortunately it only increased her annoyance at having her offer of doing teas for the Flower and Gardens Festival ignored.

'We're all geared up for doing teas now,' she complained, attempting to count the various lavenders. 'And yet nowhere on the information leaflets that I've seen does it say that teas are available here. Does it?'

'Er, no.' Rosemary was not anxious to be drawn into this particular battle.

'Apart from anything else it looks bad, as if we're not helping the village effort.'

Rosemary regarded Susie's bent back with affectionate amusement. 'And I suppose the tea customers couldn't be expected to buy stuff from the shop and garden, could they?' she remarked naughtily.

'Whose side are you on?' Susie demanded, with mock indignation. 'I told that Daphne Stalker woman we'd do it on a not-for-profit basis, and she was quite keen at first. But then it seems my dear mother-in-law put her oar in, and persuaded the organising committee to go for the Village Hall only. Not that they had the decency to tell me. Oh damn, the 'Hidcotes' have all got mixed up with the 'Twickel Purples'. Hang on, I'll have to sort them out.'

'Are you sure Julia did that?' Rosemary objected hesitantly. 'It doesn't sound like her.'

'She's dead against this place,' Susie's voice was resentful, 'she just wants it to fail, and then she thinks I'll give up, and concentrate on producing a son and heir.'

'And would you? If it didn't work out, I mean.'

'Well to be honest, I'd like another child, and so would Clive. And of course it would be lovely if it was a boy. But not for her reasons.' She screwed up her face. 'It's not practical though. We've just got to earn some money. Okay, that's three 'Twickel Purples', and six 'Hidcotes'. I must get some more Twickel Purples in quick, before we run out. They're obviously popular. Besides,' she went back to their conversation, 'I don't like being told what to do, especially with the inference that if I came from the right background, I'd know my duty. She's such a snob.'

'Oh come on,' Rosemary defended Julia. 'She doesn't seem like a snob to me. After all she's...'

She stopped abruptly. 'Say, I wonder how the lavenders got muddled up. And how are you going to stop that happening again?'

But Susie was not to be distracted.

'After all she's what?' she demanded, straightening up. 'What were you going to say?'

Me and my big mouth, Rosemary chided herself. 'Well, because she's... according to Mrs Chitting that is, she's, um... seeing Mike Swathe.'

'*What*?' This was clearly news to her daughter-in-law. 'Oh that's rich, that is,' she exclaimed. '*I'm* not good enough, but a jumped up scrap metal merchant is!'

'Now who's being a snob?' suggested Rosemary mildly. 'In the States, we reckon someone who makes it up from the bottom of the heap deserves the kudos for showing brains and initiative.'

'Well, yes,' Susie backtracked hastily, 'I'm not saying he isn't...' She left a list of the man's positive attributes hanging in the air, as she shook her head in disbelief at this nugget of information. Then, as some of the implications sank in, she looked at Rosemary with dawning satisfaction.

'Just let her try insinuating that, because I come from a different background to Clive, I don't know how to behave, that's all,' she said in triumph. 'Huh! Just let her try.'

Chapter Eighteen

On Wednesday morning, with unaccustomed patience, Zinnia let twenty minutes elapse after she watched Elaine's car go past the gate, having collected Veronica. Time enough, she thought, for the discovery of a handbag left at home, or the sudden realisation that the house hadn't been locked up. Then, certain that by now Elaine and Veronica would be halfway to Stockleigh Health Club, wittering away to each other like a couple of schoolgirls on an outing, she walked up the lane and casually turned in the Thornway's drive.

To make it look good, should anyone be watching, she first rang the front door bell, waited theatrically for a few moments, tried the door of the large conservatory at the side, then went round to the back and surveyed the garden.

She smiled to herself as she recalled Basil Berriman's pained insistence that he had designed Gerry's garden strictly to the client's specifications, and greatly against his own inclinations. It certainly showed. At the end of a large paved patio was a rectangular pond, complete with a voluptuously undressed maiden struggling to control a retching dolphin. Water marginal plants had been placed at measured intervals in plastic baskets on the shallow ledge round the edge, and enormous koi carp restlessly cruised the water, a fake heron regarding them with understandable apprehension. From the patio, a vista had been created, past island beds filled with heathers and conifers of assorted colours and shapes, through to a gazebo at the end, housing a couple of cane chairs and a table. As a trysting place this would have been about as inspiringly private as a concrete bus shelter, but somehow Zinnia didn't picture Gerry and Elaine indulging much in that line these days. To the side of the gazebo, and obviously designed to be hidden by a forest of bamboo which had so far failed to oblige, was an aviary for the peacocks, and an enclosure for lawn mowings. Seeing her, the two peacocks strutted over, anticipating food, or at least entertainment.

Zinnia gave them a look of distaste. 'I suppose you did me a favour,' she told them, with the obvious gratitude of a wife given a socket set for Christmas. 'If you hadn't come scavenging in my garden there might not have been any Settlewort plants at all. But why the hell couldn't you have deposited them all on my side?'

The birds followed at a wary distance, as she quartered the garden. It wasn't hard to spot the Settlewort plants, poking through the expanses of heather and horizontal conifers, their elegant, willowy leaves seeming incongruous, like duchesses at a greyhound race meeting. Excitement at finding them was quickly overcome by gloom. This garden boasted, she counted, eight of the things, whereas the Pit Garden had just one. If only she could dig them up and establish them there…

Assessing the practicalities, she scrabbled down through the heather to the earth. These plants were more stunted in growth than her carefully nurtured specimen, but, she reckoned, probably had a bigger root system. It might be possible to transplant them, but not unobtrusively. The surrounding heather was going to be left looking thoroughly messed about.

As she stood back to consider the options, the more daring of the peacocks wandered up, and casually nipped the top off the Settlewort she had just been examining.

'Tasty is it?' she enquired thoughtfully. Perhaps that was the reason the plants were small. And maybe the peacocks would solve the problem for her, in due course, by consuming all Gerry's Settlewort plants. Though time, she told herself realistically, was just what she didn't have. Experts from Kew seemed likely to come down soon, and they would surely ask more questions than Simon. If they wanted to look in the next door garden she would be sunk.

But the bird's action had helped her come to a conclusion. I'll try and transplant as many as possible, she decided. And pull up the rest. If Gerry suspects anything, it can be put down to his precious peacocks having a fondness for the plants. She looked at her watch. Mm, a bit risky to do it now though, especially as she'd have to tackle all eight plants in one go. No good leaving some. Next Wednesday, she told herself resolutely. Rain or shine, she would come and dig them up next Wednesday morning, as soon as Elaine went off to the Health Club.

****

Elaine and Veronica enjoyed their weekly visits to the Health Club. They had started going two years ago, when Veronica, realising that the boss's wife was lonely and unhappy, had hesitantly offered the hand of friendship. Being married to the unlovely Gerry might have been considered misfortune enough, but Elaine, it transpired, was beginning to despair of ever producing a family. Tests had found no medical reason as far as she was concerned, but she had utterly failed to persuade Gerry to submit himself to any kind of procedure that might pinpoint the problem.

He brushed off her request. 'You're only thirty-five, plenty of time. And this isn't the right moment to be thinking about a family anyway. Expensive things, children, and money's a bit tight just now. Besides,' he added breezily, 'we're happy as we are. It's great to be able to fly off to Bermuda for a couple of weeks' golfing, and you like spending weekends on the boat, don't you. Couldn't do that with kids around the place.'

Elaine pictured herself contentedly left behind with two adoring small children, and said nothing. She loathed both activities, but what was the point of saying so? Her dark eyes seemed to grow bigger, and more mournful by the month, reinforcing the impression of a field mouse, timidly anxious to please. And she did her best to gain Gerry's approval. Obediently she prepared dinner parties for the people he insisted on inviting, even though she didn't know anyone, and trying to making conversation made her rigid with nerves. Actually, entertaining had rather fizzled out of late, since people seemed unable to find the time to come twice, and no-one asked them back.

She kept the house nice, tried to make her cooking more sophisticated (Veronica had been able to help there), and lately had attended flower arranging classes. She was gratified to find that Gerry approved of this. He had a feeling it was what ladies did. So Elaine had been excited to discover there was to be a flower arranging competition as part of Haydon's Gardens and Flower Festival, and decided to give it her all.

'Gerry would be so proud of me if I won,' she confided to Veronica, as they drove towards Stockleigh.

'Yes.' Veronica tried to keep the doubt from her voice. But perhaps he would surprise them all, and give his wife credit for something for once.

'The theme is "Understanding", and I've done quite a bit of thinking about it,' Elaine continued with something approaching enthusiasm. 'Before putting in an order to a florist, there was a favour I wanted to ask you.'

'Me?'

'It's your mother-in-law really, but I hoped you might ask her for me,' she said hesitantly. 'The thing is, do you think she'd let me pick some stuff from her garden? It'd just be foliage really, for the background. Only we haven't got much of that sort of thing in ours.'

'Well...' Knowing how obsessive Zinnia was about her garden, there were misgivings. 'She doesn't really like things being picked. Oh, except she does have an agreement with the wife of a local artist who paints flowers,' Veronica remembered. 'Lets them come and pick what they want. They gave her a lovely flower painting not long ago, as a thank you. So perhaps...' She knew Zinnia felt sorry for Elaine, as everyone did.

'I think it's best if you approach her yourself,' she suggested, 'the garden's going to be open on the day, isn't it, so she may not be too keen. But I'll pave the way by telling her you're going to ask.'

The two women had a tacit agreement not to talk about Thornways. The fact that Elaine was the boss's wife had the potential to wreck their friendship by itself, without the recently added reefs of Derek's participation in a Management Buyout attempt. Gerry hardly bothered to discuss work matters with his wife, but clearly he was only regarding the MBO as a fallback, should the sale of the business to Clumpings fail.

Derek, by contrast, had tried to keep Veronica in the picture, and she knew he was battered by the maelstrom of figures and projections surrounding him every day, daunted by the sheer enormity of what was involved in a Management Buyout, and worked to a frazzle. She had responded by redoubling her efforts to make him comfortable and well-fed, confident that a secure home base would help him to win through in the end. He was going to be Managing Director, she thought proudly, and he would have a loyal and supportive wife by his side.

That Wednesday evening he was unusually silent as he slumped exhausted onto a chair in the kitchen. Matthew had already eaten, and gone out. She reported how excited he was that the Heebie Jeebies had been asked to audition for a live show in Norwich, and chattered lightly about her day. But Derek wore a glazed look, and what was more concerning, had hardly touched the salmon she'd bought for a treat, and refused a slice of her strawberry shortcake.

'I've got some bad news to tell you,' he said dejectedly, pushing the food across his plate, and she looked at him anxiously. 'The Buyout's off. The venture capital people are pulling out.'

'But why?' Veronica was shocked and dismayed, all her fond imaginings of prospertiy and social elevation suddenly lying shattered at her feet.

'They've been over all the figures, and don't care for what they've found. Things are worse than even I thought. But as well as that – and they've been quite frank about this – they don't think that we'd be up to running the company successfully, and they're not prepared to draft in their own team either.'

'I like that!' she was indignant. 'After all the work you've put in. No-one knows how to run that place better than you.'

'Well...' he shrugged. 'I always had my doubts about Prentice Stalker. His commitment for a start, and whether we could pull as a team.'

The worry lines that had appeared in the last few weeks deepened. He was looking not only exhausted, but much older, she realised.

'But the thing is, they're right.' He drew trails of mayonnaise across the plate with his knife, and added tonelessly, 'Realistically, I just don't have what it takes to head up a company that size, Veronica. I'm a competent General Manager, and that's all.'

'Oh that's rubbish.' She got up to make some coffee. That would perk him up.

'In a way it's a relief,' he continued, and looked up. 'It's better to face things. And you can't make yourself be what you aren't. I'm just sorry for your sake.'

She stopped, spoon halfway out of the coffee bag. 'For me?'

'Well, I haven't been able to give you much of a life, have I? It's probably not what you pictured when we got married.'

This was certainly true, but as she looked at Derek's tired and crumpled face, all Veronica's private grousing and discontent evaporated, and she felt a rush of maternal protectiveness towards him.

'We've been happy, haven't we?' she said, crossing the room, and putting her arm round his shoulders, and her face against his. 'And we don't need much. Matthew will be off our hands soon, and that'll help. Besides,' there was pride in her voice, 'I'm going to have a bit of money coming in from my herbal jams. Perhaps I could expand it into a proper little business.'

'Would you like that?' He put his hand on hers, grateful for her warm support. 'I'd help you all I could. Of course if Thornways goes belly-up I'll have to look for something else, but maybe, in the long term, we could develop your jams into something that would support us both. That would be fun, wouldn't it.'

She kissed him, then went back to making the coffee, trying to remember how many spoonfuls she'd already put in.

Over coffee, in unaccustomed harmony and affection, they discussed a future of hazy hopes and improbable expectations. And when Matthew came in, he was mystified to discover the kitchen in a mess, the house in darkness, and his parents' bedroom door firmly closed.

****

When he'd heard about the Management Buyout not proceeding, that Wednesday morning, Gerry Thornway didn't know whether to feel glad or sorry. He hadn't liked the concept in the first place. The idea that Derek Peasmore, who'd left school at sixteen and then just got some kind of half-baked, grease monkey qualification, should think he could step into the Managing Director's shoes, was plainly ridiculous. Insulting, even. And obviously the Venture Capital people had finally seen that. On the other hand, Gerry had found the possibility of a Management Buyout a useful tactical ploy in his dealings with Clumpings.

'I don't have to sell the company to you chaps, you know,' he'd been able to say loftily to various members of the Clumpings team, when they turned up uncomfortable facts, or unexplained holes in the accounts, during due diligence. 'My management are only too keen to buy me out, and after all, they should know what a good proposition Thornways is.'

In the afternoon he drove over to the office of the company's solicitors, for the completion of the legal paperwork assigning a large chunk of the car park to Swathe's Environmental Services. He'd have to come clean to Clumpings about it now, which they wouldn't like. But the money involved was going to be a vital stopgap, he thought, congratulating himself on arranging the sale. Thornways' bank manager had become downright insolent lately. At least this would shut him up for a while.

Admittedly he hadn't achieved the price he'd hoped. Not half as much in fact. But then he'd managed to persuade Mike Swathe to part with that strip of his garden next to the Golf Club, as part of the deal. What a coup! By giving them room to make another exit, it was going to solve their acute car park problem. The Club had been trying to persuade the man to sell for years, but then they hadn't Gerry's charm and negotiating talents. He'd found Mike Swathe easy to deal with.

He smiled to himself as he parked the car where it said "Partners". Whoever the space belonged to wasn't using it, he reasoned. Anyway, serve him right to find it blocked if he returned. Clients like Gerry were more important.

After the signing was completed, he suggested a celebratory drink at the Golf Club. Waltzing in there with this notoriously sharp and formidable man as a drinking companion would have done his reputation no harm at all, but Mike Swathe declined, stating pressure of time. That didn't seem to prevent him staying to chat in the car park though.

'How are the talks with your buyer coming along?' he enquired affably. 'Clumpings International isn't it?'

'Well, they sent this team of kids in who don't know a thing about business.' Gerry's tone was dismissive. 'If their shareholders knew how incompetent the management is, their share price'd hit the deck.'

'Really?' Swathe looked suitably sympathetic, as befitted one good businessman to another. 'The important thing is not to let them walk all over you,' he advised. 'Your father wouldn't have stood any nonsense.'

Old Man Thornway would never have been selling, he thought to himself, regarding the son with contempt.

'You tell 'em where to get off, if they start being heavy-handed,' he suggested in avuncular fashion. 'These big boys just think small companies are easy meat.'

And he shook hands with Gerry, got into his car, and drove away, a faint smile hovering on his lips.

****

Gerry's morale was greatly boosted by the encouragement, especially as he had an important meeting with Clumpings' people scheduled for Friday. Emboldened by Mike Swathe's friendly respect, he planned how he would tackle them as he repaired to the Golf Club Bar.

They would try to run the company down, of course, tell him Thornways was hardly worth buying, and they'd be doing him a favour by taking it off his hands. Lately he'd been feeling that perhaps they were right. But a tough cookie like Mike Swathe knew about these things, and his advice was valuable. The team's attitude was just a negotiating ploy, and only to be expected.

He sipped his Campari, one eye on the door in case someone came in who should be waved to. He would give Clumpings a piece of his mind, he thought assertively, tell them to take Thornways on his terms or not at all. That'd make them climb down pretty fast. And, he reflected, this was probably the right occasion to announce that with Thornways came the chance to market a herb the world would soon be scrambling for.

Yes, he nodded. Now that Zinnia Peasmore had let slip where this damn plant was, well, it would be just too easy for it to disappear. Time he did a little walking, he decided. Down the lane that evening.

****

After her conversation with Gerry at the Herb Garden Tea Shop, Zinnia had taken several cuttings of the herb she'd pounced on in a plant sale before Christmas. The parent, a shrubby-looking plant with veined leaves, she now carefully removed from its large terracotta pot, and replaced in a smaller, plastic flower pot.

'Why did you do that?' Rosemary enquired curiously, looking up from her book in the shade of the greengage tree. 'I rather liked the old pot. That shape always reminds me of Ali Baba and the Forty Thieves.'

'Precisely,' Zinnia told her. 'I was afraid it would get stolen.'

'Well, that's not likely, is it? I mean you could hardly hide the thing about your person, and you'd be pretty obvious staggering down the road clasping a heavy terracotta pot to your bosom.'

'Chest, I think.'

'What?'

'Yes, you're probably right,' agreed Zinnia unconcernedly. 'But if the plant should get stolen, at least now my nice pot doesn't disappear with it. Now, where is the right place to put this?'

She surveyed the area outside the kitchen, trying to remember exactly what she'd told Gerry, and selected a spot only a few steps from the drive, just glimpsable from the kitchen window, but out of sight from round the house.

'Doesn't look nice there,' Rosemary remarked. She got up and viewed the new siting critically, from both sides. 'I preferred where you had it before. What is it anyway?'

She pulled out the freshly-written label, expecting to find a Latin name. '"My Very Special Herb!"' she read aloud, in sceptical tones. 'But you don't write labels like that!'

'Don't I?'

'No. It's always some gibberish which you insist any proper gardener would translate as, oh I don't know... "the marsh plant from St Petersburg with ear-shaped yellow flowers that stink like a rutting reindeer".'

'You have learnt a lot,' Zinnia remarked with humorous approval. 'Put it back so it's easy to read from a distance, will you.'

Rosemary's hand brushed against the greyish-green leaves as she replaced the label, and she wrinkled her nose. 'The plant's got a funny smell.'

'Yes, it has hasn't it,' Zinnia sounded happy. 'Just perfect for the job.'

'What job?' Her niece looked at her suspiciously. 'What exactly are you up to?'

'In war time, armies set up dummy tanks, don't they, made of painted cardboard or something,' Zinnia explained lightly. 'And then they get bombed instead of the real ones. This,' she fingered the small shrub's leaves encouragingly, 'is a decoy tank. By my reckoning we can expect a hostile raid any day now.'

****

The day after Zinnia had prowled about in his garden, Gerry slipped down the lane at dusk to Kiln House. He had no trouble locating the Settlewort plant that all this fuss was about. It was in a large pot near the corner of the house, just within sight of the kitchen window, as she'd described. It didn't look very special, he thought, quietly slipping it into a large Harrods carrier bag. The leaves gave off a strong odour as he did so. That was one of the distinguishing factors, he remembered. Prentice Stalker had reported smelling it in Zinnia Peasmore's garden.

She was a stupid woman, he thought scornfully, furtively retracing his steps in the growing darkness. Not only had she blabbed about where the thing was growing, but the label she'd put in was laughably easy to see through. "My Very Special Herb!" indeed!. That might work with Jo Public, but it was no good trying to fool him.

Unlike her, he would use his brains. Needed to. What he now possessed was not only very valuable but, in the strictest sense, stolen property, he thought cautiously. That meant he couldn't let Elaine find it. Or show it to Stalker. That was a pity. It would have been good to see his expression, when faced with a demonstration of how Gerry Thornway got results where he had conspicuously failed.

He turned into his gateway, wondering where to put the plant. It couldn't be anywhere in the garden. The Peasmore woman might come looking for it. Not that she was likely to suspect him of course. If it was left in the garage Elaine would see it. His car, he decided, was the best bet, and he delved into his pocket for the key fob. The plant only had to stay there for tonight. Then he would produce it dramatically at the meeting with Clumpings on Friday. As he placed the pot in the boot, still in its socially telling carrier bag, he pictured the forthcoming meeting with satisfaction. If they wanted this herb, they'd have to pay a really good price for Thornways. He'd make that shower laugh on the other side of their faces.

The following day he got Prentice Stalker to produce a write-up on Settlewort, incorporating its history as far as was known, the esteem in which the plant had been held through the ages, and the likely active constituents. Gerry then added some sweeping predictions of his own as to the business opportunities presented by any company first into the field with this herb, up to now considered extinct. Herbal teas of course, but also sweets and chewing gum, food additives and supplements. Then there were supplies to the drug companies, who would be clamouring at the door. The drawback to plant-based medicines normally was that they couldn't be patented. But if there was only one source in the world of a really important plant…well, it was simply a licence to print money.

He read through the document, made several photocopies of it himself and, with a confidence that was bordering on triumphalism, surreptitiously removed the Settlewort from his car boot, just before the meeting, and locked it inside a stationery cupboard.

****

Clumpings sent three negotiators, two of whom Gerry had met, and disliked, before. Young, university educated, and with an air of superiority about them, they acted like itching powder on his own insecurity. Swathe was right, he thought resentfully, big companies just thought they could throw their weight around. Well he'd show this lot.

But the meeting proved less than successful.

Due diligence threw up some disturbing information, the senior executive, a man by the name of Vetcher, informed him, and his tone had been decidedly disrespectful. In view of the gloomy picture Thornways now presented, they were, at considerable risk, prepared to take on the business, largely for its good name, but at less than half the price they had originally discussed.

Gerry was genuinely shocked at the offer. He'd expected a slight lowering, but this was insulting. It was completely unacceptable, he told them, out of the question.

'Then I don't think we have anything further to discuss,' Vetcher told him dismissively.

This was Gerry's moment.

'That's where you're wrong,' he announced. 'There's been an important development,' and he reached down and brought out the information sheets on Settlewort. 'I think you should read this, while I fetch something,' he said, handing them round.

He returned with the plant, by now divested of its Harrod's bag, and placed it with a flourish in the middle of the table.

'This, gentlemen, is Settlewort – Solanum regale,' he said importantly. 'I live in Haydon Settleworth which was named because it grew there, and a single plant of it has reappeared. If you've read that resumé, you will know just how lucrative this could be.'

He saw them exchange glances. 'If Clumpings wants a piece of the action, then they'll have to buy Thornways,' he told them triumphantly. 'At *my* price.'

His dramatic announcement successfully changed the meeting to one of negotiation about how, and for what length of time, the plant could be properly examined and tested, without its ownership being compromised. Not only had Gerry insisted they sign an affidavit to the effect that he was the legal owner of the plant, but he had got his secretary to take photographs of the room, with himself, the plant and the three Clumpings people, so there could be no doubt what the plant looked like, and that it belonged at Thornways. Gerry was blissfully unaware that plants could be cloned, using micro-propagation, but he had a vague idea that some plants could be reproduced from cuttings, and this worried him. Vetcher was adamant that the thing would have to be properly examined, however, and Gerry could see no help for it. They could have it for a few days only, he warned them, and then he would expect its return, plus a much revised offer for the company.

In the car that evening Gerry couldn't stop himself shouting, 'Yes! *Yes!*' and punching the air frequently on the way home, which did nothing for the standard of his driving. He had really put one over on them now, he crowed to himself, and the urge to tell everyone about his brilliance was almost irresistible. It was a crying shame that, in the circumstances, there was no-one he could safely tell.

****

That afternoon, as Gerry was following advice and ensuring Clumpings didn't walk all over him, Mike Swathe was driving towards Haydon, also in a good mood. He was now in possession of the land for his new venture, a buyer was interested in his Stockleigh house, and this afternoon he was going to discuss with a local builder what could be done with his mother's cottage. That included asking about the feasibility of knocking through and joining it with Julia's next door. It did occur to him that that might be tempting fate, but he dismissed the thought. Things were going so right.

The barley was turning soft and furry-looking, always a sign that full summer had come, and as he crested the hill and the sun played hide and seek among the overhanging branches, he noticed that the chestnut trees at the edge of Ridleys Wood were in full flower. Their cream bunches of lines always reminded him of those peculiar fibre-optic table objects that people unaccountably had as ornaments. Some things stayed reassuringly the same, he thought, remembering the childhood delight of shuffling through the fallen leaves in autumn, bringing home bags bulging with chestnuts to roast on the fire, fingers full of prickles.

But he wouldn't ever go there again. The place still made him uncomfortable, like a stretch of road where a loved one has died.

Julia had come with him, that last time he ever went chestnutting. Zinnia Whats-her-name had moved away from Haydon the previous spring, he recalled, which meant he was able to see Julia more often, although her mother would have been furious if she'd known they were spending the day together. He smiled faintly at the thought. Julia had simply said she was going riding, and he'd joined her as soon as she reached the edge of the village. She'd brought a picnic lunch, and they'd tethered Misty, and shared it, looking down on the valley in the autumn sunshine, amongst the sere and whispering grasses.

It was a beautiful day, but he remembered it with no pleasure. That was the day he asked her to marry him, and she'd said no. Even after all these years, just thinking about it still caused hurt, like the ache of a damaged joint when the weather turned damp. You're so vulnerable when you're young, he reflected, slowing down as a lorry came up the hill, things go in so deep. She'd tried to be diplomatic of course, but he'd known, with bitterness, what lay behind it. Julia wasn't prepared to rebel, and go against her parents' wishes. You might love the blacksmith's boy, but you didn't marry him. He wasn't the right sort. And he had no money.

Ruefully, Mike Swathe tried to picture himself as he had been then. Just a youth, but full of hope, and certain that he and Julia belonged together. He hadn't been blind to their social differences, naturally, but he thought they wouldn't matter, if she loved him. He shook his head. He'd never made the mistake of being idealistic again. That was the day the iron had entered his soul.

He'd bloody show her! he'd promised himself. Show the lot of them.

They were laying new tarmac on the lane down to the village, and he drew up at the temporary traffic light while a bronzed and muscled young man directed a tipper with a steaming load of asphalt.

This last month he'd been reminded how it felt to be young, and fired up with love and desire. He grimaced wryly. Thank God no-one else had ever made him feel like this.

It had taken him aback too, such a renewed flood of passion, after a lifetime of determined discipline. The discovery that Julia still cared about him was the catalyst that had changed everything. It might be just residual fondness on her part though, he'd reflected, trying to be level about the situation. If that was so, it was vital to find out. He'd suffered rejection once at her hands, and it had been the single most hurtful, humiliating moment of his life. He wasn't going to risk that happening again.

He'd decided on a plan of campaign, and made sure their outings were limited. Just a few days and evenings out together, everything very casual. Rigorous self-control meant that a peck on the cheek was the nearest he'd got to touching her.

The air conditioning was keeping the car cool, but couldn't do much about its owner. He was desperate to hold Julia in his arms, to take her to bed and show her how she could have been loved, if she'd only made the right choice. His eyes closed at the thought of her softness against him. He wanted to feel her arms round his neck, and hear her admit she'd been wrong about him when they were young.

But there were going to be no mistakes, he told himself harshly, it was too important. He'd get her used to his company, gentle her along, like you did with a thoroughbred horse, until finally it would be his ring on her finger. As it always should have been. He nodded to himself. Things would be taken slow, played right this time. She was a lady, in every respect.

That she was only titled because she'd married the 'wrong' man, was a thought he didn't care to entertain.

The light turned to green, and as he drove on, past Gerry Thornway's house, and Zinnia's, he decided to tell Julia about his new venture today, now that the land was in the bag.

It had always amazed him, the things builders ripped out of houses and gardens, and dumped in the company's skips – fireplaces, sundials, finials. He'd rescued a large garden urn once, which turned out to be Coade stone, and sold in London for a satisfyingly large sum. Retrieving such things seemed almost a duty, as well as a pleasure, and as his knowledge had grown, he'd begun selling, almost as a hobby.

But there'd been friction with Eddie about the space his stuff was taking up at Swathe's. Now he could have proper premises, he reflected, and turn the hobby into a retirement interest. Eddie's impatience to take over, and the opportunity to buy Thornways' car park, had just accelerated things. With an agreement now signed, passing control of Swathe's Environmental Services to his son, Mike Swathe was looking forward to setting up as a dealer in architectural reclamation and high class garden stonework.

He smiled. It was not quite the image of himself he'd been used to. On the other hand, there was money to be made, and rather pleasantly. The trend of wealthy Londoners buying up large places in the area was increasing, and when they wanted to make something of their houses and gardens, there was nowhere local for them, or their designers, to buy what was wanted. Stately home owners who needed to sell also had to get the London dealers in. He would fill the gap. He already had a lot of contacts, it was just a question of building the business up, especially the buying side. And he wanted Julia to join him as a part-time 'consultant'. The two of them would be flung together a lot of course, that was part of the plan. But he was certain she would enjoy it. She spoke the same language as these people, and her presence would give them an entrée.

Drawing up outside his mother's cottage, he checked the time. Ten minutes before the builder was due, just right for a casual, neighbourly chat with Julia. With assurance, he strode up to her front door and knocked loudly.

****

Julia knew, when she looked in the mirror these days, that she looked better. There was a brightness about her eyes, her skin had got back some of its glow, and her mouth seemed to smile of its own accord. She felt sprightly, instead of ageing, and the dull hopelessness of the previous months had evaporated like a puddle in hot sunshine.

Going out all of a sudden had been great fun, especially to the races, but she could have done these things on her own, or gone with friends. People had been kind in asking her out after Richard died. It wouldn't have been the same though. What was putting the sparkle back into her life, she realised perfectly well, was the man who had invited her. He was such a stimulating companion – sharp and interesting, and she had yet to find anything about which he wasn't well-informed.

It was hard to equate this wealthy and assertive man with the youth of all those years ago, she thought to herself, putting the shopping away. Yet that unpredictable, almost dangerous aura he had about him was the same, with that disconcertingly direct look. And the natural affinity that had brought them together when they were young, was unchanged. She opened the tea packet, and poured the contents into the caddy, savouring the aroma, but her mind was far away. He'd seemed to love her then with a fierce possessiveness, and his bitterness towards her after that picnic day had left her scarred. She wasn't sure it was in him to forgive her for being weak, and choosing financial and social safety instead of love with him. But how could it have been otherwise?

She threw the empty packet in the pedal bin. Now it's my turn to be lovesick. Ridiculous! I'm not supposed to feel this way, she thought, feeling almost ashamed. Not at my age. Rather guiltily, she reflected that it hadn't been like this with Richard. Liking, and love, and companionship, yes. Passion, no. But it had been a good marriage, she reminded herself firmly, and you couldn't expect everything. That was as unfair as asking a nice-natured cob to go out and win the Derby.

Like some snowbound dreamer picturing the lush fruit and warm evenings of summer, she'd found herself thinking about a second marriage these past few weeks. It would be a different vista, a new world almost. They'd be free to enjoy themselves, and each other, without money worries or family restraints. The prospect was undoubtedly inviting.

But unlikely, she told herself, putting apples in the fruit bowl. He'd been just casually friendly, no sign that he was thinking along those lines.

And part of her was glad, because of the shadow that lay between them. She'd tried to broach the subject several times, only to have him cut her short, or suddenly go deaf. But if things got serious she would have to say what was on her mind. All in all, it was better for things to jog along as they were.

The Gardens and Flower Festival was only three weeks off now, and that Friday afternoon, over a cup of tea, she and Mrs Chitting were going through the piles of things that had been donated to the Brownies' White Elephant Stall. There was no space in Carol's small modern house, and her mother couldn't clutter up any of her rooms, when she was already packing up for the move. So Julia had kindly offered her dining room as a depository.

'If we price things up now, it'll save a last minute rush,' she suggested, 'also Carol will have some idea whether they've collected enough stuff.'

They had divided the table up into price sections, and were light-heartedly discussing the questionable merits of a mock hedgehog bootscraper, and a Christmas tree stand with a wonky leg, when there was a loud knocking on the front door.

Julia greeted her visitor with surprised pleasure, and invited him in. 'Mrs Chitting and I were just having a cup of tea in the dining room, to help our thought processes,' she said. 'I'll freshen up the pot.'

'Well just a quick cup, I'm not staying,' he told her. 'Thought I'd warn you in case you heard odd noises from next door. It's only me, and a builder. He'll be here shortly.'

He followed her into the kitchen and leant against the worktop, appreciating her back view as she filled the kettle. The pale blue blouse and swingy denim skirt she was wearing emphasised her trim figure, and she still had great legs, he thought admiringly. Her natural elegance was one of the things which held him in thrall, and always had.

'Thought you might like to know that No Nannicking's running at Chepstow next Thursday,' he told her. 'Don't know if it'll be on the television, but I shall be relying on you to will him on. I'm going to be in Japan next week. It's a damn nuisance.'

'Oh I'm sure he'll win,' she said encouragingly. 'He was unlucky to have such heavy going last time out, wasn't he. You know, I keep forgetting to ask you what "Nannicking" means,' she added, reaching in the cupboard for a cup. 'I looked it up in the dictionary and it wasn't there.'

'And you a Suffolk girl!' he ribbed her. 'When you were little, did no-one tell you to stop nannicking?' He paused, and added with slight edge, 'No, I don't suppose they did. It means fooling around. So no nannicking means no messing.'

'That's your motto is it?' she smiled at him over her shoulder.

'Certainly is,' he said briskly. 'Know what you want and go for it. Don't let anyone get in the way. No nannicking.'

He looked at his watch. 'There's something else I wanted to tell you. I've decided to retire. Been toying with the idea for a while. My elder son's taking over the business. And I have a proposal, for you to think about while I'm away.'

Julia steeled herself. 'No,' she said quickly, 'there's something that has to be sorted out first. You wouldn't let me talk about it, but we have to.'

'And that is?'

'I can't...we can't...' she struggled for words, 'go any further, while you're planning to destroy Zinnia's garden.'

'*What*!'

'You must see, I can't do that to her. It's bad enough my son selling it without saying anything.'

Mike Swathe felt as if he was in a lift that had fallen forty floors.

'I don't believe it. Not her again!' he exclaimed angrily. 'She was the one who turned your mother against me. If she hadn't meddled, things might have been very different.'

'Is that what you think?' Julia was taken aback. She gestured helplessly. 'It would never have worked, my dear. Not then.'

But he hardly heard. 'You haven't changed!' his voice was bitter.

'Changed? How do you mean, changed?'

'You always put that bloody friend before me. Just because she comes from the right sort of family. I should have known.'

'What nonsense.' She was getting angry now. 'It's nothing to do with that.'

'And my business decisions have nothing to do with you,' he said brusquely.

'Yes they have,' she insisted. 'At least this one has, because it devastates her life, and she's my oldest friend. Why are you determined to destroy her wonderful garden? It's so unreasonable.'

'And of course only people who've been to the right schools would know about reason,' he shot at her.

'That's ridiculous, and you know it.'

The kettle boiled unnoticed, as they glared at each other across the kitchen.

'So when it comes down to it,' he said tautly, 'you side with her against me? Just how it always was.'

'There is another way of looking at it.' Her voice was cold. 'That you put making money before anything else.'

'That's not what it's about. You wouldn't understand.'

'Well you don't seem to understand simple loyalty,' she said cuttingly. 'I couldn't possibly marry a man who thinks money is everything, and friendship doesn't matter.'

She'd done it to him again!

For a moment his face wore the look of a small boy whose favourite toy has just been smashed in front of him, then he spun round and headed for the front door.

Opening it, he turned back to face her, eyes blazing, as she stood in the entrance to the kitchen.

'Who said anything about marriage?' he said savagely, hurt and anger making him unheedingly cruel.

She stared at him wordlessly.

'For your information, it was a *business* proposal I was going to put to you. Not that it matters now,' he added bitterly, and slammed the door behind him.

Chapter Nineteen

Daisy Chitting was not one to gossip, and her loyal discretion was one of the reasons she had long ago earned the Trugglestone family's trust. In return, she held a certain status in the village as being part of The Hall set-up, which she was not above enjoying. But overhearing such a noteworthy row was trying her self-imposed rule of silence to the limit.

Rosemary dropped in to see her the morning after. Besotted with the cottage that was soon to be hers, any pretext to visit the object of her infatuation was seized with enthusiasm, and today's excuse was to ask after the progress of Mrs Chitting's bungalow purchase. To a large extent this was dictated by how fast the legal machinery moved on the sale of Spring Cottage, Mrs Chitting being unable to pay for her new home until ownership, and money, changed hands. But there seemed little Rosemary could do to speed things up. Lawyers, they agreed amicably, sitting at the kitchen table, the morning sun streaming through the window, were like woodlice. When challenged they rolled into a protective ball, and all progress stopped.

'Zinnia says Lady Julia got so mad when she was buying her cottage, she went round to the solicitor's office and threatened to stay there until they got their act together. But it didn't help any,' remarked Rosemary, adding, 'Doesn't sound like her at all. She's so restrained.'

'She have her moments,' Mrs Chitting asserted enigmatically, offering the plate of ginger biscuits. Her discipline of silence was now struggling with a different loyalty. That Mrs Peasmore, went the reasoning, she ought to know what Lady done for her.

She opened her mouth to speak, then shut it again, and Rosemary looked at her enquiringly. Suddenly the dam of discretion gave way, and, with suitable drama and embellishment, she told her about yesterday's happening. 'Sent him packing, she did,' she ended with relish, her several chins wobbling. 'Said she didn't want no more to do with him, if he wouldn't leave your aunt's garden alone.'

Whilst not strictly accurate, this was now how the scene was replaying in Mrs Chitting's mind, and how it was, in turn, immediately conveyed to Zinnia, who was not supposed to have known that Julia and Mike Swathe were consorting in the first place.

'Can't say I'm surprised,' she said guardedly, tossing the salad for lunch. 'I saw him visiting her cottage back in the Spring. She tried to make out it was just about dampness or something, but I wasn't fooled.'

'Don't you think it's time to stop this silly feud between you?' Rosemary's tone was parental. 'Okay, so her son sold the Pit Garden, and she didn't say anything. But she was in a difficult position. And I've seen how happy she looked these past few weeks. It must have cost her some to finish with him. You owe her.'

That afternoon Zinnia knocked on Julia's front door, holding the best peace offering she could think of.

'Brought you a plant for the garden,' she said awkwardly. 'It's a very vigorous seedling pink that just appeared last autumn. May be good enough to register, especially now I've decided on a name. It's going to be called *Dianthus* 'Julia.'

The two women smiled at each other, understanding the code. Julia looked worn and tired, as if she hadn't slept, and her eyes were puffy. But she seemed to take some comfort from the healing of a rift that had been unpleasant for both of them.

'That's very pretty, and really kind of you,' she said, taking the peace offering. 'Mm, wonderful scent! Dear Basil is wedded to his colour schemes, but fortunately I'm allowed to have white! I know just the right place for it too, where I sit out in the early morning and have breakfast. You must come and see how everything's come on.'

There were still areas of constraint between them. Like the arrival of the bank statement after a row over family finances, there were certain things that couldn't be mentioned. Julia would have been interested to hear how the Settlewort story was developing, only she wasn't supposed to know of the plant's existence. And in turn, Zinnia couldn't talk about the fight for the Pit Garden, or ask too closely about the recent goings on in Julia's life. Her new garden, though, was a safe bet.

An eager Bracken preceded them through the sitting room, wagging her tail in welcome. This visitor was the one who had provided some very acceptable provender last time they met.

'Basil's really pulled out all the stops,' Julia said, opening the door to the garden. 'On the Open Day I'm not sure he isn't expecting me to display a sign saying, "Designed by Basil Berriman".'

They stepped out on to a south-facing area of York stone paving, dominated by two large containers, planted with white lilies, Paris daisies, mignonette, and pale yellow petunias. 'They're only imitation lead planters,' Julia remarked regretfully, 'but of course I couldn't take the ones from the Hall.' An elegant wrought iron bench nestled against the cottage wall, and modern, comfortable-looking seats were set about a teak table.

'It's a wonderful sun trap,' observed Zinnia.

'Yes. And completely private. The summer jasmine over there shields it from the cottage next door, and the raised bed in front makes a windbreak, and stops anyone on the river or the meadows seeing up here.'

'Certainly been a big change since I last saw the place.' Zinnia looked about her with interest and approval.

'Basil's idea was to have a separate theme for each terrace,' explained Julia. 'This top one is devoted to scent. Those lilies are only just coming out, but the perfume in the evenings is heavenly. And then he's put lavender, and thymes, and lots of things whose names I don't know, in the brick bed. The bees are mad about it. I'll plant your lovely pink there, where I can enjoy it.'

'Come and tell me what you think of the rest of the garden,' she suggested, leading the way under an archway, on both sides of which a rose had been planted, the rich apricot flowers now past their best, and shedding petals.

'Thought you didn't like 'Climbing Lady Trugglestone',' Zinnia commented, sniffing one of the blooms appreciatively.

'Well I'm not terribly keen on the colour,' Julia confessed, 'but Basil insisted, and,' she smiled faintly at the remembered diplomacy, 'he didn't get his way on everything, so I let him win that one.'

From the archway, wide, shallow steps, with a handrail set into the brick of the raised bed, took them down to the second level. Here a little breeze tempered the heat of the sun, but what seemed to cool the temperature even more was the colour scheme of green and cream. At the base of the brick wall were hostas and ferns, enjoying the dampness that seeped down from above, and the cool root run of the path in front of them. It led to a paved area against the fence, shaded with the fresh green leaves of a vine that was being trained over an arbour containing an inviting seat. On the other side of the path, hummocks of cotton lavenders were beginning to be dotted with creamy, button flowers. Curly-leaved parsley made crinkled patches of intense green, and three sorts of alchemilla frothed exuberantly. Green lavender wafted its astringent personality on the air, accompanied by clumps of the creamy Anthemis 'Sauce Hollandaise'. Dwarf hebes contributed an array of different leaf colour, and wherever there was space in the middle of the bed, nicotiana had been planted, it's buds already showing the delicate almost-green that was to come. Round the edges Helichrysum 'Limelight', and the Californian Poppy 'Jersey Cream', were living up to their names.

'Goodness, I'm impressed,' Zinnia exclaimed, with genuine admiration, which changed to slight miffiness as she discovered the bed contained things she didn't know. 'What's that grey-leaved little thing, with lime green flowers? And this?' She fingered the long, fresh green leaves of an umbellifer with star-shaped flowers of greeny-bronze.

'You know I haven't a clue,' Julia was apologetic, but secretly rather taken with the prestige of growing something rare enough to baffle Zinnia. She could be irritatingly condescending at times. 'You'll have to ask Basil, he's calling in next week. He's fussing over this garden like an old mother hen. I'm not sure whether to be flattered, or wish he'd leave me in peace to enjoy it. Come down to the riverside. That hasn't changed much, but I love sitting down there.'

A sloping path led diagonally across the garden, with a bed of young shrub roses on their left, underplanted with an eye-catching carpet of golden-leaved Creeping Jenny. On the right, various shrubs topped a steep bank, including a purple hebe, busy with bees, a philadelphus exuding its fresh sweetness, and two delicate-flowered shrub fuchsias.'

'I couldn't have a garden without "fooshas", could I?' Julia commented wryly as they passed. 'Harry was so keen to give me lots of his big, garish ones, Basil said "over his dead body", and I was left trying to keep the peace in the middle.'

A well-established weeping pear, surrounded by white violas, formed an island round which the path circled, at the top of another flight of steps leading down to the third level.

'Basil thought this bottom terrace should be much more formal,' Julia explained, as they reached the last step, 'but I wanted it to be grass, as the last people had it, with a sitting area, and the river bank and the reeds left natural.'

'It's liable to flood in a wet winter anyway, isn't it?' suggested Zinnia, as they followed the path across to a bench on the far side.

The lawn was dominated by three ancient apple trees, their trunks patched grey with lichen, leaning towards each other, like old women sharing a juicy bit of gossip.

'Basil wanted to replace them,' Julia indicated the trees, 'but I wasn't having that either. They're so attractive don't you think. And what does it matter if they don't fruit much?'

'Only so many apples you can eat,' agreed Zinnia, as they sat down on the bench, watching Bracken chasing a Cabbage White butterfly, which nonchalantly flittered out over the water, leaving its pursuer prancing in frustration on the edge. 'I think your garden's lovely, Julia,' she said with warm sincerity. 'Not only is it really attractive, and packs a lot into a small space, but it suits you.'

'Glad you like it. I'm dreading having the public tramping round it though. Don't know why I ever agreed.' She sighed wearily. 'It'll be a great relief when this wretched Garden and Flower Festival is over. The organisation's taking up so much time.' A bee with a good deal to learn about flowers came to investigate Julia's hair, and she waved it away irritably. 'Sometimes, I think I don't have a life of my own, Zinnia,' she went on. 'Every time something needs doing people say, "Oh Julia Trugglestone will help with that, ask Julia Trugglestone to be chairman, Julia Trugglestone's good at fund-raising." Frankly, I'm fed up to the back teeth with it.' There was real resentment in her voice.

Zinnia regarded her with affectionate concern. This was so out of character.

'These last few weeks I've been…going out a bit more,' Julia continued cautiously. 'And realised how enjoyable life can be. Which has just made things worse.'

She sighed. 'Trouble is, there doesn't seem to be any way out. Susan says she can't possibly do anything, she's far too busy. But then she won't accept any help up at the Hall. It's ridiculous.'

These things were obviously forming an unhappy circle in Julia's mind, and Zinnia wondered what she could do to lighten her mood. Distraction would be a start, she decided, and cast round for a safe topic of conversation.

'Talking of help, I saw round Mrs Chitting's place the other day,' she informed her brightly. 'You know my niece is buying it, for some unfathomable reason. That garden has great possibilities! Such a lovely stream, completely wasted. Just channelled into pipes!' She shook her head in bafflement at the obtuseness of the place's owners, past and present.

'Has Rosemary got plans for it then? I didn't know she was interested in gardening.'

'Well, no…'

'Nice girl,' commented Julia, stroking Bracken, who had come to be made a fuss of, 'but what does she want with a property in Haydon? I thought she was going back to the States.'

'She's supposed to be, but I think she's having second thoughts,' Zinnia confided, quietly congratulating herself on a successful manoeuvre. 'There's this young man she's got to know at Kew, who seems to have taken a shine to her. Came down about ten days ago to see her, and I'm... well, I'm rather hoping things might develop.'

She shot a glance at her friend, and then made a confession. 'You'll scoff at me for going soft, Julia, but it would be lovely to have her stay in the village. I've really enjoyed having her here.' She smiled ruefully. 'Feel free to say "I told you so".'

****

Zinnia received her long-awaited telephone call from the young man in question the following day. Simon was bringing a Kew expert, and someone from the Chelsea Physic Garden, down next Thursday to see the Settlewort, he told her. They'd been impressed and fairly convinced by the leaf he'd shown them, apparently, but needed to see the plant for themselves. Meanwhile the Kew authorities had been putting wheels in motion about getting protected status for the site. It all sounded very hopeful.

She was now in a dilemma. If the plants were left growing in Gerry's garden, the visiting experts might discover them, after which the Pit Garden would lose its significance – and promised protection. But if she dug them up, and transplanted them to the Pit on Wednesday, they would stand out like pale bodies on a Mediterranean beach. It would hardly fool anyone, let alone experienced botanists. Regretfully, she came to the conclusion that her best interests lay in destroying Gerry's eight Settlewort plants, leaving hers as the only one in existence.

She deemed it unnecessary to convey this train of thought to Rosemary, and was having trouble quieting her conscience too. If Settlewort really was a plant with powerful medicinal properties, her dutiful self insisted, then the discovery of eight of them far outweighed the importance of saving one private garden, however unusual and precious to its owner.

'Well, perhaps I'll just try and transplant them then,' she thought to herself unwillingly, and on the Wednesday morning, when her niece had gone into Ipswich for some shopping, and Elaine and Veronica were pumping iron, or whatever they did at the Health Club, she gathered together a spade, fork, gloves, and a pair of secateurs, and put them into a large black rubbish bag. This would also conceal the molested plants when the dark deed was done, but she racked her brain for a persuasive excuse for such implements, if she was caught. Looking for a lost cat was hardly going to be convincing, she thought with self-mockery. And what was that police charge? Oh yes, "Going equipped to burgle".

Mind you, remembering the 'inexplicable' disappearance of the decoy plant from her front garden, she had her doubts whether Gerry would want to cut up rough about a little trespassing to garner a few unwanted weeds. Digging up his precious heathers might be another matter, she thought, amused at the notion of wanting any such plants, let alone stealing them.

She had attempted to check on Gerry's movements, with a casual question to Derek, two days before, about how things were going at Thornways, and what his unloved boss was doing at the moment.

'Clumpings are supposed to be coming back to him with their final offer on Wednesday,' he informed her. 'Gerry's very upbeat about it. Can't imagine why,' he added dispiritedly. 'He's the only one who thinks this place will survive. Half the workforce are already searching the local paper for jobs.'

Big white clouds were drifting across the sky with steady purposefulness, as Zinnia made her way up the lane, trying to look as if she always went for a walk accompanied by gardening tools poking out of a rubbish sack. Only once did she have to hide it hastily behind a tree, when Daphne Stalker's Honda appeared round the bend, and, prompted by guilt, Zinnia was ashamed to find herself waving cheerily. Retrieving her swag-bag as soon as the car was out of sight, she made it at a fast pace to the Thornway's gateway. This time she didn't bother with the charade of knocking on the door, but walked straight round to the back, wondering how much growth the Settlewort plants would have made in a week.

The koi carp gathered, gulping expectantly, at the end of the pond as she stood beside it, gazing at the undulating beds of heathers and conifers, in confusion. The peacocks were pecking desultorily at some scattered corn over by their enclosure, but of the Settlewort plants there was not a sign. A swift walk round the garden confirmed it. They'd disappeared. Someone, in the last six days, had either pulled or dug them up. Zinnia didn't know whether to feel pleased, or cheated. But she did want to know what had happened.

A visit to the compost heap, behind the inadequate bamboo screen, soon revealed the answer. There, beside a cascade of fresh grass cuttings, were the wilting remains of the Settlewort plants she had come for, pulled up by the roots. Elegant green-grey leaves drooping pathetically, their once juicy stalks bore more than a passing resemblance to the limp bunch of celery Rosemary had firmly turfed out of the fridge only that morning. The roots, she noted with interest, were thick and fleshy, with a slightly yellowy tinge, and there still lingered about them the faint scent of peaches. She regarded the sad remains thoughtfully, wondering if she couldn't make use of them somehow. But she still came back to the conclusion that it was better for the Pit Garden to be growing the only one in existence, at least while the botanical bods were sniffing round the place. In any case, these shrivelled specimens really did appear past retrieval. As if giving a decent burial to the battle fallen, she proceeded to cover up the desiccated roots and stalks with grass cuttings.

At the same time, she became aware of a vague sense of unease that she couldn't focus on. Something was not quite right.

She'd forgotten about the peacocks, and now one of them let out its piercing cry just a few feet away. Zinnia jumped as if she'd trodden on a snake, and swore loudly, while the bird cocked its head at her, like an insolent schoolboy who has just put one over on the teacher. She regarded it with a jaundiced eye, but, her nerve suddenly undermined, picked up the burglar's bag of tools, and making a gloopy face at the koi carp in passing, retreated down the lane.

It was only when she was almost back at Kiln House that the niggle in her mind crystallised into a thought which stopped her dead in her tracks. Last Wednesday she'd counted eight Settlewort plants in Gerry's garden. But on his compost heap today she'd covered up the remains of only seven. Where on earth was the other one?

****

The fact that Clumpings were coming back to him only five days after taking the Settlewort for scientific examination was an excellent sign, Gerry thought, with satisfaction. They'd obviously done their homework, and were anxious to get in smartly, before Thornways, and Settlewort, slipped through their fingers.

He'd given much thought to the price he should stipulate for the company, in the light now of its unique selling proposition – a phrase he had heard bandied about in the past few weeks, and now used, shortened to USP, at every opportunity. Double what he'd been asking before, he decided would be a realistic price. And he would threaten to sell the place to Clumpings' main competitor if they didn't play ball. He'd show these young cubs what it was to negotiate with someone who held all the cards.

He was looking forward to the meeting, and had dressed with care. His gold cufflinks in the shape of golf clubs, plus a Calvin Klein tie and Tommy Hilfiger shirt, recently bought in Bermuda, would give the right impression, he thought. There would be a bigger team coming down from Clumpings this week, no doubt, and probably more important people. So he was put out to observe, that afternoon, the arrival of just one car, from which emerged only that supercilious Vetcher creep.

Gerry had had glasses and notepads laid out, and expensive champagne was on ice, in anticipation of toasting a successful deal. But Vetcher took in the scene with an expression of scornful distaste, as he came in.

'Your plant is hereby returned, Mr Thornway,' he said, putting it on the table, and indicating that Gerry should sign a receipt. 'It's been thoroughly examined by experts both within the Group, and from outside, and I'm sorry to have to tell you that it certainly is not Solanum regale, as you maintained.'

'Not! You don't expect me to believe that!'

'I'm afraid so. It's certainly a herb that was used in the ancient world, but it's not particularly rare.' A suspicion of enjoyment was discernible as he went on. 'It's Cassa acutifolia, or senna. Popularly used as a laxative.'

'But...' Gerry was speechless.

'And I also have to convey to you the withdrawal of Clumpings' offer for your company. We are not now interested in the possibility of acquiring Thornways,' Vetcher said bluntly. 'After due examination we no longer consider it synergistic with our other brands. You will of course be receiving that decision in writing.'

Twenty minutes after he'd left the premises, the news was winging its way round the company, courtesy of Gerry's secretary who'd found it necessary to be working in the room next door. In his office Derek sighed resignedly, and started work on his c.v., while Prentice Stalker tried to make some sense of having been asked to write a résumé on Settlewort, and the departure last week, and arrival back this afternoon, of a Clumpings' executive carrying a wholly different plant.

****

Botanists and gardeners were two different species, Zinnia had long ago decided, and both were inclined to despise the other. Botanists peered at flowers, examining their private parts through a magnifying glass, whereupon they declared that their botanical names would have to change. Gardeners, on the other hand, enjoyed the whole plant, got to know its habits and preferences, admired its attractions, and tried to match it with congenial companions. It was, she thought, the difference between analysing what made a person attractive, and falling for them. She did not expect to like the two men that Simon arrived with next morning, but then that wasn't the point. If their position and prestige were going to protect the Pit Garden from becoming a rubbish tip, a little false obsequiousness was a small price to pay.

Rosemary came down to breakfast that morning wearing a slim-fitting, cotton dress instead of her usual shirt and jeans.

'You look very nice,' Zinnia observed, adding innocently, 'Any special reason for the glad-rags?'

'It's going to be a lovely hot day, that's all', she shrugged. 'I notice *you've* put on a skirt. Now that is telling!' and they smiled at each other affectionately.

Simon had said to expect them about mid-morning, and just before eleven a car turned into the drive, and he introduced a thin, bearded man as Doctor Sieva of Kew, accompanied by a small and rather bird-like representative from the Chelsea Physic Garden, fortuitously named Professor Peck.

'I'm just going to be the ignorant, but keen, gardener,' Zinnia had declared cheerfully at breakfast, and she now proceeded to chat carelessly to the two august visitors, as she led them down to the Pit Garden, with Rosemary and Simon bringing up the rear.

The first few hot days of July had brought a subtle difference to the garden, as if it had changed gear. The roses that cascaded flirtatiously from the trees were fast losing their looks, and peonies, abutilons, rock roses and the plentiful Sweet Rocket were going over in sympathy. But big shrubby mallows were opening their bright pink flowers, spreading drifts of day lilies trumpeted their presence, and hebes of various shapes and colours were covered in their long, fuzzy blooms. Everywhere there were patches of double, white Feverfew, contrasting with startling royal blue, where self-sown larkspurs were just opening their elegant flowers.

'What an amazing garden', the Professor exclaimed. 'I've been to the quarry garden at Highdown in Sussex of course, but this seems even bigger. Wonderful planting too. A real achievement.'

He immediately went up several notches in Zinnia's estimation, but she was careful to continue her role as unassuming amateur, surprised to be harbouring a plant which was arousing so much interest.

And of their interest there was no mistake, particularly the Professor's. The grey-leaved deadnettle had now gathered strength, and not only filled the ledge, but hung over the edge, covering the base of the Settlewort entirely. The result, Zinnia was gratified to note, was most natural, as if the seed had germinated and the growing plant had pushed its way up through the groundcover. It was now about three foot tall, and several flower buds were just beginning to form on the side branches.

'This is *most* exciting! Really quite extraordinary,' Peck declared, after he and his companion had stood in front of the Settlewort for some time, examining it closely, and comparing its characteristics with descriptions they had brought with them.

'I just noticed it growing one day,' Zinnia volunteered, not untruthfully.

'Tell them about the plant occurring here when you were a child,' Simon suggested, and Zinnia related her story of the wartime appearance of the plant, thought to be Settlewort, leaving out the bit about her future father-in-law's attempt to grow the seeds.

'And that was just up the lane was it? Could we look at that area?' Dr Sieva enquired. 'After all if it's suddenly regenerated here, there's a chance it might have done the same there.'

'Oh no, the bomb crater was filled in not long after, and there's a house on the site now,' Zinnia hastily informed him.

'And it's never been found growing in the area since that time?' he persisted.

'Not until now. Of course I keep searching for seedlings. You never know, they might just pop up,' she said with an ingenuous smile.

'I have had a good look around the village, and up on the hill,' Simon chipped in helpfully. 'There was nothing that I could see.'

'Extraordinary longevity, some seeds have,' Dr Sieva remarked, fingering the leaves reverently. 'They managed to germinate some solanum seeds recently from a two thousand year-old tomb in China. Quite remarkable.'

'The things won't be able to struggle through tons of rubble though,' said Zinnia, and told them about the imminent tipping of building waste in the Pit. 'Planning permission has already been granted to the new owner,' she finished. 'He could start at any time. Probably just about where we're standing. The track comes across the field above here.'

Rosemary's sceptical eye was upon her, but the visitors did not appear to detect any theatricality.

'I don't think you need have any worries about that now, Mrs Peasmore,' Dr Sieva assured her. 'The Botanic Gardens have already asked the Department of the Environment to prepare an injunction stopping any such activity, in advance of it being declared a Site of Special Scientific Interest. It just needed our verification that the plant was indeed Solanum regale, and of course that it was growing nowhere else. And my colleague and I are now satisfied with its identification.'

'But legal things take ages,' commented Rosemary. 'What if he starts tipping next week?'

'If I have the man's details, we'll write informing him of the situation,' Sieva promised. 'Let's see, today's Thursday, and I'm away tomorrow and Monday. But I'll write to him on Tuesday. And if anything untoward should happen between now and then, get on the phone to Simon Forb.' He nodded approvingly in Simon's direction. 'This is a most important find,' he added, 'we certainly can't have it put in jeopardy.'

Zinnia regarded him with high favour, and decided she might have been a little harsh on botanists.

'The Chelsea Physic Garden's records show investigations into the plant's medicinal properties as far back as the eighteenth century,'

Professor Peck told her enthusiastically, as they walked back to the house. 'But now, with modern knowledge and methods, we can learn much more. And of course put the findings to good use. This reappearance is really very exciting.'

'Naturally we shall very soon have to consider the possibilities of propagating the plant,' Sieva added. 'You know, I'm sure, that it's not believed to be frost hardy, and opinion is even divided as to whether it's an annual or a biennial. Either way, we need to spring into action immediately it sets seed. We'll be in touch about that.'

****

Zinnia was exultant. Her precious Pit Garden was saved, and what's more it was through her own efforts. Unfairly brushing aside Rosemary's part in finding the Settlewort seeds, she began to think in grandiose terms. She could open the garden to the public and make lots of money. The limitations of increasing age swiftly forgotten, she even resurrected the idea of expanding the garden into the adjoining Little Pit. With money, it occurred to her, she could employ labour to clear the undergrowth, and her mind was happily envisaging an enlarged and financially productive garden, famous throughout the gardening world, as she cut off some of the spent Sweet Rocket heads, that afternoon.

When Basil Berriman hailed her from the top of the ramp, she greeted him so effusively he wondered if she hadn't been at the sherry.

'Wonderful garden you've made for Julia,' she enthused, straightening up as he approached. 'Saw it for the first time last week. I love that green and cream colour scheme.'

'Well a lot of it is annuals and tender things of course, because of it being open on the Gardens Day,' he said modestly. 'In the autumn we'll replace them with more perennials and shrubs. Glad you like it. I'm going round to see if it needs any titivation this afternoon.'

'Very original,' she complimented him, lifting a bundle of Sweet Rocket stalks onto a carrying mat. 'And I really would like some seed of that green umbellifer.'

'Oh, the bupleurum, certainly.' Praise from Zinnia was worth having, and he was genuinely pleased to be able to give her a plant she didn't know.

'You haven't been for weeks,' she reproached him, taking off her gloves. 'I trust you've brought your camera today.'

'Ah yes,' he said, shifting uncomfortably, remembering what he had to tell her. 'I'll get it out of the car in a moment, but do you remember last time I was here, I trod on a plant by the greenhouse – the one you thought was a weed of some sort? And it had an odd, fruity smell.'

'Ye-es,' Zinnia said cautiously.

'Well it reminded me of something I'd been reading about, and I was going to look it up. But could I find that wretched book anywhere? Turns out Maurice had been using it to prop up the projector while he sorts out his talk.'

'I thought you were the one who gave talks.'

'He's gone completely over the top with his vegetables.' Basil made a gesture of exaggerated despair. 'And now he's putting together a talk about their history. Not without interest actually. He was telling me this morning about some complete craze at Louis XIV's court for eating green peas. But it's hardly going to rivet the Women's Institute is it?'

'Well...'

'And of course I've been roped in to do the photography for the slides,' he went on. 'My dear, I swear even Cecil Beaton couldn't make a radish look attractive.'

Zinnia picked up her secateurs, and hid a smile. 'What was it you were going to tell me about this... this weed?'

His face fell. 'Oh yes. Well, when I finally retrieved the book and re-read it, I came to the conclusion – you're not going to believe this – that that thing just might have been Settlewort! You know, Solanum regale, the famous herb that's been extinct for over a century.'

'Really?'

'Yes, only the awful thing is of course that I killed it! I went to look just now, and there's only the blackened stump still visible.' He put his hands to his face, in a dramatic gesture of remorse. 'How could I have been so clumsy? Dear Zinnia, I would quite understand if you never spoke to me again.'

'I'll show you something.'

She took his arm, and led him across the garden to where, just two hours before, the distinctive looking plant growing on a ledge had received its official endorsement.

'There was another seedling,' she said quietly, 'and you're right. It is Settlewort.'

He looked at her incredulously, then back at the plant, and reached up to touch one of its willow-like leaves.

'There were experts from Kew and the Chelsea Physic Garden here this morning, and they've confirmed it. Just as well too,' she added, and told him how the threat of tipping had hung over the Pit Garden.

He was horrified. 'But that's unthinkable!'

'Well it is now,' Zinnia nodded happily. 'I can tell *you*,' she added, 'although it's unofficial at this stage, so don't spread it around, but they're issuing an injunction. And then it's going to be designated a Site of

Special Scientific Interest. So the new owner won't be allowed to tip after all. Isn't that wonderful?'

Chapter Twenty

Three days later the Pit Garden's new owner settled into his seat on the London-bound 747, as the lights of Tokyo airport shrank and disappeared below. He hated flying. It was the feeling of not being in charge that was so alien, and the prospect of sitting passively for hours with a herd of sheep-like passengers. He was thankful to have got an aisle seat, and the Japanese businessman beside him didn't look the chatty type, which was something.

At least I'm on the way home, he thought with relief. Eddie had wanted him to show the way things were going in Japan which, like Britain, had problems of high waste and land shortage. But incinerators and the disposal of chemical waste were miles away from the kind of business he had built up, and he could raise no interest. It was the way of the future, according to Eddie, and the direction Swathes Environmental Services should be going. That had been a contentious issue between them for years, but now that Eddie had been given his head, there was no point in further objection. The lad was ambitious. He must be allowed to get on with running things his way. But Mike Swathe would be glad to have no part in it.

I must be getting old, he thought, watching the flight attendants working their way down the aisles, with drink trolleys. With her shiny brown hair, one of them was rather reminiscent of his daughter-in-law. She'd be in the air right now, of course, flying to meet up with Eddie in Hong Kong. They'd fancied a holiday there before the handover to China next year. It was the sort of thing he and Julia would have enjoyed doing.

Oh hell. That unguarded thought acted like water on the quick lime of his resentment, and he began to seethe again. In the last eight days, he'd refused to think about the row with Julia, pushing it away to concentrate on helping Eddie. As founder of the firm and head of the family, he had status in Japanese eyes, which must be used. Now a long flight stretched ahead of him, and when he landed, it would be to a life where all his recent hopes and expectations had been ripped to pieces.

I'll get drunk, he thought to himself savagely, as the glossy-haired hostess served the row in front. But by the time she reached him his strategy had changed, and he shook his head at the proffered spirits dismissively, and chose sparkling water. Better to think it through. Otherwise the hurt and anger would only fester inside.

It was the sense of betrayal that stung so badly. She'd put that bloody friend before him. It was such a slap in the face. He unscrewed the bottle, and poured fizzing water into the glass, reflecting bitterly on what was lost. They could have lived happily in his and Julia's joined cottages. Although that, he was honest enough to admit, was possibly a rather rose-tinted picture. Because there would have been problems, no getting away from it. They'd have had to adjust to each other's way of life, for a start, and certainly Julia would have found it awkward dealing with that Zinnia friend.

He didn't have close friends, never felt the necessity of a best mate. You didn't need one, if you were strong enough yourself. And self-reliance meant no-one would let you down. But, he mused, women were different. Like chemical elements, they seemed to have a natural affinity. Maybe it stemmed from the primitive need of help in childbirth. He sipped the water, feeling the bubbles effervesce in his mouth. And that Zinnia woman had been a lifelong friend. Perhaps, he conceded grudgingly, he could have been more understanding about Julia's warring loyalties.

Not to the extent of backing down over tipping in the pit, of course. And it wasn't just about money either. He felt anger rising again, and poured himself more water, slopping it over his hand. How dare she accuse him of that. It wasn't true. The whole thing was about pride and self respect. That place was a symbol of the past he had overcome.

The satisfaction of making sure no-one ever played on that tennis court again would be sweet, he reflected. It would show the world, as well as himself, how far he had come, a fitting revenge for his humiliation all those years ago. And earning a fat profit from the tipping only made the whole thing better.

Show who, exactly? a part of his brain enquired sarcastically. They're all dead, those people who snubbed you. There's only Zinnia and Julia left.

It was an uncomfortable thought, and he ignored it.

The Japanese businessman was now watching The English Patient, and Mike Swathe was distracted by the picture on the neighbouring screen, of a light aircraft skimming the desert dunes, heroine's scarf trailing in the wind. Having seen the film, he knew that at the end you realised she was dead. An unaccustomed pang of sympathy for the fictional hero struck him. He was experiencing for himself the desolation of losing the woman he loved.

The difference, the same rebellious part of his mind suggested, is that you can change things.

No, he pushed the thought down again. She had to take him on his terms. 'Go for what you want, don't let anyone get in the way.' That was how he was, Julia knew that. And she was getting in the way.

'Have you made your choice, sir?'

They were taking orders for the meal. He shook himself back to the practicalities of picking something, although he wasn't hungry, and the flight attendant passed down the aisle.

Have you made your choice? The words hung in his mind. Was he guilty of woolly thinking, insisting he could have everything? Maybe, he admitted reluctantly, there was some choosing to do. He mulled over the problem. Taking things down to the simplest factors, was the best way of tackling business dilemmas. What would this situation boil down to? Compromise, and life with Julia, versus... assuaging his pride with a profitable hole in the ground. Which Eddie didn't even want to bother with now.

'*Don't let anyone get in the way of what you want,*' he said slowly to himself. My God, you're the one who's getting in the way, you fool! You don't need to bury that bloody tennis court if you've got the girl who played on it. That's a far better triumph.

As the thought sank in, it was like understanding a magician's trick, and he couldn't believe the simplicity of it. Why had he never seen it that way before?

But hold on, it was more than just Julia versus an old quarry. His pride was at stake, and the question of whether she loved him. He sure as hell wasn't going to be humiliated again. She'd put her friend's interests first, after all, and said some hard things.

Unwillingly, he thought back to their quarrel, trying to remember exactly how it had gone. Suddenly words he'd hardly taken in came back to him. '*It would never have worked, my dear.*' He frowned, perplexed. Did she really think that?

For the first time since, as a youth, bruised and thwarted, he had walled away an idealised picture of himself marrying Julia, he tried to imagine honestly how it might have been.

Her parents would have been dead against it of course – that mother of hers furious, the father scathing. That would have hurt her, and caused a lot of friction. Those first years, too, when he was selling scrap iron, and even after starting Swathe's Skips, money had been very tight. The business had needed long hours, and he was hardly ever at home. His mother-in-law had looked after the kids then, while Doreen took a job at Thornways, so at least they had one steady income. He grimaced. Julia could hardly have been asked to do that. Maybe, if they'd married, he would even have had to give up on the idea of his own business, and taken a job. She'd have expected to have a decent house and lifestyle. And, with him resentfully stuck in some dead-end job, wouldn't they have had rows? Divorced even?

As if some knot inside him had suddenly loosened, he faced the stark truth for the first time. Could it be that Julia was right? They really wouldn't have stood much chance.

A young couple across the aisle caught his eye. Scruffy-looking backpackers, it seemed unlikely they could afford to fly Club Class. Probably been upgraded. Wasted on them though, he thought dryly, watching them share a secret world of togetherness. It didn't matter to them where they were. Their love made them blind to everything else.

Julia had loved him all those years ago, of that he was certain. But not enough to lose sight of practicality. Well, that was all in his favour this time. He'd got money and enjoyment to offer. And he deserved her. She ought to be the prize for what he'd made of his life.

'*Not then.*' He suddenly sat up, remembering her words last week. '*It would never have worked, my dear. Not then!*' Why had she added that, if she didn't think they could make a go of things now? And what's more, it seemed she thought he was going to ask her to marry him.

The captain's voice came over the intercom to announce that they should be prepared for some air turbulence.

Fastening his seat belt in response, Mike Swathe's mind was experiencing disturbance of its own. He was recollecting the stricken look on Julia's face as she stood in the doorway, while he snarled at her, 'Who said anything about marriage?'

When they were young, he thought guiltily, she had refused him gently, trying to make it less hurtful. And what had he done? Reacted like a boorish oaf, kicking a kitten. He was filled with remorse. How could he have treated her like that? Oh no, even worse, he closed his eyes in shame as he remembered, that Chitting woman had been in the next room. It was unforgivable.

Suddenly overwhelmed by a desire to leap the distance, he wanted to rush and tell Julia he didn't mean it, that he loved her. He wanted to stroke her hair, and kiss the hurt away. He would say her friend could keep the bloody garden, he didn't care, so long as they could be together.

He gave an inward snort of self-mockery. It wasn't just young love that made you go soft.

But it wouldn't be possible to go to Haydon straight away. There was this Thornways business to sort out first, he thought, trying to rank things in time order. Vital to get in before Gerry Thornway made an approach to someone else about buying the company. He must be getting desperate, Mike Swathe reckoned with all the sympathy of a hawk preparing to stoop on a particularly foolish rat.

As asked, his younger son Ian had faxed them in Japan with developments, and he and his father had had long telephone conversations. Working in Clumpings' Strategic Planning department, he could get hold of the reports on Thornways without difficulty. They made clear that the conglomerate had now decided to bide its time till Thornways went into receivership, which was a virtual certainty. That would save them paying any redundancy money to the employees, and they could walk away with the brand name, which was all they really wanted anyway. Ian had scruples about making use of this information though.

'Cobblers to that,' his father had told him unequivocally. 'As long as Clumpings have taken their offer off the table, you're in the clear. This is for you, after all. Do you want the chance to run your own company, or not?'

****

Gerry Thornway was surprised to see Mike Swathe parking outside the company on the Monday morning, and came down to Reception to greet him, a rare privilege, had his visitor but known it. Gerry normally liked people to be escorted up to his office, with ceremony.

Ensconced in the luxurious office, Mike Swathe got straight down to business.

'I gather Clumpings have decided not to go ahead with their offer for the company,' he said.

'How did you hear that?'

'My younger son works for Clumpings, and keeps his ear to the ground. They told you they were no longer interested in Thornways, didn't they?' He paused. 'You may like to know that's not true. They want the brand name anyway.'

Gerry perked up. 'So it was just a negotiating ploy? I knew it was all along, of course.'

'No. They've decided to wait until you go under,' Swathe said bluntly, 'then pick up what they want from the receiver, for next to nothing.'

He waited, for extra effect, monitoring Gerry's expression. 'We can't let them do that, can we?' he commented in kindly tones.

'We? You'd be prepared to help me?'

'Your father was very good to me. Gave me encouragement, a loan to get started, and land to rent. I owe him a lot.' Mike Swathe ladled on the sentimentality. 'It would break his heart if he could see Thornways closed down, the workforce out on their ear, with some big conglomerate using the name.'

'Yes.' Gerry found it irritating the way people kept banging on about his father, but if Swathe had an unexpectedly soft spot for the old man, it was worth exploiting.

'What I really need is a large loan,' he suggested eagerly. 'Just to tide things over, you know. The bank won't help. But if you...'

'I'll do better than that,' his visitor said crisply. 'I'm prepared to take the company off your hands. Then you'll be free to launch out in other directions. Stockleigh Golf Club could do with a shake-up, couldn't it. Needs some new blood, someone with energy and vision.' He looked with clear approval at Gerry, who glowed. This man really appreciated his talents.

'I'm not going to bother with due diligence,' Swathe continued. No need to mention that he was perfectly well aware of Clumpings' figures. 'I don't want to mess around, and nor do you. This is the deal I'm prepared to offer you.'

He passed a sheet of paper over to Gerry, who seemed to deflate, like a ball spiked on railings.

Mike Swathe watched him. 'We're already getting sheaves of job applications from your employees,' he said. 'So speed is important, or you won't have any work force left. Which isn't a great selling point.'

'It's a lot less than Clumpings were offering,' Gerry blustered, 'I don't think I could consider...'

'They have, of course, withdrawn that offer,' Mike Swathe cut in. 'And going into receivership would put paid to your business career for the foreseeable future,' he added pleasantly.

Gerry was silent, fidgeting, trying to do sums in his head.

'As a clincher, and to show good will, I'm prepared to give up on tipping in the old pit at Haydon. Then you need have no more worries about it affecting the value of your house.'

On the plane yesterday, the pit's owner had found this little touch pleasing as soon as he'd thought of it.

It was only a matter of time. They both knew that. Gerry was in a no win situation. Half an hour later they emerged from the office, for a tour round the company.

Derek was taken by surprise when Gerry opened the office door, and introduced his General Manager to Mike Swathe, whose sharp eye took in the c.v. lying on the desk. Derek Peasmore, he'd noted, was named in Clumpings' reports as about the only the reason the company was still keeping its head above water.

'Perhaps Mr Peasmore here could show me round the rest of the place,' he suggested firmly to Gerry. 'I want to ask about the packing machinery, for instance, and I'm sure you've got more important things to do. I'll come back to your office afterwards.'

'But first,' he told Derek, sitting down after a ruffled Gerry had departed, 'I'd like to talk to you. You'll know soon enough, so you might as well hear it now. I've reached an agreement to buy Thornways. The company's likely to be modernised and expanded, and,' he nodded towards the c.v., 'your knowledge and organisational ability will be badly needed.'

Derek hardly knew what to say.

'You should also be aware,' Mike Swathe continued smoothly, 'that I'm no longer planning to make use of the old chalk pit that your mother currently uses as her garden. She'll be able to continue as before. So there's no reason for bad blood between us. You won't be subject to a conflict of interest.'

'That's wonderful news,' Derek's wariness changed to a broad smile.

'My son will be coming in as Managing Director. He's been in the food industry for some years. Got a business degree and all the theoretical stuff they seem to cram into them these days.'

Derek's apprehensions about the possibility of another Gerry must have shown on his face.

'I have a high opinion of his abilities,' Swathe assured him. 'But he'll need someone steady and experienced as his right hand man. Would you be prepared to do that? You won't regret it.'

At the end of a blurred morning, Derek finally got a few moments to himself. First he telephoned Veronica to tell her that his job was safe, and the future suddenly rosier than he could have hoped. Then he rang his mother.

'Great news about The Pit Garden,' he began.

'Yes, *isn't* it,' she interrupted happily. 'I'm thrilled to bits. I've kept quiet in case it all went wrong, but it's certain now. Such a relief. Good old Settlewort.'

He didn't quite see the connection, but let it pass, and went on to tell her about Thornways being bought, although he tactfully soft pedalled on the identity of the buyer. Any new owner intending to invest in the firm would have been welcome, but Derek had been surprised to find that this businesslike man talked straight and inspired confidence. The fact was he liked what he'd seen of Mike Swathe. He just didn't think Zinnia needed to be told that.

****

At her sitting room desk after lunch that day, Julia Trugglestone was writing a letter of condolence to an acquaintance who'd just lost her husband. Over the years something of a formula had developed for such duties, but she was feeling so raw herself at the moment that the usual words seemed particularly trite. She gazed out of the window, pen poised unproductively. The weather front bringing the morning's rain had passed through now. Glistening drops were still adorning the yellow petunias, but the patio paving was changing from brown to cream as it dried patchily.

That's what happens after a death, she reflected. Your dark state of mind evaporates gradually, as time and events conspire to lighten it. She had thought of the process as a steady progression, and up to ten days ago it seemed as if, for her, the sun was at last breaking through. But that was before…no, it was time to stop dwelling on that, she told herself sternly, and turned her attention back to the note.

It was difficult to offer any comfort, when she felt so bruised herself. The green shoots that had been tentatively growing towards a new life had been cruelly crushed, and now she was lost. There were so few things to be sure of, she reflected unhappily. You spent your married life with the security of husband, house and children. But for her those had proved impermanent, and she had clearly been naïve in seeing another marriage on the horizon. He'd made that humiliatingly clear. More than ever, she needed to cling to the fixed things of life.

Bracken was asking to go in the garden, and she got up to open the door. 'Take you out shortly,' she promised, and sat down again at the desk.

Honesty and generosity were the watchwords of her natural personality, as well as upbringing, and now it seemed to her they were the only certainties worth clinging to. To try and protect her friend's garden, that had surely been right? Even though, she thought with sad realism, Zinnia would never understand how much that loyalty had cost in happiness.

She bit her lip. The galling thing was it might all have been for nothing. According to Basil Berriman, who had conveyed the news confidentially on Thursday, an injunction had now been issued, forbidding Mike Swathe from any kind of despoilation of the Pit Garden. So the timing of their quarrel had been really unfortunate. Another few days, and she wouldn't have needed to say anything.

Except, she reflected, holding the pen up to the light, and trying to remove an annoying hair from the nib, that to be a prisoner of the idea of making money, whatever the cost to other people, was a trait she couldn't be comfortable with. And what other reason could there be for his insistence on destroying Zinnia's beautiful garden by tipping? Love of money was notoriously corrosive, and perhaps a lifetime dedicated to making it had had a warping effect.

She considered herself a good judge of character but, she reluctantly admitted now, she must have been guilty of seeing in an old love what she wanted to see, rather than what was actually there.

This wasn't getting the task done. *Family and friends rally round and give great support*, she wrote, *they carry you through*.

Trouble was, she thought dolefully, although her family and Zinnia had been wonderful after Richard's death, she couldn't talk to them about her current heartache, and the death of her hopes. She had to cope with this on her own.

The sun was making its way through gaps in the cloud now, lightening the room and reflecting softly off the polished desktop. Outside Bracken's nose was dampening the glass door to the garden, as she looked in hopefully, tail wagging.

Yes, we both need some fresh air and exercise, Julia responded. It'll help me feel more positive. Although, she told herself with a concluding sigh, avoidance is really the answer. Yes, that's it. I won't see him, won't have anything to do with him. Her shoulders straightened determinedly. It was a fanciful, foolish affair in the first place, she chided herself, and you should have known better, my girl.

Glancing down at the half done letter on the desk, she smiled ruefully, imagining the recipient's reaction if the words she really wanted to write went down on the paper. *You will be very susceptible emotionally for some time. Take it from me, keep well away from an old flame, you'll only get burned.*

****

Mike Swathe tried Julia's front door just after three, with no result. He was still standing by it, frustrated and considering what to do, when Mrs Chitting walked past on her way back from the village shop.

'Lady's out,' she called to him, adding with satisfaction, 'and a good thing too.'

'Do you know when she'll be back?'

Mrs Chitting put her shopping bag down, and eyed him with disfavour.

'She don't need you to make her more unhappy. Haven't you done enough damage?'

The antagonism was fully deserved, he reminded himself, keeping a hold on his temper.

'I've come to mend fences,' he told her with unaccustomed meekness. 'Do you know where she's gone?'

Mrs Chitting sniffed. 'Dunno,' she said unhelpfully, and picked up her shopping. 'She's took the dog for a walk.'

After a moment's thought, he locked the car and walked down towards the river. The early July sun shone hot on his shoulders, but the dampness of the morning's rain lingered at the road edges, and in the shadow of Julia's garden wall. A magpie was strutting importantly across the playing field, on the other side of the road. They weren't most people's favourite bird, but he rather liked their clean lines, and in-your-face plumage. What was that rhyme of his mother's, about magpies? 'One for sorrow, two for joy.' Load of nonsense. Strange what lingered in the memory.

He reached the kissing gate beside the bridge, and leant against the post. As a small boy he'd enjoyed swinging on that gate. It was a wooden one then, replaced years ago by the present metal gate, which now squealed plaintively on its hinges. He swung it to and fro, with a half smile, as if trying to recreate that childish pleasure. It wasn't often he allowed himself time to idle.

It was good to be here, after the strangeness of Japan. He looked back at the village, at the church tower, rising proudly above the rooftops, the familiar row of cottages along the river, and, like a fading sinner embracing religion, finally admitted to himself that this was where he belonged. All his adult life he had wanted to keep away from Haydon, tainted as it was by conflict, unhappiness, and what it said about where he'd come from. Now he would move back here to live, he thought with satisfaction. Come home. With Julia at his side, there wouldn't be anything left to prove.

A movement caught his eye, and he smiled with pleasure at the sight of a figure in the distance on the river path, accompanied by a dog. There was no mistaking either of them and, causing the gate hinges to squeal once more, he set off to meet them.

But as she came level with the old dry dock, Julia disappeared from view, leaving a puzzled Bracken loping in circles on the path above.

No record existed of a boat builder in Haydon, but once there must have been someone who built or repaired boats, hauled up in a little inlet flanked by brick walls. Hidden from the path above, the long-disused dry dock had always been a favourite trysting place for the lovelorn of the village, and probably still was, what remained of the wall acting as an adequate, if uncomfortable, seat. The ground was covered with detritus left by the river in spate, and from beneath it grass struggled to grow, with the persistence of a selfish idealist seeking the perfect partner. Brambles and a wild rose draped themselves down the walls, and above a sturdy alder tree ensured cool shade and seclusion.

Leaving the footpath, Mike Swathe stood by the tree above the dock, and looked down with a smile at Julia's slight figure pressed against the bank to avoid detection. The green patterned dress she was wearing was actually quite an effective camouflage. A late rose, hanging from above, had dropped petals which now adorned her hair, white against silver, and she looked almost girlish, he thought tenderly. The knowledge that she had taken refuge there in order to avoid him was a stab to the heart. But soon everything would be put right between them.

She jumped at the sound of his voice.

'It's no good you trying to be invisible. That dog of yours is a dead give away.'

He made his way round the tree, and down the short path to the dock.

'Is there room on there for two?'

'No, I rather think not,' Julia told him defensively, unprepared for the assault that just his presence made on her resolve. He rolled a log over and sat down at her feet instead.

'Odd that,' he observed. 'Long time since you and I sat here together. Getting on for fifty years. But as I recall there was room for two then.'

'Since when have you taken to going for walks along the river?' enquired Julia stiffly. It was banal, but slightly better than commenting on the weather.

'I've come to apologise,' he said simply. 'I don't know what went wrong, but I'm very sorry. You're the last person I would want to quarrel with,' and he held out his hand. Her instinct was to take it gladly, the recent determination to stay well clear already crumbling, but she stopped herself. Principles mattered.

She looked away awkwardly. 'We probably both said things we didn't mean, but that doesn't solve the problem, does it?'

'Ah yes,' he assured her, injecting a little humour. 'I also came to tell you that I've thought about what you said, and although you aren't right, it might look like that.'

'What?'

'You said money was what mattered to me above...everything else. That hurt, and it isn't true either. And to prove it I've decided to call off the tipping in the old chalk pit.' He paused. 'Isn't that what you wanted?'

Her face was not expressing the response he had anticipated.

'I'd much prefer you to be straight with me.'

'What do you mean?'

'I don't like being taken for a fool,' she said stonily, brushing a fallen twig from her skirt.

'Julia, there are many things I might take you for, but a fool is not one of them.'

'Then stop insulting my intelligence.'

He stared at her, thrown. 'Have you moved the goalposts or something? You flew at me to protect your friend's garden, and now you've got what you wanted. Isn't that enough?'

'You know perfectly well why it isn't.'

'My God, woman, what is it you do want?' He stood up, puzzled and resentful. 'I don't do grovelling, you should know that.'

'Nobody asked you to, but a bit of honesty wouldn't come amiss.'

'Honesty? Do you want me to tell you how I thought it all through, and decided you were right, and I was...'

'No,' she cut in coldly. 'No, I specially don't want that. I'd far rather have the truth. Maybe you don't know what that is any more.'

'Meaning?' His tone was dangerous.

'You seem to think that telling me what I want to hear makes everything all right. It doesn't. If you can't be straight with me, I don't think we have anything more to say to each other.'

Bracken, worried by the antagonism in the air, put her paw on Julia's knee, as Mike Swathe stared in hurt and baffled anger.

'And that's it?' He looked as if he was about to boil over, then, like a milk saucepan with the heat turned off, suddenly subsided, shaking his head in despair.

'I give up. What's the use of even trying to understand you, Julia? he asked bitterly. 'I never will.'

And he turned and made his way back to the footpath, without looking back.

Chapter Twenty One

With less than two weeks to go now to Haydon's Garden and Flower Festival on the nineteenth of July, Julia found herself grateful for the myriad organising tasks that seemed to fall her way. Although neither would willingly have admitted it, she and Daphne Stalker formed a good team for getting things done, despite lack of personal empathy. Daphne barked instructions, and harried at people's heels, like a persistent terrier, while Julia employed tact, charm and persuasion, backed up by discreet use of her social standing.

On occasions she also had to smooth the ruffled feelings of those who found Daphne's abrasive manner too much to take. Relations were less than cordial, it transpired, between her and the Chairman and Secretary of Stockleigh and District Flower Club, and the day after Julia's walk by the river, simmering discontent erupted into an open split. The rebellion was a real threat to the Flower Arranging Competition. This would have been financially disastrous, with the marquee irrevocably booked, and Haydon relying on attracting good numbers of the region's keen flower arrangers, both as competitors and visitors. It was expected that having Loretta Moss in attendance would be a big draw.

Hastily, the two indignant officials were invited over to afternoon tea with Lady Julia Trugglestone, in an effort to placate them. Afterwards, exuding warmth and friendly interest, she showed them round the garden, taking care to ask their opinion on everything. It didn't fail, as she knew it wouldn't.

She was less adroit at mending rifts nearer home. The coolness with her daughter-in-law had been exacerbated by Susie's annoyance at The

Herb Garden not being designated, in the programme, as an official place for teas. Somehow Julia had not put her mind to sorting this out, and now it was too late, the programmes were all printed.

Rosemary did her best to make Susie feel better about it. 'You'll hardly be able to cope with the rush of customers as it is,' she pointed out reasonably. 'And at least this way no-one can say that you're cashing in on the event.'

'But we were going to give the profits to the fund anyhow. Now they'll just say we didn't pull our weight with helping to raise money for the village hall,' complained Susie, who was feeling decidedly ragged. Work had at last started at Trugglestone Hall on the improvements necessary to turn it into a conference centre, and trying to maintain family life amidst the dust, noise, and trampling workmen, liable to breach their privacy at any time, was proving a strain. She was also pre-occupied with a threatened disaster at the Herb Garden.

'We've got red spider mite in the big greenhouse,' she told Rosemary, with an anxious expression.

'A mighty spider, huh!'

'Well no, actually it's tiny – and not even a spider either, just looks like one. I'll show you.' Susie led her into the greenhouse. 'See... all the yellow spots on the leaves, where they suck the sap, and look, underneath,' she turned up the leaves of a scented-leaf pelargonium to display a reddish tinge along the veins. 'Through a magnifying glass, you can see thousands of the little buggers.'

'Can't you kill them with some kind of chemical spray?' suggested Rosemary, who couldn't see what the fuss was about.

'No, that's just the problem. Berriman's always used to spray, but we can't.'

'Why not? You said you weren't going to claim to be organic.'

'Well, we're not allowed to label ourselves organic, because we buy in plants from sources that aren't,' Susie explained, 'but I don't use chemicals on plants once they're here. For one thing I don't approve of them, and for another, customers are hardly going to be happy about taking herbs home for cooking, with insecticide recently sprayed all over them, are they?'

'Might not be too smart,' Rosemary agreed.

'But it's more than just the plants in the greenhouse,' Susie went on gloomily, picking the yellowing leaves from an exotic basil. 'With people coming in here to pay at the till, any outside plant they bring with them is liable to get infected too. I've tried using a soap spray, but the wretched bugs are still multiplying. I'm really worried about it.'

'But why do you need to have stock in here anyway? Surely it's hot enough outside now?' The greenhouse temperature seemed oppressive.

'Pressure of space, pure and simple. There's nowhere else to put the plants.'

'Isn't there a lizard or something who'd relish the thought of mighty red spiders for lunch? Rosemary tried to lighten things up. 'You could label this place The Reptile House, and make it an extra attraction.'

Susie raised a small smile. 'Well not a lizard, but there is another mite that eats it, and I've sent for details. Trouble is, it should have been introduced earlier, and it won't be able to cope with an infestation this bad.' She surveyed the sick-looking plants unhappily. 'I'll have to spray first. Then wait before putting the predator in. And the Flower and Gardens Festival is only ten days away,' she lamented. 'It was going to be such a showcase for us.'

Rosemary's scepticism turned to sympathy, at the obvious worry. Susie had been so pleased and relieved about the Herb Garden's initial success, and this was clearly a serious setback.

'What does Harry Trench think about it?' she enquired. 'Surely it must have happened before.'

'Oh no good asking him, he's wedded to his sprays,' Susie dismissed the idea. 'And before modern insecticides, they used really pernicious stuff, like nicotine, which we wouldn't dream of using nowadays. Anyway, the old boy thoroughly disapproves of what's been done here, so I don't want to involve him.'

She shut the greenhouse door. 'Let's go and have a cup of coffee in the kitchen at home,' she suggested. 'It's about the only place that's habitable. Come and see what they're doing, and I want your advice about a colour scheme for the main conference room. Clive and I can't agree.'

'Are you sure you'll able to afford it?' Rosemary teased. 'My interior decoration consultations don't come cheap, you know.'

'Probably cost about the same as we charge for viewing historic Trugglestone Hall. So we'll call it quits, shall we,' parried Susie, more cheerfully.

Although the sky was overcast, the air was sticky and warm as the two of them set off down the drive, attracting the attention of the herd of heifers grazing in the parkland meadow. They came over to investigate, egging each other on to a gallop, skittishly bucking and kicking.

'I don't know why you're so hard on Harry Trench,' Rosemary remarked, uneasily surveying the post and rail fence and wondering if it would survive the assault of fifteen excited young cows. 'I think he's a nice old boy. He has a kind of solid stillness. Reminds me of a backwoodsman my father got to know in Michigan.'

'Well... I do feel rather guilty about him, to be honest,' Susie admitted reluctantly. 'It's just that he'd had the gardens to himself for so long. And when I appeared, he seemed to think I shouldn't have anything to do with them. And as for making changes...! It was hard enough fighting Julia's opposition to setting up the Herb Garden, without Harry making me feel like a cross between Genghis Khan and Attila the Hun.'

The heifers proved to have braking powers, and were now keeping pace with them on the other side of the fence, jostling for prime position, their big eyes dark and questioning.

'Couldn't you have let him help you, or at least think he was?'

Susie shrugged apologetically. 'Perhaps I should have done. But it seemed easier to make a clean break. Trouble was, no-one would tell him he ought to retire, and I certainly can't.' She looked glum. 'There he is stuck in that cottage too, which I could badly do with. It would make all the difference if we could store stuff upstairs and have the till for plant sales in there.'

'Well where's he supposed to go? Your cupid's arrows aimed at him and Mrs Chitting don't seem to have hit their target yet, do they?' Rosemary still found this objective amusing, despite discovering that the two already had a symbiotic relationship steadier than many married couples.

'One of the village almshouses might be coming up in the next few months. Now that really is waiting for dead men's shoes! And he's on the list for a council house. But I don't hold out any hope there.' Susie sighed. 'Fact is, I can't see any way out of the problem. And when we meet he has this look of silent reproach. Makes me feel awful.'

****

Rosemary decided to drop in for a chat with Mrs Chitting on the way home. They could celebrate the exchange of contracts which was due to happen next day, and discuss when would be the most suitable completion date. But she was also aware that Harry had his lunch at Spring Cottage on Thursdays, officially as a reward for a morning's work on the garden.

She stood in the road and gazed adoringly at the property that was soon, amazingly, going to be hers. With all but the dormer windows flung open to catch the air, it was as if the cottage had woken up, and was watching eagerly for her. The front garden was a blaze of flowers now, with multi-coloured antirrhinums on either side of the front path, reminiscent of wedding guests in their finery lined up to throw rice over the happy couple. In the bed bordering the road there was a blizzard of red, white and pink blooms, their flat faces turned upwards like so many gaily coloured coins, and the path round the side of the cottage was outlined in a little blue flower, which also tumbled over the edges of two plastic tubs, containing Harry's beloved fuchsias. He was bending over a standard fuchsia with puce and pink flowers as she walked down the path, his jacket discarded as a concession to the oppressive warmth of the day, but cap still firmly on his head.

'Mornin. Tha's moosey old weather we're havin',' he greeted her, touching his cap, a gesture she had once thought subservient, but now found endearingly old-fashioned.

'Mm. Might have a thunderstorm this afternoon.' Rosemary had learnt that you couldn't start any conversation without the weather preliminaries. And it wasn't done to be too upbeat either. Measured gloom was the correct tone, especially with Harry.

'Getting ready for the big day?' she enquired. 'The garden's looking great. You've sure got a lot of flowers out. What are these?' she indicated the fancy coinage.

'Them's Busy Lizzies. Give a good bit o' colour,' he declared unnecessarily. 'Cheer a body up, that do.'

'Do your plants get, er, eaten by things?' she asked innocently.

'Eaten?' Examining the fuchsia, he began pinching out the shoots. 'Rabbits, you mean? Can't say as they do. Not like up at the Hall. A good tidy few up there. Old Fred Chitting took his gun to 'em, but didn't do no good.'

'No, I meant, sort of, pests. Insects.'

'Not so's a body'd notice.'

'What about red spider mite?'

Straightening up, he looked at her with the incurious benevolence of an elderly sheep dog. 'Tha's a thing as you mos'ly find in a glasshouse.' He dropped the pinched-out fuchsia shoots into a plastic bucket, half full of weeds, and turned to survey the improved shape of the bush.

'Did you have trouble with it in the big greenhouse...where your fuchsias were in the winter?' she persisted. 'Only, um, a friend of my aunt's got a real problem with red spider mite. And I thought you might know how to get rid of it.'

'Tha's not gen'lly a problem in there,' he assured her, revolving the pot in order to get a different view. 'Leastways, not if you treat it proper.'

'How do you do that?'

There was no immediate reply, but Rosemary resisted the urge to prompt. Trying to speed Harry's speech process was like stirring molasses.

'Well, seems that ol' mite, he don't like it dank, y'see. An' if you get a touch of it, all you got a do is flood the place.'

'Flood it?' She looked puzzled. 'Won't that cause problems with the plants?'

'No, that 'ont.' He had found more sprigs of growth that spoilt the fuchsia's shape, and was picking them off. 'Them ol' boys what built that place, they knew a thing or two. Made grut big sections, they did, an' you flood 'em. Like a turkey bath in there, it is. Spray the plants with water night and mornin', and after a few days tha's the innd on it.'

'Harry, you're a marvel!' she exclaimed, and kissed him impulsively.

He managed to look both pleased and embarrassed. 'Course, your friend, she prob'ly don't have that kind of greenhouse,' he added. 'Jus' have to try pails of water, and keepin' the ol' plants wet.'

As soon as she got back to Kiln House, Rosemary picked up the phone and called Susie.

'I've discovered that Harry Trench knows exactly how to cure the Mighty Red Spider,' she said triumphantly, 'and it's very simple.'

''Oh wonderful,' was the delighted response. 'What is it? What do I have to do?'

'Now that would be telling,' Rosemary told her, rather enjoying being disobliging. 'See, I figure you should ask him yourself.'

She put the phone down, bubbling with the news of Susie's problem, and how she had managed to crack it, but Zinnia had her own troubles, it seemed. Apparently a letter from the Features Editor of Country Harvest had arrived in the post that morning, which had been less than effusive about her column.

'He says I've got three months to alter the tone of it,' she reported indignantly, opening the door of the washing machine and pulling the clothes out into a basket.

'Is that the New Broom who came here in the Spring, and was given the er, brush off?' Rosemary flopped down on a chair at the kitchen table. 'Got staying power then, has he? You said these magazine guys were never around for long.'

'Long enough,' complained Zinnia gloomily. 'He's had this great idea – why do they always want to change things? Says instead of writing about plants, readers would like it if I took them through the making of a garden from scratch.'

'What's wrong with that? I think it's rather a good idea.' Dutifully Rosemary got up, and prepared to carry the basket of wet clothes out to the washing line. 'I wouldn't have a clue what to do.'

'Well, the trouble is,' Zinnia unhooked a bag of clothes pegs and followed her out, 'I don't have that sort of imagination. I can write about plants because it's something I know, but pontificating about creating a garden...' She shrugged. 'It's just not me. Sounds suspiciously like all these television makeover programmes too.'

Zinnia handed out a bundle of pegs, and companionably they began hanging the clothes on the line outside, one at each end.

'Couldn't you just imagine that you're advising me?' Rosemary suggested. 'After all, I'll be needing all of the help you can give. In fact,' she warmed to the idea, 'you could describe the garden at Spring Cottage, and the changes you're going to make.'

'*I'm* going to make?'

Rosemary looked innocent. 'Well what I know about gardening could be written on a flea's fingernail. I'm relying on you to help.'

'I'm not falling for that one,' retorted Zinnia, pulling out the sleeves of a shirt. 'Advice, yes. But as for doing any work, absolutely not. This place takes all my time as it is.'

'Your garden's looking so good,' Rosemary told her, with real admiration as well as diplomacy. 'It'll just slam-dunk visitors on the day.'

'No, it won't.' Zinnia's face was hidden behind a towel, but her voice had the deliberate lightness of a two-timing spouse. 'I've decided to withdraw the garden.'

'Oh you're kidding! Why, for heaven's sake?'

'Security,' she said shortly. 'That Settlewort plant is all that stands between me and the destruction of the Pit Garden. I just can't risk some dratted member of the public saying "Ooh, in't that luvly", and digging it up.'

'But they wouldn't, surely.' Rosemary hunted for a second sock in the basket. 'I mean, it's up on a ledge, for a start. There'll be lots of people around as well. No-one's going to risk being caught stealing plants. And then they'd have to get it past the people taking money on the gate.'

'Well, I'm not chancing it. Too much at stake.'

There was silence, while Rosemary thought disappointedly of all that time spent fact-finding about the Pit's history for the visitors' information leaflet. Not that that was likely to sway her aunt, she reckoned, any more than her responsibility to the village appeared to have done. But loyalty to Julia just might.

'That'll be a real smack in the face for poor Lady Julia,' she pointed out reproachfully. 'She's put such a lot of time and effort into organising this event. The programmes have gone to the printers, and everything. Have you told her yet?'

She'd hit the right button.

'Er, no, not yet.' Zinnia sounded uncomfortable. 'Oh drat it, I must have missed a tissue in a pocket somewhere. There are bits of white mush everywhere.'

'I noticed,' said Rosemary succinctly, 'and don't think you can slip a change of subject in that easily.'

Only her aunt's underclothes were left in the basket now and she decided, with tact, that these were not pegging tasks for her. Standing back, she watched Zinnia, before deciding to speak her mind. 'You have to tell Lady Julia right away,' she said. 'And I sure don't think you should kick her in the teeth like that, after what she did for you.'

****

Julia came up next day to try and persuade Zinnia to go back on her decision, and laid stress on how much the village was relying on the day to be a success, and that the garden at Kiln House was going to be a big attraction.

She wouldn't have insulted Zinnia by using the deliberate flattery worked on the flower arranging ladies, but as they walked down the ramp she did exclaim, quite genuinely, about how good the garden was looking.

Achilleas and osteospermums in soft shades were mixed in with drifts of double, white tanacetums and Shasta daisies, and clematis were flowering exuberantly, making the trees and shrubs they draped seem dressed for a gala. Huge pom-pom poppies of the darkest maroon had found niches for themselves in the sunnier places, their rich colour complementing the royal blue of larkspur. The day lilies, salvias and tall campanulas were at their best now, and on the south-facing quarry wall bushy clumps of wall germander, and sheets of little pink and white daisies that had somehow rooted themselves into the chalk, were alive with bees.

'You really should let people come, you know,' she declared looking round, adding astutely, 'the real gardeners among the visitors deserve to see something this good.'

'It's the security I'm worried about,' protested Zinnia, pleased in spite of herself. 'I've already had one plant in a pot stolen.'

'That did come back a week later though, didn't it.' Rosemary wasn't having the plant put out to tempt Gerry used as ammunition. 'Maybe it just went on vacation.'

Zinnia appeared not to hear her. 'I haven't told you before Julia,' she said as they walked round the pond, 'but the most extraordinary thing has happened. A plant of Settlewort has appeared here! And the botanical world is jumping up and down about it.'

'Settlewort! Good heavens, who'd have thought it?' exclaimed Julia, aware that Rosemary was suddenly taking a deep interest in the goldfish. 'Do show me.'

Zinnia led the way towards the base of the cliff. 'An injunction's been taken out which is going to protect the garden from...' she suddenly realised this was sensitive territory. 'Well, anyway, I just don't want to put the plant at risk. Someone might try and dig it up.'

'Gardeners wouldn't do a thing like that though, would they?' Rosemary put in mischievously.

Julia spotted the Settlewort from some way off. 'That tall, striking thing – is that it?' she asked. Goodness, I never thought I'd see one.'

'Nor did anyone else,' murmured Zinnia, as they came up to it.

'You know there's a tapestry up at the Hall which depicts the plant growing,' Julia remarked, 'but it's very stylised. I don't think I'd have recognised it.'

Zinnia fingered the glossy leaves lovingly, turning them up to show the grey underside. 'Didn't you see the one that appeared in the bomb crater when we were young? At least people thought that's what it was.'

'I don't remember that. Can't have been interested.'

The Settlewort had grown rapidly and branched, so that it looked bushier. The glossy green upper surface of the leaves reflected back the sun's rays, and it seemed to be soaking up the heat, spicing the air with its strange peachy aroma.

'There's a flower just opening round this side,' announced Rosemary, 'look, isn't it beautiful!'

There were several clusters of buds, each rather like an elongated Chinese lantern, and one was just opening out, to reveal a white cup-shaped flower, with curious purple stripes dividing it into five sections.

'Now that is the clincher!' Zinnia enthused excitedly. 'Must have opened this morning.' Thrilled, she examined the flower closely, announcing, 'It's exactly as the books describe. You see how I can't risk the public coming in here. It's just too important.'

'I tell you what, how about roping off this bit of the garden,' suggested Julia practically. 'We can say there's a danger of rock falls, or something.'

Zinnia shook her head. 'That wouldn't deter someone who really fancied it.'

'Well I'd be prepared to stand guard some of the time,' Rosemary offered nobly, and couldn't you bribe Matthew to do a stint?'

'No, you've forgotten that the Heebie Jeebies are playing during the afternoon. Besides,' Zinnia looked at her kindly, 'it'd be a shame for you to miss the full extent of English village eccentricity, even though we're not having a proper fete this year. You'll have to report it all back to Bill, you know. Give him a good laugh.'

Rosemary had a sudden image of her fiancé as an Easter Island statue, being unsuccessfully tickled by an ostrich feather. Realistically, he'd be likely to find her account of the Gardens Day more baffling than amusing, she thought regretfully. He'd be irritatingly superior about it all.

'If I arrange for three instead of two people to man the gate,' Julia tried again, 'then they can take it in turns for one of them to stand guard down here, and see that no-one approaches it. How would that be?'

'I'm not at all happy about it...' Zinnia seemed unconvinced.

'Oh do say yes,' Rosemary tried, persuasively. 'All that fact-finding I did, about chalk and lime. You wouldn't let it go to waste!'

'For the sake of the village,' Julia said quietly, and they all knew that wasn't the loyalty actually on test. She'd already made her sacrifice in the name of friendship.

Zinnia looked at her wan face, and softened. 'Well...perhaps...oh all right then,' she agreed, with the fading resistance of a wilful pony finally coaxed into a horsebox. 'But if anything happens to my precious Settlewort...!'

****

There was avid interest in the weather forecasts in the week leading up to the Gardens and Flower Festival. The outlook didn't seem particularly promising, but the general opinion was that Haydon had special weather anyway, a fact of which the meteorological office in London were for some reason unaware.

Matthew, already ambivalent about the HJ's performing at such an uncool venue, had gloomy visions of them being forced to perform under large brollies, to complete the loss of face. That was until he suddenly thought what a great advertisement the umbrellas would make for his computer services, commandeered all the large ones family and friends could provide, and adorned them with stuck on letters in luminous orange. "Y2K Bug Buster!" they screamed, followed by his telephone number.

'It sounds disgusting,' Veronica remonstrated with him. 'People will think we're running some kind of insect infestation service.'

'Wasps nests a speciality,' Matthew assured her, taking a couple of oranges from the fruit bowl, and juggling with them. 'And as for computer viruses... phh!, they don't stand a chance. Ollie and I are working on a programme that'll wack 'em dead. We're turning it into a game as well. It's a whiz. I'll bring it home. Even you'll be able to play it.'

His mother heaved a theatrical sigh. 'Games are all very well...' she began, in familiar vein.

'No, this one's going to make our fortune,' Matthew forestalled her. 'Ollie's dad's looking into the marketing possibilities. Whoops.'

He crawled under the table to retrieve the independently minded orange, but escaped the anticipated rebuke. Veronica was trying to keep too many balls in the air herself to continue nagging Matthew to the expected standard, and had noticeably let up on her pressure now for Zinnia to move into one of the new bungalows. She had spent hours cooking, almost filled the freezer with cakes and scones for the school's fund-raising stall at the Gardens and Flower Festival, and could hardly keep up with the demand for herbal jams to sell in The Walled Garden's shop. At the school she was helping with the Fourth Form's dancing display, and was also making fancy dress costumes for some children whose mothers were too busy, or too inept with a needle, to provide the necessary accoutrement.

Nigella Picket would have been mortified at the notion that anyone else should have to make Angelica's costume. The original idea of a milkmaid had been discarded as too common, and she was now going as the arachnophobic Miss Muffet who, according to the nursery rhyme, sat on a tuffet, eating curds and whey.

'What's a tuffet?' Angelica sensibly wanted to know, and as the dictionary defined this as a mound, her mother settled on a foam rubber cushion intended for invalid drivers, covered with imitation grass from the greengrocer in Stockleigh. A market stall that Nigella would normally have deemed not worth a glance, selling all sorts of vulgar, knick-knacky toys, provided Miss Muffet's eight-legged tormentor, on a long piece of elastic. The repeated sight of it was giving Angelica bad dreams, and she was considering quietly jettisoning both tuffet and tarantula on the day, and simply declaring herself to be a milkmaid.

Nigella was also organising a Plant Stall, and had badgered any villager who was known to take the slightest interest in gardening to give plants for it. This had simply provided an excuse for everyone to offload the progeny of packets of seed they'd been unable to resist buying, but hadn't got room, or time, to plant. As a result her drive was now overflowing with yoghurt pots, ice-cream containers, and trays containing distressed-looking lavateras, cornflowers, nasturtiums, sweet peas, French beans, cucumber and marrow plants, plus a good number of seedlings with no label at all. Although she had dragooned a couple of people into manning the stall on the day, no-one seemed to be willing to harbour the stock beforehand. The resulting untidiness of her drive, and the thought that visitors might conclude she had grown these lacklustre specimens herself, was beginning to upset her. The garden just had to be perfect on the day.

Prentice Stalker was fairly sure of perfection. He had been beavering away for weeks at information and display boards, and had reorganised his collection of carnivorous plants to illustrate which parts of the world they came from. Bladderworts from Australia were divided from the Asian species, Caribbean and South American natives were now grouped separately, and the North American pitcher plants were all clearly labelled as either species or cultivars. To avoid crowding in the greenhouses, he had arranged for a queuing system outside, with lots of information on the plants people would see, plus rules about what visitors would, and would not, be allowed to do. There was a large sign forbidding the feeding of the plants, but how he was going to stop the curious from exhausting the sundews by continually teasing them into closing, he wasn't quite sure.

He and Daphne were, for different reasons, both now channelling their best efforts into the big day, which was as well, since marital harmony might otherwise have been at risk from her testiness. There were so many things demanding her attention, and she knew from experience that if she didn't personally check up on everything mistakes were made. You just couldn't rely on people to do things thoroughly. It troubled her that the Flower Arrangement Competition was largely out of her control, and efforts to remedy this situation had been firmly rebuffed. In the Chairman of Stockleigh and District Flower Arranging Club, Daphne had come up against a desire to organise quite as strong as her own. She had been permitted to make the practical arrangements – hire the marquee, provide rubbish containers and a supply of water – but beyond that knew very little of what was going to take place, which was decidedly irksome.

Elaine Thornway wasn't much the wiser, although she had been a member of the Club for over a year. Overawed by the prima donna status and brisk professionalism of the demonstrators, she had kept her head down at meetings, listening with misgiving to the calculated backbiting of members of different cliques, none of whom welcomed or took any notice of her. She had a great deal to learn, that was obvious, but was determined to do her very best in this, her first, flower arranging competition. The fact that it was in Haydon, and everyone in the village would view her efforts, was another spur. And if she could just persuade Veronica's mother in law to let her use some of the unusual flowers from her wonderful garden, at least her effort would stand out from the rest, and might gain extra points.

Veronica had dutifully conveyed Elaine's request, choosing a moment when Zinnia seemed to be feeling reasonably mellow, with the result that permission had been given for flowers to be gathered, as long as it was under supervision. Accordingly, four days before the great day, Elaine went round to see her neighbour, to get some idea of what would be available, and was given a conducted tour of the garden.

'It's a difficult time of year, isn't it,' Zinnia said kindly, meeting her by the garage, and leading the way into the garden. She had nothing against Elaine, and thought it was a good sign that she was doing something on her own, away from Gerry's bullying influence.

'There isn't much to pick in our garden at the moment,' admitted Elaine, giving her apologetic little laugh. 'Gerry wants it to be easy-care, you see, he likes heathers and things. I've put an order in to the florists in Stockleigh of course, but lots of people will do that, and I would like to have something a bit different.'

'How about concentrating all on one colour?' Zinnia suggested, trying to be helpful. 'Blue for instance. This dwarf lupin's just recovering from an attack of the American Lupin aphid, so it's flowering late. It would look spectacular with larkspur. You could have all different shades, and call it "A Bout of the Blues".'

'Oh no, you see we have to stick to the theme on the schedule,' Elaine explained awkwardly. 'The title is "Understanding".'

'Understanding!' Zinnia stood still in scorn. 'How on earth is a vase of flowers supposed to indicate something so completely abstract?'

'I don't know,' admitted Elaine, adding timidly, 'but I'm only a beginner.'

'Well I never heard anything so ridiculous.' Zinnia thought she detected the overweening hand of Loretta Moss, and immediately determined to do her best for the girl. She took her round suggesting things that would be useful for foliage effects, whilst pointing out flowers that were particularly out of the ordinary.

'This Francoa 'Confetti', she said generously, as they toured the Pit Garden, 'you can have several spires of that if you like. It's so elegant. Choice as well.' A pleasurable thought struck her. 'Even Loretta Moss isn't likely to know what the thing is, if her latest column in Country Harvest is anything to go by.'

'What's that?' Elaine pointed at the Settlewort, now decorated with several striking white flowers, the divided leaves hanging with the haughty languor of a thirties model posing with a cigarette holder.

'Ah, that.' Zinnia sounded casual. 'Don't know. Probably something exotic that germinated from your peacocks' birdseed. But I'm afraid it's not to be picked. *At all.*'

'It's pretty,' Elaine commented. 'I'm definitely going to use mine, although it does have rather a strong smell. Do you think that would lose marks?'

'You've got one in your garden?' asked Zinnia faintly.

'Oh we had quite a few of the things springing up. Gerry thought they were untidy and told our gardener to pull them up, but I asked the old boy to put one in a pot for me. It scents the whole conservatory,' she went on happily. 'I was hoping you might know what it was called, in case I'm asked.'

Roger the Lodger had been shadowing them at a discreet distance, and now he sauntered past, lightly brushing his tail against Zinnia's leg, to signal ownership.

'Oh hello Blackie.'

Imaginative names were evidently not Elaine's strong point. The feline rebel disdainfully kept his distance as his erstwhile owner bent down to try and stroke him, and she was thus entirely oblivious of the consternation on her neighbour's face.

'I don't think Blackie liked it when Gerry got the peacocks, and that's why he ran away,' she went on, with a generous lack of resentment. 'He looks well, doesn't he.'

Zinnia felt like a holiday maker who's suddenly realised that at home the front door has been left wide open.

'Tell me a bit more about this competition,' she prompted carefully, as they moved on. 'What exactly is going to happen? And when will you be picking flowers, and, er, doing the actual arranging?'

****

Later that afternoon Matthew obeyed a mysterious summons from his grandmother, while Rosemary was asked to come back early from her walk, and they arrived at the back door of Kiln House simultaneously. It was a hot day, and the inviting coolness of the kitchen was enhanced by the fact that the door of the large and venerable fridge stood open, while Zinnia, hammer in hand, tried to knock ice chunks off the inside.

Rosemary, who had several times volunteered to defrost it only to be told there was absolutely no need, raised her eyebrows.

'Door wouldn't shut,' explained her aunt unblushingly. 'Otherwise it's fine. Now, I'm going to need your help.'

'A load of hot air from Rosemary should do it,' suggested Matthew, perching on the table.

'No, not with the fridge. Wretched child!' his grandmother berated him fondly. 'Listen, we've got to think of some way to get hold of a Settlewort plant that's going to be in one of the flower arrangements on Saturday,' and she told them about Elaine's revelation. To her irritation they both seemed to find it amusing.

'Oh, I'm sorry to laugh,' Rosemary spluttered, 'but there's you luring Gerry into stealing a plant of yours, and now you want to do the same to him.'

'I can't see why it matters anyway,' said Matthew, bending down to tickle Roger under the chin. 'Your Settlewort has made sure they aren't going to tip in the Pit Garden. What difference does it make if Elaine Thornway has another one?'

'It matters a lot.' Zinnia tried to prise off a large block of ice. 'The Pit's being protected because it's the only place that's Settlewort grows, in the world. At least it's supposed to be,' she added, giving up, and looking round for the hammer. 'If there turns out to be another Settlewort, the site won't be unique any more, will it? Questions will be asked, and it'll come out that there were far more in Gerry's garden than here.'

'Well there's going to be an auction of the arrangements afterwards. What's wrong with just buying Elaine's entry?' enquired Rosemary practically. 'After all, no-one will know what the Settlewort flowers are. And later we can think of some way of getting hold of the actual plant in the conservatory.'

'Your usual judges of country flower arrangement competitions might not know what it is,' replied Zinnia, between hammer bangs, 'but unfortunately Loretta Moss is coming round in the afternoon. The country's queen bee of flower arranging. True, it'll be strange to her, but you can be damn sure she'll find out what it is. She'll ask Basil for a start, and he's useless at lying.'

'We could let Elaine think it was deadly poisonous,' suggested Matthew, 'and then she wouldn't want to touch it, would she?'

'Trouble is, I've already told her I haven't a clue what the plant is,' Zinnia said regretfully. There was a metallic clang as a large chunk of ice collapsed onto the shelf. 'Gotcha!' she exclaimed with satisfaction, then sat back, considering.

'You're right, we need some reason to stop Elaine using it,' she said slowly, 'or if we can't do that, getting rid of the entry so that the Moss woman doesn't see it.'

'That's a bit tough on poor Elaine, isn't it?' objected Rosemary. 'Seems she's not too hot in the confidence line as it is.' She surveyed the fridge's contents laid out on the work top, picked up a can of beer, and mimed downing it at Matthew, who nodded.

'Well, she won't miss out on the judging, because that's in the morning. And I'll find some way to make it up to her,' conceded Zinnia. 'It's just vitally important we get hold of that plant. Trouble is I'm going to be tied up here, because of the garden being open.' She looked at them. 'I'm relying on you two.'

There was a pss! as Matthew pulled the ring off the can Rosemary handed him, and chucked it towards the bin. He missed, and Roger the Lodger abandoned his bored act, and sent it skittering under the dresser.

'No worries Gran,' Matthew said in an exaggerated Australian accent, taking a swig of his tinny. 'You just leave it to us. We'll think of something, won't we Rose?'

****

Before breakfast the following morning, at what she would once have considered an indecently early hour, Rosemary went down to the Pit Garden with her camera. The coming of full summer had somehow taken her by surprise, but lately she'd become more conscious of the passing days, making her anxious to record everything. Like a squirrel gathering nuts, she felt the need of something to nourish her through what might be barren days to come.

Not that she wanted to think about the future. Her mind shied away from it, preferring to enjoy what seemed a golden time, suspended between the awkwardness of her first few weeks, and the end of summer, when she would have to go back. Curiously, this knowledge had no trouble coexisting in her mind with the picture of herself moving joyfully into Spring Cottage, lavishing care on the cottage and its garden, and living there happily ever after. Any shrink worth half his fee would have probed the contradictions painfully.

The garden was so magical at this hour of the morning, she thought, standing by the pond and drinking in the air's freshness and the beauty of the flowers. The early light, soft as a mother's glance, quietened colours and emphasised the clumps and leaf shapes. Cut off from the rising sun by the high sides, the Pit Garden seemed even more a world on its own, out of time with the rest. Beside the path, pale yellow Evening Primrose flowers greeted the day, putting a brave face on the extinction it would bring, while day lilies opened new buds to compensate.

Living with Zinnia and watching the garden drift into summer, had brought home to Rosemary how little she knew about flowers and their names, but she was able to appreciate what she saw, without being aware of how it was achieved.

She didn't lack artistic flair herself, and enjoyed composing her pictures, whilst realising that nothing would adequately convey the size and special atmosphere of the Pit Garden. She'd photographed the Settlewort before of course. Heck, the thing was historic. It hadn't had so many flowers on it though, and a few more shots would be in order, she reckoned. But standing in front of the plant, looking through the view finder, something struck her as being amiss. The stems were surely thicker than they should be, and somehow it wasn't holding itself with the usual confidence. It looked...sick.

Lowering the camera, she stepped up to the plant for a closer examination. Swarming over the stalks, forming a thick and repulsive layer, were a mass of little grey bugs, feasting on one of the rarest plants in the world.

Summoned urgently, Zinnia took one horrified look, and diagnosed the problem.

'Hell's teeth, that's the American Lupin Aphid!'

'But it's not a lupin.'

'Well, the little buggers go for other things as well. Completely demolished my broccoli plants last summer. Goodness knows why they've started appearing over here, but they're really bad news - multiply like nobody's business. Oh and the Settlewort, of all plants!' she wailed. 'Can you run and get the insect spray. Under the greenhouse workbench. *Quick!*'

Later that morning, Rosemary drove down to Matthew's house, carefully harbouring on the front seat a large ice cream container, lid tightly closed, inside which were a few broccoli leaves, and a quantity of voracious, grey, and rather lucky American emigrants. Back in the Pit Garden, their compatriots had begun to feel decidedly off-colour.

'Is Agent 003 and a Half up yet?' she enquired of a distracted Veronica, knee deep in bilious coloured crepe paper, making the cabbage costume for some luckless child coerced into entering the Fancy Dress as a Cabbage Patch Doll.

'Could you please tell him 'M' is here? We have some mission planning to do.'

Chapter Twenty Two

The day of Haydon Settleworth's Flower and Gardens Festival dawned fine, but 'scattered showers' were forecast for the afternoon, a get-out phrase which, according to Zinnia, neatly covered the weather service even if it poured for several hours. That would merely have been a slow-moving shower.

Daphne Stalker had of course insured the event against it being rained off, and Clive Trugglestone obligingly arranged for two tractors to be on stand-by to pull cars out of the mud, should the fields designated as car parks become quagmires. He and Derek had rather enjoyed practising their towing and manoeuvring skills a few days before, and felt they were now well-qualified to act as White Knights, should the heavens open. They were in quiet agreement too, that volunteering to oversee the parking gave them an excellent excuse to decline anything else they might otherwise have been marked down for. In Derek's case this could well have been manning the microphone, but Toby Picket was now deputed to do the announcements, keeping up the relentless jollity of a tipsy uncle at Christmas all afternoon.

'Fingers crossed for good weather,' Susie suggested to Rosemary, who somehow doubted that digit twisting had much meteorological effect. It would have been disloyal not to comply though, with Susie hoping that the Walled Herb Garden would be really busy, introducing it to a host of repeat customers who otherwise mightn't have been aware of its existence.

In addition to her usual weekend helpers, Susie had promises of help from Rosemary and Matthew in the morning, and after some hesitation Mrs Chitting had agreed to join the tea team in the afternoon. Her loyalty had been torn between supporting Harry Trench at Spring Cottage, Lady

Julia, with her garden open, or joining in at the Herb Garden. Julia had been reproachfully taken aback to learn of her decision, but Daisy Chitting felt it was high time Lady made things up with her daughter-in-law, and said so. In any case the gardens would each have two volunteers to oversee and guide visitors, so she would only have been there for moral support. There was also the small matter that Susie would be paying for Mrs Chitting's services.

Proud that Toby was to be the microphone maestro, Nigella Picket was confident that she could manage without his help. She had put a lot of thought into how visitors should see her garden, and produced a leaflet on the computer, comprising a map, showing all her different 'gardens'. Where possible Before and After photographs had been scanned in, plus a plant list for each one. She had decided on a Best-Way-To-View system, which was shown on the map, and had put up notices everywhere, indicating the route visitors should take. She would of course be on hand to answer their questions, and was determined that everyone should find it a learning experience, whether they intended to or not.

The large marquee which was to house the Flower Arranging Competition had been dominating the playing field down by the river for several days now. A water bowser arrived the day before, plus staging, and a container for the disposal of greenery, stalks, or unwanted accessories that seemed to be de rigeur for the successful arranger these days.

Elaine Thornway had been wondering what she could do in the accessories line, and had thought of buying some contorted-looking driftwood out of a Flower Arranging Catalogue. But Gerry scoffed at the idea, on the basis that everyone would do that sort of thing. She should use something like peacock feathers, he instructed. Now they *would* be different. The word 'prestigious' wasn't added, but he certainly thought that. After all, the hoi-polloi simply didn't have peacocks strutting round their gardens. It would show all the flower arranging ladies that the Thornways were not just as good as they were, but a whole lot better.

Unconvinced, but not daring to say so, Elaine obediently added the exotic feathers to the flowers and leaves gathered under Zinnia's careful tutelage the night before. These, together with some eustoma and long-stalked roses collected from the florist, and branches of Settlewort carefully cut from the plant in her conservatory, were taken down to the marquee early on the Saturday morning.

She found herself ticked off on a list, given a badge, and told which bit of staging she had been allocated. All around her, entries were being put together, while people chatted to each other guardedly, as if playing a parlour game in which one of their number had been designated the murderer.

'I'm Sheena,' the competitor on her right introduced herself, 'It's going to be exciting having Loretta Moss coming round this afternoon, isn't it?' On her left a smartly-groomed, blonde-haired woman in a turquoise jacket gave her a brief smile, while opening what seemed a huge box of carefully packed flowers and accessories.

Elaine had selected a tall, cut-glass vase that had been a wedding present, and in which she often arranged flowers at home. Sheena observed her choice with a raised eyebrow, but forebore to mention that this was unlikely to find favour with the judges if they were at all old fashioned, and disapproved of stalks and water being visible.

Zinnia hardly ever picked flowers for the house herself, preferring to see them in the garden, but Elaine's timid lack of confidence had triggered her instinctive support for an underdog, and she'd been generous with both flowers and foliage. The result was that Elaine was in the happy position of having almost more than she could sensibly use, even without the bought-in flowers.

She became absorbed in making the arrangement, forgetting about the competition schedule, and the exhortations of various demonstrators at the Flower Club evenings. She had brought a notebook full of jottings about how to work frontals, and bring about balance, contrast, texture and colour. She had been told about Hogarth Curves, and should have deliberately counteracted the forward pull, created a light and airy skirt, and remembered her heavy leaf balance.

But instead she just did what seemed good to her. The mid-blue of Brodiaea 'Queen Fabiola', and a Jasione Zinnia had grown from seed mixed pleasingly with the subtle, misty mauve of Nepeta 'Dawn to Dusk'. Fibigea clypeata contributed its extraordinary, fleshy seedheads, Larkspur made stabs of dramatic colour here and there, and lacy Selinum leaves gave the whole thing a light, ethereal touch . She put in the peacock feathers, roses and Eustoma, but quickly concluded that they just didn't look right, and took them out again, adding instead the white spires of Francoa 'Confetti'. These were nicely set-off by the Settlewort's graceful, grey-green leaves, while its flowers, with their extraordinary purple lines down the ice-white petals, drew the eye like a supermodel.

The woman in the turquoise jacket had been watching without comment, as they worked. She had a feeling her neighbour's arrangement would be marked down for not interpreting the title well, nor filling the allotted space.

'Don't you want those?' she asked, and was given the spare flowers to add to her own imposing arrangement of orange gerberas, with curled bergenia leaves, and Bird of Paradise flowers pecking through a plaster arch on which was perched a mortar board and graduation certificate. Sheena, on the other side, had gone for a shout of yellow – huge lilies, carnations and chrysanthemums, with variegated ivy trailing over a leather-bound book. The arrangements were all arresting in their way, but Elaine's had the fresh, natural beauty of a native girl, unaware of her effect, flanked by knowing, made-up, city sophisticates.

'What's that?' Sheena pointed to the Settlewort. 'It's rather effective, isn't it. Bit of a strong smell though.'

'I'm afraid I don't know.' Elaine felt embarrassed by her ignorance, even though her authoritative gardening next door neighbour apparently couldn't put a name to it either. 'It's just a weed that came up in the garden.'

Zinnia had made it clear that Rosemary shouldn't feel obliged to put in any time at all at Kiln House, and as they were both, for their own reasons, anxious to see the flower arrangements before judging, they went down to the village together at about ten o'clock. The day was warm but overcast, the clouds harried by a breeze, and every now and then the sun managed to peek through, like a child jumping for the occasional glimpse of a parade over adult shoulders.

Haydon had an unaccustomed bustle to it, with various stalls being set up on one side of the main street. Yellow, *No Parking* cones marched commandingly down the other, which the locals were ignoring with the confident certainty of ownership. It was their village. The cones could only be instructions for visitors.

Outside The Oak the publican was setting up a blackboard sign with 'Meals Served All Day', chalked on it in fancy letters, and underneath, 'Fresh Country Fayre'.

'That'll be the day,' commented Zinnia sceptically, as they drove past. 'Straight out of Stockleigh's Cash and Carry, more like.'

Lacking an official windscreen sticker, she was, to her annoyance, turned away from the playing field, where competitors were allowed to unload, and waved on to the official car parking area over the river. Derek strolled over as Zinnia was locking the car.

'Five pounds keeps your car safe, lady,' he said in a threatening wheedle, holding out his hand.

'Oh yes? Ten pounds keeps the secret of all your floozies safe from Veronica,' his mother countered cheerfully. 'I didn't think you'd be here till after lunch.'

'Had to escape the house.' Derek shook his head in mock despair. 'Veronica's buzzing around like the proverbial blue-tailed fly, and would you believe Matthew got up this morning at *seven o'clock*, so he and his chums could have a practice session in his room before he went to the Herb Garden. The din!'

'Good heavens. I thought he was like Cinderella in reverse,' his grandmother commented drily. 'Only turned into a human after ten o'clock in the morning.'

Rosemary found her aunt's reinterpretations of aphorisms and nursery tales most endearing. She laughed. 'You don't think it might have been the coach that changed?'

'And with Matthew I would question the word "human",' added Derek unkindly. 'Anyway, I thought I'd come and keep the flower arrangers in line. As it were.' He winked at Rosemary. 'Been laying on the charm, in the hopes of making a conquest. Do you reckon it'd be better with a cap to touch? I could probably find one on the Brownies' Stall over there. They've got masses of stuff.'

As they walked across the bridge, they could see a sign saying 'Competitors Only', outside the marquee. Daphne Stalker was observed across the field, ensuring the St John's Ambulance first-aid post was sited exactly as planned, while a television crew waited impatiently for her attention, and Zinnia decided that particular string was not worth pulling.

'Press,' she told the clip-boarded Flower Club official at the tent entrance, firmly. 'I write for Country Harvest magazine. This is my secretary. And she sailed in, Rosemary in her wake.

The scent of a thousand flowers mingled memorably with that of warm canvas and trampled grass, as they walked slowly up the gangways, squeezing past people, stepping over handbags and boxes of flowers, trying not to kick buckets and watering cans. There was an excited buzz of female voices, although here and there a man was engrossed in a floral creation. Less than half the arrangements were finished, or nearly so, but already the eye was assaulted by colour and spectacle on every side.

'I hadn't realised it was going to be so big,' Rosemary remarked, jumping over the lead of a small dog, tied to the staging.

'Julia said the Stockleigh Flower Club wallahs were very pleased with the response,' answered Zinnia, looking back. 'Seems they've had entries from Flower Clubs all over the region'.

They found Elaine at the end of the marquee, and even if neither of them had had a personal interest, her arrangement would have caught their attention. It was just so different.

'But that's beautiful, my dear!' exclaimed Zinnia, with unalloyed admiration, and some surprise. 'Really lovely.'

Elaine's pale face flushed with pleasure. 'Oh that's very kind of you Mrs Peasmore. It's nearly all your flowers of course. You gave me such super things. I'm ever so grateful.'

Zinnia indicated the Settlewort. 'I see you've used that odd flower to good effect,' she said in a guarded tone, before turning to Rosemary with a meaning look.

'This is quite something, isn't it.' Rosemary waved her hand at the busy scene, giving Elaine a friendly smile.

They didn't stay long, but as Rosemary was arranging with Mrs Chitting's daughter to buy back the bellows from the Brownies' stall near the marquee entrance, Zinnia found herself accosted by Daphne Stalker.

'Ah, Mrs Peasmore,' she called, 'all ready for the great invasion?'

'Oh this'll be the big attraction, won't it?' Zinnia indicated the floral marquee. 'Kiln House garden can't possibly compete.'

'Nonsense, it's the jewel in our crown,' said Daphne briskly. 'Although there has been a slight disappointment with regard to your garden, and the Thornway's.'

'Disappointment?'

'Yes, I've been meaning to tell you. As you know I had arranged with Mr Swathe for car parking to be in the field he owns further up the lane – as he allowed when the bird-watchers came. You remember?'

'Only too well.' Zinnia's lips tightened at the memory of the fanatical interlopers.

'Well the thing is, he's now withdrawn that permission. I've been having quite a battle with him.'

'Join the club,' muttered Zinnia.

'I'm afraid he's adamant. I'm not quite sure why.'

It wasn't difficult to fathom. Being given the brush off by Julia, and losing over tipping in the Pit, were not calculated to sweeten the man's temper. Hardly surprising that he should react by being uncooperative.

'So where are visitors going to park?'

'That's just it, there isn't anywhere else,' Daphne said resentfully. She didn't take kindly to defeat. 'We've had to alter the programme, telling people they'll just have to walk up there. Although I'm laying on a minibus service every fifteen minutes during the afternoon for people who can't manage on foot. I'm sure you'll still get lots of visitors, but it might be a bit less than if they could have taken their cars. That's what I wanted to tell you.'

Zinnia drove back to Kiln House, the bellows, woodworm now treated, on the seat beside her, leaving Rosemary to walk along and help Susie. But before doing so, having taken more than a passing interest in the immediate surroundings as they stood in front of of Elaine's flower arrangement, Rosemary casually wandered round to the back of the tent, and examined the way the canvas sides were pegged to the ground.

Looking round warily, she bent down and carefully loosened several, then, turning the plan over in her mind, set off to do her stint at the Walled Herb Garden.

Before starting in the shop, she sought out Matthew in the plant sales area, where he had just come on duty as car-loader, heavy-weight-carrier, and anything else Susie might want. She briefed him about the location of Elaine's flower arrangement, and reported on the loosened pegs.

'And if you're not outside that tent at exactly the right time to take the flowers when I pass them through, I'll murder you.' She shook her head wonderingly. 'How did I get mixed up in this crazy idea of yours? It'll never work. I mean, if you're setting up the band, how are you going to have time to do it? Or you'll forget. I know you.'

'You vould qvestion ze great Peasmore Plan? How can zis be?'

Rosemary regarded what was evidently a European professor with affectionate irritation.

'Matthew, has anyone ever told you you're impossible?'

'*Me?*' his eyes widened in amazed innocence. 'Please, vhat is zis vord, "impozeeble"?'

It was just impozeeble to be mad at Matthew, thought Rosemary, laughing, as he pulled a face at her. He was as disarming as a toddler's giggle.

Susie was waving at him from the till, and he made to go. 'Do not vorry,' he gave a most unprofessorial grin. 'Trust in me, my child.'

****

So far the day had been even worse than Basil Berriman feared. Maurice had taken such a lot of trouble with the lunch too, nobly raiding his prized potager for vegetables. But the globe artichokes, followed by schnitzel with new potatoes, glazed onions, and carrots scarcely out of playgroup, took no account of Loretta's assumption that good time-keeping was just a framework for cockerels, aeroplanes and dull little office workers. Certainly nothing that need concern her.

The meal dried up and ruined, his dear sister had then dominated the conversation, as she always did. Tact never had been her strong point, although it was scarcely perspicacious of Maurice to broach the subject of slide lectures. He'd just told her enthusiastically about his first talk booking, and she swept away with the conversation, adding crushing remarks about rank amateurs, and hammering them with how successful her latest lecture tour of America had been. Really she was too bad. As a small boy, Basil had had a recurring nightmare that the dough, set in loaf tins in the warm kitchen, kept on rising, and rising, till it expanded to fill the whole room, crushing him against the wall. His older sister had always given him much the same feeling.

Sitting in the car, waiting to drive her over to Haydon, he was uncomfortably aware that they should have set off some time ago. Why was it the wrong kind of people who became famous? he pondered ruefully, his hand hovering pusillanimously over the horn. Not only that, fame succeeded in exaggerating exactly those qualities which made them unsuitable in the first place. Loretta simply didn't need hordes of star-struck flower arrangers telling her how wonderful she was. She'd been convinced of it from birth.

He was just summoning the courage to go in and remind her of the time, when she appeared at the top of the steps, her cerise outfit, with matching lipstick and earrings, cut just that bit too low for a woman of her age, her determinedly blonde hair sprayed into submission. Behind her Maurice hovered, and their eyes met in silent commiseration. Maurice's mother was a visitor desperately to be avoided too, so at least they could call it quits.

On the twenty minute journey, wondering how many weeks it would take for the car to be rid of her perfume, he tried to fill her in on Haydon's important personalities.

'There's Lady Julia Trugglestone of course. Her new garden is open, so I don't know whether she'll be at the Flower Show or not. But I hope you'll go and see what I've done for her. The company are going to use photographs of it in their Garden Design brochure next year. In fact my instructions are to be on hand there in case potential clients make enquiries, so I won't be able to come round with you.'

'I'll just visit a few of the gardens, to show willing,' Loretta decided. 'Which ones should I avoid?'

Basil considered. 'Well you won't like the Thornways', even though it's one of mine. But it's next to Zinnia Peasmore's, and that's wonderful. You know who she is, of course? Writes the gardening column in Country Harvest. A special friend. Oh dear!' Large drops were spattering on the windscreen. 'I do hope it's not going to rain.'

But the shower had evidently not been routed via Haydon Settleworth. The village was dry, and briefly bathed in sunshine as they came into it. People thronged the main street, sauntering along, sampling the various stalls, and the car could only drive at walking pace down towards the river, with people casually spilling off the pavement, like a swarm of ants secure in its numbers. The sound of music grew louder as they approached the playing field, and turning in the entrance they were confronted by a group of primary school children in someone's idea of traditional dress, performing country dances.

'Save us!' commented Loretta Moss acidly, before switching to a tight smile as they drew up in front of the marquee.

Relief was clearly discernible on the faces of Daphne Stalker and the Flower Club Chairman as their guest of honour disembarked. The film crew, who had been recording the childrens' somewhat ragged rendering of 'Gathering Peasecods' were now torn in the demands for their attention.

'We'll go with the Red Pepper,' Jeremy the producer informed his colleagues ungallantly. 'We can get the kids to do the prancing bit again, if necessary. You've got the lights set up in the marquee, haven't you?'

Meanwhile Rosemary, waiting round the back of the marquee, had given up cursing her cousin, and had graduated to praying. Seeing the car arrive, she realised with agitation that Loretta Moss would now be beginning her tour of the Flower Competition. Any minute now she could reach Elaine's arrangement, and catch sight of the Settlewort flowers. But where was Matthew?

She was bending down to peer under the canvas side when he came up behind her, and announced pompously, 'You'll have to come along with me, Miss. I'm arresting you for loitering with intent. Well, nearly in tent.'

'Where the hell have you been?' she demanded furiously.

'Oh, just talking to one of the girls on the Brownie's stall,' he told her nonchalently. 'Friend of mine.'

Rosemary looked at him in exasperation. 'Matthew, I'm tearing my hair out here, and you've been chatting up a girl friend. You are the limit!'

'That's very nice of you to say so,' he responded modestly. 'Always glad to be of service.'

'Have you got the insects?' she asked urgently. 'We've got to hurry!'

'Nope.' He shook his head, enjoying her expression.

'Why not!'

'Put 'em on already, haven't I.'

She stared at him. 'But I was supposed to do that. You said I should wait here and then transfer them to the Settlewort because I would arouse less suspic...' She broke off, putting her hand to her head. 'Oh what's the point?'

'Well, they were all trailing behind that woman,' he shrugged casually. 'It was a good opportunity... Very happy little insects now, they are. Anyway, you should be pleased, I've done half your job for you.' His eyes danced mischievously. 'Better get a move on, hadn't you.'

At that moment they became aware of voices from nearby in the marquee, and looked at each other.

'There's no time to go round the front now,' hissed Rosemary. 'Maybe I can get under the gap. Quick, help me.'

He held up the canvas as she squeezed through, to find herself underneath the trestle table that was the staging for Elaine's exhibit. Cautiously she lifted up the overhanging tablecloth and to the left, a little distance away, could see people crowding round a figure in red as she made her way slowly up the aisle, commenting on the various arrangements. The camera crew, though, had stopped following Loretta

Moss, and were making their way towards Rosemary, evidently intending to set up a different angle. There wasn't any time to lose.

She crawled forward, trying to straighten up as she reached the aisle, only to discover, with annoyance turning to panic, that she was caught on a protruding nail. Struggling to release herself, she was beginning to feel like a stuck beetle waving its legs on a cactus spike, when suddenly there was a ripping sound, and she was free. Scrambling to her feet, she found herself in front of Elaine's striking creation, and had just grabbed hold of it when the celebrity entourage moved on towards her. Clutching the glass vase, Rosemary ducked down under the staging, and crouched there enveloped in the Settlewort's pervasively peachy scent, her heart beating fast as feet came into view. Childhood memories of a game of hide and seek, when she'd taken refuge on the bathroom window ledge, assailed her uncomfortably. It was such bad luck that her friend's mother should have come in to use the john, only to leap up with a sudden shriek on sighting the clandestine figure. Now the ensuing guilt and embarrassment seemed to echo down the years, as Rosemary studied the footwear just a few inches away.

'What *are* you doing?'

Unwillingly she looked up, to discover that the woman in red at the centre of an eager crowd – a woman strangely familiar – had lifted the cloth, and was glowering down at her like a double-decker London bus intimidating an injudiciously parked bubble-car.

'What are you hiding under there? Come out!' she commanded.

This can't be happening, Rosemary's reeling brain told her, as, shaken and dishevelled, she slowly crawled out from under the staging, and stood upright, holding the flower arrangement. As she did so, she became aware that all eyes were riveted upon her, and it was not her face they were looking at.

'*You again!*' Loretta Moss fired at her, and confronted by the supporting battery of faces and a television camera, Rosemary registered two things in icy slow motion. First, that Loretta Moss was none other than the woman she'd sat next to on the plane coming over, and secondly that her torn blouse was no longer doing what blouses are supposed to do.

Quickly she put the flower arrangement down on the staging, and grabbed at the torn garment, as Loretta Moss swung round in anger on the television crew.

'Think you're very clever, don't you,' she accused them caustically. 'Trying to trick me into appearing in your disreputable film. Well, let me tell you, if you dare to include any footage of me in your smutty little production, I'll *sue*!'

The producer's jaw dropped, while his colleague, with admirable devotion to duty, swung the camera off Rosemary's not altogether successful attempts at modesty, and followed the indignant celebrity as she prepared to flounce away. But she found her route blocked by a bespectacled man in a brown raincoat and faded trilby hat pulled down over his eyes, who was pushing through the throng of people.

'Let me through,' he called loudly. 'This is important.'

The crowd, hopeful of more drama, closed ranks behind him, and pressed forward eagerly, as he reached Rosemary.

'Young lady, are you anything to do with this flower arrangement?' he enquired in an officious tone, indicating Elaine's creation on the staging beside her.

Rosemary gazed at him in shock. 'Good,' he said, not waiting for a reply. 'Because I'm an inspector from the Ministry of Agriculture.'

From his pocket he pulled out a Suffolk College Student Card, and waved it importantly under her nose.

'We have reason to believe that those white and blue flowers are infected with Gransectis horrendis. Ah yes, there they are,' he reported with satisfaction, scraping a few fat, grey aphids off the Settlewort petals with his finger, and showing them quickly to the crowd, like a magician waving a suspect ace at his audience. Squashing them ostentatiously, he turned back to Rosemary. 'I have to tell you this is a very serious pest,' he declared sternly. 'Probably imported on rush matting from Kilimanjaro. As a potential threat to British agriculture, and in the interests of safety, I'm afraid I must impound this whole flower arrangement.'

He swept the flowers out of the vase, holding them well away from himself to avoid the drips. And of course contamination.

'What about the other entries?' the Flower Club Chairman asked anxiously, awful visions of the whole tent being deemed infectious exercising her imagination. 'Is it likely to have spread elsewhere in the marquee?'

The Ministry official paused and looked back. 'No, you're quite safe there,' he assured her blithely. 'Little buggers only thrive on this particular flower. Attracted by the smell, you see.' And he made his way towards the entrance, the crowd parting for him in some alarm.

Studiedly ignoring Rosemary, Daphne Stalker and the Flower Club Chairman closed protectively round Loretta Moss, and ushered her away, attempting to restore the atmosphere of obsequious welcome, like a hostess valiantly distracting attention from flat champagne. The hangers on followed, casting furtive glances back at Rosemary, who found herself alone with the film crew.

'Did you get all that?' a jubilant Jeremy asked his camera and sound colleagues. 'There is a God after all! That'll spice the whole thing up no end. What's your name, love?' he asked Rosemary.

'You must be kidding,' she told him, glad to discover her voice still worked. 'But you'll find out when *my* lawyers issue an injunction. You can forget about using any of that.' She tried to think of some easy explanation for what they'd just witnessed, but her thinking process had curdled. 'Why don't you go and film the local group that's just about to start playing,' she suggested instead. 'People are saying they're the new Beatles.'

'Now that'd be a great link,' he commented delightedly, and they moved off, the cameraman looking back with what he hoped was an inviting smile. A teenage girl stood aside for them in the aisle, and then rather hesitantly approached Rosemary, who managed to recognise her as Mrs Chitting's granddaughter, Tracy, last seen serving in the pub in markedly less demure attire.

'You're Matt's cousin, aren't you?'

'I try not to think about it.'

His admirer's smile didn't falter. 'He asked me to give you this.' She held out a scarlet and yellow striped poncho, with miniature Mexican hats bobbing on black tassels all round the edge. 'He bought it off the Brownies' stall for you. At least he said you'd pay for it – and the hat and raincoat he took earlier. And a pair of glasses.'

'Oh he did, did he. Suppose I might as well clear his debts before I murder him.'

Rosemary was regarding the distinctive garment with a mixture of disbelief and thankfulness, at the same time realising that she couldn't spare any hands from their necessary function of maintaining decency.

'Could you help me on with it, do you think?'

Tracy kindly obliged. 'He gets up to things, doesn't he,' she giggled fondly. 'He's taking me to the Bonfire Supper this evening. 'Are you going?'

'You bet. Doing a strip act.'

But Tracy only looked puzzled. 'Well, I must be getting back to Mum's stall,' she said. 'Oh, I nearly forgot. Matt's left something in a black rubbish bag behind the stall for you to collect when you come and pay. Said you'd know what it was.'

Gerry Thornway had chosen this moment to come and look round the marquee. News had filtered through at lunch time that Elaine's effort had not won any prize, which came as no surprise to her, but he felt was some kind of snub. These judges had their favourites, that's what it was. He was also put out that only a trickle of people had so far come to visit their garden, and had left Elaine in charge while he came down to the village to look round the flower tent, and assess visitor numbers.

Rosemary saw him coming with a sinking heart, for the first time welcoming Matthew's odd choice of attire. Surely Gerry wouldn't recognise her amidst the gaudy stripes?

But she'd already been pointed out to him as the girl who had tried to save his wife's entry from confiscation by the Ministry of Agriculture, and he caught up with her as she tried to slip away.

'What's all this about Elaine's arrangement being taken away?' he demanded. 'What's the matter with it?'

'Oh well, seems there was a little beetle that was bad news on some of the flowers.' Damn, why hadn't she managed to escape when she saw him coming.

'I told Elaine she should have gone to a better florist,' he complained, then a thought struck him. 'Wait a minute. Half the stuff came from your aunt's garden.' He looked at her accusingly.

Well actually, the insects were on the white flowers with the purple stripe. The, er, Inspector said they were attracted by the smell.' Rosemary was choosing her words carefully. Both these statements were perfectly true.

'That awful thing that stank the conservatory out? he exploded, and people looked round. 'Right, that's it! I'm going straight home to chuck the damn plant on the bonfire.'

'Oh don't do that. It's so pretty.' Rosemary realised the opportunity was too good to miss. 'My aunt'll have it if you don't want it,' she suggested lightly. 'She rather likes the one in her garden.'

'Well she's welcome to it,' retorted Gerry grabbing the cut glass container, now standing empty and forlorn between its neighbours, and he turned to go.

'Please tell Elaine that I thought her arrangement was wonderful. The best thing in the show', Rosemary called after him, with sincerity. 'I'm real sorry the public aren't going to see it.'

So, mission accomplished after all, she thought to herself with satisfaction, following him at a judicious distance towards the entrance. Things might not have gone to plan, but if the end result was achieved did it really matter? She glanced down at the unlikely attire, and her sense of humour began to reassert itself. What must she look like? Just wait till Susie saw this garish poncho! And Zinnia would be highly amused to hear about the encounter with Loretta Moss. What's more, with all that out of the way, she was now free to enjoy the whole afternoon.

Like a bungee jumper reacting to the outpouring of adrenalin immediately the ordeal was over, her spirits were lifting by the minute as she made her way through the crowds of people. She carefully chose the aisle furthest away from the celebrity party, and emerged from the marquee just as the Heebie Jeebies began to play 'The Sun Has Got His

Hat On'. It seemed a ridiculously old-fashioned number for five young guys to be playing, but at the same time their youthful zest and enjoyment matched the spirit of the song exactly, and Rosemary joined the crowd that soon gathered.

The film crew had adopted her suggestion, she noticed, and they appeared to be specially taken with Matthew. He connected so well with the audience as he played the guitar, his blue eyes sparkling, face alight. It didn't take him long to spot the poncho, and the delighted grin he sent his cousin was like a flash of electricity between them. Rosemary watched him, any hard feelings displaced by pride, and deep affection. Then, remembering that this charming minstrel had left her with debts to pay, she wandered over to the Brownies' stall. Declining offers of help from various small girls in brown uniform, she waited patiently till Tracy should be free, and able to tell her what was owed for the various items of clothing.

'Well, look who I've found!' There was a voice at her shoulder, and she turned to see a tall figure in blue shirt and chinos.

'Simon! What are you doing here?'

'Oh just thought I'd sample the pleasures of the country, and see how the Solanum regale was coming along. And hoping to see you of course', he told her. 'I've got some news.'

'Would you mind keeping Matthew's trash bag behind the stall for a while longer?' Rosemary asked Tracy quietly, as she paid the £4.50 owed. 'I'll collect it later.'

Then she turned to Simon with a glad smile. 'I was just going to make a tour of the open gardens in the village. Do you have time to come round with me? Oh, by the way,' a shadow of anxiety crossed her face, 'you weren't in the Flower Tent a little while ago, were you?'

'No, I was going to give that a miss. Flower arranging isn't exactly my thing. Why?'

'Oh, nothing, just checking. Now, where shall we start? Let's have a look at the map on your programme.'

Lady Julia's garden was the nearest, so they went there first. Rosemary happily paid out for a programme which gave entry to all the gardens and the Flower Show, even though she didn't need to. As the person largely responsible for selling its advertising space, and a family member of one garden owner as well, she should have been exempt.

Julia was already beginning to experience visitor fatigue, and greeted Rosemary with relief, tinged with surprised amusement at her unexpected attire.

'Matthew gave this to me,' she explained, pirouetting merrily, before remembering that it mustn't fly up too high. She saw Julia's expression and laughed. 'It's a long story.'

'Who's Matthew?' Simon enquired, as they walked along to Spring Cottage afterwards.

'My cousin, sort of. Now, I want to know what you think of this next cottage. Isn't it just something!'

Without interest he surveyed the delightfully crooked roof and huge chimney of Spring Cottage, taking in its friendly expression, lichen-smudged tiles and air of ancient wisdom.

'Mm. Okay I suppose. What's special about it?'

Rosemary had been going to enthuse about the place, telling him how thrilling it was to be buying such a lovely old cottage. But she recoiled from his indifference, like a touched snail.

'Oh, I just like the look of it,' she said defensively. 'Come and see the garden. It's the pride and joy of a great old character.'

Harry Trench was receiving many compliments for the colourful display. Fuchsia enthusiasts had gathered round him, anxious to jot down the names of some of his most striking ones, only to be disappointed when he told them, 'Oh, that's jus' one as I were given twenty year ago. Never did know the name on it.'

He was clearly enjoying himself, and gave no sign of recognising Rosemary amongst the people strolling round the garden.

She and Simon dropped in on The Walled Herb Garden, partly out of politeness, but also to see how Susie was faring. If she had problems though, they were clearly brought about by success. With the second official car park located in the parkland behind, there was never going to be a lack of visitors, although she'd reckoned they wouldn't necessarily be in buying mood, either in the shop or the plant sales area. But there were queues of people waiting at both tills, the tea tables were already filling up, and the herb garden itself was coming in for much admiring comment.

'So much for Susie's complaints about not getting the official endorsement for teas,' Rosemary remarked. 'And imagine how she'd cope if they'd had a plant of Settlewort to display.'

'Was that likely?' Simon sounded surprised.

'Not at the moment of course, but she certainly wants to be top of the list when Zinnia gives out seeds and cuttings.'

'I'm looking forward to seeing it in flower,' he said, his voice indicating enthusiasm for the first time.

'Do you mind if we call in on one more garden first?' asked Rosemary. 'I wanted to check out this one, here.' She pointed out The Old Forge on the map. 'It's on the way anyhow. Belongs to the chief organiser of this event, and her bearded weirdo husband. At least he's crazy about weird plants, according to Zinnia.'

'Weird plants?'

'Yeah. Man eating things, or something.'

The crowds of people strolling beneath the bright bunting strung across Haydon's main street, gave a delightfully festive air. The villagers, urged on by Daphne Stalker, had obviously taken special trouble, and gardens fronting the road were gay with tubs, bedding plants and hanging baskets. Rosemary felt proud to be part of the community, and the whole event.

Walking along beside Simon, she also became aware that his presence was awakening in her an odd feeling, and she searched for what it was. The answer came when he put out a protective arm, as a car she hadn't seen nosed its way up the street behind them. It was nice to have a man beside her, that's what it was, she realised somewhat awkwardly. To be part of a couple, however tenuous, felt good. She pushed away this discovery, for later dissection, and asked about his forthcoming trip to India.

'Well we've got a date now, all the permissions and things are going through and it's looking fine, except that the girl who was going to do the cataloguing of the information and specimens, is laid up in hospital, so she's cried off.' He looked at Rosemary and said slowly. 'I was wondering if you would like to come along instead?'

'Me!' She stopped in surprise. 'You're kidding. I don't know a palm tree from a pawpaw.'

'Really? And what about all those witches' herbs you were so interested in?' he asked blandly.

It was confession time, there was no help for it.

'Simon, when a woman next to us in the Herb Garden asked what that thyme was, I looked at my watch!' she admitted candidly. 'Sorry to disappoint you, but I don't know the first thing about herbs, as used by witches or anyone else. Only what I picked up by researching Settlewort.'

'I know.'

'Then why did you ask me about the Indian trip?'

'Well we don't necessarily want another person with botanical knowledge,' he assured her. 'We need someone who knows how to catalogue information efficiently. And you're a librarian.'

She had rather forgotten that she was.

'Besides,' he added, 'I thought you might like to come along. You'll see parts of India the tourists never get to. Although you'll probably have to pay your way. Would that be a problem?'

'Er, no.' Rosemary was still bemused by the suggestion.

'Well? What about it?'

'Jeez, I don't know. I'll have to think it over.'

They'd reached The Old Forge, and joined what promised to be a slow-moving queue to a large greenhouse. But after a couple of minutes with no progress, Rosemary discerned the reason. Through the green-slimed glass, a figure in a cerise outfit could be seen in earnest conversation with

Prentice Stalker, and like shop assistants avidly discussing last night's soap, both appeared quite oblivious to the customers they were inconveniencing.

'I think it's too long to wait,' Rosemary concluded hastily, 'we'll go on up to Kiln House. Zinnia will be pleased to see you.'

Zinnia's prejudices had been both shaken and reinforced alternately since lunch time. It had been delightful to encounter several, clearly knowledgeable, 'proper' gardeners, and she was gratified by the obvious pleasure they took in her garden. She'd noted down names and addresses, so that seeds or cuttings of various admired plants could be sent in the autumn, and been promised desirable things in return. Several gardening acquaintances had also made an appearance, and for one with misanthropic tendencies she had enjoyed a very sociable afternoon.

Even though the garden was now inaccessible by car, however, a surprising number of hackle-raisers had also made it up to Kiln House. Some of them had evidently been attracted by the description of Gerry Thornway's heather and conifer garden next door, and thought they might as well get their money's worth by having a look round both properties. These people could be overheard complaining about the size of the goldfish in comparison with his koi carp, the lack of hard landscaping and statuary, and the narrowness of the paths.

'Funny place to make a garden,' one woman remarked disparagingly, and added, looking up at the steep quarry sides, 'I'd get rid of those tree seedlings, for a start'. Zinnia was tempted to enquire how, exactly. Others, more irritating in their way, felt impelled to show off what they evidently felt was expertise, succeeding only in revealing the opposite.

The Settlewort had been roped off, so that visitors couldn't get nearer than several yards away, but even so she was plied with questions about the lovely plant with the fruity smell, as she hovered protectively near it, with one of Julia's designated helpers as back up the other side.

The striped poncho could be seen coming down the ramp some time before Zinnia recognised her niece enfolded in it.

'Don't ask,' Rosemary held up her hand with a laugh. 'I'll tell you later. Look who's here,' she indicated Simon, then smiled teasingly at Zinnia. 'Will you tell him visitors are not allowed to examine the Settlewort closely, or shall I?'

'Oh, I was hoping to...' he began earnestly.

'Simon!' she reproached him. 'That was a joke.'

He was thrilled to see it in full flower. 'Isn't it just wonderful! I can't get over it,' he exclaimed, with an enthusiasm which somehow had a familiar ring to Rosemary. Bill used the same tone of voice when he spotted some rare avian specimen through his binoculars, she was taken aback to realise.

'I've got some news for you,' he told Zinnia, as he stood reverently in front of the horticultural wonder. 'They reckon this is so important, Kew have persuaded the Government to nominate the whole pit as a World Heritage Site.'

'Good heavens! I thought only places like Venice and the Taj Mahal qualified for that sort of thing.'

'Well no, apparently Unesco rather favours industrial heritage and natural landscapes now,' said Simon seriously. 'Anything that's unique. And you can't get more special than a place which has the only example in the world of a very important plant, can you?'

For some reason Rosemary was looking ill at ease, but Zinnia rather liked the concept.

'That really will put paid to the idea of tipping then,' she remarked, with satisfaction.

Simon stroked the plant's leaves reverently. 'There is a slight drawback from your point of view,' he said hesitantly. 'If it becomes a World Heritage Site you, um… you won't be able to use it as a garden any more.'

'What!' Zinnia was aghast. 'You can't mean it. Why ever not?'

'Well the idea is to let the plant regenerate in its preferred natural conditions. They'd keep the quarry from getting overgrown, but continuing to use it as a garden would be out of the question. It'll be an inconvenience to you of course,' Simon commiserated, 'but that's just the price of being its custodian. I'm sure you'll put the interests of Solanum regale first. You know how important it is.'

'How easy would it be to get the nomination withdrawn? And what if the owner won't agree?' asked Rosemary, looking at the dismay on her aunt's face.

'I think the owner's been informed,' Simon said vaguely, 'but he can't veto it anyway. And they've already made the application, so there's no possibility of going back on it.'

He seemed to become aware of Zinnia's distinct lack of enthusiasm for the first time.

'On a purely monetary basis, you should be very pleased,' he told her encouragingly. 'Your house'll shoot up in value. Make an ideal Field Studies Centre or something. Or, as the owner of the only access to a World Heritage Site, you could really clean up'.

'How do you mean?' She was finding it hard to take all this in.

'It'll attract a lot of visitors. Really put Haydon Settleworth on the map. And you could do Bed and Breakfasts, cream teas, sell guide books to the area, give talks about the Pit. All sorts of things.'

Rosemary was torn between sympathy, and private enjoyment at the unlikely vision of this jolly landlady, who bore no resemblance to any relation of hers, when she caught sight of a figure in red walking briskly along the path by the pond towards them.

'Oh heck, that's Loretta Moss!' she alerted Zinnia. 'Don't let her see the Settlewort flowers. Tell you why later.' And she shrank behind Simon, who looked disconcerted as his audience melted away like sherbet lemon.

'Mrs Moss?' Zinnia launched forward gamely. 'I'm Zinnia Peasmore. It's wonderful to meet you at last. I've heard such a lot about you from Basil,' and she guided the visitor off towards the summer house.

'Well, I might as well get on my way,' Simon said, with slight huffiness.

'Oh, won't you stay for the Bonfire Supper this evening?' suggested Rosemary. 'Susie and Clive are hosting it, and I'm sure there'll be some tickets left. We could put you up here afterwards.'

'No, it's my mother's birthday tomorrow. I only called in on the way to visit her in Norfolk,' he informed her stiffly. 'You'll let me know what you decide about coming to India won't you? I need to hear in the next week or so.'

Rosemary watched his tall figure walk across the garden and up the ramp, and was aware of feeling a little bereft.

Chapter Twenty Three

Apart from a few spots of rain towards the end of the afternoon, the scattered showers appeared to have been warned off Haydon Settleworth, and by early evening the low cloud cleared to the east, leaving only fluffy vapour trails, like past thoughts, lingering in the pale sky. As Zinnia and Rosemary walked down from Kiln House the low sun caught the side of the church tower, and highlighted angles of the tiled cottage roofs, giving them a warm glow, as if they were clustered round some cosy fire.

Rosemary felt a real pleasure at being part of the scene, as the two of them were acknowledged by various people heading the same way. To belong to a community, she reflected, must be a basic human need. The breeze had died away with the rain clouds, and the air was pleasantly warm and still as a good proportion of the village's inhabitants gathered in the field beside the Walled Herb Garden, where a large bonfire had been ceremoniously lit by Lady Susan Trugglestone. An excited babble of voices and laughter could be heard as they approached, and Rosemary was reminded of the aftermath of exams, with everyone bursting to relate their experiences of the day.

Susie seemed in no need of alcohol to aid her spirits, which were clearly as high as the day's takings.

'Who'd have thought it would go so well!' she exulted, as they stood watching the flames take hold. 'We couldn't have asked for better weather really. Not too hot. And you must have done a fantastic job on the publicity, Rosemary. Do you know we had people from as far away as Norwich!'

'I think that might be down to Nigella,' responded Rosemary modestly, 'or at least Toby Picket. She made the poor man distribute flyers on his train to London.'

They glanced round at the microphone maestro, now pulling his weight on the barbecue team, turning out hamburgers and sausages, while his wife held court some distance away, and exchanged an understanding smile. 'I shouldn't let Nigella rope you in on her latest project,' advised Susie.

'Oh, what's that then?' Zinnia enquired, catching the end of the conversation as she joined them.

'She's all fired up with some suggestion one of the visitors made this afternoon,' Susie reported. 'Actually you might like to take part. She wants to start up a Gardening Club at the school, to get the children interested.'

'I thoroughly approve of that, it's an excellent idea,' commented Zinnia, 'but not the getting involved bit. They'd be welcome to come and visit my garden, but that's about it.' Her face fell as she suddenly remembered the day's news about the fate of the Pit Garden, and she began to tell Susie about it, knowing hers would be a sympathetic ear.

Rosemary saw Veronica carrying a tray of plates piled high with what looked like cocktail eats, and sprang forward to clear a space for it on the nearest trestle table.

'Did you make those? Don't they look great!' she exclaimed, pleased that truth and expedience coincided. Veronica always responded well to praise. Like the choke on an old-fashioned car, it got any conversation with her off to a good start. But in fact lately there seemed to have been an appreciable loosening up, which was to be welcomed. Even Zinnia had noticed it.

'Matthew was telling me the other day you were looking at one of those 'seedbed' units on the Stockleigh Industrial Estate,' Rosemary continued, a savoury pastry melting in her mouth. 'Are you really going to set up in business? How exciting.'

'Well, at this stage we're just looking at all the costs and possible outlets,' Veronica said with self-conscious pride. She'd rather taken to the role of budding entrepreneur. It gave immediate status, without burden. 'It's not the sort of thing to go into without very careful planning. But now that the Gardens Day is out of the way I'll be able to spend more time on it. I'm going up to London next week to see what sort of jams places like Harrods and Fortnums stock.'

'That's a good idea. Shall I help pass those eats round?' suggested Rosemary, adroitly sliding out of what might have ended as a prolonged dissertation on the establishment of Veronica's herbal jam business.

'I'll have one of those. I'm starving!' Matthew had materialised, and helped himself to three at once. Tousled curls indicated that his idea of party preparation didn't stretch to a hair brushing, nor a change in attire. 'Don't Let It Bug You!' was emblazoned across the front of his tee shirt, with a fierce-looking Millennium Bug, and on the back it announced "Bug Busting", with his telephone number. 'I like the outfit,' he grinned at her, nodding at the poncho, 'suits you. You saw the film crew this afternoon, didn't you?'

She was about to remark how it was more a case of the film crew having seen her, but he rushed on enthusiastically, 'They really liked the HJ's. Producer guy said he might be in touch.'

Rosemary opened her mouth to tell him sardonically, 'They all say that', but a half-formed thought gave her pause. 'Looks like Tracy's searching for you,' she said instead, nodding towards a figure by the barbecue. 'I don't suppose it would occur to you to take her something to eat, instead of stuffing yourself?'

But before he could reply, two girls launched themselves at him from behind, with loud squeals. 'Matt! There you are! You said you'd meet us at the entrance with tickets. We had to buy our own!'

As they bore him away, one on each arm, he glanced back at his cousin with an eloquently helpless shrug, eyes dancing. She watched him go, shaking her head, irresistibly reminded of a naughty puppy. And puppies were so damned cute.

Lady Julia was sitting at one of the nearby tables, flanked by her granddaughters, anxious to fill her in on their day.

'We'd practised that dance at school ever so many times,' Anthea was telling her, 'and Miss Timmins was very pleased. We knew them all really well.'

'Trouble was,' her sister put in, 'there was this molehill...'

'Yes, and, and...' Anthea wanted to get the story in first, 'and Pip Wilson tripped over it, and then...'

'We all fell over him!' finished Hazel, and they both laughed merrily.

Rosemary liked Susie's girls, and smiled at their infectious good humour, proffering the plate to the three of them.

'I missed the Fancy Dress Parade,' she said, 'who won?'

'Oh there were lots of prizes,' Hazel told her, '"cept we didn't win anything. Peter Prager got one for being a mobile phone. I thought that was silly.'

And one of the Playgroup Children went as a black beetle with red spots, and she got a prize. What is a badylird?' asked Anthea, puzzled.

'Why don't you sit down Rosemary,' Julia suggested. 'I'm sure the girls will take that plate round for you.'

Her granddaughters accepted the role with enthusiasm, and Julia fondly watched them depart. 'They're staying with me tonight, and I don't know how I'm going to get them to sleep. Now tell me, did Zinnia do well for visitors? I expect she was overwhelmed wasn't she?'

'Well she'll want to tell you herself. She's here somewhere.' Rosemary swept the crowd unsuccessfully. 'Oh, but I'd better explain about the Tent Incident, or you'll get such a garbled version you'll never let your granddaughters speak to me again!'

She launched into an account of the rescue attempt in the marquee, embroidering the more ridiculous aspects, and was rewarded by making her listener laugh. 'And that's why I ended up wearing this crazy outfit,' she finished, standing up and giving the striped poncho a twirl, revealing a practical, and all-covering, sweater underneath. 'Thought I'd wear it this evening. I'm quite fond of it now,' she declared, none too seriously. 'It'll feel right at home in Mrs Chitting's garden.'

'That reminds me,' Julia remarked, 'have you heard the news about Harry Trench? He's decided to move in with Daisy Chitting when she goes into her bungalow. At least, they've decided between them.'

Someone brought round a tray of small sausages on cocktail sticks. Julia shook her head, but Rosemary took one eagerly.

'Hey that's great,' she exclaimed, discovering too late that her mouthful was burningly hot. 'True love wins through!'

'What's love got to do with it?' Julia was amused. 'You're the reason why.'

'Me?'

Well you see, at the moment Mrs Chitting gets help from Social Security. But you're going to pay her all that money for Spring Cottage, and the bungalow she's buying is cheaper. So she won't qualify any longer. Too much capital.' Julia put out a hand to steady her empty glass as someone knocked against the table. 'But if Harry Trench moves in as her paying lodger, that tops up her income nicely. And he'll get Social Security payments instead. To help him pay the rent.'

She smiled faintly at Rosemary's expression. 'Doesn't do to be a romantic, you know. Country people will soon put you right.'

'On a purely practical note then,' Rosemary suggested good humouredly, 'can I get you another drink? I've never had cider like this before, but it's rather good, isn't it.'

'Thank you, but no, I'm going home.' Julia looked round for her stick, and stood up wearily. 'Could you please tell Susan or Clive not to be late bringing the girls along. They may not be tired, but I am exhausted.'

Rosemary saw her disappear into the throng, wondering if offering to walk home with her would be ridiculous. She had the wilted look of a flower too long out of water, and sounded apathetic and strained.

Her own glass was in need of replenishment, and she made her way towards the bar, set up outside the Herb Shop and Tea Room, but spotted Daphne Stalker heading in the same direction, and had a change of mind. Better deliver the message first, she thought hastily. Perhaps Susie was still talking to Zinnia.

House martins weaved acrobatically above, scooping insects out of the evening air and calling gleefully, as Rosemary perused the chatting groups. It didn't take her long to locate her aunt, but she found that Derek had replaced Susie.

'Well, and how's our little matador!' he greeted her genially. 'I've been hearing about your bravura performance this afternoon. Wish I'd seen it.'

She made a face at him.

Zinnia had obviously been in full flow, and continued with only a token break. 'So I was wondering if it can be true that the owner has no say in this Heritage Site thing,' she said. 'Surely he has some rights. Is there any possibility you could talk to Swathe, Derek?'

'I'd rather keep out of it,' he told her. 'He assured me the day he agreed to buy the company that I wouldn't be subject to a conflict of interests, and I don't want to start mixing family affairs with work now.'

He finished his beer, and was putting out his hand for Rosemary's empty glass, when his mother said slowly, 'What do you mean, he assured you?'

'Well, he said he'd decided not to tip in the Pit. I told you. You said you already knew.'

There was a shower of sparks as a big branch shifted on the bonfire, and smoke was suddenly deflected towards them.

'I knew he wasn't going to be *allowed* to,' Zinnia waved away the smoke, staring at him. 'But at that stage he couldn't have known...' Her voice tailed off. 'Are you telling me that Mike Swathe had already changed his mind about the tipping before he even received the injunction?'

'Looks like it. You know Mum, the man's not this great ogre you've built up in your mind,' Derek pointed out. 'He wants his own way, yes, and clearly doesn't suffer fools, but he listens, and he's fair-minded. I like him. It's only been two weeks, but what he and his son have got planned for Thornways is really going to make a difference.'

He glanced at Rosemary, understanding and amusement dawning. 'That does explain one thing though.'

'What?'

'Well, I didn't see why a second plant of Settlewort was so important that you had to lure young Rosemary into baring her all in public this afternoon, just to get it back.'

'Couldn't stop her,' Zinnia declared dryly. 'These Americans can be a touch too liberal for our country ways.'

'Is that why nobody stayed behind to pay me?' Rosemary joined in with enjoyment. 'And there was me thinking it was just the meanness of you English hicks.'

She was gratified to find that quite a few people there had found her leaflet about the history of the Pit interesting, and wanted to talk to her about it. That, together with the contacts made when seeking advertising for the Programme, meant that she had no trouble mixing and feeling part of the celebration. Nevertheless, later in the evening she was happy to volunteer for escort duty, taking Hazel and Anthea along to their grandmother's.

Having seen them home, she walked unhurriedly back along the darkening street, the scent of wood smoke hanging pleasingly on the still air. An interlude of solitude was not unwelcome before rejoining the animated chat of the Bonfire Party. She waved as Derek's car passed her halfway, and reaching Spring Cottage she stopped to lean on the gate and gaze up at it reflectively. The disappearing sun had snatched back the light from the buildings now, and the cottage's great chimney and irregular roof were solid outlines against the glowing sky. It had an air of reassuring permanence, she thought, almost a friend to talk to.

'You all right?' Derek appeared beside her. 'I've just driven Mum home, but we couldn't find you. And there you were pacing the village street all on your own. What happened to whoever you were with this afternoon?'

'Oh that's Simon,' she explained. 'It's his mother's birthday, he had to go back.'

'Mm. Demanding things, mothers.'

'He's invited me to go to India with him,' she confided.

'What backpacking?'

'No, as hanger on to a scientific group looking at traditional plant remedies.'

'Sounds interesting. Are you going?' Derek joined her on the gate.

'I don't know.' She paused, and added, as if it followed, 'He doesn't like this cottage.'

'Ah, that is a black mark,' Derek said with understanding. 'I've always thought it was the nicest one in the village. Will you be coming to live in it?'

'I haven't figured that out either.' She attempted a laugh. 'I half thought Zinnia might like to, but...' she shrugged, and looked at him. 'Would that would be a good idea?'

'I think it's an excellent idea, but she'd never agree. Veronica's been harping on about her moving into the village for ages.'

The orange sunset had deepened to an ember red, and a light came on downstairs in Spring Cottage, as they admired both in companionable silence.

'My father would have loved the place,' she said wistfully. 'I wish you'd met him. You'd have had a lot in common.'

'Yes, I'm sorry too. I don't think he and Mum were particularly close when they were young, were they. Come on,' he gave her a friendly pat on the shoulder. 'I prescribe more alcohol. Back to the party.'

****

Rosemary slept late the next morning, waking with a guilty start and the memory of promising to help Susie and Clive with the clearing up. She got herself some breakfast, and while feeding Roger, who was giving the indignant impression of having been wilfully ignored, her eye rested on the primrose painting beside the dresser.

She toured the garden looking for Zinnia. Many of the roses were into their second flowering now, and the air was heavy with scent. She had rather given up asking the names of flowers, almost all of which were completely new to her. Not knowing what something was called didn't spoil her enjoyment of a garden, she reckoned, any more than being unaware of what ingredients made a special dish so delicious.

Drawing a blank near the house, she walked down the ramp into the Pit Garden. Seen from above the place gave the impression of a Persian carpet in 3-D, and the way it changed subtly with each passing week fascinated her. In the last few days spikes of white Rosebay Willow Herb had opened out in one of the big beds, their icy elegance showing up the discolouration of the chalk cliff, like an advert for more effective washing powder. In various parts of the garden heleniums in yellow and burnt orange had now taken over the colour lead from the day lilies, and penstemons were making little pools of blue and mauve. A late-flowering honeysuckle entwined itself possessively in one of the trees, its scent wafting down intoxicatingly, and by the old tennis court flat-headed achilleas were a mass of eager hoverflies. Over them all the white and mauve-flowered Settlewort reigned serenely, like a highlighted motif in the pattern.

She found Zinnia uncharacteristically relaxing with the Sunday newspaper on the summer house bench, in contrast to the hectic activity of the past few weeks.

'I've had gardening up to here,' she declared robustly, 'August is my closed season as it is – I'm just reckoning it's come a week or so early. Anway I'm damned if I'll bust a gut keeping this place up to scratch if they're just planning to let it go.'

She folded up the newspaper as Rosemary joined her on the bench. 'What are we going to do about this World Heritage Site nonsense?'

Rosemary rather liked the 'we'.

Beside them pink lilies in a pot were giving off an intoxicating perfume, and the buzzing of happy insects formed a low, background hum. It was difficult to imagine how the place must have been before her aunt started work, Rosemary thought looking about her, but what she had produced was beautiful, really special. No wonder the prospect of not being able to continue was upsetting.

'Now that Mike Swathe's changed his mind about the tipping, couldn't you just confess everything?' she suggested. 'After all, they only think the Pit's unique because Settlewort apparently germinated there. But it didn't, did it?. Why not tell them exactly what happened?'

'Hmm. It's tempting but…' Zinnia shifted uncomfortably, as if sitting on a pebble. 'Well you can just see the newspaper stories, can't you – "Gardening Writer Dupes Authorities". I'm supposed to have some standing in the horticultural world. Not a lot, I'll grant you, but I do write a gardening column, and dispense advice.'

'It would get you noticed though.'

'Oh it'd do that all right,' agreed Zinnia with exaggerated lightness. 'But has it occurred to you that not only the horticultural big-wigs, but your Simon, would end up looking complete fools?'

'Oh yes, I wasn't thinking.' Rosemary felt a twang of guilt, then added with slight irritation. 'He's not "my" Simon, you know.'

A flock of long-tailed tits were squeaking frenetically as they chased through the tree branches, like excited mice on a treasure hunt.

'I'll go and discuss it with Julia this morning,' decided Zinnia, thinking aloud. 'She's always a good sounding board, and she can talk to Mike Swathe for me.'

'Why not approach him yourself? Rosemary suggested, craning her neck in an effort to locate the vociferous little birds.

'Because somehow I don't think I'm flavour of the month with our friend Mr Swathe,' remarked Zinnia getting up. 'But I'm sure Julia won't mind approaching him for me. Things can't be that bad between them.'

'I'm going over to the Herb Garden this morning,' Rosemary told her, picking up the newspaper. 'I can run you down to the village.'

'You know something,' she remarked, as they walked back to the house. 'I've remembered what Elaine's beautiful flower arrangement reminded me of. It's been bugging me.'

'Perhaps not the most fortuitous expression, under the circumstances,' observed Zinnia.

Rosemary laughed. 'No, I guess not. But you know how much I like that painting in the kitchen? Well I realised this morning, that's what her creation reminded me of. Your picture.'

'Now that's a brilliant idea,' Zinnia said slowly,

'What is?'

'Why didn't I think of that?'

Things weren't any clearer to Rosemary.

'Well, you remember I told you the artist's wife is going blind, poor woman,' Zinnia explained. 'She arranges the flowers for him to paint, or rather, did. Last time we spoke he didn't reckon he could carry on without her, because no-one else had her flair. But you're right. Elaine has exactly the same natural style.'

'Say, that's neat. Might help to boost her confidence,' Rosemary remarked, thinking of Elaine's submissive manner. 'Do you think she'd be willing to work with him?'

'Well, we can ask her. She's bringing her Settlewort plant round this afternoon. Gerry's refusing to have it on the premises any longer.' Zinnia smiled, savouring the irony of that situation. 'It'll make me feel better too, about what happened to her arrangement yesterday,' she added. 'What did you do with it, by the way?'

'Brought it back here in a bag, and put it in the trash can,' Rosemary confessed regretfully. 'I felt real bad about it.'

'Well he only lives this side of Stowmarket, it wouldn't be far for Elaine to travel,' said Zinnia. 'And I think she'd enjoy doing arrangements for him. I'll ring him at lunchtime and see what he says.'

****

Rosemary dropped Zinnia off in the High Street, ignoring the remaining No Parking cones, most of which had anyway been removed to the pavement by the drivers now congregating in the church. Julia opened the door to her with a guarded expression, which changed to relief as she saw who the visitor was.

'Oh, I thought it was Prentice Stalker back again,' she exclaimed, 'he really is a dry old stick.'

'What's he doing visiting you on a Sunday morning?' Zinnia wanted to know, following her friend into the sitting room, as Bracken pranced around excitedly.

'Well he called in on his way to church to let me know what we managed to raise yesterday. The preliminary figures anyhow, so that I can tell all the helpers.' She sighed resignedly. 'I've got to ring and thank them all today. But I shouldn't malign him,' she repented leading the way out onto the patio. 'He's an excellent Treasurer. And he was delighted to meet Loretta Moss yesterday.'

'A closet flower arranger is he?' Zinnia stood looking down at the garden, with the river forming a peaceful boundary, its water sparkling in the sunshine. The fields on the far side of the valley were golden now. It would be harvest time any minute. The view gave her a little shot of pleasure, and she wondered if the effect wore off when you saw it every day.

'Well apparently he's offered to help with the chapter on exotics in her latest book, and in return La Moss is going to lobby the Royal Horticultural Society about getting him appointed to some committee or other – I'm sure you'd know.' Julia picked up a glass and almost empty jug of iced orange juice from the table. 'I'll just top this up.' On her way to the kitchen she called back, 'She's also suggesting he has a stand at one of the RHS shows, or something. The man's thrilled.'

Zinnia sank into a comfortable cane chair, made an appropriate fuss of the dog, and looked about her with appreciation. Summer jasmine, colonising the fence behind her, perfumed the air exotically, against which the subtleties of the mignonette in the planters managed just the odd note. Her special white pink, she was pleased to see, was flowering now, enjoying its sunny position and the good soil Basil had put in the brick bed at the end of the patio. His design skills, and the natural advantages of the site, had combined to give an impression of cosiness with refinement, like a comfortable armchair in a fashion salon.

'I want to hear all about your visitors yesterday,' said Julia, reappearing with the replenished jug and another tall glass, the sunlight through the jug turning a patch of her blue dress to green.

'Before that I'd like your advice,' Zinnia told her. And she recounted the true story, for the first time, of the regeneration of Settlewort, to which Julia for some reason showed not much surprise, and finished with the latest development, the proposal that the Pit be designated as a World Heritage Site.

'What do you think I should do?' she asked. 'Being a Site of Special Scientific interest was fine, that just protected it. But this is nonsense.'

'You really want to know?' Julia said wearily. 'There isn't much point in telling you, because you won't like it. But the fact is, Zinnia, I think you should face reality. You won't be able to keep that garden the way you want it for much longer anyway, be honest.' She sipped her orange juice. 'And the future was going to be that you would have more and more of a struggle, only to see the ivy and sycamores winning the battle. Then, when you were finally forced to admit defeat, the place would have gone back to nature. No-one would remember there was ever a garden there.'

Zinnia opened her mouth to protest, but Julia gestured at her. 'No, let me finish. If this thing goes through, it seems from what you've been saying that they won't allow any more actual gardening, but just keep it clear of encroaching vegetation. Is that right?'

'So Simon said.'

'Well that's not so bad, is it? The Pit Garden won't go on looking as wonderful as it does today. Of course not. But it'll still recognisably be a garden, the undergrowth will be kept at bay for the foreseeable future, and your name would always be associated with it. Kiln House'll probably go up nicely in value as well. So my advice is to accept the situation, sell up and buy something with a manageable garden in the village. Start a new chapter.'

'You sound like Veronica,' said Zinnia crossly. 'She's always on at me to move into the village. I'd far rather fight the whole silly proposal.'

'Well you asked for my advice,' Julia seemed slightly nettled. 'I told you you wouldn't like it.'

'Hmm.' Zinnia leant down to stroke Bracken, considering how to put the next request. 'I was wondering if you could talk to Mike Swathe about it for me,' she asked in a casual tone. 'See what he thinks can be done.'

'*No*! I couldn't.'

There was uncharacteristic vehemence in her voice, normally so soft and calm.

The nuances of people's emotions generally passed by Zinnia unheeded, like drivers of oncoming vehicles, but there was no denying Julia didn't seem herself. She gave her a searching look. All the liveliness had gone from her expression, and her face wore the bleak, closed look of a child covering up a private misery.

'What's the matter Julia?' she asked with concern. 'My niece thinks you look ill. Are you?'

The word Rosemary had actually used was 'unhappy'. Recovering from great sadness herself, she was sensitive to it in others.

'No. No I'm fine.' Julia fiddled with the gold chain round her neck, and was about as convincing as a badly fitting wig.

Zinnia raised her eyebrows sceptically, and a thought occurred. 'Why haven't you and Mike Swathe made things up, now that tipping in the Pit isn't an issue?' she enquired with caution.

Julia looked at the ground, and didn't answer for a long moment.

'Oh all right, if you must know,' she said in a rush. 'He tried to pretend that giving up on the tipping was his own idea. That he'd changed his mind because I asked him to.' She stopped, and ran her finger nervously round and round the rim of her glass. 'Quite apart from the fact that it showed him in such a bad light, my confidence has taken a knock, because I thought I was a good judge of people. I'm obviously not,' she added in a small voice.

In the ensuing silence the nasal laugh of a duck drifted up from the river, while Zinnia had a short battle with herself, loathe to clear the name of someone she still regarded as an enemy. But honesty and friendship won.

She leant forward. 'Julia, I was told something yesterday that I think you ought to know.' Her voice had the encouraging kindness of a hospital visitor. 'It seems he did decide not to use the Pit for tipping after all, a couple of days before he received notice of the injunction.

What's the matter? Doesn't that makes things better?'

Julia hardly seemed comforted, quite the reverse in fact.

'Oh no! I called him a liar.' She put her hand to her mouth. 'Said such hurtful things! I sent him away.'

'Well... surely you can just apologise, and tell him it was all a misunderstanding.' It was Zinnia's turn to dish out the unpalatable advice.

'No, it wouldn't make any difference. Not with him.' Julia sighed with beaten finality. 'The timing's always been wrong,' she added enigmatically, sinking back in her chair. 'Some things are just not meant to be.'

****

Rosemary parked her car in the field behind the Walled Herb Garden. Wisps of smoke still curled from the smouldering remains of the bonfire, and flecks of white ash covered the trampled grass, like an unseasonal snow flurry. She was surprised to discover Harry Trench fighting an uncooperative trestle table, which was refusing to fold flat, and went to help him.

'Hi Harry, I thought you'd be repairing the damage visitors must have done to your garden yesterday. There were some badly behaved kids weren't there?'

'Mornin'. He touched his cap, and she caught the table as it wobbled under his one-handed grasp.

'No. Fact is young Lady, she asked me to help this mornin', and tha's a pleasure. Mind your fingers now.'

Rosemary stood back while he succeeded in collapsing the table, and then helped him carry it over to lean against the wall. She was glad to notice he was back in his comfortable clothes – well worn jacket over a faintly striped white shirt, and corduroy trousers of an indeterminate brown. Seeing him all spruced up in a suit yesterday had seemed unnatural, and not altogether nice, like a plaited and beribboned work horse.

'It was a good thing you were able to help her clear up that spider problem in the big greenhouse,' she remarked.

'They don't teach 'em nothing at Horticulcher College, y'see,' he asserted mildly as they took one end each of the next table. 'She'll larn soon enough though,' he added with approval, 'she have a good way with plants. Asked me to help her, she has, if I can spare the time of a Friday.'

'This table's all sticky with something, I'll get a cloth,' Rosemary suggested, as they approached the third trestle.

She fetched one from the Tea Room, and he stood and watched her wipe the table in silence. Like the use of electric hedge trimmers, small talk was something he saw no necessity for.

'I heard you're going to move out of your cottage,' she remarked conversationally. 'Be able to start a whole new garden at the bungalow. Will you enjoy that?'

'I ain't ever made a garden from nothin' afore,' he confided. 'Be easier on my poor ole back though, bein' on the level, tha's for sure.' Creakily he bent down to unfasten the clip on the table. 'A conservtree for me fooshas, it have. And young Lady, she say as how she'll get pavin' stones for paths that bit cheaper for me.'

Relations between the two had clearly taken a considerable turn for the better, and Rosemary congratulated herself on having at least started them on the road to reconciliation.

When the tables were all folded and the chairs stacked, they went together to tell Susie that the task was completed. They found her tidying up the plant sales area, while it was still quiet. Her short hair was bleached by the summer sun, and when she looked up and smiled, it seemed to Rosemary that under the tan her skin had a special glow to it.

'Oh that's wonderful, thank you,' she said. 'But I don't know where Matthew is. He was supposed to be helping. And he promised to bring his father's trailer, so we can take them back to the village hall. I don't want them collapsing on some inquisitive child.'

'What about some of the little horrors yesterday?' suggested Rosemary, who had yet to be swept off her feet by maternal instinct.

'Yes, you're right,' agreed Susie laughingly, 'death by trestle table would have been far too good for them.'

Harry went in to have a cuppa with Mrs Chitting in the Tea Room kitchen, until Matthew should turn up and they could load the trailer, and Rosemary started a Hairy Bittercress hunt among the plant pots, as she now knew how to do. 'Wretched weed,' Susie cursed it. 'Damn thing sets seed as soon as it sees the light of day, and sprays them everywhere. I'm determined to offer clean plants if I can.'

'We've sold such a lot,' she exclaimed, inspecting the sales area and running her eye over the few origanums that were left. 'These have been popular. We'll have to get more in.'

'Some things have been slow though, haven't they,' observed Rosemary. 'No-one seems keen on those Woad plants.'

'No, well, it's all a learning process,' admitted Susie. 'But it's been such an encouraging start. I do hope we can keep up the momentum next year. Yesterday was fantastic. Clive and the girls have gone into Stockleigh to find a bank deposit thingy. We didn't dare have so much money on the premises.'

'Jeez, this one's about to seed,' Rosemary exclaimed, closing her hand over a sneaky bittercress that had grown unnoticed in a pot of lemon balm. 'Do you have something to put it in?

Quickly Susie fetched one of the carrier bags hanging by the till, and held it open.

'You and Matthew have been such a help,' she said gratefully, as Rosemary put in her fist, and cautiously released her grip on the seed capsules while Susie held the bag closed. 'You don't fancy staying on to help run the place I suppose? If your aunt's garden really does become a World Heritage Site we should be overrun with visitors.'

'Sure. But you'll have to wait while I go off and get several years' training,' Rosemary joshed back. 'And my fees'll be real high.'

They smiled at each other. 'Actually, I really will have to get someone in by next spring,' Susie confided, adding almost shyly, like a schoolgirl, 'I'm…well, I'm pregnant.'

'Oh congratulations!' Rosemary beamed at her, and then realised this might not be in order. 'At least, if you're pleased about it.'

'Well, I can't say it was intentional,' confessed Susie, 'but, yes…now it's happened we're very happy about it. And with the Herb Garden doing so surprisingly well, we could just about afford someone in to help. Clive thinks we should let out Harry's cottage rather than use it in the business, so that'll help pay for someone, at least part-time.'

Rosemary paused in her bittercress search, considering the implications. 'Have you told your mother-in-law?' she enquired tactfully. 'She'll be thrilled, won't she.' Then she shot Susie a naughty glance. 'I sure hope it's going to be a boy. It is your duty you know.'

Susie laughed. 'Too bad if not. Three children is quite enough, believe me. That is *it*!'

'And you don't need to tell her it was, er, a happy accident, do you?' suggested Rosemary, with wisdom. 'That is if you don't mind her assuming she's won the argument.'

'You could be right,' conceded Susie, who was coming round to the view that truth and pride might be a small sacrifice to pay for better family relations. It would make poor Clive happier. He'd been an unfortunate pig in the middle these past months, she thought guiltily. Besides, willing grandmotherly assistance was certainly going to be needed in a few months time. Perhaps she could afford to be magnanimous, particularly as Julia'd been looking so down in the mouth since that unlikely romance of hers had folded.

Matthew sauntered in a little while later, and was full of injured protestations. 'You've done all the tables and chairs,' he said in an apparently hurt tone. 'Why didn't you wait for me?'

When they'd been successfully loaded into the trailer hitched to Derek's car, Matthew drove off to the village hall, with Rosemary beside him.

'Meant to tell you,' she remarked casually, as they drew up outside. 'I overheard the film crew talking about you yesterday.'

He stopped searching in his pocket for the village hall key, 'I told you the HJ's blew 'em away, didn't I.'

'No, not the HJ's. You specifically.'

'Me?' He looked at her eagerly. 'What did they say?'

'Oh, well... I only caught a snatch,' she said vaguely. 'But it was something about you being perfect for a part. I'm not sure, but I think they were talking about a film.'

'I thought they were just gathering stuff for a programme about country life or something.'

She shrugged. 'Doesn't stop the producer being involved with other projects though, does it? He's probably freelance.'

Matthew's eyes sparkled. 'Oh ace! Wonder what kind of part it was? Hollywood here I come!'

Rosemary gave a little smile at his reaction. 'Expect you'll be hearing from them,' she remarked lightly. 'Come on, where do we have to put these tables?'

****

After leaving Julia, Zinnia walked through the village to the Herb Garden to see if there was a chance of a lift back with Rosemary. Unable to find her, she wandered round the walled garden, noting the various herbs with interest, then toured the plant sales area. Even at this stage of the season, and despite yesterday's depletions, there was still a good selection of things, she thought approvingly, and you could see they were well grown and cared for. She was critical of the explanatory boards beside each plant though, which she considered lacked background and history. Zinnia liked plants to be put into context.

A rather earnest young couple were also going round, selecting plants for their trolley, and from the overheard conversation it was clear they were specifically seeking perennials for their new herb garden.

'I think you'll find that's only an annual,' she couldn't resist remarking, pointing at a pot of Borage they had just decided on. 'Mind you, it'll seed prolifically, so you'll never be without it, and it has always featured in herb gardens. Mothers of Roman soldiers are supposed to have made their sons borage tea for courage, before they went off to war. And now science has found it really does affect the adrenal gland.'

She smiled at them, and was about to walk away but the girl exclaimed, 'Oh you know about herbs – could we ask you about this one...?'

From the till, where she was dealing with another customer, Susie noticed the couple's impromptu tutorial, and was delighted when they subsequently arrived brimming with enthusiasm, and a trolley full of plants.

'You are good for business,' she told Zinnia, as soon as they'd gone. And when Rosemary returned from a litter hunt with a bag full of rubbish dropped the day before, she found the two of them deep in plant talk.

In the car on the way back to Kiln House though, conversation was unexpectedly limited. Zinnia had much to think about, and Rosemary, with a half smile on her face, was already enjoying composing a letter.

Chapter Twenty Four

Elaine appeared bearing the Settlewort plant from her conservatory just as they were finishing their lunch. Her specimen had a rather stumpy look, all the flowers having been harvested for the competition arrangement, and its cut stalks exuded the peachy smell strongly. This certainly would have made it less than ideal as a conservatory plant, but Zinnia was looking at it through different eyes.

'That's very kind of you Elaine. Just put it down by the door would you,' she suggested with careful restraint, 'and come and join us for a cup of coffee. I've had an idea you might be interested in.'

When this had been explained, Elaine was flattered to think that her flower arranging skills might be good enough to be immortalised in paintings, and thrilled to hear that Zinnia's artist friend was keen to meet her. She stood up and studied the primrose painting.

'It's lovely, such a natural arrangement. But I couldn't do anything as good as that,' she said uncertainly.

'Well I think you have a real gift. Anyway, no harm in going to see him is there?' Zinnia encouraged her. 'I said you'd ring in the next few days. And tell him he's always welcome to flowers from Kiln House. That is if I have any garden left,' she muttered under her breath.

The afternoon was hot and still, an invitation to take a book into the garden and drift off into unrepentant sleep. Rosemary disappeared upstairs, saying she had to e-mail Bill, and Zinnia decided on a walk, a luxury she didn't normally find time for. But it would help her think, and just at the moment her mind and mixed up emotions needed some settling, like the pond after she'd been pulling up water lily roots.

An unseen skylark trilled joyously above the trees as she passed the Thornway's house, smiling at the thought of having managed to help her artist friend and Elaine simultaneously. Giving a hand to an underdog always appealed to her, even though she found Elaine's under-confident nature hard to understand. Zinnia prided herself on being strong and self-reliant. You had to stand up for yourself. No-one else was going to do it for you.

And I'm not one to give up, she said to herself proudly, stepping up on to the bank as a car came down the lane. Never have been.

The temporary defeatism that followed her bruising encounter with Mike Swathe two months ago, had conveniently faded from memory.

Further up the lane a bramble caught at her washed out cotton skirt, and she paused to free it. Not so long ago she would have worn shorts on a hot day, but for the last two summers had grudgingly swapped them for a skirt. Some concessions to advancing age and leatheriness just had to be made. But Julia's wrong about giving up on the Pit Garden, she thought with irritation, her pace slowing a bit as the hill steepened. I've got years of gardening left in me. Why shouldn't I go on enjoying the garden I made?

As she emerged from the trees the sun was hot on her head, and she wondered why she hadn't thought of wearing a sun hat, as Julia would have done. At a bend in the road, beside the field that ran along the top of the Pit, a large ash tree cast a cooling shadow, and she paused for breath, despising herself for needing to. New fencing now securely protected man and beast from the edge, she noticed, and four horses were swishing their tails peacefully as they cropped the grass. Mike Swathe must have let the grazing.

A World Heritage Site! It was such a fantastic thought. Places like Ayres Rock and the Scottish island of Iona were World Heritage Sites. Rosemary had looked it up on the Internet. But a disused chalk pit in a small Suffolk village! It just didn't seem credible. Except, she thought wryly, that it was being proposed because a very rare and important plant had spontaneously re-grown there, and nowhere else. Supposedly.

Rested, she set off again, admiring the creamy yarrow, purple knapweed and yellow ragwort that mixed with pink mallows to make a multicoloured ribbon along the verge. Not colours you would think of putting together in any other context, she reflected, but somehow they worked. She turned left off the road and climbed over a stile on to the old drover's track that skirted a field of barley. A pheasant called raucously from the copse on the other side, and her nose picked up the slightly acrid scent of warm leafmould rising subtly into the air from under the trees.

I should go out walking more, Zinnia thought to herself, enjoying the sense of relaxed freedom . Trouble was finding the time. There were always so many pressing things to do in the garden.

Her life revolved around it, she freely admitted that. And it was why the potential loss of the Pit Garden came so hard. Julia simply didn't understand what gardening meant to her. I'll fight, she assured herself. Only this time it's bureaucratic institutions I'm up against.

Things had taken such a strange turn, she mused, stopping to shake a stone out of her sandal. Who'd have thought that Julia would persuade Mike Swathe to change his mind about the tipping? Well, he was one major obstacle out of the way. Now, if it was possible to knock this World Heritage Site proposal on the head, she could carry on as before.

But for how long? The thought insinuated itself into her mind, like a sly splinter whose painless entry belied the trouble it could cause. There was no denying Julia was right in the long term, she admitted to herself realistically. Although not a welcome prospect, she wasn't fool enough to think she could stop nature encroaching for ever. And then what?

A hunting kestrel caught her eye, and she stopped to watch it, wings fluttering, as it hovered intently over the ripe barley, and Zinnia expected to see it dive down and catch a meal. Instead it gave up, and performing a graceful arc, took up a hovering watch some distance away.

Probably the mouse had retreated down its hole, she thought, walking on again. Birds were such pragmatists. They adjusted without fuss to what was, rather than what they would like. Absently admiring the sky blue of a Sheep's Bit Scabious growing by the side of the path, she extended the thought. Wasn't that what Julia was urging her to do? she asked herself. Make use of what had happened, instead of kicking against it. Was she perhaps staring an opportunity in the face, and stubbornly ignoring it? Unwillingly, like a child faced with a new and suspect food, she toyed with this possibility. Kiln House would shoot up in value, if it came with access to a World Heritage Site, no doubt about that, and the money needing to be spent on it wouldn't matter.

She remembered her pleasure at the view from Julia's patio that morning. Perhaps, it suddenly occurred to her, if she sold Kiln House advantageously, she might be able to afford one of the cottages along the river, with a terraced garden that went down to the water. Like Julia's and Rosemary's. Basil had made an excellent job of Julia's, but she could do even better. She could make a wonderful garden with walls, sunny terraces and shade areas. Maybe a little, cascading stream...

From up here Haydon was hidden by the curve of the hill, except for the top of the church tower. Now the clock striking three could be heard distantly, and she turned to gaze at the view. Hidden by alder and willow trees, the river wandered lazily across the valley it had scoured out over thousands of years. The water meadows had lost their intense freshness now, and taken on the muted green of late summer, while across the other side the first combine harvester trailed a cloud of dust, its muffled clatter as insistent as an annoying insect.

She loved this valley, and felt part of it. Julia's suggestion that her name would always be associated with what remained of the Pit Garden was an engaging thought. You couldn't wish for a better memorial really. And yes, it would be based on a lie, she reflected with an inward shrug, but the regeneration of Settlewort couldn't have happened without her.

From under her feet almost, a rabbit darted out from a stand of nettles, and swerved away down the track in panic, scut bobbing madly. It must have lain hidden, hearing her approach and judging its moment.

Maybe, she thought seriously, pausing to let her nerves recover, maybe this is my moment. Make a dash for it. Go with what's happening. It was certainly one way of looking at it. Food for thought anyhow.

The shadows had lost their form, and she became aware that the sky had hazed over, and the sun was disappearing behind a deepening cowl of cloud. She cocked a speculative eye at the sullen sky, and decided an about turn might be wise.

Heading back along the track, she tried to look at the situation from another angle. One of the factors in the equation, she mused, was not knowing what Mike Swathe had been told, and what he thought about it all. He was the Pit's owner after all. What's more, he had money, and accompanying influence. He was altogether in a better position to resist, if that's what he wanted to do. Since neither Derek nor Julia would talk to him about the situation, it seemed she would just have to tackle him herself. Remembering their last meeting, the idea beckoned like fillings at the dentist, but there was no help for it.

Zinnia didn't hate the man himself any longer. Strangely, that had evaporated when they'd finally met. But she was well aware that he had every reason to dislike her. Perhaps she could put him in a good mood by telling him that Julia and he had simply quarrelled over a misunderstanding. It didn't seem likely that Julia was going to.

Reaching the stile, she sat on it for a while, considering. According to Rosemary, Julia positively bloomed when she and Mike Swathe first got together, and Zinnia had found her friend's obvious unhappiness that morning perturbing. Julia had always been wonderfully steady, someone who could be relied on for calm and sensible advice. They'd been friends for such a long time, first as children, and then throughout the whole of their married lives. They'd seen each other through joys and storms, and knew the other's faults and circumstances so well, it was as if they were family, she reflected, picking a blackberry to see if it was ripe.

But it seemed there was a part of Julia she didn't know about, which was hurtful in itself. She pulled a face at the blackberry's sourness. What had been going on between her and Mike Swathe?

It was true that when they were young Julia had a soft spot for him, even though he was a no-hope village youth with ginger hair and annoying manner. Zinnia bit her lip, remembering how she'd out-manoeuvred him then, so that he wouldn't take her friend. And something Julia said this morning indicated things between them had developed after Zinnia's family had left Haydon. It couldn't have been serious though, because she got engaged to Richard not long after. But this must be different, Julia didn't go in for triviality. It was in her nature to feel things deeply.

She climbed down on to the road, remembering with a shock of humility that Julia had loyally tried to protect the Pit Garden, and sent Mike Swathe packing. Real friendship demanded that loyalty went both ways. If Zinnia could mend things between those two, then she shouldn't hesitate. Except...

The horses, restless at the oppressive turn in the weather, began walking over to inspect her, but Zinnia, deep in thought, hardly noticed them.

Romance in all its forms was not something that had ever impinged on her consciousness much, and certainly not now. Solitude and self-reliance were far preferable. She had plodded through a marriage, and been secretly relieved to find herself on her own. But occasionally one encountered people who meant so much to each other that it pushed the world and everyone else out of focus. Some instinct told her that if Julia and Mike Swathe became a couple, nothing would ever be the same again. She would be permanently excluded.

Perhaps I don't need to say anything, she told herself uneasily. It never does to interfere in other people's love lives. He owns the cottage next door after all. They'll have plenty of opportunity to get together again.

Like the sound of scrumpled paper relaxing, a few raindrops pattered down on the undergrowth, and left splodges of darkness on the warm road. Zinnia quickened her pace.

I'll think about it anyway, she concluded, always her get-out phrase when she didn't want to do something. But I will telephone Mike Swathe to see if it makes the situation about the Heritage Site any clearer. The worst he can do is take no notice.

She reached the house just as the drops gathered frequency, and went straight to the telephone in the hall, while her mind was made up. But he wasn't listed in the telephone book. Instead she rang Swathe's Environmental Services, forgetting it was Sunday, and found herself speaking to an answering machine.

'This is Zinnia Peasmore from Haydon Settleworth,' she announced awkwardly, 'with a message for Mr Swathe, to ask if you would please get in touch with me.' It hardly sounded persuasive, given the circumstances. She hesitated, then added, 'And you might learn something to your advantage – as they put in solicitor's letters.'

As soon as she replaced the receiver she regretted it. 'Damn, why on earth did I say that?' she asked herself, and could find no satisfactory answer.

****

Rosemary had managed to make the cold bedroom, which had first seemed so strange and unwelcoming, into somewhere she felt relaxed and at home. An old armchair, gently mouldering in the garage, had been appropriated for the space by the window, and she'd covered it with a brightly patterned throw, and bought several cushions, so that there was somewhere comfortable to sit and read if she felt the need for solitude. Books, and files of old e-mails, correspondence about Spring Cottage, and the information gleaned for the leaflet about chalk and lime were stacked in a corner, together with a strew of clothes, an untidiness Bill would have frowned on. Next to a treasured photo of her dad, a small pot of roses beside the bed scented the room delicately, and her own enlarged, framed photographs of Haydon and the river adorned the wall opposite. A music centre, and the heater which had saved her life occupied another corner. And in a secondhand furniture shop in Ipswich she had bought an office chair, and a table to use as a desk. Above it was a poster of Tower Bridge and the Thames on a misty morning, which looked attractively romantic, and not at all how she had experienced it.

Sitting at the table, she dutifully typed out a scrappy e-mail to Bill, condensing the happenings of the village's Gardens and Flower Festival down to a brief, and colourless outline, which only touched on her own doings. He would have scoffed at it all, even if she had tried to make things amusing for him. The possibility of going to India was omitted too, on the grounds that she hadn't made up her own mind about it yet. She finished with a convenient 'Must rush…' logged on and sent it off, turning with relief to a task that was much more fun.

Where was it film companies clustered? She tried to remember. Some famous area in London – she'd have to check later. She made up an address, and after some thought typed a letter from Lashings Entertainment Worldwide Division, to Mr Matthew Peasmore.

Dear Mr Peasmore, it said, We are currently seeking a talented young man to play the chief protagonist in an important forthcoming production. Your name has been brought to our attention by a freelance producer who saw you performing recently, and we would like to consider you for the part. The film's Casting Director, Desiree Flynge is to visit Norwich on Thursday this week, and I have asked her to break her journey in order to meet you. The producer suggests a pub named The Oak, in Haydon Settleworth. Should you be interested, she will be there at twelve thirty that day, carrying a copy of this letter.

Yours truly, E. Roticke

She ran a draft copy off on the printer that Matthew's computer guru friend Ollie had found for her, and was reading it through when there were footsteps on the stairs, and a rather damp-looking Zinnia knocked and came in.

'Wondered if you'd like a cup of tea?' she enquired, raising her eyebrows as her niece quickly tried to hide the sheet of paper.

'When Matthew came to the airport,' Rosemary explained sheepishly, uncovering the letter and waving it in her direction, 'he played a lousy trick on me. And I've just thought of a great way to get my own back.'

'Good for you.' Zinnia glanced at it without obvious interest, then noticing splashes on the sill, went over to close the window. Absently she gazed out through the rain which was now steady, although not heavy enough to prompt bucket drill. 'You know, this bedroom is the only room in the whole house with even a glimpse of the valley,' she remarked wistfully. 'I'm very fond of the little wood opposite, but I'd love a view.'

Rosemary noted the remark, filing it away for future use. 'I've got a question for you,' she said. 'I was thinking about it after Elaine left. What exactly are you going to do with the second Settlewort plant, now you've got it?'

'What?'

'Well, you can't very well plant it in the Pit Garden and pretend it was there all the time and you didn't notice, can you?'

She had Zinnia's full attention now. 'Good heavens, I hadn't really thought about it. No, of course not. It would unravel the whole story, and I'd be left appearing a complete fraud.'

Rosemary shot her a quizzical look.

'Well, all right, I am a complete fraud,' Zinnia acknowledged with a twinkle. 'The whole thing is. But only you and I and the family know that.'

'And Susie,' Rosemary pointed out. 'I was wondering,' she added hesitantly, 'if perhaps you couldn't give it to her. It'd sure be a big draw for the Herb Garden.'

'Hm.' Zinnia sat down on the bed. 'And how would she explain where she got it? No, that wouldn't solve things at all. I'd like to help her of course, but the horticultural world would smell a rat, not to mention the press, and she'd be in an impossible position. It'd still be traced back to me.'

The bedroom door was pushed open slowly, and Roger the Lodger poked his head round enquiringly. Observing a family gathering, he sauntered over to Zinnia, tail waving, and jumped up on the bed.

'Perhaps,' Zinnia thought aloud, fondling his ears, 'we could plant it in Spring Cottage's garden. When are you going to get possession?'

'We're due to complete a week tomorrow,' Rosemary told her, unable to keep the pleasure out of her voice. 'I'm not sure that would be a smart move though. I mean, where would I have got it? She swivelled the chair to and fro. 'As I see it, wherever that plant is, people are going to want to know where it came from. And we can't tell them.'

Roger rolled on his back in a bid for further attention, which was not forthcoming, and he began washing his under-fur to show that that had been his intention all along.

Zinnia ignored him. This was something she should have thought through. In her effort to retrieve the plant, what to do with it afterwards simply hadn't featured. She was berating herself for being so woolly-minded, when Rosemary shrugged.

'You could give it to Mike Swathe,' she suggested jokingly. 'It'd be his problem then.'

Zinnia was about to reject this derisively, but her response solidified in transmission, like the drip on an icicle. 'Do you know,' she said in slow surprise, 'there really could be something in that. He owns the land, after all. It's plausible that he might root around, find another seedling and remove it. No-one would think of associating it with me.'

'And he just bought a company selling herbal products,' Rosemary pointed out astutely. 'Say, that's neat. He could use it to help Thornways.'

'Derek said Settlewort tea would be a sensation even if the company didn't have the field to themselves,' his mother remembered with growing satisfaction. 'And Thornways would have a monopoly on it for years...'

Impulsively she turned to Roger and energetically rubbed his tummy in delight, giving him a fright. 'That's the answer,' she enthused, 'I'll give the plant to Mike Swathe.'

Dignity affronted, Roger jumped down, and went and sat by the door, with his back to them.

'How could Thornways grow it commercially?' asked Rosemary, holding out her hand with amused sympathy to the cat, who didn't deign to respond. 'After all, you had a deal of trouble getting the seeds to germinate. And they'd need to grow fields of it, wouldn't they?'

'They'll have to get it micro-propagated. I told you, remember – it's a process where they produce thousands of tiny offspring using slivers of tissue from the parent plant, under laboratory conditions. Berrimans have a unit. Basil showed me round once, it was fascinating and faintly repulsive, I thought, all these minute plants growing in gel. There's a local commercial microprop unit as it happens, near Stowmarket. I'll tell Mike Swathe about it.'

She was now completely sold on the idea. Rosemary was right, it was neat.

'As a matter of fact I've just rung and asked the man to get in touch with me,' she remarked with satisfaction, getting up off the bed. 'What's more I left a message saying he might learn something to his advantage,' she added, looking pleased.

Rosemary frowned in puzzlement. 'What was that then?'

Zinnia's smile faded a little. 'Oh, nothing,' she said. 'Just a ploy.'

****

Mike Swathe sat in Gerry's office, opening the post early on Monday morning. It hadn't been difficult to bribe the unlamented Gerry into departing immediately. He was now reportedly spending much of his time at the Golf Club, had had his house valued, and put his boat up for sale. But whether his attempt to buy in to the place was going to be successful or not, Mike Swathe neither knew nor cared. With Gerry gone, and Ian needng to work out his notice at Clumpings, his father necessarily had to step into the breach at Thornways. That suited him just fine.

It was something to throw himself into, and he was also using it as an excuse to put his architectural reclamation business on hold for the time being. He told himself it was because he had to spend all his time at Thornways until Ian could take up the reins, but the truth was that these past two weeks his relish for the business he'd planned to share with Julia had gone, as if it was a dish tainted with something bitter. Deliberately he shut it away in his mind.

The sale of his house had gone through unexpectedly quickly, the week before. Selling to a monied London lawyer had its advantages, he thought, slitting an envelope. No messing about with tardy solicitors for a start. He'd left without any regrets. Doreen liked that house, but he'd never really felt at home in the place. It hadn't helped that the neighbours were almost all from the professions, and keen golfers to a man, socialising enthusiastically in the Club bar. His lip curled in disdain at the thought.

He'd hired a removal firm to pack everything up and put it into store, abstracting just a few of his belongings to instal in the Blue Boar, Stockleigh's not particularly comfortable old coaching inn. To the despair of the local estate agents, he showed no interest in looking for somewhere else to buy for the moment, and had also refused the invitation to perch temporarily with Eddie's family. He wanted time alone.

Under these circumstances it was a relief for his energy and attention to be fully used. Having no reason to stay away, he went into Thornways early and stayed late, spending long hours trawling through the books in the silence of the empty building. To turn a business round, you first needed to know exactly what had gone wrong.

It was a principle that applied to most things. But where his personal problems were concerned, anger seemed to be getting in the way. He boiled whenever he thought back over that last altercation with Julia. Nobody speaks to me like that. Nobody! he told himself, and yet his hurt fury was tinged with puzzlement.

Unseeingly, paper knife poised over an envelope, he went over it once more, as he did so often, lying sleepless in bed. Why had she reacted in that unexpected way? What was it she wanted that he hadn't understood? But however many times he analysed it, things never became any clearer. It was as if he were faced with a picture on a television whose horizontal hold was faulty. The whole thing was distorted, and he could make no sense of it.

The sound of voices in the corridor outside brought him back. No firm was going to be pulled round by someone whose mind wasn't on the job, he told himself brusquely, got up and went to the window, watching as the staff arrived. One of the first things he'd ordered to be done was the removal of Gerry's beloved Managing Director's parking place. Mike Swathe's car arrived well before anyone else's anyway, and that sort of self-importance was not his way of gaining respect.

He had no doubts that Thornways could be built up again. Business meant to him what a garden did to Zinnia, something instinctively understood and cared about which, given hard work and talent, grew and rewarded you. Going through the books and records, his contempt for Gerry Thornway increased with each revelation of greed, lost opportunity and incompetence, resulting in the near destruction of what his father had spent a lifetime creating. Thank goodness his own sons were not like that, he thought, watching the car park fill up. Eddie and he might not have agreed about the future direction of Swathes, but at least it was in safe hands.

The young woman who had been Gerry's secretary drew up in her Japanese sports car, parking it where her former boss's prized slot had been. A lazy, silly girl, as might have been predicted, Mike Swathe wouldn't have kept her on for five minutes, but it wasn't up to him to change the personnel. He smiled, remembering her shocked reaction when he'd asked her to arrange the replacement of Gerry's swanky, black leather sofa and armchair with a low table and four modest chairs. She was also greatly offended when told that her new boss wanted to open the post himself in future. He always had at Swathes. It was one of the ways to keep a finger on the company's pulse.

He went back to the desk, and continued the task, scanning a letter from a complainant whom Prentice Stalker had evidently failed to mollify. That was someone who hadn't made a wonderful impression to date either, he thought. His future was open to question, but then you had to balance performance against the advantages of continuity. And the man might do better with a really good Sales and Marketing Manager in situ. Recruiting one was an urgent priority, along with a sharp Finance man.

Ian would have to make all the major decisions to turn this company round, when he took over, that was important. So was the fact that his son's position was not usurped in the meantime, Mike Swathe fully realised. But the workforce needed to be reassured and enthused, and he had spent plenty of time on the shop floor, talking to people, finding out exactly what went on, and building up their confidence. He did this with Derek Peasmore's full co-operation, careful not to undermine his position either, and was pleased to note that Thornway's General Manager was both liked and trusted.

He had formed the same opinion himself. The man was good at his job, steady and capable, just what Ian would need. Never get any further, mind you. He wasn't hungry enough.

He glanced at the clock. Derek was due to come for a meeting shortly, to discuss the outline Recovery Plan that he, Ian and himself were putting together. They had formed a good relationship, and Mike Swathe was prepared to have his proposals questioned vigorously, provided Derek could back up his arguments. In turn he knew he would get straight answers from his General Manager.

There was one thing, however, he held back on, causing a lightly covered chasm of silence to lie between them. Having promised Derek at the outset that he would not be subject to a clash of interests, Mike Swathe refrained from asking him about the two reports by Prentice Stalker on Settlewort, which he had found on Gerry's desk.

The first, earlier one, concluded that if Settlewort had regenerated anywhere in Haydon, then Derek's mother, Zinnia Peasmore, was likely to have something to do with it. That had proved true, in as much as it was apparently growing in the old chalk pit that she was using as a garden. His land, ironically. Not that it was doing him any good, he reflected wryly, binning a load of junk mail. The horticultural top brass had seen to that, by rushing to protect it.

The subsequent paper, the one which Gerry had sent to Clumpings, outlined, in decidedly rosy terms, the business opportunities that possession of the plant presented to Thornways. It was clear Gerry was under the impression that he already had a specimen in his possession, a fact which had turned out not only to be wrong, but derisively so.

To Mike Swathe there were several things about the whole situation which simply didn't add up.

It was just too convenient, for a start, that the moment Zinnia Peasmore found her garden under threat, she should discover a unique plant growing in it. Secondly, how was it that Gerry Thornway, who would have won Ignorant Twit of the Decade by a mile, had apparently, without Stalker or anyone else knowing, managed to get hold of a plant he was convinced was this elusive money-spinner? And thirdly, why was Derek Peasmore keeping so quiet about it? You could understand him not wanting to tell Gerry about this apparent gold mine that was growing in his mother's garden, but everything had changed now. There'd been the failed attempt at a management buyout of course, but they'd talked about that, and the man's loyalty was not in doubt now, he felt sure.

He was gathering up the pile of opened mail, still pondering the matter, when the telephone rang on his desk.

It was Eddie, back from a weekend away, wanting to congratulate him on No Nannicking's second place at Doncaster on Saturday.

'He's certainly coming on,' his owner responded with pleasure, enjoying the situation. Eddie made no secret of the fact that he thought keeping a racehorse was tantamount to pouring money into their own waste-disposal systems. Having failed to inherit his father's love of horses, he simply couldn't fathom his satisfaction at owning No Nannicking, and the thrill when he did well.

Julia would have understood completely. The thought jolted through him, painful as an electric fence.

They talked about matters at Swathes for a few minutes. It pleased his father how carefully Eddie was treading, now that he had full control. And he appreciated being kept informed and consulted. In fact relations between the two of them were much better now than they had been for ages.

'Oh, I nearly forgot,' Eddie concluded. 'There was a message for you left on the firm's answerphone over the weekend. You really will have to get your own place, so your lady friends can ring in private,' he added jocularly.

Mike Swathe's heart leapt. Julia! It had to be Julia. He kept his voice uninterested.

'Oh yes?'

'It was Zinnia Peasmore.

Dad? Are you still there? She's the woman who's been causing all the trouble over that old chalk pit at Haydon, isn't...'

'I know who Zinnia Peasmore is,' his father interrupted testily. 'What did she want?'

'Asked you to contact her. Oh yes, she said you might learn something to your advantage. Sounds promising!'

'She'll be lucky,' retorted Mike Swathe dismissively, 'I've got quite enough on my plate without tangling with that ruddy woman again.'

But as he put the phone down his eye fell on the report about Settlewort that Gerry had sent to Clumpings. He picked it up thoughtfully, flicking through the pages, before tucking it under a pile of papers, so that it shouldn't stare Derek in the face when he came in. Then he opened his diary, and finding Thursday afternoon free, he scored a line across, and wrote firmly 'No Appointments'. A few moments later Derek knocked on the door.

Chapter Twenty Five

Rosemary debated whether to take a trip up to London, just to ensure her spoof missive to Matthew bore the correct postmark, but in the end decided it wasn't worth the effort. The likelihood was that he'd see through the whole thing anyway, she reckoned, but if he should be taken in by the letter, then he'd be unlikely to give the envelope close examination. Most of the stuff Zinnia received bore postmarks that were illegible anyway. So she mailed it on Monday in Ipswich, when she went to have her hair cut.

As Wednesday wore on without him appearing, waving the letter at her with a dismissive comment, her hopes of success grew, but she didn't see him around the village. Meeting Veronica in the post office that afternoon, casually she enquired after her cousin.

'Oh the last couple of days he's been whizzing off every morning to help Ollie, his computer friend,' she told Rosemary. 'They're very excited about this game they've invented. Looks as if one of the Japanese companies is interested. But how anyone has time to sit for hours playing computer games I don't know, do you?'

She didn't wait for a reply. 'You'll probably have him ringing Kiln House asking for a lift in the morning, because I can't let him have the car tomorrow. I'm going to visit a farm that specialises in growing herbs for the wholesale market,' she explained importantly.

Nigella Picket joined the queue behind them, and Rosemary considered not bothering to wait for the stamps she'd undertaken to buy Zinnia, but was relieved to find, after a brief greeting, that it was Veronica she wanted to talk to. Evidently the idea of a Garden Club had taken firm root in Nigella's mind, and she was eager to discuss the practicalities with someone involved with the school. Rosemary listened with interest and amusement to her ideas of what the children should be taught, saving it up to tell Zinnia. The chat then turned to the success of the Flower and Gardens Festival, whereupon the postmistress and the elderly gentleman renewing his television licence and car tax disc – the cause of the queue – joined in.

'I seen the report in the East Anglian Daily Times,' he remarked. 'Shame about the children's dancing. They should never have took that photo.'

'The day raised a tidy pile, I hear,' the postmistress, a diminutive woman in outsize glasses commented. 'We've got to equal what the Millennium Commission's prepared to put up, so Mrs Stalker was saying. But she reckoned a couple of jumble sales, and the usual Bank Holiday Event in August should do it now. Oh and the Fun Run. How about you going on one of the runs Mr Nayler?' she enquired playfully, raising her voice.

'Oh much better now, thank you,' he assured her, finally locating his wallet. 'Think it must have been something I ate.'

Late the next morning Rosemary walked down to the village with enjoyment. Her lambs had long since grown big and solid looking, and been moved elsewhere. Although whether that was to another part of the farm, or somewhere less pleasant to contemplate, she didn't dwell on.

Helped by the shower on Sunday, the grass was beginning to show life again, while thistles dotted the empty field like exclamation marks.

It was bright, with a few businesslike clouds here and there to remind the sun that it wasn't all powerful. She swung along the road, stooping to collect some of the tiny, green conkers shed by the large horse chestnut tree, half way to the village. They were such works of art, she thought, admiring the little round maces before tossing them into the hedgerow. It was a shame they wouldn't develop, but evidently the tree felt it had made too many. Perhaps its estimating skills weren't too hot.

At the roadside, where the verges had been cut earlier in the year, there was still a fresh greenness, but further back the tall stalks were straw-coloured, and here and the briars of wild roses burst triumphantly out of the hedges, their bottle-shaped hips turning subtly from green to shades of red.

As the road levelled out and rounded the bend, she paused, struck as always by the pleasure of seeing Haydon village street stretched out before her. Just as attractive in its way as the trees and fields, it seemed natural somehow, with its double ribbon of old houses, and the solid, flint-decorated church hustling them together, like a teacher with a gaggle of schoolchildren.

The heavily-beamed Oak inn had, over the centuries, achieved a fond lean towards its neighbour on one side, while on the other an entrance, just wide enough for a cart or carriage driven by the uninebriated, led through to a paved area and lawn. This was the 'Family Beer Garden' which the chalked blackboard announced on the pavement outside. Plastic chairs had been put out around white metal tables, each with a furled sunshade in the centre, and on the grass two small children were squabbling over possession of a flaccid-looking ball, while the family dog, tied to a table, yelped in frustration.

Outside the Saloon Bar door, Rosemary's nose wrinkled in distaste at the stale smell of beer, and she hesitated. It was kind of awkward to go into a pub on her own. And she wasn't at all certain how she was going to play this anyway. Matthew hadn't rung about a lift for this morning, in fact there hadn't been any communication between him and Kiln House since Sunday. She looked at her watch. Twelve fifteen. Would he really turn up, expecting to meet some mythical casting director who'd make him a star? Or more likely, had he seen through the tease and be about to turn the joke round on her? Quailing, she rather wanted to forget the whole thing. But then she would never know if Matthew had taken the bait. You can't chicken out now, she told herself severely, and pushing the door open, went in.

After the bright sunshine it was cool inside, and the light was subdued, with varnished wooden tables and chairs crowding the room, a dark red carpet, and beamed walls displaying a variety of smoke-stained prints, and a large Ordnance Survey map of the area. A fire was laid in the inglenook fireplace, the room's natural focal point, awaiting the first chilly evening of late summer, and the sound of someone playing a fruit machine in the public bar beyond mixed with the quiet background chatter of conversation .

It being midweek and early lunchtime, there were only seven or eight people in the saloon. The likely owners of the Beer Garden inhabitants were ordering food, while a group of men in suits chatted at the bar. Salesmen having an unofficial get together, by the look of them. At one table a young couple were attempting to eat chicken nuggets while undressing each other with their eyes. Rosemary was thankful to discover Tracy serving behind the bar, and exchanged pleasantries while ordering a sardine salad. Then she took her plate and a ginger ale to a table in the corner, from where she could watch the door.

She didn't have long to wait. The door opened and Matthew bounded in, rather breathless, as if he'd been hurrying, yet he appeared tidier than usual, his curls newly-brushed, chinos and tee shirt suspiciously unrumpled. He looked carefully at everyone there, and seemed taken aback to spy his cousin.

'Hi Matthew,' she waved at him guilelessly. 'Come and join me.'

This seemed to throw him. 'Well no…that is…um…' he looked round for inspiration, 'I…I've just come to talk to Tracy.'

He went up to the bar, and although the conversation was inaudible, judging by Tracy's expression as he bought a Coke, he was out of favour there. After a minute or two, reluctantly he sat down at Rosemary's table.

'Shouldn't two-time girls, you know,' she chided him lightly. 'You left her high and dry at the bonfire party.'

'How was I to know those two ravers were expecting me to look after them? he protested with an air of injured innocence, keeping an eye on the door. 'They were too,' his grin was irrepressible. 'Bit of a handful really!'

Rosemary tackled her salad, watching him fidget uncomfortably. 'This is very good,' she remarked, enjoying every moment. 'I didn't know you came in here at lunchtime.'

'Well, no, I don't usually. Er, that is, you know, just thought I would.' He checked his watch. 'What time do you make it?'

'Why, are you waiting for someone?'

'No. Well, that is…um…possibly.'

'*Oh*!' understanding dawned exaggeratedly in Rosemary's voice. 'It wouldn't have been a smartly-dressed woman in a sports car, would it? She was in here earlier, and we got chatting. Now what was the name,

Dolores, or something...' her forehead wrinkled with the effort of remembering.

'Desiree?' he said eagerly.

'Oh yes. Yes that was it. Bit old for you though, isn't she?'

'She was here early?' he looked crestfallen.

'She left you a message though,' Rosemary told him comfortingly. 'Asked me to give you this.'

From her jeans pocket she withdrew a blank, sealed envelope and handed it to him.

Luckily Matthew didn't seem to think this odd, and with a beatific smile she watched as he eagerly ripped it open and unfolded the sheet of A4 paper.

On it was typed in large letters, *To Matthew Peasmore, Please note Lashings Entertainment Worldwide Division (L.E.W.D) is a subsidiary of Explicit Films Inc.*

HA!

His face was a picture, like a small child startled by a mechanical toy, and she broke into a peal of delighted laughter.

'Oh nice try,' he acknowledged, looking up with a smile, shaking his head. 'You almost had me, too.'

'*Almost*? You lying hound! We're quits now, okay?'

'Yeah, okay,' he smiled at her, and pinched a tomato wedge off her plate. 'Bit of a relief really. It would have been a problem, because Ollie's asked me to go in with him. Man it's all happening now! He and his Dad are setting up a company to market this game we've come up with, and one of the big boys is showing interest. It's ace.'

Over the shepherds pie and peas that Rosemary bought him, he told her eagerly about the unlimited prospects for this fledgling company, while she listened, pleased to see him so enthusiastic. It'd probably come to nothing, she thought, but even then Matthew would be bound to land on his feet somehow. He fizzed with life. And charm. Hell's bells, she was not immune to it herself, she was taken aback to realise, watching him with enjoyment. This cousin of hers was never going to lack for female company. Out of the corner of her eye she could see Tracy repeatedly glancing his way.

Afterwards Matthew went home to work on his computer, and Rosemary, in a really good mood, and still laughing to herself, turned down towards the river. The marquee had left a bilious footprint on one side of the playing field, and the rest of the grass looked mussy and scuffed, as if it had slept rough. She wandered down to the bridge, and leaned on the brick parapet. With the soil's summer dryness, Sunday's rain didn't seem to have filtered through to the river, and the current was so slow that every now and then a little breeze blew the surface detritus back upstream. It stirred the willows, their twisted trunks impossibly split and bent, like sinewy old men with whom age has called a truce. In the cleft of one a bramble had taken root, and it arched down, dangling in the water, the ripening blackberries out of reach of all but wildfowl, who weren't interested.

In a secluded little bay beside the bridge, two white ducks were resting, with their heads kinked back but, she noticed, one eye each was never quite closed. They looked decidedly comical. She waved at them, the eyes opened a bit wider, and she laughed, stretching her arms along the parapet and raising her face to the warmth of the sun. It was good to be alive.

I'm...over...it. The realisation seeped slowly into her brain. I've come out the other side.

Gradually, like drops of warm milk on a sugar lump, this village, her family and friends had softened and leached away her grief, and she felt positive again. Ready to live life with the eagerness Dad would have wanted.

Opening her eyes, she found that one of the ducks had given up on an afternoon siesta, and was preening its feathers fussily.

Now what? she asked it. Tell me what to do next.

But it waddled unconcernedly to the river, launched itself with a casual waggle of its tail, and disappeared underneath the bridge.

****

Zinnia regarded the flowering of the hollyhocks beside the front door with mixed feelings. It marked the beginning of the end of summer, she always felt, and already they were in full flower, the lowest blooms limp and wasted. Mostly she wasn't a stickler for deadheading – in any case the time to do it would have been a fine thing – but she considered removing the spent hollyhock flowers was worthwhile. Apart from making them look so much better, it stopped the things seeding everywhere. Besides, she passed them most days on her way to and from the garage.

As she snipped off the lowest flowers after lunch on Thursday, she pondered her situation. It was annoying that Mike Swathe hadn't made contact. Knowing what he thought about the World Heritage Site proposal would at least have helped her make up her own mind what to do. She didn't feel like ringing again. I'll leave it a bit longer and then maybe write, she decided.

Prompted by Rosemary, she'd telephoned a local builder that morning, asking him to come and give an estimate for repairing Kiln House's roof. He'd warned her he was snowed under with work, (what builder ever admitted he wasn't?) but promised to come in the next few days if possible, to look at the problem.

Gathering up the snipped flowers to take to the compost heap, she was wondering gloomily how it would help to have a figure put on a bill there wasn't a hope of affording, when an obviously hard-worked, maroon Ford pick-up backed in off the road, and stopped a few yards away. Leaning against the driver's cab, loosely tied on with rope, were what looked like fence posts.

No-one got out and, secateurs in hand, she approached the driver's open window.

'My, that was quick, I wasn't exp... Oh!' she broke off, taken aback. 'I thought you were the builder.'

This might have been taken as less than complimentary by a millionaire who was, oh dear, also Derek's new boss, and she added hurriedly, 'I mean I thought you always went around in that big green thing.'

'Did you.'

Mike Swathe stopped searching for something on the front seat, and opened the door. He was wearing faded work jeans and a check shirt, and would have passed without question on any building site. He got out, without further comment, and reached over to check the tightness of the rope fastenings on the posts.

Zinnia watched him, feeling awkward. 'I didn't think you'd come, specially when you didn't return my call.'.

The lashing evidently didn't pass muster, and he began untying a knot. 'Thought I'd drop in as I was coming this way,' he said. 'They're unblocking the fireplace at my mother's old cottage next week, so I'm going to shore up the ceiling with these, just in case.'

'Are you going to live there?' She tried to oil the social wheels. 'It's got a lovely view.'

'No. It's being done up for sale,' he told her, adding with strong emphasis as he gave a couple of pulls on the rope to tighten it. 'Going to shake the dust of *Haydon* off my *feet*. Should have done it years ago.'

Zinnia felt a stab of joy. The man was leaving! Quitting the district. He and Julia wouldn't have the chance to get together after all. It was going to be all right.

'Can I get you a cup of tea?' she enquired, as he refastened the knot, and gave the props an experimental push to ensure they couldn't move now.

'No.' He paused just long enough for it to be significant. 'Thank you.'

He locked the pick-up and looked at her for the first time. 'But I would like to see this plant that all the fuss is about.'

Zinnia turned to lead him past the house. The man was decidedly daunting. He couldn't possibly have suspected about the Settlewort jam. Could he?

The aim was to extract information from him, but so far he seemed to be wrong-footing her. As they walked along the brick path towards the Pit Garden she felt some explanation would help. It was important to keep Derek out of it too.

'First of all I want to say that my son Derek doesn't know I contacted you,' she began. 'He reckons work and family affairs should be kept apart.'

'I wouldn't argue with that,' Mike Swathe said shortly. After a few moments, in a more conciliatory tone, he added. 'I think well of your son, you know. Thornways probably would have gone under without him.'

Zinnia warmed to the man a little. He'd had no need to say that.

'He's very pleased you've taken it over,' she told him. 'He believes the company's got a great future now.' She seized the spur hurriedly. 'And it was the future I wanted to talk to you about. This proposal that the Pit becomes a World Heritage Site, what are you going to do about it?'

'What do you expect me to do?'

'Well, I rather thought you'd want to fight it.'

'Why would I do that?'

He seemed considerably better at asking questions than answering them, and she was floundering.

'I thought…you wouldn't want to lose control over it.'

'And what good is control of this place doing me now, with tipping prohibited anyway?' he enquired, as they walked down the ramp, the gentle movement of air giving way to the Pit's stillness and sense of private enclosure. 'Now, my turn to ask you some questions. This thing that's appeared, Settlewort, it'll produce seed, will it?'

'Yes, it already is.'

'I see. And what's going to happen to them?'

'Well, I think Kew are hoping it'll regenerate itself in quantity, if the soil's undisturbed and the vegetation cut back. But obviously they'll try and germinate some seeds themselves. Although,' she added, 'it seems to need to go through the body of a bird.' A smile hovered. 'They don't necessarily know that. Look, those are the berries, forming now.'

They had skirted the pond, and now stood in front of the Settlewort. Quite a profusion of the attractive white flowers with their strange blue stripe were opening, with plenty more buds forming, and the colour scheme against the grey-green two-tone leaves would have found favour with the most discerning of tastes. Where the earliest flower clusters had finished, juicy-looking green berries were developing, one or two already showing a hint of yellow. The thing was now over three feet high, and almost as wide, and Zinnia had driven several skewers into the cliff beside it, to support a cradle of twine for the plant to lean against.

'You're looking at something everyone thought was extinct,' she informed him with pride.

He examined the plant for a few moments without speaking, then turned to her.

'It was amazingly lucky,' he said lightly, 'that it should appear just when this place changed hands. Wasn't it?'

Zinnia found his penetrating gaze fixed on her, and gave him a little smile.

'Very lucky,' she said.

Mike Swathe turned back to the plant. 'Something else is... curious, shall we say. A few weeks ago Gerry Thornway thought he'd got hold of a Settlewort plant. Made a big song and dance about it to Clumpings, saying how much money it could make for Thornways.'

'Really?' Zinnia was enjoying the sparring now. 'And was he right?'

'About its money-making properties, quite possibly yes. About the plant he'd got hold of being Settlewort – no.' He held her gaze. 'Do you know anything about that, by any chance?'

The corners of her eyes were crinkling as she dodged the question. 'Dear me, what a disappointment for him.'

Knowing the end game gave her a pleasing sense of control. She was going to answer all his questions, but only in the way she saw fit. And the Settlewort would be given to him because that was the way she wanted it. The fact that circumstances made it something of a necessity was conveniently swept aside.

Reaching out thoughtfully to finger a leaf, she decided this was probably the right moment.

'There was... is, another plant of Settlewort,' she announced quietly. 'It's in a pot up by the house.' She paused, then said, dead pan, 'I'm proposing to give it to you.'

Mike Swathe's face gave nothing away.

'Are you now.' For a long moment Zinnia found herself subjected to a cool, assessing look. 'Why?'

'I think you'd better hear the whole story,' she said, 'that is if you're not in a hurry. Come and sit down.'

They made their way over to the summer house bench. He listened intently as she related the Settlewort saga, from the finding of the seeds, which must have been collected from the plant that appeared during the war, to the final irony, of Gerry ordering the destruction of the Settlewort plants in his garden, and then jettisoning the one his wife had taken into the conservatory.

'So you see,' she finished, 'it's far better for everyone if you take that plant. No-one will suspect you of any shenanigans. It's your land after all. They'll just think you rooted around and dug up another seedling without saying anything.'

'And you don't mind me getting a reputation for ignoring every conservation rule in the book?'

'Do you?' This asking questions game could work both ways.

Mike Swathe thought for several moments, reviewing the story and its implications.

'That does explain a lot of things,' he said slowly and his lips twitched. 'So Gerry had this thing all along and chucked it out. Oh yes, I like it.'

He looked at Zinnia. 'Has the phrase "hoist by your own petard" ever come to mind?' he enquired, amusement clearly taking hold.

'I've never known exactly what a petard was, but yes,' she agreed ruefully. 'If I'd just done nothing...' She broke off, not wanting to go into the reason he'd changed his mind about tipping, and quickly altered tack.

'So you're not going to protest about this World Heritage Site thing?' she asked.

'I see no reason to,' he told her, standing up. 'I suggest you cash in on the situation. Owning the access to it, you could hardly be better placed.'

She was going to say, 'Just what Julia says', but stopped in time. Now was not the moment to mention her. In fact I'll keep well away from their quarrel, she decided, as they began to walk back across the Pit Garden. Julia would get over it, she told herself with self-interested deception. As soon as Mike Swathe was no longer around.

The staccato drilling of a woodpecker echoed across the Pit as they walked up the ramp, the sound magnified in the enclosed space. They took the path round to the side of the house where, under the sitting room's bay window, in the sun, Elaine's Settlewort had been secreted. In its truncated state, it seemed like a country frump compared to its supermodel cousin in the Pit.

'Just needs a bit of TLC,' Zinnia remarked, as they stood looking at it. 'Tender Loving Care,' she explained in response to his questioning look. 'You'll need to get it micropropagated too,' she added, and told him about the local firm. 'And as soon as possible. To be honest no-one's even sure that the thing is perennial.'

Problems began to occur to the plant's designated new owner. 'How should it be looked after?' he asked uncertainly. 'I haven't a clue how to grow things.'

She shrugged. 'Nobody alive today really knows anything about Settlewort. Prentice Stalker will probably be able to look after it though, he knows about growing things in pots better than I do. And I'll always be happy to help, if I can.' She added with a laugh, 'The only thing I can't do is own the blessed thing.'

He regarded the stubby-looking plant with caution 'I'd be happier to have something in writing, to the effect that you've freely handed this over to me,' he said, giving her a sideways look. 'Being accused of theft is not amusing.'

He suspected a trick, she realised. Hardly surprising really.

She shook her head. 'Can't do that, sorry. I'm not supposed to have had it in the first place, remember.' Then she looked him in the eye. 'You'll just have to trust me – that I won't turn round and shout "Stop Thief!". And I have to trust you that you won't spill the beans and jeopardise my horticultural standing. How's that for an agreement?'

He considered, then nodded, and put out his hand with a smile.

'That has to be the strangest bargain I've ever shaken on,' he remarked, picking up the large pot. 'My word this thing pongs. What's the quickest way back to the car?'

They walked round the house to the pick-up, and he unlocked the passenger door, carefully placing the flowerpot on the floor. Zinnia stood beside one of the large urns at the side of the porch, as he went round to the back of the vehicle and looked for something to wedge the plant upright.

What kind of friend are you to Julia? the honourable part of her was demanding. You know what you've got to do. Get on with it. But the rest of her protested defiantly, I don't have to give him everything. Why should I?

Almost as a displacement activity, she began deadheading the tawny-green violas that bloomed all summer in the urn. She always planted Viola 'Irish Molly' there. Such a strangely coloured variety, jealousy personified, Julia always said.

Mike Swathe lifted out a couple of bricks from the back as she watched. A shrewd, abrasive man who'd made a lot of money, he must have everything he wanted, she thought. Why should I let him take something that matters so much? He'll never know, if I don't tell him.

'So, that was the something to my advantage, was it?' he said conversationally, taking the bricks round.

There was a pause. 'Yes.'

'Good thing I came.'

A cloud moved unexpectedly to blot out the sun, and with it went the warmth and joyful light of a summer afternoon, and Zinnia had a sudden recollection of the bleakness on Julia's face. If ever anyone deserved some happiness…

Do it. Do it now, she ordered herself.

He fetched a couple more bricks and some empty plastic sacks, and placed them firmly round the Settlewort.

Nipping the heads off the spent flowers, Zinnia still struggled. Then with reluctance she made up her mind.

'No, that wasn't it,' she said in a monotone. 'I only thought of giving you the plant afterwards.'

'Well?' he glanced up questioningly.

Zinnia looked at him, and drew a deep breath. 'How are you and Julia getting on?'

It was like poking a tiger with toothache.

'I don't think that's any of your business,' he said curtly, slamming the passenger door and walking round to the driver's side..

'Perhaps not, but I don't like to see her so unhappy.'

'*She's* unhappy!' He swung round on her. 'And whose fault is that? She's the one who practically called me a liar to my face. Nothing more to say to each other… that's what she said.'

'Well she would.'

'*What!*'

'How would you have treated someone you thought was taking you for a ride?'

He stood still, hand on the door. 'I'm not with you.'

'Somebody – not me – jumped the gun and mistakenly told her an injunction had been issued, forbidding any tipping. And then when you told her you'd changed your mind, she thought you were just stringing her a line.' Zinnia gave a little shrug. 'Julia doesn't like deceit.'

He stared at her. 'And is she still under the impression…?'

'Not now, no. I found out on Sunday that was the reason you'd quarrelled. So I told her you couldn't have known about the injunction till later.'

The sun escaped from behind the cloud, flooding the drive with warmth, as the darkness of Mike Swathe`s world suddenly lifted. He'd felt as if he was lost underground, and now she'd handed him the string that led out.

'So why hasn't she contacted me?' he asked with apparent gruffness. 'I should have thought an apology was the least I could expect.'

'Could be waiting a long time then,' retorted Zinnia. 'She thinks you aren't the kind to forgive. Not twice. That's what she said anyway. I don't know what it means, but presumably you do.'

She paused to let him think about it. 'Of course if you're going to be as obstinate as she is, you'll both have a lonely old age, and thoroughly deserve it,' she added tartly, just as Rosemary walked up the drive.

Zinnia hastened to forestall any possible mistakes about the identity of the caller. 'This is Mr Swathe,' she told Rosemary, and turned to him. 'My niece Rosemary.'

'Oh we've met,' he recalled, nodding to her across the bonnet, and a flicker of amusement crossed his face. 'When you charged me for the privilege of touring my own property.'

He opened the car door, and before getting in, looked directly at Zinnia. 'Many thanks for the Settlewort, I'll see it's well cared for. And...thank you,' he said, with emphasis.

'What was all that about?' Rosemary asked, intrigued, as the pick-up turned out of the drive, heading towards Haydon.

Zinnia sighed. 'Penance,' she said resignedly, running her hand over the velvety coolness of the violas. 'For something done a long time ago.'

****

Julia was sitting on the bench at the end of her garden, trying to compose a report on the Flower and Gardens Day for the Parish Magazine. The difficulty was to convey thanks adequately to all the people who had helped, but without including names, otherwise it would just end up as a long list. And even if she didn't forget someone, those responsible for a great deal of work would be incensed to find themselves lumped in with others who'd just done a token amount. 'Oh dear,' she said to Bracken, lying at her feet, 'whoever said village life was simple?'

It was a huge relief that the whole thing was over now, it had been a real burden. Trouble is, she thought, I'm just a sitting duck for anyone organising anything in the village. Everyone can see my life just consists of committees and local organisations. And I've had enough. I'd like to resign from the whole wretched lot. Surely to goodness they can find someone else. They would if they had to.

She was rather regretting being tempted to sit down by the river. It was lovely when the sun was out, but every so often when it went behind a cloud, a breeze sprang up and ruffled her notepad, and she had to pull the cardigan round her shoulders. If she'd stayed on the top patio, it would have been more sheltered. But probably too hot in the sunny spells. We never do get perfection, she reflected, the wonder of it is that we keep looking for it.

The river was a distraction too, but also soothing. In the middle a grasslike weed reached up from the bottom, forming mats of bright green. She found herself watching a blue damsel fly which kept returning to hover choosily, then settled on one of the verdant islands. It must have fulfilled requirements, for suddenly the insect's abdomen bent over like a hairpin, as she delicately deposited her eggs. A new cycle of life beginning, thought Julia. As it was in her own family, with Susan finally agreeing about trying for a boy to carry on the title. Curiously, she'd kept quiet about the change of mind too, until she was actually pregnant. What had been the point of secrecy? It would have improved relations between them to have known.

She'll need me to help more with the children, Julia reflected. But it's not *enough*. I must pull myself together and find something to fill my life. Perhaps I could find a charity or something to work for. That'd be a good excuse to resign from everything else too.

What's the point of telling Zinnia to start a new chapter, if I can't take my own advice? she asked herself sternly. And it's no good hankering after what might have been. The whole thing with Mike Swathe probably had Failure written on it from the start.

If she saw him she would try and apologise, she decided. But he couldn't feel the way she did, his humiliating snub in front of Mrs Chitting showed that. There was no hope that he would forgive being spoken to in like manner, either. Self-made men seemed to carry an allergy all their lives, so that even small slights raised angry red weals across their self-esteem. He still seemed to be bitter about the path she'd chosen, all those years ago.

There was a whirring sound, and a couple of swans winged their way down river, a few feet above the water. She watched them until they rose and turned away in the distance, the sun glinting on their white wings with each upbeat. The likelihood was she wouldn't see the man again anyway, she thought with a sigh.. According to one of the workman, his mother's cottage was being done up for sale in the autumn.

She pulled herself up short. This wasn't getting anything written, and the deadline for contributions was tomorrow. Just a bit of effort and she would be rid of the thing for good. Then perhaps I'll go away for a while, she thought. On her last Christmas card an old schoolfriend, now in Canada, had said how lovely it would be to meet again. She might really have meant it. Widows have to face up to doing everything on their own, she told herself. Travelling would be no exception.

The sun sparkled on the water, and in the warm shallows at the edge her eye was caught by hundreds of little shadows, darting about. She put down the notepad and looked closer. It had to be minnows casting the shadows, but it took a while for her eye to adjust and see the tiny little bodies, like a host of floating needles suddenly energised by an unseen magnet.

Becoming absorbed, she failed to observe Bracken sit up alertly, tail wagging, as the dog became aware of Mike Swathe making his way through the overgrown shrubs at the end of the next door garden. He reached the fence and stood silently, studying Julia, as she sat, fascinated by the tiny fish.

She was wearing the same blue denim skirt that she'd worn, he remembered with a pang of guilt, when they'd their first bust up a few weeks ago, and a blue and white blouse, with a fawn cardigan draped over her shoulders. He smiled. She was the quintessential upper class English lady, no-one could have mistaken her for anything else.

'I don't like to see her so unhappy,' Zinnia had said, and even from there she appeared strained and wan. As he watched, the anger and resentment softened inside him, like butter on a warm hearth. To hell with apologies. He just wanted to love her, and show the world she was his. I'll make her happy, he promised himself.

Bracken gave a little whine, and Julia looked up and suddenly saw him there.

'Oh!' she exclaimed, hand at her throat, 'you gave me a fright.'

'Again! Getting nervy in your old age,' he mocked. 'I tried knocking on the front door, and decided you were probably in the garden. Now,' he said, 'I shall attempt to get over this thing without falling in the river.'

She watched him walk down to where the wooden fence changed to wire at the water's edge. Why was it, she wondered ruefully, that she normally had no difficulty with coherent thought, but just his presence managed to reduce her to a mess of feelings?

'When I was young I used to climb out in the evenings, and through this garden to the road,' he confided, panting a little as he clambered over, hoping not to make a fool of himself half a century later. 'You could do it when the river was low.' He gave her a teasing look. 'Used to go and meet a certain girl at the old Dry Dock. She'd have been in a lot of trouble if her parents had found out.'

Julia smiled at the recollection. 'They never did though,' she said nostalgically.

He completed the obstacle course with some relief, and responded to Bracken's pleased greeting, then looked at Julia. 'Is there room on *that* seat for two?'

Her heartfelt smile of welcome as she moved to one side, told him what he needed to know. He walked across, bringing with him an interesting aroma of peaches, mixed with river mud. And as he sat down, his knee, by happy chance, ended up touching hers.

'I wanted to say...' she began, but he held up his hand.

'No, listen to me,' he said firmly. 'I've been talking to your friend Zinnia. And it seems that last time you and I met there was some misunderstanding. So I suggest we just forget about it, and wind the tape back. How about that? Start again.'

'Oh yes.' The idea of visiting a schoolfriend was unaccountably losing appeal.

'First of all, I have a business proposition to put to you.'

'Oh.' It was as if someone had opened the oven door on her rising hopes.

'No, you've got me wrong, Michael,' she said quietly, 'I haven't any capital to invest.'

'It's not your money I'm after,' he told her.

Just the way she used that name dissolved him. No-one else had ever called him Michael.

He explained about the statuary and architectural reclamation business he planned to expand, after Ian took over at Thornways. 'And I'd like you to come in with me,' he said. 'There'd be no need to get involved in the day to day stuff, but you could come with me to visit potential buyers and sellers. We'd have a great time together.' He smiled at her. 'It'd be an excuse to visit all sorts of places, and of course we'd have to sample the local restaurants. That's only right.' He'd been going to add 'and hotels', but thought the better of it.

'Sounds fun,' agreed Julia warmly, 'but I really don't see how I'd be much use to you.'

'You can talk to these stately home people on their own terms,' he suggested. 'They'll be happy to see you – you're a Lady, after all. You'll give the business a bit of status.'

'Oh *that's* why you want me,' she parried playfully, allowing herself to hope that it wasn't.

In answer he reached for her hand, and slowly traced each finger, coming to rest meaningfully on her wedding ring, then he looked up.

'Can you think of any other reason!'

He wouldn't put it into words, she realised, not with a history of rejection. But her answering smile showed that she understood.

'Yes. I'd very much like to… join you,' she informed him, somewhat ambiguously, and paused. 'But there's one condition.'

'Oh yes?' He sounded wary.

'Yes. You'll have to promise to be less touchy.'

For a moment he looked at her searchingly, then his expression relaxed.

'Touchy is it?'

He caressed her arm, with a possessive intensity that did strange things to her stomach, and gave her a long smile.

'I'll show you touchy,' he said.

Chapter Twenty Six

Four days later, the date Rosemary had been looking forward to arrived, Completion Day, the moment Spring Cottage would become hers. It was also to be the day that Mrs Chitting took possession of her bungalow in the Sleepy Hollow development, and Harry Trench finally left his tied cottage to go and lodge with her.

'It's like a game of draughts, isn't it,' Rosemary remarked happily to Zinnia as they cleared up the breakfast things, 'everybody moving on to different squares.'

'And is Spring Cottage the square you're going to end up on?' her aunt enquired, plonking a wet plate in the drying rack.

'You know I haven't decided right now,' Rosemary put the milk and butter back in the fridge. 'Just going to play it by ear.' She almost tripped over Roger the Lodger on her way back to the table, and bent down to give him an apologetic stroke. 'I need to discuss it all with Bill when he gets back...'

'But you haven't even told him yet that you're buying it! Have you?' Zinnia had given up trying to understand the workings of that relationship, and indeed Rosemary's intentions.

'Well, no. It might not have come off. And I guess he'd just think I'd gone crazy anyway.' The topic made her uncomfortable, and opening the larder door to put away the marmalade, she rehearsed the day instead. 'I'm going down there this morning to help Mrs Chitting. Although her daughter and son-in-law will be doing most of the furniture shifting. Then we ring the solicitor to check it's all gone through, and ... that's it. Susie and Clive are going to move Harry Trench's things. Don't think he'll be able to do much. His rimmitis don't half give him jip,' she mimicked in a passable Suffolk accent.

'Just wait till you get old, my girl,' Zinnia chided good-humouredly, pleased to see her in such high spirits.

Rosemary took a cloth off the Rayburn's rail, and came to dry the cutlery. 'You will come down and celebrate with me, won't you? There's a bottle of champagne to open. Might be a bit on the warm side but...'

'Yes, of course I will,' her aunt assured her. 'Got to write my Country Harvest column first. They made so many objections about the one I sent in, damn them, that it's simpler to start again. But I'll come down afterwards.'

'Another reject,' Rosemary waved a teaspoon, and handed it back. 'Covered with egg yolk, you don't have your glasses on.'

'Out!' ordered Zinnia in mock outrage. 'Tiresome child, go and buy yourself a cottage!'

Rosemary breathed in deeply as she emerged from the back door shortly afterwards. The sky was overcast, but the lack of a breeze enhanced the mingling scents from the garden, and house martins swooped, squeaking delightedly, above her head. She glanced up at the bobbly, mud nests beneath the roof eaves, and smiled to see the heads of the babies peeping out. They were almost as big as their parents now, and seemed to enjoy flying practice. Just as well. They would be winging their way to Africa before long.

As she was getting into the car, her aunt appeared from the house. 'Simon's on the phone,' she reported. 'I told him I might just catch you.'

'Too bad you didn't,' responded Rosemary easily. 'I don't want to talk to him right now.'

Zinnia gave her a questioning look. 'He says he needs an answer about the Indian trip.'

'Yeah, well I'll...' Rosemary shrugged, 'I'll think about it today and call him this evening.'

You have to make up your mind, she told herself, turning out of the drive. Trouble is, Bill isn't going to be happy about me running off to India with some guy I just met. She imagined her fiancé's disapproving expression, as he read her e-mail in explanation. *I'll just be part of a scientific group, Bill. No different to you going off to the Antarctic.*

The difference was, she allowed herself to admit, that she did quite fancy Simon, and had a feeling that was probably mutual. He and his long-time girlfriend had bust up nearly a year ago, she'd established, and the discovery enhanced his attraction. It made him a damaged soul, chary of being hurt again. The role excused his lack of animation too, and his focus on work to the exclusion of much else. She remembered his thrill at seeing the Settlewort for the first time, just like Bill when he saw a rare bird. He was rather similar to Bill, in many respects, she thought idly, and almost as...

Rosemary braked hard. Boring! She'd been going to say 'boring'. Unseeingly she drove towards the village, as inwardly the cataracts melted away. What was it she could say she liked about Bill? she asked herself incredulously. Wide-ranging interests? Character? Teasing humour? No, no and *no*! He'd been a shoulder to lean on when Dad died of course. But otherwise – heck, the man was about as interesting as yesterday's milk carton.

Was he always like that, she wondered, and why hadn't she seen it before?

The countryside had taken on the muted shades of full summer now, like an ageing matron adjusting her wardrobe. The Queen Anne's Lace had gone to seed, and a flock of goldfinches feeding on thistle heads flew off as the car passed. Such a difference from when she'd first walked down the lane, back in March. She shook her head as she concluded, Bill hasn't changed. I have.

Passing The Oak, she compared his stolid righteousness with Matthew's stimulating joi de vivre, and guiltily remembered how attractive she'd found her mercurial cousin a few days ago. Matthew would make some poor girl a rotten husband, she reflected affectionately. He'd be impractical, unnoticing, hopeless with money, and almost certainly unfaithful. But he'd make you laugh. And in between bawling him out you'd be loving him to bits. Living with Matthew would never be dull. Life with Bill would be tedium writ large.

She parked the car outside Spring Cottage, and sat there thinking, still not used to her new vision. I don't want someone like Matthew, she realised. But why would I want to marry Bill either? They're opposites. I need something in between, godammit. And Simon sure as hell isn't it.

From reckoning that she needed to choose between two men, she reflected, with rising relief, the unexpected conclusion was that she couldn't be bothered with either of them. Hallelujah. Decision made.

Heck no it wasn't. Why pass up the idea of going to India? If she wasn't in danger of falling for Simon, and didn't care what Bill thought, then she was free to go and enjoy herself. The trip promised to be very interesting, and much more fun if she was wasn't moping about in an anxious state.

A figure in an orange patterned dress, holding a carrier bag, was walking towards her, unmistakably Veronica. Rosemary was torn between giving her a friendly wave, and hoping that she wouldn't be noticed. Veronica was not the most observant of people. But she was out of luck.

'Today's the day then,' Veronica greeted her unnecessarily, and Rosemary wound down the window. 'When you take possession, can I come and have a look round? All the years we've lived here, and I've never been inside Spring Cottage.'

'Sure. But it's going to need a deal of work.' Rosemary was fairly confident that the unsophisticated state of the place would arouse pity, not jealousy, in her house-proud relation. Probably just as well.

'I wanted to ask your help,' Veronica confided, as Rosemary reached for her sweater on the back seat. 'This school Garden Club that Nigella's so anxious to have, the Headmaster's asked me to see how it could be organised.'

Such an obvious choice, Rosemary thought with mild sarcasm, given Veronica's known love of gardening.

'Like to, but I don't see how I can help,' she commented, getting out of the car. 'Zinnia's the one to speak to, surely.'

'Exactly. She'd be perfect for helping them to start a garden, and talking about plants and things. But...' Veronica hesitated. 'Well it's just that...she'd take more kindly to the suggestion coming from you.'

Rosemary looked at her in surprise. There didn't seem to be any antagonism in the tone, which was generous to someone who was just a Johnny Come Lately.

'Getting Zinnia to do anything she doesn't want is no pushover,' she agreed sympathetically, 'but you're right, she'd be good at it, and probably enjoy it too. Explain to me what you had in mind, and we'll both try and persuade her, shall we? Hard guy, soft guy,' she added humorously, but it sailed over Veronica's head.

The morning passed quickly and enjoyably. Rosemary had wondered if she would be resented, or in the way, but found herself welcomed into the Chitting family like a friend.

'I'm glad the old house is going to someone who'll love it,' Mrs Chitting's daughter Carol told her sincerely, as they packed saucepans into a large cardboard box. 'I was born here, so it has lots of memories, and I didn't like the idea of it going to the original couple who were buying. Proper townies, they were.'

'Didn't you want to move back in yourself?' asked Rosemary, immensely flattered.

'Heavens no, it's cold and draughty. I like me comforts,' Carol laughed. 'And Mum'll be much better off in a nice new bungalow.'

At ten-thirty, phone calls confirmed that all the legal and financial arrangements had successfully gone through, and Mrs Chitting was handed the key of her new home by the estate agent. Rosemary felt slightly hard done by not to have an equivalent key ceremony, but then Spring Cottage was not locked, and she was already inside it.

She helped to ferry all the boxes and plastic bags full of stuff over to Sleepy Hollow, while the large items of furniture were put on a borrowed trailer, towed by Carol's husband's car. As the cottage emptied of Mrs Chitting's busy belongings, so its atmosphere began to change. The rooms seemed larger, and developed an echoing sound. It reminded Rosemary of the empty snail shell she had found beside the drive that morning, thick and limey. Houses needed to be lived in just as much, she thought, heaving herself up on to the draining board to take down the kitchen curtains, which had somehow been forgotten. She must do right by this old cottage, it was her responsibility.

'Can I come in?' a voice called, and a few moments later Lady Julia appeared in the doorway, holding two packages in gift wrapping. She was bright-eyed, and there was life and colour in her face. Like a magazine makeover that'd actually worked, Rosemary thought with pleased surprise.

Hard to believe you were susceptible to romance at her age, but the change in her was unmistakeable.

'My goodness, you have got on well!' Julia exclaimed. 'It's so odd to see it empty. I'm on my way to ask if there's anything I could do for Mrs Chitting, and thought I'd pop in with a house-warming present.'

Rosemary climbed down off the draining board, wiping her dusty hands on her jeans, and took the proffered package. 'It's real kind of you,' she said sincerely, and opened it to reveal a framed, nineteenth century print of Haydon street, with Spring Cottage just discernible at the end.

'That's just great!' she thanked her, touched by the gift. 'My first possession in the house.' She found a convenient hook on the wall, and hung the picture. The delight was obvious, and Julia smiled at her pleasure.

'Where's Zinnia? I thought she would be helping you. Or at least casting a critical eye over the place.'

'Oh she had to finish her column. She'll be here any time soon,' Rosemary explained. 'Can I ask your advice?'

She told Julia about the proposed school Garden Club, and how Veronica and she both thought it would be a shame if Zinnia were not involved. But her aunt was unlikely to see it that way.'

'What do you think would be the best approach?' she asked. 'Appeal to her vanity, or sense of duty to the village?'

'Duty?' Julia queried, with amused asperity. 'Zinnia?'

****

With misgiving, Zinnia sat down at her desk after Rosemary had left. Relations with the Features Editor of Country Harvest were approaching mid-winter. He didn't know anything about gardening of course, that went without saying. But he couldn't seem to grasp the fact that gardening was a slow process of picking up facts, she thought impatiently. You learned as you went along. Partly it was the plants that taught you – where, how and when they wanted to grow. But gardeners also gleaned valuable information from articles, books and talks. Then, when you had been gardening for most of your life, you naturally passed on what you'd learned to new generations.

At first she'd been diffident about writing for a magazine. It seemed scarcely possible that she was senior enough to give advice to other people. But her confidence had grown as she realised, with surprise, what a lot of knowledge had accumulated over the years. The money Country Harvest paid for the column was badly needed, but she also drew satisfaction from feeling that at least she was doing her bit in passing information on to newer gardening recruits.

Now this wretched man was insisting that his readers wanted advice on how to start a garden from scratch, like some slick television programme, and Zinnia's imagination wasn't running to the task. *It just isn't me.* And how could I do it? she asked herself resentfully, gazing out of the window. *I don't know anything about tackling an ordinary plot from the beginning.* The garden surrounding Kiln House had been mature when she inherited it, as regards the layout anyway, she'd only altered the planting. And the creation of the Pit Garden was scarcely typical of usual gardens.

'Why not do it as a journal, month by month,' the Features Editor had suggested. 'That'd show our readers what they could be doing, and they'll be able to connect with you more. If you can't adjust, then I'm afraid we'll have to part company. You're too highbrow for them at the moment.'

Huh! Zinnia snorted scornfully. What did he know? Stupid man. She wound a sheet of paper into the typewriter, and began a piece about plants that inexorably died away in late spring and summer. Bearing in mind his jibe about loftiness, she wrote humorously about how she had desperately tried to keep sickly-looking camassias from apparently dying in midsummer, and had mourned the loss of a newly-acquired Bloodroot, after its exquisite flowers had finished, only to discover, sheepishly, that dying down when everything else was growing was exactly what it was meant to do.

You can't buck Nature, she wrote, *it only makes a fool of you if you try. Now I use these plants' habits by partnering them with late things like Toad Lilies, eucomis, and the fascinating Balloon Flower, Platycodon grandiflorus, which comes up just as its neighbours are dying down. Twice the value in one spot.'*

A fly was buzzing at the window, and Zinnia got up to open it. Deprived by the cloud cover of his favourite garden sunbathing spots, Roger took advantage of the situation, and jumped onto the sill, and in through the window.

'Now sit quiet,' she told him firmly, settling into her chair. 'I'm trying to get this done, so I can go down and drink warm champagne.'

But the cat had broken her train of thought, and her attention wandered. 'You can't buck Nature'. The phrase was resonating in her mind.

Am I making a fool of myself? she wondered uncomfortably. Trying to hang on to Kiln House and the Pit Garden when it's time to let go? Julia certainly thinks so.

Julia. Knocking on her door on Saturday morning, she'd found her friend hurrying to get ready before Mike Swathe arrived. They were going to have lunch out, then visit his racehorse's stables in Newmarket. She'd thanked Zinnia for helping to mend the rift, but didn't have time to chat, and it was clear her interest was elsewhere. Julia's animation and obvious happiness were heart-warming, and made Zinnia feel proud of herself. But, like the clouds of an on-coming front rolling across the sky, she could see that her instincts had been right. The exclusive, sunny days of their friendship were over.

When she and Julia were estranged over the sale of the Pit Garden, Zinnia had suffered a taste of life without a close friend in the village, and found it disconcerting. But at least then Rosemary had been around to talk to. She'll be going off soon, back to America probably, Zinnia thought with regret.

'I shall end up a sad old woman with just a cat for company,' she informed Roger, who was now sitting on the windowsill with his eyes gently closed. This scenario conveniently excised a loving son and dutiful daughter-in-law from the picture, but Zinnia despised people who were a burden to their offspring.

At the sound of her voice he opened his eyes, and the curled tail twitched. 'And you came purely because it suited you,' his new owner reminded him. 'Just upped sticks and moved. And ever since you've had a lovely life.' The idea of a cat pulling up tent pegs rather amused her, and she looked down at her article, mind refreshed. *You can't buck Nature, it only makes a fool of you if you try*, she read, and suddenly, like donning spectacles, everything seemed to come into focus.

That cottage, Zinnia thought, when Rosemary goes back, she'll need someone to live in it, after the place is done up. And she'll certainly want someone to sort out the garden. It's all planted with tender stuff at the moment. Why not me? She pursed her lips in concentration. Once this World Heritage thing is definite, I could sell Kiln House for a really good price, perch temporarily at Rosemary's place, and buy a riverside cottage myself, as soon as one comes on the market.

A second fly had appeared from somewhere, and was buzzing at the window, watched with close interest by the cat. Zinnia pulled the typewriter's spacing lever to start a new paragraph. What's more I could do what this wretched man wants, it occurred to her as she stared at the paper. Write a journal about making the garden. And, she thought with sudden cheerfulness, perhaps with public interest in Settlewort, my standing might rise enough to write a better column. In a magazine read by proper gardeners.'

Roger pounced, cleverly outwitting the fly, which he promptly ate.

'You're revolting,' Zinnia told him. 'And you'll have to decide if you want to move down to the village with me.' Unexpectedly she found herself hoping that he would.

Wryly she pictured Veronica's face on hearing that they'd be near neighbours. Well, at least I never agreed to go into one of those ghastly bungalows she's been going on about, she told herself. That's something.

I could make a small garden, packed with really special plants, she thought, with growing anticipation. It's just the right time for taking cuttings of everything now. And I'd have a lot more time. The possibilities were beginning to crowd in. Perhaps I could put in some hours at the Herb Garden, with Susie able to do less. That would help the old income as well, and make up for the generous amount Rosemary had insisted on paying into the housekeeping budget these past few months. I'll get more involved with the village, as well, she promised herself. The fact that she was now unknown or irrelevant in a community she'd considered herself part of, had come as an unpleasant discovery.

Running her eye down the unfinished article, she decided the right way to conclude would be to say that she herself was going to bow to Nature and move to a smaller garden. But she'd have to talk to Rosemary first. She glanced at the clock. Good heavens, time she was going down there anyway.

****

Walking up the path to Spring Cottage, she looked about with new eyes. Colour assailed her from every side, with Busy Lizzies, lobelia, petunias and Harry Trench's beloved fuchsias fighting to trumpet their presence. The little front lawns would be one of the first things to go in the autumn, she decided immediately. They're a nonsense. But the old rosemary by the porch fully met with her approval. Good placing, and very apt in the circumstances. Perhaps add another one the other side to give balance, she thought, knocking for form's sake on the open door, before going into the cottage.

She was surprised to find Julia chatting to Rosemary in the kitchen, one curtain half hanging off the rail. The room didn't seem quite as empty as the others, since the fifties-style, blue-painted cupboards had been left behind. The new bungalow had everything fitted. But the old kitchen was looking decidedly scruffy, patterned linoleum showing where fridge and cooker had stood, and even particular Mrs Chitting couldn't clean underneath. Where pictures had been removed there were smudges on the walls, and the stains of plant pots showed clearly on the windowsill, the tile lines between the circles making it resemble a row of binary code.

'Champagne time!' Rosemary declared happily, after greeting her. 'Heck, I forgot there wouldn't be any glasses here.'

Like a barrister triumphantly producing indisputable evidence, Zinnia brought out of a pocket in her rain jacket, a stack of four plastic beakers, with a coffee brand name on the side. 'Waste not, want not,' she remarked cheerfully, 'I always keep them when I go up on the train to London. Brought them in case.'

She laid out three on the draining board and, advised by Julia, Rosemary eased off the constraining wire. The champagne was released with a satisfactory pop and fizz, and the coffee beakers filled.

'To Spring Cottage,' Zinnia proposed, and they drank to that, looking out over the river, dove grey like the sky, and still.

'Such a lovely view,' Zinnia murmured, half to herself.

'Lot of work to do,' observed Julia, glancing round, 'this old place is in something of a time warp. But then you must have taken that into consideration.'

'Sure, but I just loved the place. Veronica will be horrified when she sees it,' Rosemary laughed, and told them about their meeting earlier. It reminded her of their conversation.

'Veronica has, um, been asked to organise this Garden Club for the school,' she said casually. 'Nigella Picket is real keen. Going to instruct them about making a trompe d'oeil, and Japanese gardens, and all that stuff, green and red colour schemes, cottage gardens...' She looked at Zinnia, expecting indignation. 'That is unless Veronica can find someone else to do the instructing...'

'You mean me,' her aunt observed evenly. 'I never saw so many bushes being beat about. She only has to ask. Yes, it would be quite fun. I'll talk to her about it.'

'The times I've asked you to help with village things, and you say you haven't a moment to spare,' Julia exclaimed, with indignation that wasn't entirely put on. 'Have you had a road to Damascus moment or something?'

'If that's what you want to call it.' Zinnia regarded them innocently. 'The fact is I'm hoping to have a bit more time in the future, because I've made a decision. This cottage, Rosemary,' she turned to her, 'instead of putting a tenant in when the builders have finished squandering your money, would you let an aged relative perch here instead?' She smiled at their expressions. 'I'll do the garden for you.'

'Say, that's just great!' Rosemary responded with enthusiasm.

'Just till I can buy somewhere along the river myself.'

'You're going to sell Kiln House?' Julia put down her cup incredulously.

'Well you suggested it.'

'And when have you ever taken my advice?'

'About as often as you've acted on mine,' Zinnia batted back happily. It wasn't the champagne that was making her mellow. She felt oddly relieved at having made the big decision. She smiled at Julia teasingly. 'I might even help you out with one or two of your village committees.'

'You would? Oh bless you, that's wonderful! I'm desperate to shed some, what with Susan expecting, and…other things.'

'Mind you,' Zinnia laid down conditions with good humour, 'I refuse to sit on anything with that dreadful Stalker woman. Which probably rules out most of them.'

'She's not on the Haydon Village Association. In fact you might quite enjoy that,' Julia started the selling job right away. 'And it would be good to have someone who's lived in the village such a long time.'

A knock on the front door, and a man's voice, announced the arrival of an electricity meter reader, and Rosemary left them discussing the high turnover of village inhabitants, while she went to see what was needed. Fortunately he knew where to find the meter, since she certainly didn't, and after he'd jotted down the electricity readings, she saw him to the door.

As he got into his van, on impulse she stepped out into the garden, following the path round to the back of the house. Her house. She hugged the thought to herself. Harry's beloved fooshas decorated all sides of the little square lawn beneath the kitchen window, with scarlet geraniums in pots on either side of the steps down. They'd be taking them later of course. Mrs Chitting's new little conservatory was unlikely to have room for sitting in. Slowly she walked down the concrete steps to the next level, where Harry was growing potatoes, carrots and runner beans, with sweet peas on a wigwam of sticks. Their scent was overpowering, almost too sweet she thought, as she sat on a shallow ledge that formed a seat in the brick wall, beneath which emerged the little spring from which the cottage took its name.

Clumps of large, crinkled leaves were growing at the base of the wall, near the moisture, and recognising them gave her a start of pleasure. Primroses! In the spring there'd be primroses. With a smile she remembered helping Matthew chase off the primrose-eating peacocks in Kiln House garden. Heck that was only four months ago! Like a butterfly harking back to chrysalis days, she felt it was simply a different era.

The sun was working hard to burn its way down, but only here and there was blue peeping through, and a plane growled on its way, unseen above the cloud cover. It was difficult to imagine people up there in the sky, sitting comfortably in their seats, as remote from her as if they were undersea creatures. That was me, not so long ago, Rosemary thought, remembering with embarrassment how scared and alone she'd felt at London airport, when it seemed no-one had come to meet her.

What a vulnerable, scaredy cat! I don't know who I am now, she reflected sagely, only that it's not the same person. Sure has to be a good thing. And I've got a place to come back to, an anchor, she thought with pleasure. And family.

All I have to figure out now is what to do. To hell with being a librarian! she told herself, bending down to trail her hand in the cold spring water. But perhaps I could put the training to use, as Simon says. I'd like to find out more about the effects of healing plants. That'd be fascinating, and there must be a job in there somewhere. Dad would have been interested too. He'd have said it connected so many fields. She nodded to herself. Maybe this Indian trip would help to find a niche she could fill.

The sun had found a thin spot in the cloud cover, and like water pushing at a weak bank, it seemed to flood through with increasing confidence, the rays pleasantly warm on her head.

Heck, Zinnia and Julia were still in the kitchen! She must go back. But standing up, she saw Julia cautiously making her way down the concrete steps, stick in hand, followed by Zinnia, who was looking about her with the eager restiveness of an Arab horse.

'I should put a firm ceiling on the money to be sunk into this garden, Rosemary,' suggested Julia with a smile, as she reached the bottom. 'There isn't a thing Zinnia is leaving untouched. And that's only the first level!'

'Well, at the risk of sounding like Capability Brown,' Zinnia defended herself cheerily, stopping halfway down the steps, 'this has got amazing possibilities.'

Rosemary indicated the wall seat, and Julia sat down.

'These people who have designs on your garden, they're fanatics,' she said, with a teasing glance up at Zinnia. 'Take it from me Rosemary, never let them get the upper hand.'

But Zinnia's attention was elsewhere, caught by movement down on the river level, and the soft maundering of poultry contentedly discussing the day. Julia followed her gaze.

'Oh those belong to next door. Mrs Chitting never minded them coming through.'

'Hens,' murmured Zinnia, with a little smile. '*Hens.*'

The other two exchanged glances.

'Now do you suppose,' she mused with a casualness she probably thought was deceptive, 'that hens might have a taste for Settlewort seeds?'